Michelle Smart's love affair with books started when she was a baby and she would cuddle them in her cot. A voracious reader of all genres, she found her love of romance established when she stumbled across her first Mills & Boon book at the age of twelve. She's been reading them—and writing them—ever since. Michelle lives in Northamptonshire, England, with her husband and two young Smarties.

Susan Stephens was a professional singer before meeting her husband on the Mediterranean island of Malta. In true Mills & Boon style, they met on Monday, became engaged on Friday and married three months later. Susan enjoys entertaining, travel and going to the theatre. To relax she reads, cooks and plays the piano, and when she's had enough of relaxing she throws herself off mountains on skis or gallops through the countryside singing loudly.

Discover more at millsandboon.co.uk.

BILLIONAIRE'S BRIDE FOR REVENGE

MICHELLE SMART

THE SHEIKH'S SHOCK CHILD

SUSAN STEPHENS

MILLS & BOON

First Published in Great Britain 2018
by Mills & Boon, an imprint of HarperCollins*Publishers*
1 London Bridge Street, London, SE1 9GF

ISBN: 978-0-263-93536-3

MIX
Paper from
responsible sources
FSC **FSC™ C007454**
www.fsc.org

Printed and bound in Spain
by CPI, Barcelona

BILLIONAIRE'S BRIDE FOR REVENGE

MICHELLE SMART

This is for Tilly & Eliza.

Follow your dreams. xxx

CHAPTER ONE

BENJAMIN GUILLEM CAST his eye over the heads of the people scattered around the landscaped garden of the Tuscan-style villa in the heart of Madrid, an easy feat considering he was a head taller than most. The only guest there without a plus-one, he was also the only guest in attendance with no intention of celebrating Javier Casillas's engagement.

He snatched a flute of champagne from a passing waitress and drank it in one swallow. The bubbles felt like jagged barbs down his throat, magnifying the hot, knotted feeling that twisted inside him.

Javier and Luis had betrayed him. The Casillas brothers had taken advantage of their lifelong friendship and ripped him off. All the documentary evidence pointed to that inescapable conclusion.

He hoped the evidence was wrong. He hoped his instincts were wrong. They had to be. The alternative was too sickening to contemplate.

He would not leave this party until he knew the truth.

Benjamin took another champagne and stepped over to the elaborate fountain for a better view. He spotted Luis at the far end of the garden surrounded by his usual entourage of sycophants. Javier, Luis's non-identical twin brother and host of the party, was proving far more elusive.

Javier would be hating every minute of this party. He was the most antisocial person Benjamin knew. He'd always been that way, even before their father killed their mother over two decades ago.

Thoughts of the Casillas brothers swiftly evaporated when a dark-haired woman walked out of the summer room, capturing his attention with one graceful step onto the flourishing green lawn. She raised her face to the sky and closed her eyes, holding the pose as if trying to catch the sun's rays on her skin. There was an elegance about her, a poise, a way of holding herself that immediately made him think she was a dancer.

There were a lot of dancers there. Javier's new fiancée was the Principal Dancer at the ballet company the brothers had bought in their mother's memory. Benjamin wondered if the fiancée knew or cared that she was only a trophy to him.

Benjamin had never cared for the ballet or the people who inhabited its world. This dancer though...

The sun caught the red undertones of her hair, which hung in a thick, wavy mass over glimmering pale shoulders. Her features were interesting rather than classically pretty, a strong, determined jaw softened by a wide, generous mouth...

Her eyes suddenly found his, as if she sensed his gaze upon her, two black orbs ringing at him.

A slight frown appeared on her brow as she stared, an unanswerable question in it, a frown that then lessened as her generous mouth curved hesitantly.

His knotted stomach made a most peculiar twisting motion.

No, not classically pretty but striking. Mesmerising.

He couldn't look away.

And she couldn't seem to tear her gaze from him either, a moment in time existing only for them, two eye-locked strangers.

And then a shadow appeared behind her and she blinked, the sun-bound spell woven around them dissolving as quickly as it had formed.

The shadow was Javier emerging from the sunroom to join his own party.

He spotted Benjamin and nodded a greeting while his right hand settled proprietorially on the dancer's waist.

It came to him in an instant that this woman, the slowly forming smile on her face now frozen, was Javier's fiancée.

By the time Javier had steered the dancer to stand before him by the fountain, Benjamin had swallowed the bite of disappointment, shaken off the last of that strange spell and straightened his spine.

He wasn't here to party or for romance. He was here for business.

'Benjamin, it's good to see you,' Javier said. 'I don't think you've met my fiancée, Freya, have you?'

'No.' He looked straight at her. A hint of colour slashed her high cheekbones. 'A pleasure to meet you.'

Under different circumstances it *would* have been a pleasure but now the spell had broken all that remained was a faint distaste that she should have stared so beguilingly at him when engaged to another man.

But that was all the introduction Javier deemed necessary between his oldest friend and new fiancée, saying, 'Have you seen Luis yet?'

'Not yet but I am hoping to rectify that now.' Then, dismissing the striking vision from his consideration, Benjamin added evenly, 'We need to talk. You, me and Luis. In private.'

There was a momentary silence as Javier stared at him, eyes narrowing before he nodded slowly and caught the attention of a passing waiter. 'Find my brother and tell him to meet me and Senor Guillem in my study.' Dropping his hold on his fiancée's waist, he turned and strode back into the summer room without another word.

Two months later...

Smile, Freya, it's a party and all for a worthy cause.
  Smile for the cameras. Smile for your fiancé, still not

here but expecting you to turn on the charm even in his absence.

Smile for the gathered strangers, pretend you know them intimately, let them brush their cheek against yours as you greet each other with the fake air kisses that make your stomach curdle.

Smile, there's another camera. Smile as you nurse your glass of champagne.

Smile at the waiting staff circling the great ballroom with silver trays of delicious-smelling canapés but do not—not—be so gauche as to eat one.

Just. Smile.

And she did. Freya smiled so much her face ached, and then she smiled some more.

Being promoted to Principal Dancer at Compania de Ballet de Casillas came with responsibilities that involved more than pure dance. Freya was now the official face of the ballet company and at this, its most exciting time. The new state-of-the-art theatre the Casillas brothers were building for the company opened in a couple of months and it was her face on all the billboards and advertisements for it. She was the lead in the opening production.

Her, Freya Clements, an East London girl from a family so poor that winters were often a choice between heating and food, a Principal Dancer. It was a dream. She was living her dream. Marriage to Javier Casillas, joint owner of the ballet company, would be the…she almost thought icing on the cake but realised it was the wrong metaphor. Or was it the wrong simile? She couldn't remember, had always struggled to differentiate between them. Either way, she couldn't think of an appropriate metaphor or simile to describe her feelings about marrying Javier.

Javier was rich. Very, very rich. No one knew how much he and his twin Luis were worth but it was rare for their names to be mentioned in the press without the prefix *bil-*

lionaire. He was also handsome. He had chosen her to be, as he had put it, his life partner. When she looked at him she imagined him as her Prince Charming but without the title. Or the charm.

It didn't matter that he was morose and generally unavailable. It was better that way. Marrying him gave her deteriorating mother a fighting chance.

In exactly one week he would be her husband.

The entire ballet company was, as of that day, on a two-week shutdown so the new state-of-the-art training facilities and ballet school that went hand in hand with the new theatre could be completed. Javier had decreed they would fit their nuptials in then so as not to disturb her training routine.

Where was he? He should have been here an hour ago. She'd snuck away to the Ladies to call him but found her phone not working. She couldn't think what was wrong with it but she had no signal and no Internet connection. She would try again as soon as she had a minute to herself.

The media were out in force tonight, ready for their first public glimpse of the couple, beside themselves that Javier, son of the ballet dancers Clara Casillas and Yuri Abramova, a union that had ended in tragedy and infamy, was to marry 'a ballerina with the potential for a career as stratospheric as his mother's had been'. That had been an actual quote in a highbrow Spanish magazine, translated by her best friend, fellow ballerina and flatmate, Sophie, who had mastered the Spanish language with an ease that made Freya ashamed of her own inadequacies. In the two years she had lived and worked in Madrid she had hardly picked up the basics of the language.

Many of the company's *corps de ballet* were in attendance that night, window dressing for the attending patrons of the arts whose money and patronage were wanted. Sophie had begged off with a migraine, something she'd been suffering with more frequently in recent weeks. Freya wished she were there. Just having Sophie in the same room soothed the nauseous panic nibbling in her stomach.

Just smile.

So she stretched her lips as wide and as high as she could and accepted yet another fake air kiss from another of Europe's richest women and tried not to choke on the cloud of perfume she inhaled with it.

A tall figure stepped into the ballroom of the hotel the fundraiser was being held in.

Her stomach swooped.

It was *him*. The man from her engagement party.

Benjamin Guillem.

The name floated in her head before she could stamp it out.

It was a name that she had thought of far too often since the party two months ago. His face had found itself floating into her daydreams too many times for comfort too. And in her night dreams...

Suddenly aware of the danger she was placing herself in, she shifted her stance so he was no longer in her eyeline and smiled at an approaching elderly man.

She must *not* stare at him again. If he came over to speak to her she would smile gracefully exactly as she had to the other guests and this time she would find her tongue to speak in the clear voice she had cultivated through the years; chiselling the East London accent out of herself so no one in this moneyed world ever doubted she belonged.

She'd never been so tongue-tied before as she had the first time she'd seen him. She had literally been unable to say a word, just stared at him like some kind of goofball.

Her senses were on red alert, though, and as hard as she tried to concentrate on what the elderly man was saying—something about his granddaughter being a keen dancer—her skin prickled with electricity.

And then he was there, a step behind the old man, waiting his turn to speak to her.

She didn't look directly at him as she laughed politely at a joke the old man said. She hoped it was a joke. She could barely hear her own words let alone his. Blood pounded hot and hard in her head, a burning where Benjamin's gaze rested on her.

He was well mannered enough to wait for a natural pause in the conversation before stepping forward. 'Mademoiselle Clements?'

To her horror she found her vocal cords frozen again and could only nod her acknowledgement at the simple question.

'We met at your engagement party. I am Benjamin Guillem, an old friend of your fiancé.'

He had the thickest, richest French accent she had ever heard. It felt like set honey to her senses.

Unlike the other guests she'd met that evening he made no effort to pull her into an embrace, just stared at her with the eyes she'd found so unnervingly beautiful at her engagement party. Olive skinned, he had messy thick black hair and thick black eyebrows, a rough scar above the top lip of his firm mouth and a sloping nose. He reminded her of a *film noir* star, his dark handsome features carrying a disturbingly dangerous air. Where the other guests wore traditional tuxedos, Benjamin wore a black suit and black shirt with a skinny silver tie. If he were to produce a black fedora it wouldn't look out of place.

The only spot of colour on him were his eyes. Those devastating eyes. A clear, vivid green, they pierced through the skin. They were eyes that didn't miss a thing.

'I remember,' she said in as light a tone as she could muster, fighting through the thumping beats of her heart. 'You stole him away from me.' She'd been thankful for it.

Javier had put his hand to her waist. His touch, a touch any other woman would no doubt delight in, had left her cold.

She prayed fervently that by the time they exchanged their vows in exactly seven days her feelings for her fiancé would have thawed enough for her to be receptive to his touch. Javier had yet to make a physical move on her but she knew that would change soon.

They both knew what they were getting into, she reminded herself for the hundredth time. Theirs would be a loveless marriage, the only kind of marriage either of them could accept. She would continue to dance and enjoy her flourishing career for as long as she wanted and then, when *she* felt the time was right, give him babies.

She would be Javier's trophy, she accepted that too, but was hopeful that once they got to know each other properly, friendship would blossom.

And even if friendship didn't blossom, marriage to Javier would be worth it. Anything had to be better than the pain of watching helplessly while her mother withered away. Marrying Javier gave her the chance to extend her mother's life and ensure it was a life worth living.

Benjamin inclined his head, those eyes never losing their hold on hers. 'Unfortunate but necessary. We had business that could not wait.'

'Javier said the same.' That was all he'd said when she had tentatively probed him on it when he'd returned to her an hour later. The tone in his voice had implicitly told her to ask no more.

Her fiancé was a book that wasn't merely closed but thickly bound too, impossible to open never mind read.

His disappearance with his brother and friend had only piqued her interest because of the friend. This friend. Benjamin. She'd had to hold herself back from peppering Javier with questions about him, something she'd found disturbing in itself.

It occurred to her that she was lucky she felt nothing for Javier. If her heart beat as rapidly for him as it did for this Frenchman she would have thought twice about accepting his proposal. She knew Javier would have thought twice about proposing if she'd displayed any sort of feelings for him too.

The Frenchman showed no sign of filling her in on their meeting either, raising a shoulder in what she assumed to be an apology.

'I'm sorry if you're looking for Javier but I'm afraid he hasn't arrived yet,' she said when the silence that fell between them stretched like charged elastic. She had to remind herself that people were watching her. 'I don't think Luis is here yet either.'

Benjamin studied her closely, looking for signs that Freya knew about the enmity between him and the Casillas brothers but there were no vibes of suspicion. He hadn't expected Javier to take her into his confidence. Javier did not do confidences.

But there *were* vibes emanating from her, as if her skin were alive with an electricity that sparked onto him, an intensity in her dark eyes he had to stop himself from being pulled into.

He had a job to do and could not afford the distraction of her striking sultriness to delay him at a moment when time was of the essence. He'd planned everything down to the minute.

Tonight, her dark hair had been pulled back into a tight bun circled with tiny round diamonds, her lithe figure draped in a sleeveless deep red crushed velvet dress that flared at the hip to fall mid-calf. Her pale bare shoulders glimmered under the ballroom lights just as they had done under the hot Madrid sun and there was an itch in the pads of his fingers to touch that silky looking skin.

He leaned in a little closer so only she could hear the

words that would next spill from his tongue. The motion sent a little whirl of a sultry yet delicate fragrance darting into his senses. He resisted the urge to breathe it in greedily.

'I already know Javier isn't here. Forgive me, Mademoiselle Clements, but I have news that is only for your ears.'

A groove appeared in her forehead, the black eyes widening.

He turned his head pointedly to the huge swing doors that led out of the ballroom and held his elbow out. 'May I?'

Her throat moved before she nodded, then slipped her hand through the crook of his arm.

Benjamin guided her through the guests socialising magnificently as they waited for their hosts, the Casillas brothers, to arrive and for the fundraising gala to begin in earnest. They would have a long wait. The wheels he'd set in motion should, if all went as planned, delay them both for another hour each. He felt numerous eyes fall upon them and bit back a smile.

When Javier did finally get there, he would learn his fiancée had disappeared with his newly sworn enemy.

He had never wanted it to come to this but Javier and Luis had forced his hand. He'd warned them. After their last acrimonious meeting, he had given them a deadline and warned them failure to pay what was owed would lead to consequences.

Freya was collateral damage in the ugly mess *they* had created, the deceitful, treacherous bastards.

When they were in the hotel's lobby, Benjamin stopped beside a marble pillar to say, 'I am sorry for the subterfuge but Javier has encountered a problem. He does not wish to alarm the other guests but has asked me to bring you to him.'

'Is he hurt?' She had a husky voice that perfectly matched the sultriness of her appearance.

'No, it is not that. He is well. I only know that he has asked me to take you to him.'

He saw the hesitation in her eyes but gave her no chance to act on it, taking the hand still held in the crook of his arm and lacing his fingers through hers.

'Come,' he said, then began moving again, this time towards the exit doors.

Her much shorter, graceful legs kept pace easily.

A sharp pang of guilt punched his gut at her misplaced trust, a pang he dismissed.

This was Javier's fiancée.

Benjamin's sister, Chloe, worked as a seamstress at the ballet company and knew Freya. She had described her as nice if a little aloof. Intelligent. Too intelligent not to know exactly the kind of man she had chosen to marry.

Money and power in the world you inhabited were mighty aphrodisiacs, he thought scathingly.

What he found harder to dismiss were the evocative tingles seeping into his bloodstream from the feel of her hand in his and the movement of her lithe body sweeping along beside him.

His driver was waiting for them as arranged at the front of the hotel.

Benjamin waited until she was sitting in the car before following her in, staring straight into the security camera above the hotel's door as he did so.

'Do you really not know what kind of trouble Javier is in?' she asked with steady composure as the driver pulled away from the hotel.

'Mademoiselle Clements, I am merely your courier for this trip. All will be revealed when we reach our destination.'

'Where is he?'

'In Florence.'

'Still?'

'I understand there was some delay.' An understanding brought about by his own sabotage. Benjamin had paid an aviation official to conduct a spot-check of Javier's private plane with the promise of an extra ten thousand euros if he could delay him by two hours. He'd also paid a contact who worked for a mobile phone network to jam Freya's phone.

As they drove into the remote airfield less than ten minutes later she suddenly straightened. 'I haven't got my passport on me.'

'You don't need it.'

Benjamin's own private plane was ready to board, his crew in place, all ready to get the craft into the air the moment he and Freya were strapped in.

He ignored another wave of guilt as she climbed the metal steps onto his jet, as trusting as a spring lamb.

Within half an hour of leaving the hotel they were airborne.

He inhaled properly for what felt the first time in half an hour.

His plan had worked effortlessly.

Sitting on the reclining leather seat facing her, Benjamin watched Freya. Her features were calm, the only indication anything was worrying her the slight tapping of her fingers on her lap. He would put her out of her misery soon enough.

'Drink?' he asked.

Her eyes found his and held them for the longest time before blinking. 'Do you have tea?'

'I think something stronger.'

'Do I *need* something stronger?'

Not yet she didn't.

'No, but a drink will help you relax, *ma douce.*'

Her throat moved, the generous lips pulling together. Then she loosened her tight shoulders and nodded.

Benjamin summoned a member of his cabin crew. 'Get

Mademoiselle Clements a drink, whatever she wants. I will have a glass of port.'

Soon their drinks had been served and Freya sipped at her gin and tonic. Her forehead was pressed to the window, her gaze fixed on the dark night sky. She covered her mouth and stifled a yawn.

'You are tired?' he asked politely.

A quick, soft shake of her head that turned into a nod that morphed into another yawn. When she met his gaze there was sheepish amusement in her eyes. 'Flying makes me sleepy. I'm the same in cars. Are you *sure* Javier is okay?'

'Very sure. Your seat reclines into a bed. Sleep if you need to.'

'I'll be fine, thank you.' Another yawn. Another sip of her drink.

He observed her fight to keep her eyes open, the lids becoming heavier followed by a round of rapid blinking, then heavying again.

A few minutes later her eyes stayed closed, her chest rising and falling in a gentle rhythm.

He leaned forward and carefully removed the glass from her slackening fingers.

Her eyes opened and stared straight into his.

A shot of something plunged into his heart and twisted.

Her lips curved in the tiniest of smiles before her eyes fluttered back shut.

Benjamin closed his eyes and took a long breath.

There was something about this woman he reacted to in a way he could not comprehend. It unnerved him.

Through all the legal battles he'd been going through these past two months and as the full extent of the Casillas brothers' treachery had become sickeningly clearer, Freya's face had kept hovering into his thoughts.

He stared at it now, watching her sleep through the

dimmed cabin lights, absorbing the features that had played in his mind like a picture implanted into his brain.

It was fortuitous that she should sleep. It would make the difficult conversation they must have easier if they weren't thirty-five thousand feet in the air.

Let her have a little longer of oblivion before she learned she had been effectively kidnapped.

CHAPTER TWO

A BUSTLE OF movement in the cabin woke Freya from her light slumber to find Benjamin's gaze still on her.

A warm flush crept through her veins.

For the first time since infancy, full sleep hadn't taken her into its clutches.

He gave a tight smile. 'I was about to wake you. We will be landing shortly.'

'Sorry.' She smothered a yawn and stretched her legs, flexing her feet before noticing her shoes had slipped off. 'Travel has always had a sedative effect on me.'

It had been the case since she'd been a baby and her parents had taken turns walking her in the pram to get her to sleep. Once she had outgrown the pram the walks had continued with Freya in a buggy, sleeping happily along the same daily walk, which had taken them past a local ballet school. She had always woken up then. Her first concrete memory was pointing at the little girls in their pink tutus and squealing, 'Freya dance too!'

Those early walks had given birth to two things: her love of dance and her unfailing ability to fall asleep in any mode of transport.

Planes, trains, cars, prams, they were all the same; within ten minutes of being in one she would be asleep regardless of any excitement for the destination.

That she had managed almost half an hour before the first signs of sleep grabbed her on Benjamin's jet had more to do with him and the terrifying way her heart beat when she was in his presence than it had about any fears she might have for her fiancé.

She'd had to keep her gaze fixed out of the window to

stop herself from staring at him as her eyes so longed to do. When her brain had started to shut down into sleep it was images of this man flickering behind her eyes that had stopped her brain switching off completely.

Her fingers still tingled from being held in his hand, her heart still to find a normal rhythm.

Rationally, she knew there couldn't be anything too seriously wrong with Javier. Benjamin had told her Javier was unhurt and that there was nothing for her to worry about...

But there was a tension in the Frenchman now that hadn't been there before.

A prickle of unease crawled up her spine and she looked back out of the window.

When she'd last looked out of the window they had been high above the clouds. Now the earth beckoned closer, dark shadows forming shapes that made her think of mountains and thick forests, beyond them twinkling lights, towns and cities bustling with late-evening life.

None of it looked familiar.

The unease deepened the closer to earth they flew and she kept her eyes peeled, searching for a familiar landmark, anything to counteract the tightening of her stomach and the coldness crawling over her skin.

She hardly noticed the smoothness of the landing, too busy straining through the darkness to find something familiar in the airfield they had landed in.

As she whispered words of thanks to the cabin crew and climbed down the metal stairs to the concrete ground, she inhaled deeply. Then she inhaled again.

She had been in Florence as part of her ballet company's European tour only the week before. Florence did not smell like this. Florence did not smell of lavender.

Benjamin had reached the ground before her and stood at a waiting sleek black car, the back passenger door open.

'Where are we?' she asked hesitantly, not at all liking the train of her thoughts.

'Provence.'

It took a beat for that to sink in. 'Provence as in France?'

'Oui.'

'Did I misunderstand something? I thought you said Javier was still in Florence.' Freya knew she hadn't misheard him but told herself her ears were unused to Benjamin's thick accent and therefore she must have misunderstood him.

Slowly, he shook his head. 'You heard correctly.'

Through the panicking spread of her blood she forced herself to think, to keep calm and breathe.

She had only met Benjamin once before but knew he was Javier and Luis's oldest friend. Their mothers had been best friends. They had grown up thinking themselves as family. She knew all this because of a costume fitting she'd had before Compania de Ballet de Casillas had gone on its most recent tour, the one that had taken her to the beautiful city of Florence. A new seamstress had been tasked with measuring Freya, a young, dazzlingly beautiful woman called Chloe Guillem. When Freya had casually asked if she were any relation to Benjamin, she'd learned Chloe was his sister. She should have been glad of the opportunity to speak to someone who knew Javier and taken the opportunity to learn more about her fiancé. It shamed her that she'd had to restrain herself from only asking about Chloe's brother.

'Where is he, then?'

Benjamin looked at his watch before meeting her eye again. The lights shining from his jet, which still had the engine running, made the green darker, made them flicker with a danger that clutched in her chest.

'I think he must now be in Madrid. Very soon he is going to learn you have disappeared with me. He might have already.'

'What are you talking about?' she whispered.

'I regret to tell you, *ma douce*, that I have brought you here under false pretences. Javier did not ask me to bring you to him.'

She laughed. It was a reflex sound brought about by the absurdity of what he'd just said. 'Is this a joke the pair of you have dreamt up together?'

But Javier didn't joke. She had seen no sign whatsoever that her fiancé possessed any kind of sense of humour.

Benjamin's unsmiling features showed he wasn't jesting either. The dark shadows being cast over those same features sent fresh chills racing up her spine.

The chills increased as, pulling her phone out of her bag, she saw it still wasn't working.

There was the slightest flicker in his eyes that made her say, 'Have you got something to do with my phone not working?'

'It will be reconnected tomorrow,' he said steadily. He took a step towards her. 'Get in the car, *ma douce*. I will explain everything.'

Her heart pounding painfully, she took a step back, taking in the darkness surrounding them. High trees edged the perimeter of the huge field they had landed in, the only sound the jet's engine. The vibrant civilisation she'd glimpsed from the window could be anywhere or nowhere.

To the left of the runway sat a small concrete building, its lights on.

When Freya had exited the plane she had seen a couple of figures in high-visibility jackets walking away from them. She had to assume they'd gone into that building. She thought it safe to assume that building contained, at the very least, a working telephone.

'I'm not going anywhere else with you until you tell me what is going on,' she said in the steadiest voice she could manage while sliding her hand back into her small shoulder bag. She put her non-functioning phone back into it and groped for the can of pepper spray.

He must have seen her fear for he raised his hands, palms facing her. 'I am taking you to my home. You have my assurance that you will come to no harm.'

'No. I want to know what's going on *now*. Here. No more riddles.'

'We have much to talk about. It is better we talk in privacy and comfort.'

'And I prefer to discuss things now, before I get back on that plane and tell the pilot to take me back to Madrid.' To get to the plane, though, meant getting past *him*. A lifetime of dance had given her an agility and strength most other women didn't possess but she didn't kid herself that she had the strength to match this man, who had to be a foot taller than her own five foot five and twice her breadth.

She caught a glimmer of pity in those dangerous green eyes that made her blood chill to the same temperature as her spine.

Her fingers found the pepper spray.

She might not have the strength to match him but she would bet her life she was quicker than him.

She pulled the weapon out and aimed it at him, simultaneously stepping out of the heels that would hinder any escape. 'I *am* going back to Madrid and you can't stop me.'

Then, not giving him a chance to respond in any shape or form, Freya took off, racing barefoot over the runway and then over the dry grass to the safety that was the concrete building with its welcoming lights. Not once did she look over her shoulder, her focus solely on the door that would open and lead her to...

A locked door.

She tugged at it, she pushed it, she pulled it. It didn't budge.

'This airfield belongs to me.' Benjamin's voice carried

through the still night air that was broken only by the running engine of his jet. 'No one here will help you.'

She turned her head to look back at him, surprised to find herself more angry than fearful.

Surely this was a situation where terror rather than fury should be the primary emotion?

He had lied to her and deliberately taken her to the wrong country.

No one did that unless they had bad intentions.

She should be terrified.

Benjamin hadn't moved. He stood by the car watching her impassively. For the first time she realised the car had a driver in it.

And for the first time she realised his jet's engines were still running for a reason. Not only that but it was moving...

Open-mouthed, fighting back despair, Freya watched it increase in speed down the runway.

A moment later it was in the air.

It soared into the night sky, the roar of its engines decreasing the further it flew until it was nothing but a fleeing star.

And then there was silence.

'Come with me.' This time there was no other sound but Benjamin's voice. 'You will not be touched or harmed in any way. I give you my word.'

'Why should I believe you?' she called back.

He gave what she could only describe as a Gallic shrug. 'When you get to know me, you will learn I am a man of my word.'

She shivered at words that sounded more like a threat than a promise and looked around the airfield for a route that could be her pathway to freedom. As far as she could tell they were in the middle of nowhere.

She could run. She had a good chance of making it to the perimeter before his car could catch her and then she could disappear. But where would she disappear *to*? She had no idea how far she was from civilisation, no money, a phone that didn't work…she didn't even have her shoes on.

She either took her chances and ran off into the unknown or she went with Benjamin into another unknown.

The question was which unknown held the least danger.

Benjamin watched Freya rub her arms as she stared back at him, could see her weighing up her options.

Then her spine straightened and she stepped slowly towards him, holding the spray can outwards, aimed at him.

When she was two metres from him she stopped. 'If you come within arm's reach of me I will spray this in your face. If you make any sudden movements I will spray this in your face.'

He believed her. The fear he had glimpsed before she had run had gone. Now there was nothing on her face but cool, hard resolve.

If he'd believed she was a woman to fall into a crying heap at the first sign of trouble he would never have taken this path.

Everything he had learned about her backed his instinct that Freya had grit. Seeing it first-hand pleased him. It made what had to be done easier.

'I have given you my word that you will come to no harm.'

'You have already proven yourself a liar. Your word means nothing to me.'

He turned to the open car door. 'Are you getting in or do I leave you here?' He didn't like that he'd had to lie and had swallowed back the bile his lies had produced. That bile was a mere fraction of the sourness that had churned in his guts since he'd accepted the extent of the Casillas brothers' betrayal.

She glared at him and backed into the car.

By the time Benjamin had folded himself into the back

next to her, she had twisted herself against the far door, still aiming the spray can at his face.

'Don't come any closer.'

'If I wanted to hurt you I would have done so already.'

Her jaw clenched and her eyes narrowed in thought but she didn't lower her arm or relax her hold on the can. He was quite certain that if she were to spray it at him it would temporarily blind him. It would probably be painful.

'Do you always carry that thing with you?' he asked after a few minutes of loaded silence had passed while his driver navigated the dark narrow roads that led to his chateau.

'Yes.'

'Why?'

She smiled tightly. 'In case some creep tries to abduct me.'

'Have you ever used it?'

'Not in anger but there's a first time for everything.'

'Then I shall do my best not to provoke you to use it on me.'

'You can do that by telling your driver to take me to the nearest airport.'

'And how will you leave France on a commercial flight without your passport?'

Her lips clamped together at this reminder, the loathing firing from her eyes hot enough to scorch.

The car slowed over a cattle grid, the rattling motion created in the car one Benjamin never grew tired of. It was the motion of being home.

After driving a mile through his thick forest, they went over another cattle grid then stopped for the electric gates to open.

For the first time since they'd got into the car, Freya took her eyes off his face, looking over his shoulder at the view from his window.

Her eyes widened before she blinked and looked back at him.

'You can put the spray down,' he informed her nonchalantly. 'We have arrived.'

His elderly butler greeted them in the courtyard, opening Freya's door and extending a hand to help her out.

Benjamin got out of his door in time to hear her politely say, 'Please, can you help me? I've been kidnapped. Can you call the police?'

Pierre smiled regretfully. *'Je ne parle pas anglais, mademoiselle.'*

'Kidnapped! Taken!' She put her wrists together, clearly trying to convey handcuffs, then when Pierre looked blankly at her, she sighed and put a hand to her ear to mimic a telephone. 'Telephone? Police? Help!'

While this delightful mime was going on, Benjamin's driver slowly drove the car out of the courtyard.

'Pierre doesn't speak English, *ma douce*,' Benjamin said. He'd inherited Pierre when he bought the chateau and hadn't had the heart to pension him off just because he spoke no other language as all other butlers seemed to do in this day and age.

She glared at him with baleful eyes. 'I'll find someone who does.'

'Good luck with that.' Only one member of his household staff spoke more than passable English and Freya had just proven she couldn't speak a word of his own language. 'Come, let us go in and get settled before we talk. You must be hungry.'

'I don't want your food.'

Turning his back to her, he walked up the terracotta steps and into the main entrance of his chateau.

'Christabel,' he called, knowing his head housekeeper wouldn't be far.

No sooner had he finished saying her name than she appeared.

'Good evening, sir,' she said in their native tongue with a smile. 'Did you have a good trip?'

'I did, thank you. Is everything well here?'

'Everything is fine and we have prepared the quarters for your guest as instructed.' Christabel's eyes flickered over his shoulder as she said this, which he guessed meant Freya had followed him inside, her bare feet muffling the usual clacking sound that could be heard when people entered the great room.

He had a sudden vision of her black high heels discarded on the runway of his airfield, a sharp pang in his chest accompanying it, which he shrugged off.

He would replace them for her.

'Thank you, Christabel. You can finish for the evening now.' Turning to Pierre, who had also followed him in, he said, 'We require a light supper, anything Chef chooses. Bring me a White Russian and Miss Clements a gin and Slimline tonic.'

When his two members of staff had bustled off, he finally looked at his new houseguest and switched back to English. 'Do you want to talk now or would you like to freshen up first?'

She glared at him. 'I don't want to talk but, if you insist, let's get it over with because I want to go home.'

He held the mutinous black orbs in his. 'Is it not already obvious to you that you will not be going home tonight, *ma douce*?'

CHAPTER THREE

FREYA STARED INTO the green eyes that only a few hours before she had been afraid to stare too deeply at because of the strange heat gazing into them produced. Now, her only desire was to swing her small bag into his face. She'd put the pepper spray back into it and her fingers itched to take it back out and spray the entire contents at him.

'When will I be going home?' she demanded to know.

A single brow rose on his immobile face. 'That will be determined shortly. Come with me.'

'Come where?'

'Somewhere we can talk in comfort.'

He walked off before she could argue. She scowled at his retreating figure but when he went through the huge double doors and disappeared, she quickly got her own legs moving. This chateau…

She had never seen the likes of it before other than on a television screen.

Walking past sculptures and exquisite paintings, she entered another room where the ceiling was at least three times the height of a normal room, with a frescoed ceiling and opulent furniture and more exquisite works of art. She caught sight of Benjamin going through a door to the left and hurried after him. It would be too easy to get lost in this chateau, a thought amplified when she followed him through a third enormous living area, catching sight of a library—a proper, humongous, filled with probably tens of thousands of books library—on the way.

Eventually she caught up with him in yet another living area. It was hard to determine if this living area was indoors or outdoors. What should have been an external wall was missing, the ceiling held up by ornate marble pillars, opening the space to the spectacular view outside.

Her throat caught as she looked out, half in delight at the beauty of it all and half in anguish.

The chateau was high in the hills, surrounded by forests and fields that swept down before them. Far in the distance were the twinkling lights she had seen on the plane. Civilisation. Miles and miles away.

'Are you going to sit?'

She took a long breath before looking at Benjamin.

He'd sat himself on a huge L-shaped soft white sofa with a square glass coffee table in front of him.

Staring at her unsmilingly, he removed his silver tie then undid the top two buttons of his shirt.

The wrinkled old man who'd greeted them on arrival appeared as if from nowhere with two tall drinks. He placed them on the coffee table and indicated one of them to her. Then he left as unobtrusively as he had come.

Benjamin mussed his hair with a grimace then took his glass and had a long drink from it. 'What do you know about my history with the Casillas brothers?'

Surprised at his question, she eyed him warily before answering. 'I know you're old family friends.'

His jaw clenched as he nodded slowly. 'Our mothers were extremely close. They had us only three months apart. We were playmates from the cradle and it's a bond we have shared for thirty-five years. I was raised to think of Javier and Luis as cousins and I did. We have been there for each other our entire lives. You understand?'

'I guess.' She shrugged. 'Is there a point to this story?'

His eyes narrowed. 'The point to this story is the key to it.'

'You're talking in riddles again.'

'Not riddles if you would bother to listen to what I am saying to you.'

She caught the faint scent of juniper. Although only a moderate drinker—very moderate—Freya loved the refreshing coolness of a gin and tonic. Usually she limited herself to only the one. But usually she hadn't been practically abducted. And she'd fallen asleep before she could finish the one on his jet.

And she really needed something to calm the ripples crashing in her stomach.

Giving in, she picked it up then sat on the opposite side of the sofa to him, at the furthest point she could find, using all the training that had been drilled into her from the age of three to hold her core and enable herself to be still.

Never would she betray how greatly this man unnerved her but beneath her outward stillness her pulses soared, her heart completely unable to find its usual rhythm. She wished she could put it down to fear and it unnerved her more than anything to know the only fear she was currently experiencing was of her own terrifying erratic feelings for this man rather than the situation he'd thrown her into.

She took a small sip then forced herself to look at him. 'Okay, so you grew up like cousins.'

Before he could answer the butler reappeared with a tray of food.

The tray was placed on the table and she saw a wooden board with more varieties of cheese than she'd known existed, fresh baguettes, a bowl of fruit and a smaller bowl of nuts.

'*Merci*, Pierre,' Benjamin said with a quick smile.

Pierre nodded and, just as before, disappeared.

Benjamin held a plate out to her.

'No, thank you,' she said stiffly. She would choke if she had to eat her captor's food.

He shrugged and cut himself a wedge of camembert.

'It's not good to eat cheese so late,' she said caustically.

He raised a brow, took a liberal amount of butter and spread it on the opened baguette. 'You must be hungry. I took you from the gala before the food was served. You do not have to eat the cheeses.'

'I don't have to eat anything.' She truly didn't think she could swallow anything solid, doubted her stomach would unclench enough for food until she was far from this beautiful prison.

Staring back out over the thick trees and hills casting such ominous shadows around the chateau, she resigned herself to staying under his roof for the night. As soon as the sun rose she would find something to put on her feet and leave. Sooner or later she would find civilisation and help.

He took a large bite of his baguette and chewed slowly. His impenetrable green eyes didn't move from her face.

'If you will not eat then let us continue. I was telling you about my relationship with Javier and Luis.'

Freya pushed her fears and schemes aside and concentrated. Maybe Benjamin really had gone to all this trouble to bring her here only to talk. Maybe, come the morning, his driver would take her to the airport without any fuss.

And maybe pigs could fly.

If Benjamin wanted nothing more than to talk he would have conducted this chat in Madrid.

Either way, she needed to pay attention and listen hard.

'Like cousins,' she clarified. 'A modern-day tale like *The Three Musketeers*, always there for each other.'

'*Exactemente*. Do you know the Tour Mont Blanc building in Paris?' He took a bite of creamy cheese.

'The skyscraper?' she asked uncertainly. World news was not her forte. Actually, any form of news that wasn't related to the arts passed her by. She had no interest in any of it. She only knew of Tour Mont Blanc because Sophie had been fascinated with it, saying more than once that she would love to live in one of its exclusive apartments and dine in one of its many restaurants run by Michelin-starred chefs and shop in the exclusive shopping arcade.

He swallowed as he nodded. 'You know Javier and Luis built it?'

'Yes, I knew it was theirs.'

'Did you know I invested in it?'

'No.'

'They came to me seven years ago when they were buying the land. They had a cash-flow problem and asked me to go in with them on the project as a sleeping partner. I invested twenty per cent of the asking price. When I made that first investment I was told total profits would be around half a billion euros.'

She blinked. Half a *billion*?

'It took four years for the building work to start—there was a lot of bureaucracy to get through—and a further three years to complete it. Have you been there?'

'No.'

'It is a magnificent building and a credit to the Casillas brothers' vision. Eighty per cent of the apartments were sold off-plan and we had eleven multinational companies signed up to move into the business part before the roof had been put on.'

'So it's a moneymaking factory then,' she said flatly. 'I take it there's a reason you're boring me with all this?'

The piercing look he gave her sent fresh shivers racing up her spine.

'We all knew the initial profit projections were conservative but none of us knew quite *how* conservative. Total profit so far is closer to one and a half billion euros.'

Freya didn't even know how many zeros one and a half billion was. And that was their *profit*? Her bank account barely touched three figures.

'Congratulations,' she said in the same flat tone. It was

a lot of money—more than she could ever comprehend—but it was nothing to do with her and she couldn't see why he thought it relevant to discuss it with her. She assumed he was showing off and letting her know that his wealth rivalled Javier's.

As if this chateau didn't do a good enough job flaunting his wealth!

Did he think she would be impressed?

Money was nothing to brag about. Having an enormous bank account didn't make you a better person than anyone else or mean you were granted automatic reverence by lesser mortals.

Freya had been raised by parents who were permanently on the breadline. They were the kindest, most loving parents a child could wish for and if she could live her childhood again she wouldn't swap them for anyone. Money was no substitute for love.

It was only now, as that awful disease decimated her mother's body, that she wished they'd had the means to build a nest egg for themselves. She wouldn't have felt compelled to marry Javier if they had.

But they had never had the means. They had worked their fingers to the bone to allow their only child to follow her dreams.

'I invested twenty per cent of the land fee,' Benjamin continued, ignoring her sarcasm. 'I have since invested around twenty per cent of the building costs. How much profit would you think that entitles me to?'

'How would I know?' she said stiffly. 'I'm not an accountant.'

'Take a guess.'

'Twenty per cent?'

'*Oui.* Twenty per cent. Twenty per cent investment for a twenty per cent profit. Twenty per cent of one and a half billion equals three hundred million, do you agree?'

'I'm not an accountant,' she repeated, looking away from him, her lips tightening mutinously.

'You do not need to be an accountant to agree that three hundred million euros is a lot of money.'

Her slim shoulders rose but other than a flash of colour on her high cheekbones, the mutinous expression on her face didn't change.

'I have received all of my investment back but only seventy-five million euros of the profit. The equivalent of five per cent.'

Her eyes found his stare again. 'Am I supposed to feel sorry for you?'

'You are not expected to feel anything.' Benjamin stifled his growing anger at her cold indifference. He hadn't expected anything less from the woman engaged to the coldest man in Europe. 'I am laying out the facts of the situation. Javier and Luis have ripped me off. They owe me two hundred and twenty-five million euros.'

He had earmarked that money for a charity that helped traumatised children.

The irony of why he had chosen that charity would be funny if the situation were not so damn serious. The memories of Javier and Luis's traumatisation at the death of their mother at the hands of their father had haunted him for years.

Benjamin had almost bankrupted himself investing in the Tour Mont Blanc project. He'd spent seven years clawing his way back, going higher than he had ever climbed before, investing and expanding his fine food business across the globe until he had reached the point where he didn't owe a cent to anyone. All his assets, his business and subsidiaries were his alone and could never be taken from him. Now he could do some good with the great wealth he had built for himself and Javier and Luis had stolen his first significant act from him, just as they had stolen his money, his trust and all the memories he'd held dear.

'Take it up with your lawyers.'

'I have.' Benjamin remembered the green colour Andre had turned when he'd had to tell his most lucrative client that the Casillas brothers were correct in their assertion that he was only owed five per cent of the profits.

It had been there in black and white on the contract he'd signed seven years ago, hidden in the small print. It could have been written in the largest font available and he doubted he would have noticed it back then. He had signed the contract without getting his lawyer to read it first. That was his own fault, he accepted that. It was the only contract he'd ever signed without poring over every word first. The brothers had been given until midnight to come up with the full asking price or the land would have been sold to another interested party and they would have lost the substantial deposit they'd already paid at that point.

They had come to him for help on the same day Benjamin's mother had been told there was nothing more the medical team could do to stave off the cancer ravaging her body. Although not a shock—she had not responded well to any of the treatment she'd been given—it had been the single biggest blow in his life.

Benjamin had signed with only a cursory glance at the document and transferred the money there and then. If it had been anyone else he would have refused to even contemplate the investment but it had been Javier and Luis asking. Men he regarded as kin. Men his mother had regarded as kin. Men he'd trusted unconditionally. At the time he hadn't cared that it would eat into his own cashflow and that the chateau he'd intended to buy outright for his mother to pass the last of her days in would need him to take a hefty mortgage. It was that knock-on effect that had almost bankrupted him.

'From a legal point of view there is nothing more I can do about it.' The words felt like needles in his throat.

He'd refused to accept Andre's judgement and had fast-tracked the matter to a courtroom. The judge had reluctantly agreed with Andre.

Benjamin's rage at the situation had been enflamed when Javier and Luis successfully applied for an injunction on the reporting of the court case. They didn't want the business world to know their word was worthless or the levels to which they would stoop in the name of profit.

'Have you brought me here to tell me this thinking I will speak to Javier on your behalf?' she asked, her disbelief obvious despite the composed way she held herself.

He laughed mirthlessly and took a paring knife off the tray. He doubted very much that Javier cared for Freya's opinion. She was his beautiful prima ballerina trophy not his partner. Benjamin's hope was that her value as a trophy was greater than two hundred and twenty-five million euros.

Cutting into the peel of a fat, ripe orange, he said, 'I am afraid the situation has gone far past the point where it can be resolved by words alone.'

'Then what do you want from me? Why am I here?'

'Every action has a consequence. Javier and Luis have stolen from me and I am out of legal options.' He cut the last of the peel off the orange and dropped it into a bowl. 'In reality, the money is not important...'

She let out a delicate, disbelieving cough.

He cut into the flesh of his peeled orange. 'I am a very wealthy man, *ma douce*...'

'Well done.'

'And if it was just the money I would write it off,' he continued as if she hadn't interrupted him, cutting the orange into segments. 'But this is about much more than money, more than you could understand. I am not willing to let it go or let them get away with it. You are my last bargaining chip.'

'Me?' For the first time since she had entered his home, her composure made an almost imperceptible slip. 'But I had nothing to do with it. I was still in ballet school when you signed that contract.'

'*Oui*. You.' He looked at his watch and smiled. 'In three minutes it will be midnight. In three minutes Javier will receive a message giving him exactly twenty-four hours to pay the money owed.'

She swallowed. 'Or…?'

'If the Casillas brothers refuse to pay what they have taken from me then by the laws of natural justice I shall take from them, starting with you. If they do not pay then, *ma douce*, the message Javier will receive any moment tells him his engagement to you will be over and that you will marry me instead.'

CHAPTER FOUR

THE BURN THAT had enflamed Freya's brain earlier returned with a vengeance. She gazed into the resolute green eyes that gave nothing away and felt her stomach clench into a pinpoint.

Freya had no illusions about her lack of intellect. Ballet had been her all-consuming passion since she could walk. She couldn't remember a time in her life when she hadn't breathed dance and her education had suffered for it. She had one traditional educational qualification and that was in art.

But this didn't mean she was stupid and she would have to be the dimmest person to walk the earth not to look into those green eyes and recognise that Benjamin was deadly serious.

This was revenge in its purest form and she was his weapon of choice to gain it.

She was his hostage.

Her kidnapper stared at her without an ounce of pity, waiting for her response to his bombshell.

She responded by using the only means she had at her disposal, *her* only weapon. Her body.

Jumping up from the sofa, she swept an arm over the coffee table, scattering the crockery and glasses on it, but didn't hang around to see the damage, already racing through the non-existent wall and out into the warm grounds. Benjamin's surprised curse echoed behind her.

Security lights came on, putting a spotlight on her but she didn't care. She would outrun them. She dived into the thick, high shrubbery that she hoped surrounded the perimeter of the chateau and hoped gave adequate camouflage until she found the driveway they had travelled to reach the chateau and which she would follow until she found the road.

She had run from Benjamin earlier. She had reluctantly gone back to him because she had thought he was the unknown that posed the least danger.

She had made the wrong choice. Her heated responses to his physicality, the strange chemical responses that set off inside her every time she looked into his green eyes had stopped her recognising the very real danger she was in.

How big was this chateau and its grounds? she wondered desperately as she cut her way through the trees and hedges, trusting her sense of direction that she was headed the right way.

It seemed to take for ever before she peered through the shrubbery to find the courtyard Benjamin's driver had dropped them off at. The night was dark but there were enough ground lights for her to see the electric gates they had driven through.

Quickly she looked around it and saw the gate, a high wrought-iron contraption with spikes at the top that linked the high stone wall she would have to scale if she were to get away.

Keeping to the shadows, Freya treaded her way to the wall, her heart sinking the closer she got.

It was at least twice her height.

She stepped cautiously from the high tree she'd hidden behind for a better look. The wall was old. It had plenty of grooves and nooks for her to use to lever herself up. If she kept to the shadows she'd be able to scale it away from the estate lights...but then she wouldn't be able to see what was on the other side if she were in the dark.

Determination filled her. If she didn't climb this wall she would never escape.

She took one deep inhalation for luck then darted forward.

The moment she stepped off the thick, springy ground of the woods and onto the gravelled concrete, it seemed as if a thousand lights suddenly shone on her.

Not prepared to waste a second, she raced to the wall, found her first finger holes and began to climb.

She'd made it only two feet off the ground when she heard shouts. Aware of heavy footsteps nearing her, she sped up. The top of the wall was almost within reach when she stretched to grip a slightly protruding stone and, too late, realised it was loose.

With a terrified scream, she lost her hold entirely and fell back, would have crashed to the ground and almost certainly landed flat on her back had a pair of strong arms not been there to catch her as assuredly as any of her dance partners would have done.

Instinct had her throw her arms around Benjamin's neck while he made one quick shift of position to hold her more securely.

She squeezed her eyes shut and tried her hardest to open her airwaves.

She couldn't breathe. The shock of the fall and the unexpected landing had pushed all the air from her lungs. But her terrified heart was racing at triple time, tremors raging through her body.

How had he reached her so quickly? He must have run at superhuman speed.

'Do you have a death wish?'

His angry words cut through the shock and she opened her eyes to find his face inches from her own, furious green eyes boring into hers.

He was holding her as securely as a groom about to cross the threshold with his new bride but staring at her with all the tenderness of a lion about to bite into the neck of its prey.

Then he muttered something unintelligible under his breath and set off back to the chateau.

'You can put me down now,' she said, then immediately wished she hadn't spoken as now that she could breathe again she could smell again too. Her face was so close to Benjamin's neck she could smell the muskiness of his skin under the spicy cologne.

He shook his head grimly.

She struggled against him. 'I'm quite capable of walking.'

His hold tightened. 'And have you run away and put yourself in danger again?'

'I won't—'

'What were you thinking?' he demanded. His footsteps crunched over the gravel. 'If I hadn't been there to catch you...'

'What did you expect?' Her words came in short, ragged gasps. The feel of his muscular body pressed so tightly against her own made her wish he were made of steel on the outside as well as the inside. Damn him. If he were a robot or machine she could ignore that he was human and that her body was behaving in the opposite manner that it should to be held in his arms like this.

Her lips should not tingle and try to crane closer to the strained tendons on his neck, not to bite but to kiss...

'I expected you to listen, not run into the night. The forests around the chateau are miles deep. You can spend days—weeks—lost in them and not meet a soul.'

'I don't care. You can't kidnap me and hold me to ransom and think I'm going to just accept it.' She squeezed her eyes shut to block his neck from her sight.

If only she could block the rest of him out too.

God, she could hardly breathe for fear and fury and that awful, awful awareness of him.

Pierre had the door open for them. As Benjamin carried Freya over the threshold, the butler saw her feet and winced. Benjamin sighed inwardly before depositing her onto the nearest armchair and instructing Pierre, who really should have long gone to bed, to bring him a bowl of warm water and a first-aid kit.

'Telling him to bring handcuffs so you can chain me in your horrible house?' his unwilling guest asked snidely.

'That's a tempting idea, but no.' Tempting for a whole host of reasons he refused to allow himself to think of.

Holding Freya in his arms like that had felt too damn good. The awareness he'd felt for her from that first look had become like an infection inside him.

He must not forget who she was. Javier's fiancée. His only possible means of getting his money back and giving Javier a taste of the betrayal he himself was feeling.

Kneeling before her, he took her left foot in his hand. She made to kick out but his hold was too firm. 'I am not going to hurt you.'

'You said that before,' she snapped.

'The harm you have caused to your feet is self-inflicted. Keep still. I want to look for damage.'

The full lips pulled in on themselves, her black eyes staring at him maleficently before she turned her face to the wall. He took it as tacit agreement for him to examine her feet. The foot in his hands was filthy from walking bare through all the trees and shrubbery but there was no damage he could see. He placed it down more gently than she deserved and picked up her right foot. It hadn't fared so well. Tiny droplets of blood oozed out where she'd trodden on something sharp.

Pierre came into the room with the equipment he'd requested, along with fresh towels.

'Going to do a spot of waterboarding?' she asked with a glare.

He returned it with a glare of his own. 'Stop giving me ideas. I'm going to clean your feet…'

'I can clean my own feet…'

'And make sure you have no thorns or stones stuck in them.'

'You're a doctor?'

'Only a man with a sister who could never remember to put shoes on when she was a child.' And rarely as a teenager either. Chloe had moved out of the chateau a few years ago and he still missed her lively presence in his daily life.

His much younger sister was as furious with the Casillas brothers as he was and had insisted on helping that night. He'd given her the task of delaying Luis from the gala and she had risen to it with aplomb. Now she was safely tucked up in first class flying to the Caribbean to escape the fall-out.

'I'm a dancer,' Freya said obstinately. 'My feet are tough.'

'Tough enough to risk infection? Tough enough to risk your career?'

'Being held hostage is a risk to my career.'

'Stop being so melodramatic. You are not a hostage.' He took a sterile cloth and dipped it in the water, squeezing it first before carefully rubbing it against the sole of her foot.

'If I'm not allowed to leave that makes me a hostage. If I'm being held for ransom that makes me a hostage.'

'Hardly. All I require is twenty-four hours of your time. One day.' He rubbed an antiseptic wipe to the tiny wounds at the sole of her foot, then carefully placed it down on its heel.

'And what happens then? What if Javier says no and refuses to pay?'

'You have doubts?' He lifted her other foot onto his lap. 'Are you afraid his love for you is not worth such a large amount of money?'

She didn't answer.

Raising his gaze from her feet to her face, he noted the strain of her clenched jaw.

'You are the most exciting dancer to have emerged in

Europe since his mother died. You have the potential to be *the* best and Javier is not a man who settles for second best in anything. You are not publicity hungry. You will give him beautiful babies. You tick every box he has made in his list of wants for a wife. Why would he let you go?' As he spoke he cleaned her foot, taking great care in case there were any thorns hidden in the hard soles not visible to the naked eye.

Freya's assessment of her feet being tough was correct, the soles hard and calloused, the big toe on her right foot blackened by bruising.

His heart made a strange tugging motion to imagine the agonies she must go through dancing night after night on toes that must be in perpetual pain. These were feet that had been abused by its owner in a never-ending quest for dance perfection. And what perfection it was...

Benjamin had been dragged across the world in his younger years by his mother, who had been Clara Casillas's personal seamstress as well as her closest friend. His childhood home had been a virtual shrine to the ballet but he'd been oblivious to it all, his interest in ballet less than zero. He'd thought himself immune to any of the supposed beauty the dance had to offer. That had been until he'd watched a clip of Freya dancing as Sleeping Beauty on the Internet the other week.

There had been something in the way she moved when she danced that had made his throat tighten and the hairs on his arms lift. He'd watched only a minute of that clip before turning it off. He'd tried to rid his mind of the images that seemed to have etched themselves in his brain ever since.

Freya belonged to his enemy. He had no business imagining her.

And yet...

As hard as he had tried, he had been completely unable to stop his mind drifting to her or stop the poker-like stabs of jealousy to imagine her in Javier's arms that had engulfed him since he'd first set eyes on her.

'Javier knows I am a man of my word,' he continued, looking beyond the battered soles of her feet to the smooth, almost delicate ankles and calves that were undeniably feminine. A strange itch started in his fingers to stroke the skin to feel if it was as smooth to his touch as to his eye. 'He knows if I say I will marry you then I will marry you.'

'You've rigged everything to fall your way but unless you have something even more nefarious up your sleeve you can't marry me without my permission.' Steel laced her calm voice. 'Besides, you said I only have to stay with you for one day—you've given me your word too. You are lying to one of us. Which is it?'

'I have not lied to either of you. Have you not wondered *why* I had your phone tampered with?'

Clarity rang from her eyes. 'To stop me warning him. You don't want me in a position to scupper your plans by telling him the truth.'

He smiled. She was an astute woman. 'Javier will know by now that we left the gala together. I do not doubt he will hear we left hand in hand. He will know you left willingly with me and will be wondering how deep your involvement goes. If he trusts and loves you he will know you are my pawn and will pay me my money to get you back. If he doesn't trust or love you enough he will refuse to pay and cut you adrift. If he cuts you adrift the ball rolls into your court, *ma douce*. The moment Javier reaches his decision, whatever that decision may be, you will be free to leave my chateau without hindrance. If you choose to leave I will fly you back to Madrid even if your choice is to plead your case with him and throw yourself at his mercy. If, however, you decide to stick with a certainty then you can marry me. I am willing to marry you on the same terms you were going to marry him—I assume there was a pre-nuptial agreement. I am prepared to honour it. Or you can decide to have nothing to do with either of us and get on with your life.'

Benjamin put the towel down by the now cold bowl of water and got to his feet. 'Whatever happens, I cannot lose. Javier will pay for what he has done one way or another.'

While he'd been speaking, Freya's silent fury had grown. He'd seen it vibrate through her clenched fists and shuddering chest, the colour slashing her cheeks deepening.

Finally she spoke, her words strangled. 'How can you be so cruel?'

'A man reaps what he sows.'

'No, I meant how can you be so cruel to *me*? What have *I* done to merit this? You don't even know me.'

'You chose to betroth yourself to a man without a conscience. I notice you have accepted at face value that Javier and Luis stole from me. You know the kind of man he is yet still you chose to marry him. What kind of woman does that make you?'

The colour on her face turned an even deeper shade of red, her stare filled with such loathing it was as if she'd stored and condensed all the hatred in the world to fire at him through eyes that had become obsidian.

She rose from her seat with a grace that took his breath away. 'You don't know anything about me and you never will. You're the most despicable excuse for a human being I have ever met. I hope Javier calls your bluff and calls the police. I hope he gets a SWAT team sent in to rescue me.'

He reached out to brush a thumb against her cheekbone. It was the lightest of touches but enough for a thrill to race through him at the silky fineness of her skin.

He sensed the same thrill race through her too, the tiniest of jolts before the eyes that had been firing at him widened and her frame became so still she could be carved from marble.

'If he were to involve the police the news would leak out and his deception would become public knowledge,' he murmured, fighting the impulse to run his hand over her hair and pull the tight bun out, imagining the effect of that glorious hair spilling over her shoulders like a waterfall. 'But the police would not do anything even if he did go to them because I have not broken any law, just as Javier has not technically broken any law.'

'You kidnapped me.'

'How? You got into my jet and my car of your own free will.'

'Only because you lied to me.'

'That was regrettable but necessary. If lying is a crime then the onus would be on you to prove it.'

'You paid someone to disconnect my phone.'

'Again, the onus would be on you to prove it.'

Her throat moved before her voice dropped so low he had to strain to hear. 'How do you sleep at night?'

'Very well, thank you, because my conscience is clear.' Finally he moved his hand away and took a step back from her lest the urge to taste those tempting lips overcame him. 'I will get a member of staff to show you to your quarters. Sleep well, *ma douce*. I have a feeling tomorrow is going to be a long day for both of us.'

Then he half bowed and walked away.

CHAPTER FIVE

FREYA PACED HER bedroom feeling much like a caged tiger prowling for escape. The only difference between her and the tiger was she hadn't been locked in. She could walk out right now and never look back. Except it was now the early hours of the morning and her feet would rightly kill her if she tried to escape again. Third time lucky, perhaps? A third attempt to escape into the black canopy of Benjamin's thick forest? She might even emerge on the other side alive.

She slumped onto the bed with a loud sigh and propped her chin on her hands. Her feet stung, the corset of her dress dug into her ribs and she was suddenly weary from her lack of food. The pretty pyjamas on her pillow looked increasingly tempting.

A young maid had shown her to her quarters. She hadn't spoken any English but had been perfectly able to convey that the pyjamas were for Freya and that the clothes hanging in the adjoining dressing room were for her too. There were even three pairs of shoes to choose from, all of them worse than ballet slippers for an escape in the forest.

All the clothes were Freya's exact size, right down to the underwear. She guessed Benjamin's sister had passed on her measurements.

The planning he must have undertaken to get her there made her shiver.

He was remorseless. Relentless. He left nothing to chance, going as far as installing a camera outside her bedroom door. She'd seen the flashing red light and known exactly what it was there for. A warning that should she attempt to leave her quarters she would be seen in an instant. If she found a landline phone she would never get the chance to use it.

Without laying a finger on her he'd penned her in his home more effectively than a collie rounding up sheep.

But he *had* touched her.

The shivers turned into tingles that spread up her spine and low in her abdomen as she remembered how it had felt to have his large, warm hands holding her feet so securely, different tingles flushing over her cheek where he had brushed his thumb against it.

She had never met a more unrepentantly cruel person in her life and being part of the ballet world that was saying something.

But he had cleaned and tended to her feet with a gentleness that had taken her breath away. She had expected him to recoil at them—anyone who wasn't a dancer would—but instead she'd detected a glimmer of sympathy. Bruised, aching feet were a fact of her life. Smile through the pain, use it to drive you on to perfection.

She had to give him his due—in that one respect Benjamin had been the perfect gentleman. If she'd allowed any of her straight male colleagues to clean her feet she could only imagine the bawdiness of their comments. The opportunity for a quick grope would have been almost impossible for them to resist. The ballet world was a passionate hotbed, the intimacy of dancing so closely together setting off hormones that most didn't want to deny let alone bother to fight. Freya wasn't immune to it. The passion lived in her blood as it did in everyone else's; the difference was when the music stopped the passion within her stopped too. She had never danced with a man and wanted the romance to continue when the orchestra finished playing. She had never felt a man's touch and experienced a yearning within her for him to touch her some more.

Benjamin had held and touched her feet and she had had

to root her bottom to the chair so as not to betray her own body's betrayal of wanting those long fingers to stop tending and start caressing. She had had to fight her own senses to block out the thickening of her blood at his touch, had fought to keep the detachment she had spent a lifetime developing.

She squeezed her eyes shut, her brain-burn deepening at how she reacted so physically to the man who threatened to ruin *everything*.

She was caught in a feud between two men—three if she counted Luis—but it wasn't Freya who had the potential for the greatest suffering as a consequence of it, it was her mother. Her mother was the only reason she had agreed to Javier's emotionless proposal.

You know the kind of man he is yet still you chose to marry him. What kind of woman does that make you...?

It made her a desperate one.

Dance was all she knew, all she was, her life, her soul, her comfort. She had achieved so much from her humble beginnings but there was still so much to strive for, both for herself and for her parents who had made so many sacrifices to get her where she was today. Imagining the pride on their faces if she were to get top billing at the Royal Opera House or the Bolshoi or the Metropolitan gave her all the boost she needed on the days when her feet and calves seared with such pain that she forgot why she loved what she did so much.

Javier's proposal had given her hope. He would give her all the space she needed to be the very best. Marriage to him meant that if she did make it as far as she dreamed in her career then she would have the means to fly her parents all over the world to watch her perform. Much more importantly, her mother would have the means to be alive and well enough to watch her perform, not be crippled in pain with the morphine barely making a dent in the agony her body was putting her through.

But she *did* know the kind of man Javier was and that was why she had no faith he would pay Benjamin the money he owed. She didn't doubt he and Luis owed Benjamin money, although how they could have got one over the French billionaire she could not begin to guess, and right then she didn't have the strength to care.

Her forthcoming marriage was nothing more than a marriage of convenience. Javier's feelings for her ran no deeper than hers did for him.

If he didn't pay Benjamin then it meant their marriage was off. It meant no more money to pay for her mother's miracle drugs.

If he didn't pay it meant she would have to trust the word of the man who'd stolen her and hope he'd been telling the truth that he would marry her on the same terms.

Because if Javier didn't pay she would have to marry Benjamin. If she didn't her mother would be dead by Christmas.

Benjamin was on his second cup of coffee when a shadow filled the doorway of the breakfast room. He'd drained the cup before Freya finally stepped inside, back straight, chin jutted outwards, dressed in three-quarter-length white jeans and a dusky pink shirt, her glorious hair scraped back in another tight bun.

The simplicity of her clothing, all selected by his sister, did not detract in the least from her graceful bearing, and Benjamin found himself straightening and his heart accelerating as she glided towards him.

She allowed Christabel, who had followed her in, to usher her into the seat opposite his own and made the simple act of sitting down look like an art form.

'Coffee?' his housekeeper asked as she fussed over her.

'Just orange juice, thank you,' she answered quietly.

Only when they were alone did Freya look at him.

He'd thought he'd become accustomed to the dense blackness of her eyes but right then the weight of her stare seemed to pierce through him. He shifted in his seat, unsettled but momentarily trapped in a gaze that seemed to have the ability to reach inside him and touch his soul...

He blinked the unexpected and wholly ridiculous thought away and flashed his teeth at her. 'Did you get any sleep?'

She smiled tightly but made no verbal response.

'You look tired.'

She shrugged and reached for her juice.

'Have some coffee. It will help you wake up.'

'I rarely drink caffeine.'

'More for me then.' He poured himself another cup as the maid brought Freya's breakfast tray in and placed it in front of her.

His houseguest gazed at the bowls before her in surprise then smiled at the maid. It was a smile that made her eyes shine and for a moment Benjamin wished he were the one on the receiving end of it.

'Please thank the chef for me,' she said. 'This is perfect. She must have gone to a great deal of trouble.'

As the maid didn't speak English, Benjamin translated.

The moment they were alone again, Freya said, 'Has Javier been in touch?'

'Not yet.' He'd turned his phone's settings so only Javier, Luis and Chloe could reach him. He didn't want any other distractions.

She closed her eyes and took a long breath. He could see her centring herself in that incredible way he had never seen anyone else do, as if she were swallowing all her emotions down and locking them away. If he hadn't seen those bursts of anger-fuelled adrenaline when she had run away at his airfield and then when she had sent his supper flying before fleeing into the night, he could believe this woman never lost her composure.

And yet for all her stillness there was something about her that made her more vivid than any other woman he had ever met, a glow that drew the eye like a breathing, walking, talking sculpture.

What kind of a lover she would be? Did she burn under the sheets or keep that cloak of composure?

Had her exotic, intoxicating presence turned his old friend's heart as well as his loins? Had he lost himself in her...?

Benjamin shoved the thought away and swallowed back the rancid taste forming in his mouth.

He should be hoping Javier *had* lost himself in her arms as that would make it more likely for him to pay to get her back. He should not feel nauseous at the thought of them together.

That sick feeling only became more violent to think of Freya losing herself in Javier's arms.

How deeply did her feelings for Javier run?

If they had any depth then why did her eyes pulse whenever she looked at *him*?

He inhaled deeply, trying to clear his mind. He needed to concentrate on the forthcoming hours until Javier made his move. Only then could he decide what his own move would be.

In that spirit, he looked pointedly at the varying bowls of food his chef had prepared for her. He'd sent Christabel to check on his unwilling houseguest earlier and see what, if anything, she required for breakfast. He did not deny his relief to learn she'd abandoned her short hunger strike.

'What are you having?' he asked. 'It looks like animal feed.'

'Granola. Your chef has kindly made it fresh for me.'

'Granola?'

'Rolled oats.'

'Animal feed.'

She pulled a face at him and placed a heaped spoonful of berries on her animal feed, following them with a spoonful of almonds. Then she spooned some natural yogurt onto it and stirred it all together. As she raised the spoon to her mouth she paused. 'Do you have to watch?'

The colour staining her cheeks intrigued him. 'It bothers you?'

'You staring at me? Yes.'

'Why?'

'Because…' Freya put the spoon back in the bowl. She could hardly believe how self-conscious she felt sitting before him like this. She spent hours every day with her every move scrutinised by choreographers, fellow dancers, audiences and had long ago learned to tune out the weight of their stares.

Yet sitting here with Benjamin's swirling green eyes fixed upon her she was aware of her body in ways she had never been before, could feel the blood pumping through her, heating with each cycle.

It wasn't merely herself and the components of her own body that she was freshly aware of, it was Benjamin too, this Lucifer in disguise. The vibrating hairs on her nape and arms strained towards him as if seeking his scent and the heat of his skin, her senses more alert than they had ever been before.

'It just does,' she said tightly. 'Why don't you get yourself something to eat and leave me in peace?'

'I rarely eat in the morning,' he informed her.

'Cheese late at night then no breakfast…all the ingredients for health problems when you reach middle age.'

A glimmer came into his eyes. 'I can assure you I am in peak physical health.'

She could see that for herself though she would never admit it to him and felt a pang of envy at a life where you could eat any morsel you liked without scrutiny and without having to weigh up its nutritional value or energy-boosting properties.

Oh, to have the freedom to eat whatever you liked—or not—whenever you liked…

Benjamin's phone suddenly buzzed loudly.

She met his narrowed green eyes the moment before he reached for it.

'It's an email from Javier,' he said matter-of-factly.

Her stomach dropped. 'Already?'

He nodded. 'He has sent a copy to your email too.'

'What does it say?'

He studied it for a long time before sliding the phone to her.

The email contained no text. Javier had sent an attachment of two adjoining photos.

She blinked a number of times before the pictures she was staring at came into focus and their significance made itself clear.

They had been taken by one of the photographers at the gala who had spotted something intriguing about them leaving together and decided to capture it. The first shot caught the moment when they had paused in the hotel lobby for Benjamin to briefly explain the situation, the other had them walking out of the hotel hand in hand.

It was the first picture she found herself unable to look away from and, she knew in the pit of her stomach, it was the reason Javier had sent the pictures to her too.

Benjamin's face had been mostly obscured but her own features were there for all to see, and all could see her black eyes staring intently into his and her body tilting towards him. They looked like a pair of lovers caught in the midst of a most intimate conversation.

The blood whooshed up and into her brain.

That look in her eyes as she'd stared at him…

Had she really looked at Benjamin like that?

She covered her mouth, horrified.

She couldn't even bring herself to say anything when Benjamin's large hand stretched across the table to take his phone back from her.

Freya was so shamed and mortified at the expression captured on her face she feared her vocal cords had been stunned into silence for ever.

Nothing was said between them until another loud buzzing cut through the silence, a continuous buzz signalling a phone call.

Benjamin put it on speakerphone.

His eyes rested on Freya as the gravelly Spanish tones of Javier Casillas filled the room.

'You will not receive a cent from me, you son-of-a-bitch. Keep her. She's all yours.'

Then the line went dead.

This time the silence between them was loud enough for Freya to hear the beats of her thundering heart.

The room began to spin around her, the high ceiling lowering, the wide walls narrowing.

She was going to be sick.

She might very well have *been* sick had the most outrageous sound she'd ever heard not brought her sharply back to herself and the room back into focus.

Benjamin, his eyes not once dropping their hold on hers, was laughing.

'How can you think this is funny?' she asked with a croak, dredging the words from the back of her throat. 'You've lost.'

And she had lost too. Javier had emailed the pictures to her too as a message. Their engagement was over.

'Lost?' Benjamin's face creased with mirth. He threw his head back, his laughter coming in great booms that echoed around her ears. 'No, *ma douce*, I have not lost. I told you last night, I cannot lose.'

It was a struggle to breathe. 'He's not going to pay the money.'

'There was only an evens chance that he would. There were only two end scenarios: Javier would pay or he would not. This result is not my preferred one but I can take satisfaction that he will be burning with humiliation at the photographs of us so it is not a loss by any means.'

'Not a loss for you, maybe, but what about me? He's never going to take me back. You know that, right? These pictures make it look like I was encouraging you…that I was a part of it.'

Oh, God, that look in her eyes as she'd stared into his…

There was not an ounce of penitence to be found in his glittering eyes. 'You don't have to lose anything, *ma douce*. Your career is safe. You are one of the most exciting dancers in the world. If Javier is foolish enough to sack you then I guarantee another company will snatch you up.'

'You think I care only about my career?' she demanded.

His laugh was merciless. 'My sister says you are the most driven dancer she has ever met, but if it is the loss of your fiancé that grieves you then I suggest you have a rethink. If he had feelings for you he would have fought for you. If he'd believed in your love he would have fought for you. You should be thanking me. I am saving you from a lifetime of misery.'

'I can assure you, you are not. I told you last night that you don't know anything about me.'

'If he means that much to you, now is your chance to go to him and plead your case,' he said sardonically. 'He has made his choice, which means you are now free to make yours. Say the word and I will arrange transportation to take you back to Madrid. You can be back there by lunch.'

Rising from her chair, Freya leaned forward to eyeball him. She had never known she could feel such hate for someone. Her heart was beating so frantically against her ribcage she had to fight to get the words out. 'Believe me, my preferred outcome would be to leave this awful excuse for a home and never have to see your hateful face again. Quite frankly, if I were stuck on a desert island with the choice between you and a rat for company, the rodent would win every time.'

Something flickered on his darkly handsome face, the smug satisfaction vanishing.

A charge passed between them, so tangible she felt it pierce into her chest and thump into her erratic heart.

He gazed at her with eyes that swirled and pulsed before his lips curved into a knowing smile and he too leaned forward. 'The way you were looking at me in that photograph proves the lie in that.'

CHAPTER SIX

'I DON'T KNOW what you're talking about.' Freya hated that her burning cheeks contradicted her.

Benjamin rose slowly from his seat and walked around the table to her, that feline grace she had seen before taking a dangerous hue, the panther stalking towards its prey.

She twisted around so her thighs pressed into the hard wood, her usually nimble feet becoming like sludge.

And then he was standing in front of her, that strong neck her lips kept longing to press into right there in her eye line, standing close enough for his fresh spicy scent to seep into her senses.

'I think you know exactly what I'm talking about, *ma douce*.' He placed a hand on the arch of her neck and dropped his voice to a murmur. The feel of his fingers on her skin burned through her, the heat from his breath catching the loose strands of her hair and carrying through it to her scalp and down into her bloodstream. 'The camera never lies. Javier saw the desire you feel for me. I have seen it too and I have *felt* it, when I carried you back into my home and the moonlight shone on us both. You say you hate me but still you long for my kiss.'

Freya found herself too scared to move. Too scared to breathe. Terrified to make the slightest twist in her body lest her lips inch themselves forward to brush against the warm neck so close to her mouth and the rest of her body, aching at the remembrance of being held so securely in his arms, press itself wantonly against him.

Focus, Freya. The next few minutes will determine you and your mother's whole futures.

He moved a little closer so his breath danced over the top

of her ear, electrifying parts inside her she hadn't known were there. 'There is an attraction between us that has been there since we first saw each other in Javier's garden.'

She gave a tiny shake of her head to deny his words but he dragged his hand from her neck and placed a finger on her lips, standing back a little so he could stare straight into her eyes.

'Now you no longer belong to him, we are free to act on it.' Benjamin brushed the finger from her lips to rest lightly on her cheek. She truly had the softest skin he had ever touched, more velvet than flesh.

He'd always known it would be fifty-fifty whether Javier would pay up, which was why he had gone to the lengths he had to make sure that whatever the outcome, he would still win.

He hadn't expected the destruction of Javier and Freya's relationship to feel like a victory that would taste as sweet as if Javier had paid in full.

Never again would he be haunted by thoughts of Freya enjoying herself in his enemy's bed because she had been correct that Javier would never take her back. She could plead with him but Benjamin knew Javier too well. His Spanish foe's reputation and pride were the fuel he needed to get through the day. In one stroke Benjamin had battered them both and soon he would set his sights on Luis too.

Benjamin was well aware the actions he'd taken made him as bad as the men he sought to destroy but he didn't care. Why should he? Who had ever cared for him?

His mother had loved him but when he had discovered the Casillas brothers' treachery the past had come back into sharp focus and he'd been forced to accept that her love for him had always been tied with her love for them. Louise Guillem had loved Javier and Luis as if they were children of her blood because, for his mother, Clara Casillas had been the love of her life. A platonic love, it was true, but with the emotional intensity of the most heightened love affair. Benjamin had been a by-product of that love, a child to raise alongside Clara's, not wanted as a child should be for himself but more as a pet, an accessory.

His father had long gone, leaving the marital home when Louise had fallen pregnant by accident a decade after Benjamin had been born. Already fed up playing second fiddle to the World's Greatest Dancer, his father had refused to hang around and raise a second accessory. Benjamin had never missed him—you had to know someone to miss them and he had never properly known his father—but, again, with the past being brought back into focus, he had realised for the first time that his father hadn't just left his mother but his only son too. He hadn't cared enough to keep their tentative relationship going.

Then there was Javier and Luis. Their betrayal had been the most wrenching of all because it had made him look at the past with new, different eyes and reassess all the relationships he had taken for granted and unbury his head from the truth.

The only relationship he had left was with his sister but she was a free spirit with wounds of her own, a beautiful violin with broken strings.

Every other person he'd trusted and cared for had used or betrayed him.

He was damned if he would trust or care again.

This beautiful woman with eyes a man could fall into was no innocent. He regretted that he'd had to use her but it had been a necessary evil. He would not regret destroying her relationship with Javier. If she had cared an ounce for his foe she would not be staring at him as if she wanted him to devour her.

Dieu, a man really could fall into those eyes and never resurface...

But there was something else breaking free in the heady

depths of those eyes, a fire, a determination that made him drop his hand from her cheek and step back so he could study her carefully without her sultry scent playing under his nose and filtering through into his bloodstream…

The moment he stepped away she folded her arms across her chest and seemed to grow before his eyes.

'The only thing we're going to act on is your word.' Freya's husky voice had the same fiery determination as resonated in her eyes.

'You are ready to be taken back to Madrid?'

This time she was the one to laugh, a short, bitter sound. 'Yes. But not yet. Not until you have married me.'

For a moment it felt as if he had stepped onto quicksand. He shook his head. 'You want to marry me?'

'No. I would rather marry the rodent on the desert island but you told me I would have three choices once Javier had made his. He won't take me back, not even if I get down on my knees and beg. I need the money set out in our pre-nuptial agreement so going back to Madrid and resuming my single life is not an option either, which leaves just one remaining choice—marrying you. You need to honour the contract Javier and I signed on our engagement as you said you would.'

He stared into her unsmiling face, an unexpected frisson racing up his spine.

Marriage to Freya…?

He had made his threat to Javier with the full intention of acting on it if it came to it but never had he believed she would go along with it, let alone demand it of him.

He tried to envisage Javier's reaction when he heard the news but all he could imagine was Freya naked in his bed, the fantasies he'd been suppressing for two months suddenly springing to life in a riot of erotic colour.

Marriage had never been on his agenda before. He'd spent the past seven years so busy clawing his business back to health and then into the business stratosphere that any thoughts of wedlock had been put on the back burner, something to be considered when his business no longer consumed his every waking thought.

Now the thought of marriage curdled his stomach. Marriage involved love and trust, two things he was no longer capable of and no longer believed in.

'Were you lying to me when you gave me your word?' she challenged into the silence.

'I save the lies for your ex-fiancé. He's the expert at them. And I am thinking you must be good at them too seeing as you fooled him into believing you had feelings for him.'

'I didn't fool or lie to anyone. Javier and I both knew exactly what we were signing up for.'

'You admit you were marrying him for his money?'

'Yes. I need that money.'

'And what did Javier get out of marrying you other than a prima ballerina on his arm?'

Fresh colour stained her cheeks but her gaze didn't flicker. 'The contract we signed spells it out. If you're the man of your word you say you are, you will duplicate it and honour it.'

'You are serious about this?'

'Deadly serious. The ballet company is on a two-week shutdown. I was supposed to marry Javier next Saturday. I presume with all the strings you're able to pull you can arrange for us to marry then instead. Either that or you can pay me now all the money I would have received from Javier, say, for the first ten years of our marriage.' Her eyes brightened, this idea clearly only just occurring to her. 'That can be my compensation for being the unwitting victim in your vindictive game. It comes to...' her brow furrowed as she mentally calculated the sum '...around twenty million. I'll be happy to accept half that. Call it ten million and I go back to my life and we never have to see each other again.'

'You want me to pay you off?' he asked, part in astonishment and part in admiration.

'That would be the best outcome for both of us, don't you think?'

He shook his head slowly, intrigued and not a little aroused at the spirit and fight she was showing. No wonder Javier had chosen her for his wife. She was magnificent. '*Non, ma douce*, the choice was marriage or nothing. If I pay you off, I get nothing from it.'

'Your conscience will thank you.'

'I told you before, my conscience allows me to sleep well. With you in my bed every night I will be able to sleep even more sweetly.' His arousal deepened to imagine that wonderful hair fanned over his pillow, the obsidian eyes currently firing fury at him firing only desire…

'Maybe you should read the contract before assuming I will be in your bed every night. You might find you prefer to pay me off.'

'Unlikely but, even if that is the case, the knowledge Javier will spend the rest of his life knowing it is my ring you wear on your finger and not his will soften the blow.'

'You really are a vindictive monster, aren't you?'

'You insult me and speak of my conscience when you are a self-confessed gold-digger.' He smiled and closed the gap that had formed between them and placed a hand on her slender hip. There was no danger of trusting or caring for this woman, even if he was capable of it and even if she did have eyes he could sink into. 'We don't have to like each other to be good together…and I think we could be *very* good together. Marry me and you have everything you would have had if you had married Javier.'

'And you get continued revenge,' she finished for him, her tone contemptuous.

'*Exactemente*. We *both* get what we want.'

Freya could smell the warmth of his skin beneath the freshness of his cologne…

Benjamin was *not* what she wanted. He provoked her in ways Javier never had. Javier was scary but Benjamin terrified her for all the wrong reasons.

She wouldn't be swapping one rich man for another, she would be swapping ice for fire, safety for danger, all the things she had never wanted, all the things she had shied away from since she had learned sex was the only control she had over her body.

There was not a part of her external body that hadn't been touched or manhandled; a grab of her arm to raise it an inch higher, rough hands on her hips to twist her into the desired shape, a chuck under the chin to lift it, partners holding her intimately in dance… Her external body was not hers; it belonged to dance. Her body was public property but her emotions and everything inside her belonged to herself.

That the control she'd worked so hard for was in danger of slipping for this man, this vindictive, abhorrent…

She clamped her lips together to contain a gasp.

Benjamin had taken another step closer. Their bodies were almost flush.

For the first time in her life someone had hold of her hip and she could *feel* it, inside and out, her blood heating and thickening to treacle.

She closed her eyes and breathed in deeply, trying to block her dancing senses and contain what was happening within her frame.

'You know what this means?' he murmured.

She swallowed and managed a shake of her head.

'It means you and I are now betrothed. Which means we need to seal the deal.'

Before she could guess what he meant, he'd hooked an

arm around her waist and pulled her tight against him. Before she could protest or make any protective move of her own, he'd covered her mouth with his.

Having no preparation or warning, Freya found herself flailing against him, her hands grabbing his arms as her already overloaded senses careered into terrifying yet exciting new directions. She struggled helplessly to keep possession of herself while his lips moved against hers in what she instinctively knew was the final marker in the game he'd been playing, Benjamin claiming her as his in an expert and ruthless manner that…

His tongue swept into her mouth and suddenly she didn't care that it was all a game to him. Her body took possession of her brain for the very first time and she was kissing him back, taking the dark heat of his kisses and revelling in the sensation they were evoking in her. Such glorious, heady sensations, burning her skin beneath her clothes, sensitising flesh that had only come alive before for dance. She loosened her hands to wind them around his neck and press herself closer still while he swept his hands over her back, holding her tightly, possessively, devouring her mouth as if she were the food he needed to sustain himself. When his hand moved down to clasp her bottom and grind their groins together, it was *her* moan that echoed between them.

Her breasts were crushed against his chest, alive and sensitised for the first time in her life, making her want to weep that she had chosen to wear a bra when she so rarely bothered, and as these thoughts flickered in her hazy mind reality crashed back down.

All the clothes she wore, her underwear, her shoes, every item designated as hers under this roof had been bought without her knowledge.

She was a pawn in Benjamin's game of vengeance and she *hated* him.

She would not accept his kisses with anything but contempt.

When Freya suddenly pulled out of his arms and jumped back, seeming to leap backwards through the air yet still making the perfect dancer's landing, Benjamin had to blink rapidly to regain his focus and sense of place.

What the hell had just happened?

Breathing heavily, he stared at her, stunned that one simple kiss could explode like that. He'd known the attraction between them was strong but that...that had blown his mind.

He hadn't experienced such heady, evocative feelings from a kiss since...since ever, not even those illicit teenage kisses when he'd first discovered that the opposite sex was good for something more than merciless teasing.

She stared back, eyes wide and wary, her own breaths coming in shallow gulps, her cheeks flushed. Her hair was still pulled back in that tight bun but there was something dishevelled about her now that made the heavy weight in his loins deepen.

He put a hand on the table, partly to steady himself and partly to stop himself crossing the room to haul her back into his arms. His loins felt as if they had been set on fire, the burn spread throughout him but concentrated there, an ache such as he had never experienced before that threatened to engulf his mind along with the rest of him.

Had she reacted to Javier's kisses with that same intensity...?

The thought deflated the lust riding through him as effectively as a pin in a balloon.

He needed air.

'Your pre-nuptial agreement. Where is it?' he asked roughly.

A flash of confusion flittered over her features before she blinked sharply. 'In Javier's safe but I have a copy of it on an email attachment.'

'*Bien.* I will get your phone unlocked. When it is working again, forward it to me. I will get it redrafted with both our names on it. It will be ready to sign by the end of the day.'

CHAPTER SEVEN

BENJAMIN RAPPED LOUDLY on the door to Freya's quarters, his heart making as much noise in his chest as his knuckles made on the door.

It was incredible to think these would be her permanent quarters.

When he had bought the chateau seven years ago there had been a vague image of a future Madame Guillem to share the vast home and land with but it had been a secondary image. He'd bought it for his mother and, at the time, nursing her through her final months had been his only concern. Not long after her funeral, he'd found himself unable to repay the mortgage and forced to face the reality of his financial situation. Nursing his mother had taken him away from his business. The bills had mounted. Suppliers had threatened court action. He'd been days away from losing everything.

All thoughts of a future Madame Guillem had been buried. He'd dated. He'd had fun. But nothing permanent and definitely nothing serious. He'd had neither the physical time nor the mental space to make a relationship work.

It was only when he'd reached a position in his life where he could take his foot off the accelerator and slow things down enough for a real life of his own that he'd reached the inescapable conclusion that he would never trust anyone enough to pledge his life to them. As much as he'd regretted it would likely mean he would never have children, another of those vague in-the-future notions, he would not put himself through it. If he couldn't trust the people he'd loved all his life how could he trust a stranger?

He didn't have that worry with Freya. Knowing there was no trust to fake made taking this step more palatable.

Reading through the contract she and Javier had signed had made it even more so.

He had read it, shaking his head with incredulity at what it contained.

He could easily see his old friend signing this cold, emotionless contract but for the hot-blooded woman whose kisses had turned him to fire to sign such a thing stretched the realms of credulity.

But then, she was already proving to be far more fiery a woman than he'd thought Javier would commit himself to.

He hadn't seen her since their explosive kiss that morning. He'd been busy in his office organising things. She'd kept herself busy doing her own thing, his staff keeping discreet tabs on her.

He knocked again. After waiting another thirty seconds, he pushed the door open and let himself in.

Her quarters were large and comfortable, a small reception area leading to a bedroom, bathroom and dressing room to the left, and a spacious living area to the right, where the faint trace of music played out through the closed door. He opened it and paused before stepping over the threshold.

All the furniture had been pushed against the far wall to create a large empty space. The music came from her freshly working phone.

Freya had contorted herself into the strangest shape he'd ever seen the human body take right in the centre of the room. Her calves and knees were on the carpet as if she'd knelt to pray but instead of clasping her hands before her and leaning forward, she'd gone backwards into a bridge, her flat stomach arched in the air, her elbows on the floor where her toes rested, her face in the soles of her bare feet with her hands clasping both her heels and her temples.

It looked the most uncomfortable pose a person could

manipulate themselves into but she didn't appear to be in any discomfort. If anything, she seemed at peace, her chest expanding and her stomach softening in long, steady breaths.

He found his own breath stuck in his lungs. He didn't dare make a sound, afraid that to disturb her would cause her to injure herself.

After what felt like hours but in reality was probably less than a minute she uncoiled herself, walking her hands away from her feet then using them to push herself upright.

Kneeling, she finally looked at him. She showed no concern or surprise at his appearance in her quarters.

He'd been so entranced with what he'd seen that it was only when her eyes met his that he noticed all she had on were a black vest and a pair of black knickers.

If she was perturbed that he had walked into her quarters while she had hardly any clothes on she didn't show it.

But then, recalling all the years spent touring with Clara Casillas, he had never met a body-shy ballerina before. He'd seen more naked women in the first ten years of his life than if he'd been raised in a brothel. It was a fact of their life. Freya was a woman who spent her life with her body under a microscope, different hands touching it for different reasons, whether to lift, to shape or to dress.

Desire coiled through his loins to imagine what it would feel like to lift this woman into his arms as a lover...

He would bet she had poise and grace even when she slept and felt a thickening in his loins to know it wouldn't be long before he discovered that for himself.

And, as his imagination suddenly went rampant with heady thoughts of this beautiful, supple woman in his bed, those long, lithe legs wrapped around him, those black eyes currently staring at him without any expression coming alive with desire, the strangest thing of all occurred. Freya blushed.

She must have felt the heat crawling over her face for

her features tightened before she jumped gracefully to her feet, going from kneeling to standing in the time it took a mortal to blink.

'If you'll excuse me, I'll put some clothes on,' she said stiffly.

The lump in his throat prevented him from doing more than stepping aside to let her pass through the door to her bedroom.

Breathing deeply, he took a seat on the armchair while he waited for her to return, keeping his thoughts and imagination far away from sex, trying to quell the ache burning in his loins.

They had business to take care of.

Feeling more together in himself when she came back into the living room, he said, 'What were you doing?'

She'd put her three-quarter-length white jeans back on and covered her chest with an off-the-shoulder navy top. Her battered feet were bare. She sat on the leather sofa nestled next to his and twisted her body round to face him. 'Yoga. That pose was the Kapotasana.'

'It sounds as painful as it looks.'

The glimmer of a smile twitched on her lips. 'It's invigorating and, under the circumstances, necessary.'

'Why?'

'I need to keep fit. I'm used to dancing and working out for a minimum of seven hours a day. I need to keep my fitness levels maintained, I need to stretch and practise regularly or it will be extra hard when I return to the studio. This is all I have available to me...unless you have a secret dance studio tucked away somewhere with a barre?'

'I am afraid not but you are welcome to use my gym and swimming pools and sauna. There's tennis courts too.'

She pulled her lips in together. 'I have to be careful using a gym and swimming. It's what they do to my muscles—they bulk them in all the wrong places. I've never played tennis before and wouldn't want to risk taking it up without advice.'

He looked around again at the space she had created for herself in this room and knew without having to ask that this was not suitable for her to practise dancing in.

'Still, I'm sure you're not here to discuss my fitness regime,' she said, changing the subject and straightening her back before nodding at the file in his hand. 'Is that the contract?'

He'd almost forgotten what he had come here for.

Pulling his mind back to attention, he took the sheets of paper out of the folder. 'I've booked our wedding for Thursday.'

She was silent for beat. 'Thursday?'

'*Oui.*'

'I was supposed to marry Javier on Saturday.'

'At this short notice there are no slots available for Saturday.'

'Couldn't you have bribed or blackmailed someone?'

'I pulled enough strings to bypass the notice period. If it's a Saturday wedding you long for we can always wait a few weeks.' He stared hard at her as he said this. Having now read the terms of the contract he understood why she was keen to marry on the same day she would have married Javier. On the day of their wedding he would transfer two hundred thousand euros into her account, the first recurring monthly payment of that sum. According to the contract, Javier had already paid her two lump sums of one hundred thousand euros.

'No,' she declined so hurriedly he could see the euro signs ringing in her eyes. 'Thursday is fine.'

He gave a tight smile. 'I thought so. I will take you to the town hall tomorrow to meet the mayor and fill out some forms but the arrangements are all in hand. Is your passport in your apartment?'

She nodded. 'I've spoken to my flatmate. She's got it safe.'

'I will send a courier to collect it.'

'I'll go and get it. I need to collect the rest of my stuff.'

'Your possessions can be couriered over with the passport.'

'I want to get them myself.'

The thought of her being in the same city as Javier set his teeth on edge. '*Impossible*. There is too much to arrange here.'

'I need my clothes.'

'I have appointments in Paris after our meeting with the mayor tomorrow. You can fly there with me and buy whatever you need.'

'With what? Fresh air? I can't buy an entire new wardrobe with one hundred and fifty euros, which is all I have in my account.'

His lips curved in distaste. 'You have spent all the money Javier has already given to you?'

'Yes. I had…'

'I have no cares for what you spend your money on. I will give you a credit card. Buy whatever you need with it. Consider it an early wedding present. While you are there you can buy a wedding dress.'

'Something black to match your heart?' she suggested with a touch of bitterness.

'You are hardly in a position to talk of my heart when you were party to a contract like this one.'

There was the slightest flinch. 'Javier and I drew up a marriage agreement that suited us both.'

'It does not suit me.'

'You said you would honour it.'

'And I will. I have only changed one item.'

'I'm not signing unless it's the original with only Javier's name substituted for yours.'

'You will if you still want the fortune and all the assets that come with it.'

'What have you changed?'

'Look for yourself.' He handed the file to her. 'The change is highlighted in red.'

She took it from him with a scowl.

'May I remind you,' he said as she flicked through the papers, 'that it is your choice to marry me. I am not forcing your hand.'

She didn't look up from the papers. 'There was no other choice for me.'

'The lure of all that money too strong to give up?' he mocked.

But she didn't answer, suddenly looking up at him with wide eyes, colour blasting over her cheeks. 'Of all the things you could have changed, you changed *that*?'

'I am not signing away a chunk of my fortune and my freedom to spend only one night a week in a bed with my wife.' He'd read that part of the long, detailed pre-nuptial agreement with his mouth open, shaking his head with disbelief as he'd wondered what kind of a woman would sign such a document.

Scheduled, mandated sex?

And then he had read the next section and his incredulity had grown.

How could the woman who kissed as if she were made of lava agree to such a marriage?

He stared at Freya now and wondered what was going on in that complex brain. She was impossible to fathom, a living contradiction. Scalding hot on the outside but seemingly cold on the inside. Which was the real Freya: the hot or the cold one?

'I will comply in full with the rest of the contract but when we are under the same roof we sleep in the same bed. If it is not something you can live with I suggest you tell me now so I can make the necessary arrangements for your departure from my home.'

Freya stared into eyes as uncompromising as his words and dug her bruised toes into the carpet. Her skin itched with the need for movement, the hour of yoga she had done before he had walked into her quarters nowhere near enough to quell the fears and emotions pummelling her.

Their kiss…

It had frazzled all her nerve endings.

How could she have reacted to his kiss like that? To *him*?

It had been her first proper kiss and it had been everything a first kiss should be and, terrifyingly, so much more.

She had spent the day searching for a way to purge her heightened emotions but her usual method of dancing her fears away was not available to her. She'd taken a long walk through his grounds and explored the vast chateau praying that somewhere within the huge rooms would be one she could use to dance in. It had been like Goldilocks searching for the perfect porridge and bed but without the outcome; not one of the rooms had been right. The majority could work with their proportions but the flooring was all wrong, either too slippery or covered in carpet, neither of which were suitable and could be dangerous.

Meditation and yoga were her fail-safe fall-backs, clearing her mind and keeping her body limber, but they weren't enough, not for here and now when she was as frightened for her future and as terrified of what was happening inside her as she had ever been.

Her brain burned to imagine Benjamin's private reaction when he had read the section that covered intimacy in her pre-nup. Javier had insisted it be put in, just as he had insisted on the majority of all the other clauses, including the one stating they would only have a child at a time of Freya's choosing. He hadn't wanted them to ever get to a point in the future where either could accuse the other of going back on what had been agreed. That agreement would always be there, a guide for them to enter matrimony and ensure a long, harmonious union without any unpleasant arguments or misunderstandings.

The whole document read as cold and passionless, entirely appropriate for a marriage that had nothing to do with love but business and safety.

Javier had been cold but he *had* been safe. There had never been any emotional danger in marrying him.

She had never had to dig her toes into the ground when she was with him. There had been no physical effect whatsoever.

The brain burn deepened as she read the contents again, the only change being Benjamin's name listed as Party One. And the new clause stating they would share a bed when under the same roof.

Her heart thumped wildly, panic rabid and hot inside her.

When she had envisaged making love to Javier it had been with an analytical head, a box to tick in a marriage that would keep her mother alive and ease her suffering for months, hopefully years, to come.

There was nothing analytical about her imaginings of Benjamin. She had felt something move inside her in that first look they had shared, a flare of heat that had warmed her in ways she didn't understand and could never have explained.

Their kiss had done more than warm her. She could still feel the scorch of his lips on hers and his taste on her tongue. Meditation and yoga had done nothing to rid it but it had helped to a small extent, allowing her to control her raging heart and breathing when he had unexpectedly entered her quarters.

And then he had stared at her with the look that suggested he wanted to strip the last of her clothing off.

She had never been shy skimpily dressed in front of anyone before but in that moment and under the weight of that look she had felt naked for the first time in her life.

And she was expected to share his bed and give herself to this man who frightened her far more than her ice-cold fiancé ever had?

He, Benjamin, was her fiancé now...

She could do this, she assured herself, breathing deeply. She had faced far scarier prospects, like when she'd been eleven and had left the safety and comfort of her parents' home to become a boarder at ballet school. That had been truly terrifying even though it had also been everything she'd wanted.

Joining the school and discovering just how different she'd been to all the other girls had almost had her begging to go home. Having been accepted on a full scholarship that included boarding fees, she'd been the only girl there from a poor background. In comparison, all the others had been born with silver spoons in their mouths. They'd spoken beautifully, worn clothes that hadn't come from second-hand stores and had had holiday homes. Freya's parents hadn't even owned the flat they'd lived in.

Somehow she had got through the chronic homesickness and the merciless taunts that nowadays would be considered bullying by burying herself in ballet. She had learned to hide her emotions and express it all through dance, fuelling the talent and love for ballet she had been lucky enough to be born with.

If she could get through that then she was equal to this, equal to Benjamin and the heady, powerful emotions he evoked in her. She could keep them contained. She must.

She could not predict what her future held but she knew what the consequences would be if she allowed this one clause to scupper their marriage plans: a slow, cripplingly painful death for her mother. She would do anything to ease her mother's suffering. Anything. The first message that had popped into her phone when it had come back to life earlier was her father's daily update. Her mother had had 'a relatively comfortable night'. Translated, that meant the pain had only woken her a couple of times.

'If you're allowed to make a change in the contract then I must be allowed to make one too,' she told him, jutting her chin out and refusing to wilt under the swirling green eyes boring into her. She would not let him browbeat her before they had even signed the contract.

'Which is?'

'I was supposed to be moving in with Javier. My flat-mate's already found a new tenant to take my room so I'm not going to have anywhere to live when I'm at work. I want you to buy me an apartment to live in in Madrid. We're on a two-week shutdown so that's plenty of time for a man of your talents to buy one for me.'

She saw the faintest clenching of his jaw before his eyes narrowed.

'I will not have my wife working for my rival.'

'The contract states in black and white that I continue my career for as long as I like and I do what is best for me and my career. You have no say and no influence in it.'

'I can change the terms to include that.'

'You said one change. Or have you forgotten you're a man of your word?'

No, he had not forgotten, Benjamin thought grimly. It had simply not occurred to him that, having agreed to marry him, Freya would want to return to Madrid. She could work anywhere. It didn't have to be there.

'He will make your life a misery,' he warned.

'Javier has nothing to do with the day-to-day running of the company. He's rarely there.'

But Madrid was his home. The thought of Freya living in the same city as *him* set his teeth further on edge.

'There are many fine ballet companies in France who would love to employ you. I will never interfere with your career but in this instance I am going to have to insist.'

'Insist that I quit Compania de Ballet de Casillas?'

'*Oui.*'

The black eyes shot fire-dipped arrows at him. 'So you want to punish me and an entire ballet company for the sins of its owners, is that what you're saying?'

'*Non.* I am saying I do not wish for my wife to work for her ex-lover. It is not an unreasonable request.'

Something shone in her eyes that he didn't recognise, a shimmer in the midst of her loathing that disappeared as quickly as it had appeared. 'It's a request now? That's funny because the word *insist* made it sound remarkably like a demand.'

'This will be my only interference.'

Her foot tapped on the carpet but her tone remained calm. 'So I can get a job working in Japan and you won't complain?'

'You can work wherever you like.' As long as it was far from the Spaniard who had captured her long before he'd set eyes on her...

'Just not for Javier.'

'Just not for Javier.'

She sucked in a long draw of breath before inclining her head. 'I will hand my notice in but I will work my notice period. You can add that to the contract and reiterate you are never to interfere with my career.'

'How long is your notice period?'

'Two months. That will allow me to do the opening night of the new theatre. I'm on all the advertising litera-ture for it. I can't pull out. It's the biggest show of my life. I've worked too hard to throw it away.'

'*D'accord.*' He took in his own breath. Two months was

nothing. He could handle her working for Javier for that period.

He reminded himself that until that morning he had expected her to insist on returning to Madrid.

'You share my bed when we are under the same roof and hand your notice in to Compania de Ballet de Casillas. I buy you a property to live in while you work your notice and guarantee never to interfere with your career again. I believe that is everything unless there was something else you wished to discuss.'

Colour rose up her cheeks, her lips tightening before she gave a sharp nod. 'Just one thing I think it is best to make clear. I may be agreeing to share a bed with you but that does not mean you take ownership of my body. It belongs to me.'

'I think the kiss we shared earlier proves the lie in that, *ma douce*,' he said silkily.

The chemistry between them was real, in the air they both inhaled, a living thing swirling like a cloud, shrouding them.

'Think what you like.' She dropped her gaze. 'I will not be your possession.'

'I am not Javier. I do not expect you to be. But I do expect a wedding night. After that, you can turn your back to me as often as you wish. I do not forget the clause in the contract allowing Javier to take a mistress without question or explanation and, seeing as you have not requested that clause to be removed, it stands for me too. And as you know, I am a man who likes to have all options on the table.'

Her nostrils flared as she jutted her chin back out again, a sign he was starting to recognise meant she was straining to keep her composure.

Let her try and keep it. Come their wedding night he would shatter that composure and discover for himself if her veins ran hot or cold.

CHAPTER EIGHT

'YOU BOUGHT EVERYTHING you need?' Benjamin asked as his helicopter lifted into the air to fly them back to Provence after what had proven to be an extremely long day. 'It doesn't look like much.'

They had sorted out the paperwork for their wedding first thing then flown to Paris. Having work to do, he'd arranged for his PA's assistant who spoke English to take Freya shopping.

He had been so consumed in recent months with his feud with the Casillas brothers that he'd neglected his business. He'd hardly stepped through the headquarters of Guillem Foods in weeks and knew from bitter experience how dangerous it could be to take his eye off the ball. Now that the first part of his revenge had been extracted he needed to concentrate on his business for a while before making his next move. Luis would have to wait.

Yet even though he'd needed his brain to engage with Guillem Foods, he'd had to fight to keep his attention on the job because his mind kept wandering back to the woman who would be his wife in three days' time.

What was it about Freya that consumed his thoughts so much? She'd lodged herself in his mind from that first look, a fascination that had refused to shift that, now she was under his roof, was turning into an obsession.

Things would be better once he'd bedded her. The thrill of the chase and the unknown would be over and she would become mere flesh and bone.

He stared at her now, convinced she was the perfect wife for him. When the desire currently consuming him withered to nothing she would not care. Her own desire for him, unwanted as it was to her, wouldn't last either. Her heart was too cold for lust to turn into anything more. The marriage agreement she had willingly signed giving herself to two separate men proved that.

Freya was a gold-digger in its purest form. A gold-digger who at some point in the future would give him a child…

A sudden picture came into his head of Freya dancing, a miniature Freya at her feet copying her moves; the child they would have together, the child that would make the chateau he had bought for his mother to end her days in a home.

It was a picture he had never imagined with anyone in all his thirty-five years and the strength of it set blood pumping into his head and perspiration breaking out over his skin.

So powerful was his reaction to the image that it took a few moments to realise she was answering his question.

'Sophie's packing my stuff up for me. I've arranged for the courier to collect it later when he gets my passport.

'Will you not need it for your new apartment in Madrid?' How he hated to think of her returning there but a deal was a deal. The contract had been signed over breakfast.

He'd already instructed an employee to hunt for a suitable home in Madrid for her. The main stipulation was that it be located as far from the district Javier called home as possible.

'I'll decide what to take with me when I go back,' she said. 'It'll be mostly my training stuff I take.'

'Would it not be easier to have separate wardrobes for each home?' He spent the majority of the year in his chateau but had apartments in Paris and London and houses in Australia, Argentina and Chile. Each had its own complete wardrobe, allowing him to travel lightly and spontaneously when the need or mood arose.

She shrugged, not looking at him. 'That would be wasteful.'

Incredulous, he stared at her. 'You're going to have two hundred thousand euros credited to your account every month for the rest of your life on top of your earnings and you are worried about being wasteful?'

The black eyes found his.

His heart thumped in the unnerving way it always seemed to do whenever those eyes captured his.

'I learned not to waste things as a child.'

'You had strict parents?'

'No, I had poor parents.' She said it matter-of-factly but with a hint of defiance and more than a little hint of pride.

'How poor?' Sob-stories of childhoods were everywhere. Some were even genuine.

However much he might despise the Casillas brothers Benjamin would never deny how traumatic their childhood had been. It made his own seem like one of the fairy tales Freya danced to.

'So poor that when I was offered a full scholarship to the ballet school with boarding fees included, they *had* to let me board as they couldn't afford the commuting fees.'

'Did the scholarship not include travelling fees?'

'Only for me, not for them. Commuting would also have meant one of them would have had to give up one of their jobs to get me there and back twice a day and they were on the breadline as it was. They didn't think it was safe for me to travel from one side of London to the other on my own.'

'How old were you when you went to boarding school?'

'Eleven.'

Benjamin winced. That was a horribly young age to leave home. 'Were they those awful pushy parents we read so much about nowadays?'

Her eyes glinted with anger. 'No. They were wonderful. They held down two jobs each and juggled things so one of them was always home with me. They worked their backsides off to pay for my ballet lessons when I was little and then to support me at ballet school because the full scholarship didn't cover everything. They did it because they loved me and wanted me to be happy.'

'Ballet makes you happy?' It might have sounded like a stupid question but he remembered from his early childhood on tour with Clara Casillas the haunted faces of some of the dancers who had definitely not been happy with their lives.

'More than anything else. It's my life.'

He studied her in silence, their gazes fixed on each other.

He had never felt the pull of a woman's eyes the way he did with Freya. It was like staring into a black pool of unimaginable depths.

'Do you want to invite your parents to the wedding?' Their marriage had such a surreal quality to it that the thought she might want the people she loved there had never occurred to him until that moment.

'They don't travel.'

'Were they not going to come to your wedding to Javier?'

She shook her head.

'Have you told them?'

'That I've exchanged fiancés like a child swapping marbles in the playground? Yes, I spoke to my dad about it this morning. I told him you had stolen me.' The faintest smile curved on her lips. 'At least it wasn't a lie. How he interpreted it is up to him.'

'How did he take it?'

'I told you, my parents only want what's best for me. They love me and want me to be happy. Are you going to invite anyone?'

'The only person I would want is my sister but she is away.' Chloe was still in the Caribbean, taking advantage of the ballet company's shutdown for a well-deserved holiday and an escape from the fall-out.

Javier's representatives had issued a short statement that morning saying that his engagement to Freya Clements was over. No details had been provided and the press were in a spasm of speculation, the main question being whether Freya's disappearing act with Benjamin at the gala had been the cause.

'No other family to ask?' she asked.

'You are interested in me?'

'Not in the slightest. I'm merely curious as to what I'm marrying into.'

'My mother died seven years ago. My father and I are not close and never have been.' Not even when they had lived under the same roof. His mother had raised him as if she were a single parent and his father had let her, never suggesting that their only son stay behind with him rather than tour the ballet world. A second unplanned pregnancy ten years after the first had been the final nail in his parents' precarious marriage.

He'd barely noticed when his father left, let alone missed him.

'Are you sure you don't want to have anyone there?' he pressed. 'There is not much time if you do.'

'I would have said Sophie but she told me earlier that she's going to make the most of the shutdown and go off somewhere. I suppose it saves her being put in a compromising position.'

'Because she works for Compania de Ballet de Casillas?'

'Like all ballet companies it's a hotbed of gossip.'

'Then don't go back,' he stated immediately, seizing the advantage.

'Do you really think I could care less what my colleagues think of me?' she asked coolly. 'Sophie is the only one I care about. We've been friends since ballet school.'

'A long friendship then,' he observed. Not many friendships survived childhood. He'd thought those that did were the strongest. He'd learned the hard way how wrong that notion was.

'The only time we've been apart since we were eleven was when I first moved to Madrid.'

'She followed you there?'

She shrugged and turned her face to the window. Soon they would be landing back in Provence, time speeding on. 'There were vacancies for new dancers to join the *corps de ballet*. I put in a good word for her. She's the only dancer I'm close to. The others can say what they like about me, it doesn't matter in the slightest, but I will not have Sophie hurt.'

He stared at her shrewdly, nodding his head slowly. 'I can see why Javier thought you were the ideal woman for him to marry. Neither of you invite closeness. But you seem to have loyalty, which he does not possess. And there is fire in your veins, *ma douce*. There is passion. I have seen it and I have felt it. What I find myself wondering is if *he* ever saw it or if it was something you kept hidden from him.'

'How very poetic.' If not for the quiver in her voice and the tapping of her foot, he could believe the drollness of her tone was genuine.

'It is no matter.' He leaned forward. 'In three nights' time I will discover for myself how deep the fire runs inside you.'

Freya's eyes were just reaching that heavy about-to-fall-asleep stage when the motion of the car driving over the cattle grid pulled her back to alertness. She stared out of the window her forehead was pressed against; the forest that marked Benjamin's territory overhung and surrounded them, the moonlight casting shadows that made her shiver. This was a fairy-tale forest where the nightmares came out at night.

The prickling of her skin told her Benjamin, beside her in the back of the car, was watching her.

He was always watching her. As much as she wished she could claim differently, her eyes always sought his too.

It was the night before their wedding. The intervening days had been relatively easy to handle as he had spent them in Paris or in his office working. She had occupied herself as much as she could, taking long walks in the forest that scared her so much at night but which during the day came alive with wildlife and glorious colours. But there was nowhere to dance, not a single room within the multitude where she could risk putting pointe shoes on and letting her body relax in the movement that had always invigorated and comforted her.

The evenings were the hardest.

They dined together but the dishes they were served were entirely separate. Benjamin favoured dishes like juicy steaks and creamy mashed potato while she ignored the tantalising aromas and concentrated on her super-salads and grilled chicken, the meals punctuated by periodic polite conversation.

It was all the unspoken conversations that had her feet tapping and her limbs aching for movement, when their eyes would lock together and electricity would flow between them, so thick she felt the currents in her veins. She could never finish her meals fast enough to escape to the sanctuary of her quarters where, mercifully, he had not attempted to join her again.

If he did, she was no longer confined to practising yoga in her underwear; all her leotards and practice outfits had been delivered from Madrid with her passport and neatly put away.

She kept her passport on her at all times.

That night he had taken her out to the theatre to watch a play she couldn't remember the plot of, the movements and words on the stage passing her by in a blur, her concentration focused solely on the man sitting in the private box beside her.

'We are home,' he said quietly as the chateau appeared before them, illuminated in its magnificence.

'This is not my home.' Her denial was automatic.

'This will be our main marital house and the base for which we lead our lives. I want it to feel like home for you but you need to be the one to make it that. Do whatever you feel is necessary.'

Unable to help herself, she turned to look at him.

She wanted to deny his words more vehemently. She wanted to throw it all in his face, tell him that she could never make a home in the place he had basically imprisoned her in but she couldn't get the words out. The expression in his eyes had frozen her tongue to the roof of her mouth.

She had seen desire there; it was always there. She had seen loathing, she had even glimpsed pity in those green depths, but this…

This look made her insides melt into liquid and her heart race into a thrum.

This was a look of possession but not the look of a buyer appreciating his chattel. It was the possessive way a man looked at his lover, and the thought made the liquid in her insides *burn* to think that, in only one night, she would *be* his lover.

He was telling her to treat his home as her own and, more than that, he *meant it*. She could see it in the eyes she found herself continually seeking.

She could never imagine Javier saying something like that. Their engagement party had been nothing but an exercise in showing her off to his peers—he didn't have friends, he had acquaintances—and cementing their forthcoming union. She had never felt comfortable in his home and he had never done or said anything to make her feel that she should feel comfortable there. In truth, she had dreaded moving into that villa and living within the cold, emotionless walls.

Yet for all her dread at marrying him, she'd felt safe. He could touch her but he could never hurt her.

Benjamin on the other hand...

'Do you want a drink?' he asked casually as she hurried through the chateau doors. 'A last drink to celebrate the last night of our freedom?'

'No, thank you.' She shook her head for emphasis. 'I'm going up. I need to do some yoga and get some sleep.'

'Yoga at this time of night?'

She took the first step up the cantilevered stairs. 'If I can't dance it's the next best thing.'

And God knew she needed to do something. She would be marrying this man in fourteen hours.

'In that case, *bonne nuit.*'

Not looking back and holding the rail tightly, she skipped up the stairs feeling his stare on her with every step she took.

She had to remember that Benjamin had stolen her. He had *stolen* her.

Nothing he did or said could make up for that.

Marrying him was the only way she could salvage the mess that he had created for her in his ruthless game of revenge.

If she dropped her guard, he had the potential to hurt her in ways she did not have the imagination to imagine.

The wedding ceremony was simple and, best of all, quick.

Two hours after they had been pronounced husband and wife, they sat alone in an exclusive restaurant at the pretty little town they had married in, and all Freya could remember of the ceremony itself was how she'd trembled; her hands, her voice as she'd made her vows, but she could remember nothing of the vows themselves. She remembered how warm her skin had been and how certain she'd been that the mayor, who'd officiated the service, and the witnesses he'd brought in could all hear the hammering of her heart.

She couldn't remember the faces of the witnesses. She couldn't remember the face of the photographer who had taken the official picture of the newly married couple on the steps of the town hall but she could remember the butterflies that had let loose in her stomach as she'd waited for the kiss that would show the world she belonged to Benjamin, striking a further blow to the pride of the man she should have married.

She had held her core tightly in dread and anticipation. Benjamin had stared intently into her eyes but instead of stamping his possession on her mouth, had pulled her to him so her cheek pressed against his chest and his chin rested on the top of her head. She could remember the scent of his cologne and the warmth of his skin through the smart suit he'd married her in, and most vividly she remembered the dive of disappointment that the kiss she'd worked herself up for had never happened.

From that day the world would know her as Freya Guillem. It would be her professional name, just as she had agreed to take Javier's name what now felt a lifetime ago.

She could no longer remember Javier's face. She didn't think she had ever looked at it properly.

But she knew every contour of Benjamin's. His features had been committed to her memory all those months ago in that one, long, lingering look when she should never have noticed him in the first place. Her hungry eyes had soaked in all the little details since she had been living under his roof and now she knew the exact position of the scar above his lip, the differing shades of his eyes depending on the light and his mood, the unruliness of his black eyebrows if he didn't smooth them down, the faint dimple that appeared in his left cheek when he smiled, which wasn't often.

But when he did smile...

His smile had the capacity to make her stomach melt into a puddle.

Trying her hardest to hide the fresh tremors in her hand, she took another drink of her champagne and readily allowed the maître d' to refill it.

'Is the food not to your liking, madam?' he asked, staring with concern at her plate.

'It's delicious,' she replied honestly. 'I'm just not very hungry.'

She'd had to virtually force-feed herself the few bites she'd had of her challans duck with crispy pear and other little morsels of taste sensation artfully displayed on her plate.

The town they'd married in was a beautiful place of old, steep, narrow streets and chic, impeccably dressed men and women. This was rural France but with a modern twist, its eclectic shops and restaurants catering to the filthy rich. The restaurant Benjamin had taken her to to celebrate their nuptials was the plushest of the lot, its chef the recipient of so many awards he was a household name, even to her. Benjamin had hired the whole restaurant for their exclusive use.

'Has anticipation caused you to lose your appetite?' the man she had married only a few hours before asked with a gleam in his eyes, the look of seduction, the unspoken promise that the kiss he had failed to deliver on at the top of the town hall steps would soon be forthcoming.

Whatever had affected her appetite had not had the same effect on him, she thought resentfully, staring at his cleared plate. He had eaten with the same relish he ate all his meals. Apart from breakfast, she remembered. Benjamin had an aversion to breakfast.

'Anticipation about what?' she challenged. 'If you think I'm nervous about sharing a bed with you then I'm afraid I must disappoint you.'

And she wasn't nervous. She was terrified.

The gleam in his eyes only deepened. 'I don't think it is possible that you could disappoint me, *ma douce*.'

You'll be disappointed when you discover my complete lack of experience.

She knew she should tell him. It was something she had told herself repeatedly these past few days but every time she practised in her head what to say, her brain would burn and she'd get a queasy roiling in her belly. Benjamin was expecting to share his bed with an experienced woman, not a virgin.

Would he laugh at her? Or simply disbelieve her? Maybe he would even refuse to sleep with her, a thought that would have sent her into hysterical laughter if her vocal cords hadn't frozen. As if he would care. The man was remorseless.

Whatever his reaction would be she had yet to find the words to tell him and now the time was speeding up and all she could do was drag this meal out for as long as she could to delay what she knew was inevitable.

Yet staring into those green eyes that gazed so blatantly back at her, she couldn't deny there was truth in Benjamin's observation. Anticipation had laced itself within her fear. It had steadily coiled itself through her bloodstream and now she didn't know if it was fear or anticipation that had her clutched in its grip the strongest.

She had to get a hold on herself and keep her head. Keep her control, the only part of herself that would be left for herself when this night was over.

He reached over to take her hand, leaning forward as he rubbed his thumb against her wrist to stare at her with a piercing look that sent fresh tingles racing through her blood. She was certain he must be able to feel the pulse behind the skin of her wrist throbbing madly.

His voice dropped to a sensuous murmur. 'As you are not hungry for food…' He raised her hand and pressed his lips to the very spot on her wrist his thumb had brushed against. 'Time to leave, *ma douce*. Let us see if we can whet and satisfy a different hunger.'

CHAPTER NINE

THE DRIVE BACK through the winding roads of Provence to his secluded chateau seemed to take hours rather than just twenty short minutes.

Benjamin had never known his veins to fizz as wildly as they were doing right then or been so aware of the heat of his skin. Freya stared out of the window beside him, her stillness absolute. Only the erratic rise and fall of her chest showed it to be nothing but a façade.

He could not believe how stunning she looked that day. Freya's striking looks had turned into a beauty that had stolen his breath so many times he was surprised he had any oxygen left in his lungs.

She'd chosen to marry him in a simple white silk dress that floated to her ankles, with a lace bodice that sparkled under the sun's rays held up by delicate spaghetti straps. On her feet were flat white sandals that suited the bohemian effect of the dress, her dark hair loose and falling in waves over her shoulders.

The dress she had chosen had hardly been a traditional wedding dress but it had been perfect for their wedding. It had proven her commitment in the vows she was making.

Benjamin had taken one look at her and wished he'd arranged for them to exchange those vows in his chateau garden under an archway adorned with flowers of all different scents and colours.

They had left the town hall as husband and wife and stood together at the top of the steps, the photographer's lens trained on them exactly as Benjamin had instructed.

The sun's rays had bounced over Freya's skin and he had stared into eyes that were wide with trepidation, and felt that same dazzling punch in the guts he'd experienced the first time he'd set eyes on her. Just like that, the kiss he'd planned for the media's delectation and Javier's continued humiliation had seemed all wrong.

This was their wedding. Whatever the circumstances behind their vows, this was a commitment they were making to each other.

He didn't want to think about his nemesis.

Instead, he had put an arm around her and drawn her to him so her cheek rested against his chest. She had trembled in his arms.

It had come to him then as he inhaled her scent with the photographer's lens flashing at them why he needed their first kiss as husband and wife to be away from prying eyes…his need to possess Freya had become stronger than his thirst for revenge against Javier.

When he kissed her next, he had no intention of stopping.

'The first time we drove this road together in the dark you had a can of pepper spray aimed at my face,' he commented idly as his driver took them through his forest.

They were almost home.

She didn't move her head from the window. 'I wish I had used it.'

'Do you think it would have changed the outcome between us?'

She raised a shoulder in a light shrug. 'If I hadn't left the hotel with you, if I had taken my chances at the airfield, if I had made a successful escape over your wall…any of those things could have changed the outcome.'

He reached a hand out to smooth a lock of her hair behind an ear.

'Do you wish you *had* been able to change it? Do you wish it had been Javier you exchanged your vows with today?'

She stilled, whether at his touch or his question he did not know.

Her throat moved before she said quietly, 'I married you. It is pointless wishing for an alternative reality.'

A stab of something that felt a little like how he imagined jealousy would feel cut into his chest.

That hadn't been a denial.

Freya had never given any indication that she harboured genuine feelings for Javier but nor had she given any indication that she didn't.

She desired him; that had been proven beyond doubt, but that didn't mean she didn't desire Javier too.

Had she spent their wedding day wishing she had married the other man? Was she approaching their wedding night wishing it were Javier's bed she would be sharing instead of his?

He rubbed his finger over the rim of her ear. Freya had such pretty, delicate ears…he had never thought of ears as pretty before. He had never noticed *anyone's* ears before.

He noticed everything about Freya. There was not a part of her face he wasn't now familiar with in a way he had never been familiar with another.

He could hardly wait to discover the parts she kept hidden from view. That time was almost with them and if she was approaching it wishing it were with Javier then he would make damn sure to drive his rival from her mind.

Come the morning her first thought would be him and him alone.

Come the morning and she would never wish she were with Javier or think of him again.

'Drink?'

Freya nodded tightly. Her knees shook so hard they could hardly support her weight. She had been unable to speak since they had walked back into the chateau to a

vibrant display of flowers and balloons in the main reception room.

She had no idea where the staff were though. The chateau, normally bustling with unobtrusive life, was silent
enough to hear a pin drop.

The silence in Benjamin's bedroom was even more op-
pressive. She fought the urge to bolt like a frightened colt.

'Take a seat.' He strolled to a dark wood cabinet, gesturing to the cosy armchair in the corner of his bedroom.

She sat and pressed her knees together under the wedding dress she knew wouldn't be covering her for much
longer.

As terrified as she was at that moment, there was none
of the coldness in her veins fear normally brought about.
Instead there was heat, electricity zinging over her skin,
dread and desire colliding.

Benjamin's quarters had a similar layout to her own but,
where hers were painted in light, muted colours that had a
decidedly feminine feel, his was much darker with a rich,
masculine hue.

His bed…

She had never known beds that large existed. She had
never known beds could be a work of art in their own
right. Made of a dark wood she didn't know the name of,
it was clearly a bespoke creation, and covered in a beautiful silk-looking slate-grey duvet that must be bespoke too
to fit the bed.

Freya breathed in deeply, trying her hardest to keep the
trembles threatening to overwhelm her under control, looking everywhere but at that bed.

'Your drink, Madame Guillem.'

She had to hold herself back from snatching the glass
from his hand and downing it all in one.

It wasn't the first time she had been addressed by her

new title since the service but it was the first time Benjamin had said it.

She was thankful she hadn't downed her drink when she took the first big sip and tasted its potency. Benjamin had made her a gin and tonic that was definitely more gin than tonic and the one sip was enough to steady her nerves, if only momentarily.

He'd moved away from her again to return to the cabinet, dimming the lights on the way. A moment later, low music filled the room and broke the heavy, stifling silence.

She had never heard the song before but the singer's soulful baritone calmed her that little bit more. It didn't make it any easier for her to breathe though and she took another sip of her drink, her nerves back on tenterhooks as she waited for Benjamin to make his move.

He held a crystal tumbler of what she assumed to be Scotch in his hand and was wafting it gently under his nose while he stared at her, a meditative gleam in his green eyes. His gaze not dropping from hers, he drained his drink in one swallow and placed the empty tumbler on the cabinet.

Then he strode to her with a hand held out.

He didn't speak. He didn't need to.

She stared at the steady hand, so much larger than her own, taking in the masculine elegance of his long fingers before slipping her hand into it and wordlessly allowing him to help her to her feet.

At some point since they'd returned to his chateau, Benjamin had removed his tuxedo jacket and bow tie and undone the top two buttons of his white shirt. Freya had never seen him wear white before, black being his colour of choice, which she had assumed was to match his heart.

The white contrasted against the dark olive hue of his skin and even more starkly against the shadows the collar of his shirt made against his throat.

Her gaze rose with a will of its own to rest on his face

and the eyes that had become as dark as the forests that surrounded his home.

The hand still holding hers tightened and she swayed forward so their faces were close enough for the warmth of his breath to whisper against her lips and suddenly she was taken by that same burst of desperate longing that had overcome her two months before when she had first seen him standing in Javier's garden.

This was the man who had haunted her dreams for two long months, the man she had been unable to stop herself obsessing over, the last man in the world she would have chosen to marry simply because he was the one man in the world who evoked this sick, desperate longing inside her with nothing more than a look and made her heart feel as if it could burst through her ribcage and soar like a songbird to lodge itself in his chest.

Their faces still close enough together that one tiny jolt forward would join their lips together, Benjamin's hold on her hand loosened. His fingers trailed up her arm to her shoulder, burning shivers trailing in their wake.

She closed her eyes to the sensation firing through her, the beats of her heart so loud they drowned out the music playing.

His hand now drew up her neck to burrow into her hair, the other splayed across her lower back. Her lips tingled as his warm breath drew closer, filling her mouth with moisture as his lips finally claimed hers.

The first press of his mouth against hers set off something inside her, a rush of need so powerful that she fought frantically against it, clenching her hands into fists to cling onto the last of her sanity before the desire dragged her down to a place she feared—the greatest of all her fears— she could never come back up from.

Since agreeing to marry him she had imagined herself playing the role of sacrificial virgin, lying on the bed and letting him take what he wanted but giving nothing back. She had known that to remain passive would take the greatest self-control of her life, especially after the kiss they had shared, but it was only as his tongue danced into her mouth that she understood how futile a hope it had been. Her hunger for him...it was too much. With a sigh that could have been a moan, she swayed into the strength of his solid body and welcomed the heat of his hungry kisses.

Her movement set something off in him too. The hands securing her gently tightened and then she was on her toes, crushed against him, breasts against chest, pelvis against abdomen, her hands winding around his neck, her fingers digging into the nape of his neck, her tongue dancing against his. And it was his hands now sweeping over her back and up her sides, brushing the underside of her breasts, the ferocity of their kisses intensifying with every passing second. Every time he touched her bare skin she felt the mark of his skin against hers and her hunger grew.

She was so caught up in their kisses she only realised he'd pulled the zip of her dress down her back when his hand slid into the opened space and dipped down to clasp her bottom.

Her breaths shallow, she moved her face to stare at him, terror making its return.

She had to tell him, she thought wildly. If she didn't...

'Benjamin...'

But he'd taken the skinny straps of her dress and skimmed them down her arms. She had hardly spoken the last syllable of his name before gravity pulled her dress down, her lean body offering it no resistance so it fell into a pool at her feet leaving her naked bar her plain, cotton knickers.

Her arms flailed to cover her breasts, panic now clawing at her.

Nudity was no big deal to her, it couldn't be. She danced

without wearing underwear, as most dancers did. She had never been body-conscious, never been one to torment herself over her shape. She ate the best diet she could and worked hard to keep her body lean and supple so she had every tool she could to be the best dancer she could be.

But she had never been virtually naked in front of a man who wasn't looking at her as a dancer but as a lover.

She hadn't had an hour of meditation and yoga to calm her mind as she had when he'd walked into her quarters the other day.

Never, until that moment, had she felt truly naked.

Her breasts were *tiny*, she thought hopelessly. She didn't have the curves other women had.

Benjamin had stepped back to look at her, and she cringed to see the frown on his face.

Then the frown softened and his hands rested on her arms that still desperately covered her breasts. Gripping them lightly, he slowly pulled them apart to expose her for his scrutiny.

Her mortification grew when he let go of her arms so they hung by her hips, her fingers twitching to cover her breasts again.

He stepped back again then slowly walked around her. She could feel the stare of his eyes penetrating her skin and could do nothing to stop the trembling of her legs.

She was exposing herself in a way she had spent years fighting to keep covered, not her external flesh but what lay beneath it, the sensuality that lay beneath her skin, the only part of herself that was hers alone, never to be given, never to be shared, the only part of herself she'd been able to keep *for* herself.

It was slipping through her fingers and the harder she tried to keep control of it, the more it pulled away from her and into Benjamin's hands...

When he finally stood in front of her again he placed a

finger on her lips and leaned in to nuzzle his lips against her ear. *'Tu es belle, ma douce.'*

She was stunned at the tenderness in his voice even if she didn't understand the words, her breath leaving her again as he moved his finger from her lips to cover her cheeks with the whole of his hands and stare hard into her eyes.

'You are beautiful, Freya.'

His lips brushed against hers before brushing over her jaw to burrow into her neck. Then he sank onto his knees so his face was level with her breasts.

He stared at them before covering them entirely with his hands. He gazed up at her. 'They are perfect. *You* are perfect.'

She couldn't breathe. Her throat had closed, fresh sensation bubbling inside her, the hunger in his eyes driving out the panic.

Then he slid his hands sensuously over her stomach to grip her hips and covered her breasts with his mouth.

At the first flick of his tongue over her nipple she gasped, her hands flailing to rest on his shoulders.

Sensation suffused her, intensifying as he took one breast into his mouth, his obvious delight in them and the thrills shooting through her veins driving the last of her embarrassment and fear clean out of her.

Benjamin felt Freya's sharp nails dig through his shirt and into his skin, the most pleasurable pain of his life.

For two months he had dreamed of this moment; dreamed of Freya coming undone in his arms, imagined her naked and fantasised about all the things he wanted to do with her.

This was beyond anything his feeble imagination could have dreamt up, and they had barely begun.

Her breasts were the smallest he had ever seen but they were the most beautiful. He hadn't been lying when he had called them perfect. Perfectly round, perfectly high and the perfect fit for his mouth.

They had the perfect taste too.

She had the perfect taste.

Slowly he trailed his mouth down her stomach, revelling in the smooth perfection of her skin, thrilling at the quiver of her belly when he licked it and the ragged movement of her chest as she struggled to breathe, knowing it was her response to *him* causing it.

His own breaths had become ragged too. The tightness in his groin was almost intolerable, his need for relief a burn that he willingly ignored, too intent on seducing this beautiful woman—his *wife*—to care for his own needs.

His time would come.

Lower down he went, raining soft kisses over her abdomen to the band of her underwear, the heat inside him rising as he got closer to her womanly heat.

Pinching the elastic of her knickers in his fingers, he gently tugged them down her hips to her supple yet shaking thighs.

He touched his nose to the soft hair between her legs and breathed deeply.

About to nuzzle lower, he became dimly aware that her fingers, which had been digging into his scalp, had stopped moving.

Looking up, he found her staring down at him with what could only be described as terror in her eyes.

It stopped him in his tracks.

'Have you not done this before?' he asked slowly.

She hesitated before giving a jerky shake of her head.

His brain racing, he pressed a tender kiss into the downy hair, inhaled her intoxicating scent one more time and tugged the underwear back up to cover her.

Freya had less experience than he had thought…

Getting back to his feet, he pressed himself close to her

quivering body and gently kissed her, then lifted her into his arms.

There was no resistance. She wound her arms around his neck and gazed into his eyes as he carried her to the bed.

Laying her down, he kissed her again, more deeply, before dipping his face into the elegant arch of her neck and tenderly nipping the skin with his teeth.

'I have too many clothes on,' he said into her neck, then pressed a kiss against the pulse beating wildly at the base of her jawline and sat up.

The obsidian of her eyes seemed to glow with the weight of a thousand emotions. She raised a hand as if to reach out and touch him then swallowed. The hand fell back to her side.

He picked it up and razed a kiss across the knuckles. *'Tu es belle.'*

She *was* beautiful. Mesmerising.

Her lips quirked in the glimmer of a smile and her chest rose as she took a deep breath.

Not taking his gaze from her face, Benjamin proceeded to undress, first his shirt, then getting to his feet to tug his trousers and underwear off until he was fully naked. He'd been so caught up in his seduction of Freya and the headiness of the moment that he hadn't appreciated how constricting his clothes had been until he took them off and his arousal sprang free.

Resisting the urge to take it in his hand, he sat back on the bed. 'Now you are the one with too many clothes on,' he said with a lightness that belied the heavy thuds of his heart, tracing his finger in a line from the dip at the top of her neck, down between her breasts and over the flat plain of her stomach to rest on the band of her knickers.

Dieu, he could devour her whole.

Her hands clenched into fists, her breaths becoming ragged again. He took hold of both her wrists and slowly spread them up to rest either side of her head as he laid himself over her until he covered her, propping his weight up on his elbows to gaze into her pulsating eyes.

Then he kissed her.

As their mouths moved together, fused into one, the passion reigniting and deepening, he loosened his hold on her wrists and laced his fingers through hers. She squeezed in response then dragged them away to wrap her arms around his neck and pull him down so his weight was fully on her.

He groaned at the sensation of her breasts pressed so tightly against his chest and kissed her more deeply. His skin was alive with heat that seeped through his veins and deep into his bones, all thoughts leaving him except one; the one that needed to touch and taste every part of this beautiful woman who had been in his head for so long and now lay in his bed and in his blood.

With his mouth and hands he began his exploration, discovering the parts of her body that made her suck in a breath at his touch, the parts that made her moan, the parts that made her nails dig into his flesh, feeling her relax so much that when he pressed his mouth to her pelvis again, she sighed and her left leg writhed.

Encouraged, Benjamin slowly tugged her knickers down, making a trail with his tongue down her legs in its wake before kissing his way back up and inhaling the scent of her heat without any barrier at all.

She stilled.

For a long time he didn't move, waiting to see what she would do.

Then he felt the whisper of her hand on his head, her fingers threading through his hair…

He traced his tongue between the damp folds and heard her gasp. Her fingers made twisting motions in his hair that pulled when he found her secret nub and her bottom lifted.

Dieu.

With all the languid care in the world, he made love to her with his mouth, relishing the taste of her sweet muskiness on his tongue, letting her responses, which were becoming more overt by the second, guide him as to what was giving her the greatest pleasure, intent only *on* her pleasure, Freya's pleasure, Freya, this beautiful, beautiful woman he ached to make completely his.

Only when he was sure that she was nearing her peak and completely ready for him did he slide his tongue back up her stomach, nipping each of her breasts with his teeth as he went, to reclaim her mouth and gently part her thighs.

Guiding his erection to the warmth of her heat he closed his eyes and gritted his teeth.

This was a moment to savour.

Inhaling deeply through his nose, he covered her mouth with his then could hold on no longer. With one long thrust, he buried himself deep inside her...

Freya felt a momentary sharpness that she would probably have missed if she hadn't been waiting for it, then there was nothing but sensation, every single nerve ending inside her sighing and delighting in the feel of Benjamin finally inside her, filling her completely.

She gazed into the green eyes that were staring at her with such hunger, and touched his face before lifting her head to kiss him.

How she loved his kisses. Loved his tongue taking such rough possession of hers. Loved his touch. Loved the feel of his broad chest covering hers, the dark hairs brushing against her breasts. Loved what he was doing to her right then...

Ohhhhh...

Her head fell back on the pillow as he began to move. He withdrew slowly only to plunge into her again. And then he did it again, and again, over and over, somehow knowing exactly what she wanted and what she needed, all the things about herself she hadn't known.

The last of the fight had left her when he'd carried her to the bed and laid her down so tenderly, almost as if she were precious to him...

And then he had kissed and stroked all her defences and fears away until sanity had ceased to matter. Nothing mattered. Nothing apart from *this*; here, now, them, together.

She'd had no idea that she could feel such things.

And the sensations ravaging her were heightening.

As Benjamin's movements grew wilder, his breath hot on her face, his groans soaking into her skin, the throbbing ache deep within her tightened and burned into a flame. Hotter and hotter it grew, blazing into a peak that came to a crescendo...

And then she was soaring, sparks exploding through her on a riptide of pleasure she had never, never, imagined possible.

Hazily she was aware that Benjamin had let go too, burying his face in her hair with a ragged, drawn-out moan.

She held him tightly as they rocked together, holding on to the pleasure for as long as they could until, finally, they both stilled and all that was left of the explosion were tiny glowing flickers that tingled and buzzed through and over every part of her.

CHAPTER TEN

FREYA LOST ALL semblance of time as she lay there with Benjamin's weight so deliciously compressing on her. They could have lain there for minutes or hours.

She opened her eyes. She felt so profoundly different from when she had walked into this room that she half expected the room to look different too.

The dim lights were still on. The music Benjamin had put on still played, a different song now worming its way through her slowly de-fuzzing head.

'Okay?' His question came as a murmur yet cut through the silence as if he had shouted it.

Her throat closed and she had to breathe deeply to get air into her suddenly constricted lungs.

'Fine,' she managed.

He rolled off her and onto his back, though kept his head turned so he faced her. 'You are sure?'

She wanted to offer a pithy comment, something that would negate the huge whirl of emotions filling her, to deny the wondrousness of what she had just experienced and which she knew, as pathetically inexperienced as she had been, that he had shared too.

But she couldn't. Somehow this man who was still very much a stranger even if he was her husband... He had made her feel beautiful. He had recognised her fear and inexperience and made love to her as if she were someone to cherish.

She would not let fear demean or diminish it.

Slowly she turned her head to look into the eyes that always saw too much, and nodded.

He studied her for long moments before craning his neck

to kiss her gently. 'I'm going to turn the music off. Can I get you a drink?'

'No, thank you.'

He kissed her again then turned over and climbed off the bed.

She watched him stride to the sound system, completely at ease in his skin.

And no wonder. Until that moment she hadn't looked at him properly. She'd gazed at his broad chest and felt it crushed against her, seen his strong, muscular arms and felt them bunch in her hands, the rest of him only glimpsed at, even the long legs she'd wound her own around.

She'd thought of him as having the stalking grace of a panther but only now, seeing him unashamedly naked, all the components that made him Benjamin put together, did she fully appreciate his rugged masculine beauty. It made the breath catch in her throat...

'You like what you see?'

She blinked, suddenly aware she had been staring at him.

Cheeks flaming, she then became aware that she had been staring at him naked, forgetting her own nakedness.

The hazy glow of their lovemaking had gone and with it her confidence to be naked around this man.

He'd cast her in a spell. He must have done.

She had done more than bare herself to him, she had given the essence of herself. She had lost control.

He'd made her forget. Forget what he'd done. Forget who she was and all the reasons she needed to keep an emotional distance from him.

His lovemaking had been incredible...*they* had been incredible. Just as she had feared.

'I like what *I* see,' he murmured, seemingly unfazed by her silence.

She averted her eyes from his gleaming scrutiny and,

keeping her thighs together to protect her modesty as best she could, grabbed the duvet, which their lovemaking had dislodged and managed to heap into a pile, and burrowed low into it.

He laughed lightly. 'I have embarrassed you.'

She sensed him treading back to his side of the bed and wished she could escape to the solitude of her own quarters.

A breeze fluttered against her back, Benjamin lifting the duvet to climb back in beside her. As she waited for the bed to dip, holding the part of the duvet she was wrapped in tightly, she became aware of a silence.

Coldness crept up her spine that had nothing to do with her back being exposed as the silence drew out and she was on the verge of saying something to break it when he finally got into bed.

She held her breath, squeezed her eyes shut and waited for him to turn off the dim lights. If she kept her back to him and played dead he might leave her alone.

Don't touch me, she silently begged. *Your touch is too much. Please, don't make me lose any more of myself than I already have.*

But the question he posed into the silence made her wish he had touched her instead.

'You were a *virgin*?'

What else explained the small, red stain marking the under-sheet of his bed? Benjamin wondered, his mind reeling. He'd seen it as he'd pulled the duvet back and his blood had run from languidly sated to ice cold in an instant.

Freya had been more than merely inexperienced. She'd been a virgin.

His chest tightened.

Why hadn't she told him?

Slowly she rolled over, her black orbs fixing straight onto him.

The tightness in his chest turned into a cramp.

For a long time neither of them spoke.

'You were a virgin.' This time he posed it as a statement.

She gave the briefest, jerkiest of nods.

'Why didn't you tell me?'

She swallowed and blinked rapidly. 'I couldn't.'

'Why not?'

Clenching her jaw, she shrugged.

'If I'd had the slightest idea you were a virgin, I would never…'

'Never have *what*?' she interrupted, suddenly fierce, her neck and face turning the colour of crimson, the obsidian in her eyes spitting at him. 'Stolen me? Blackmailed me? Wrecked my life? Forced me to give up my job in a company I love? Does my being a virgin somehow *improve* me? Does my innocence make me a better, more worthy person?'

The tenderness he'd felt towards her vanished as a flash of lava-like anger coursed through him. At her. At himself.

At himself for blackmailing a virgin into marriage.

At Freya for putting money above her own morals, or whatever it was that had caused her to reach the age of twenty-three years untouched.

'Innocent? You signed a contract exchanging your body for money!'

'No, I signed a contract of *marriage*. You read that contract without any context and made assumptions about me because it suited your agenda. Not once did you ask *why* I chose to sign it. You were determined to punish Javier and to hell with who got hurt while you did it.'

'You wanted the money. You made that very clear.' He leaned forward so his nose almost touched hers, delivering his words with ice-cold precision. 'Paint yourself as a sainted martyr if you must but no one forced you to sign those contracts. No one forced you to marry me. No one forced you into my bed, and no one, *no one*, forced you to enjoy being in it.'

Her face became aflame with colour but she didn't back down. 'Who said I enjoyed it?'

He slid his hand around her neck and rested his cheek against hers, ignoring her attempt to rear out of his hold. Speaking into her ear, he whispered, 'You came undone in my arms, *ma douce*, and that is why you are so angry now. You hate that you desire me and you hate that what we just shared proves the self-control you take such pride in is built on sand. If I were to kiss you now, you would come undone all over again.'

'Get your hands off me,' she said with such venom her words landed like barbs on his skin. 'Do not forget my body belongs to me. I am not your chattel.'

He did more than move away from her, he threw the duvet off and climbed out of the bed to stride to his bathroom. Over his shoulder, as if delivering a throwaway comment, he said, 'I'm going to take a shower. Feel free to use my absence to return to your own quarters.'

He could feel the burn of her stare as he locked the bathroom door.

Alone, he pressed the palms of his hands tightly against the cool white tiles and took a deep breath, then another, and another, fighting the urge to punch the walls until his knuckles bled.

The world had turned itself upside down in a matter of seconds.

Dieu, she had been a virgin.

Stepping into the shower, he turned the temperature up as high as he could bear and scrubbed vigorously at his skin, determined to rid himself of the grubby, scaly feeling cloying in his pores.

When he'd finally rubbed himself raw and returned to the bedroom, Freya had gone.

* * *

'This is where you've been hiding.'

Freya looked up from the bench she was sitting on under the cherry tree, shielding her eyes from the sun with her hand.

Benjamin walked towards her, a bottle of water in his hand, a wary smile on his face.

'I've been looking for you,' he explained with a shrug.

Feigning nonchalance at his unexpected appearance although her heart immediately set off at a canter, she stretched her legs out. On this scorching summer's day, he'd dressed in black jeans and a dark blue shirt, his only concession to the sun his rolled-up sleeves. She couldn't detect an ounce of perspiration on him whereas little beads trickled down her spine even though she wore a cotton summer dress.

'I went for a walk.' She fixed her gaze on the spectacular view surrounding her.

She had woken before the sun, everything that had passed between them that night flashing through her on a reel before she'd been fully conscious, sending her jumping out of the bed and into the shower.

So early had it been that when she'd hurried to the kitchen not a single member of staff had been awake.

She'd found an avocado and a banana that would suffice for her breakfast and forced them down her cramped throat and stomach. And then she had set off, walking the forests and fields of his estate, keeping her legs moving, *needing* to keep them moving, her usual way of expelling her emotions still denied her and would always be denied when she resided under Benjamin's roof.

She had never needed to dance as much as she did then, never felt that the fabric of her being could fray at the seams without the glue she had learned to depend on.

He sat next to her and offered her the water bottle.

'Thank you.' She took it from his hand being careful not to let their fingers brush, instinctively knowing just one touch would be her undoing.

She needed to keep her focus. Had to. She would not let what was happening inside her derail the future she had worked so hard for and which her parents had sacrificed so much for.

But Benjamin awoke her senses so they all tuned into his frequency just with his presence. Her nose begged her to lean closer so she could smell his gorgeous scent better, her fingers itched to slide over and touch those muscular thighs inches from her own...

She didn't want this. Not any of it. When he'd asked after the wedding if she wished she'd married Javier instead, the answer that had screamed through her head had been a resounding *yes*.

And that had been before they had made love.

If she'd married Javier there wouldn't have been any of this angst tormenting her, there would have been only indifference. None of the hate. None of the passion.

None of the joy she had discovered in Benjamin's arms...

Hands trembling, she drank heavily from the water bottle then wiped the rim and handed it back.

Silence fell between them until he broke it by saying, 'This was my mother's favourite spot.'

Freya had discovered this unexpected patch of paradise by accident a few days ago. The bench and its overhanging cherry tree were in a small clearing accessed through a short cut-through in his forest, sitting on the crest of a hill. Fields of all colours sprawled out for miles below them.

It was just a bench under a cherry tree but there was something so calming about the setting she'd sought it out again.

'Was this your family home?' she asked.

'My family home was in a suburb of Paris. My mother

always said she would move to Provence when her children were grown up and Clara retired from the ballet.'

'Clara Casillas?'

He nodded. 'My mother was her seamstress. She worked for the ballet company in Paris where Clara first made her name. Remember I told you of the closeness between them? Clara refused to let anyone else make her costumes. They denied it but I am sure they deliberately got pregnant at the same time so they could raise their babies together.'

'You and the Casillas brothers?' she asked cautiously, afraid to break their tenuous cordiality by saying the names she knew were like a red rag to a bull.

Another nod. 'We saw the world with them.'

'You were lucky. I would have loved to have seen her perform in the flesh.'

'I found the ballet as boring as hell. I wanted to play football, not be stuck in a theatre. But I had Javier and Luis. We would sneak off together and kick drink cans in theatre car parks or try and spy on the dancers undressing. We had the run of the backstage when performances were on and we made the most of it.'

A bubble of laughter burst from her lungs. 'I can't imagine Javier doing any of that.'

He met her eye, a tinge of amusement in his stare. 'He joined in grudgingly—he was always the serious one. Luis and I were always the instigators of any trouble.'

'Did Chloe not join in?'

'We were ten when she was born. By the time she was old enough to get into trouble with us it was over.'

Neither of them needed to say why it had been over. The story of Clara Casillas's death at the hands of her own husband was still a tale rehashed *ad nauseam* by the press and ghoulish television producers. The friendship between Benjamin and the Casillas brothers had endured…until mere weeks ago.

'Did your mother buy the chateau after Clara died?' she asked.

'She was a single mother by then—my parents divorced when she fell pregnant with Chloe. I bought the chateau for her to end her days in when we learned the treatment for her cancer had failed. I would carry her here to sit on this bench when she was too weak to walk any more.' He lifted his head to look up at the branches of the cherry tree hanging sweetly over them. 'We planted this tree when she died seven years ago. Her ashes are buried under it.'

Freya jumped up. 'I'm sorry. I had no idea...'

'Sit back down, *ma douce*. This is not a shrine for her. It is a celebration of her memory, and if there is an after-life I know my mother will be delighted that you, a dancer she would have loved, were sitting in the spot she loved so much and enjoying the same views that gave her such peace. Please, sit.'

She sat back down gingerly, trying to process what he'd just revealed to her.

Benjamin had said his mother died seven years ago. Hadn't he said before that Javier and Luis had gone to him for the money they'd needed to buy the land for the Tour Mont Blanc building seven years ago too?

These were both things she already knew but only now did she put the two dates together.

Had they gone to him when his mother was dying? Had they taken advantage of the grief he must have been deal-ing with—and she knew what that felt like, a ticking time-bomb hanging over your head...?

'Javier and Luis were with me when we planted the tree,' he said, breaking into her thoughts with words that made her certain he'd been able to read what she'd been thinking. 'She loved them. I thought they loved her too. The night Clara was killed, it was my mother who com-forted them...'

'You were there that night?' That was not something she had known.

He nodded. His jaw had tightened. 'It was after the performance. We were in a hotel across the road from the theatre babysitting Chloe so none of us were there to see or hear what went on between them. My mother woke us to tell the news. She held those boys in her arms the whole night. After they were taken to Spain by their grandparents, my mother made sure they still saw us. They stayed with us many times.' Benjamin swallowed the bile forming in his throat. 'After Clara died, Javier and Luis's visits were the only things that could make her smile. She became like their second mother. They visited her when she was ill. Luis visited so many times the hospital staff assumed he was her son. She never corrected them. She liked them thinking that.'

He had no idea why he was revealing all this to her. These were things he never spoke of.

But the past had become so entwined with the present in recent months that he found it a relief to finally speak of it.

In truth, he owed it to her. Freya deserved to know.

What had she said that first night, about being able to sleep soundly? That his conscience should prevent it?

He understood now what she'd meant. His sleep had been fractured, in and out of wakefulness, his mind a constant whirl.

He still couldn't believe she had been a virgin, did not see how it was possible to reach the age of twenty-three untouched, especially in the hotbed of the ballet world. But the proof had been there, undeniable.

He'd taken her virginity and the more it played on his mind, the worse he felt, sicker in himself.

Her husky voice carried through the humid air. 'When did they ask you for the money?'

'The day she got the terminal diagnosis. They knew I

had the money.' He looked at her, his heart tugging to see the glimmer of compassion ringing in eyes that normally only rang with loathing. 'I knew my mother wasn't going to survive it even before we had it confirmed. I'd already made up my mind to buy the chateau for her.'

He'd known the romance of its architecture and its spectacular views would be a tonic to his mother's cancer-ravaged body and he'd been right. She had spent the last three months of her life there and slipped away peacefully.

He had kept the dire financial situation buying the chateau had left him in from her.

He cleared his throat before continuing. 'I had the cash available to buy it outright. It was a lot of money. The chateau had undergone a complete renovation so was priced high.'

'They knew?'

'Of course they knew.' He didn't hide his bitterness. 'They knew everything. They knew taking my money to finance Tour Mont Blanc meant I would have to take a mortgage to buy the chateau. They knew I overextended myself. They knew when I got into financial trouble over it and was on the verge of bankruptcy. They knew I only gave them that investment because it was them and I trusted them as if they were my own blood. I never blamed them for the situation I got myself in but I gave them that money in good faith and then I learned they had taken it in bad. They knew the terms we agreed verbally were different from the terms on the contract.'

'So your revenge really wasn't about the money then,' she said in the softest tone he had ever heard from her lips. 'They hurt you.'

'They did not hurt me,' he dismissed. 'They betrayed me and kept the lie going for seven years. I was going to donate the profit to a charity that helps traumatised kids. Javier and Luis had to deal with one of the most traumatic things a child could go through but they had been lucky to have family and my mother to help pick up the pieces. Other children aren't so lucky or resilient. They haven't just stolen from me but those children too. I'm fortunate that all the hard work I've put into the business in the past seven years has left me with a sizeable fortune. I'm in the process of liquidating some assets so I can still donate the money but it should never have come to this. They are thieves. They have stolen my money and robbed me of my childhood memories. Everything is tainted now. I think of them carrying my mother's coffin with me into the church and want to rip their heads from their necks.'

He closed his eyes and took a deep breath. Beside him, Freya remained silent but he could feel something new emanating from her that he had never felt before, something that was neither loathing nor desire and flowed into his skin like a balm.

'Do you feel better now you have taken me from Javier?' There was no malice in her voice, just simple, gentle curiosity. 'Do you feel avenged?'

'There is some satisfaction to be had but do I feel avenged…? When I have had my revenge on Luis too, *then* I will feel avenged.'

'What are you planning to do to him?'

'I am still thinking.' *Trying* to think. His thought process had been awry since Freya had been under his roof, her presence even when not in the same room taking all his focus.

'I don't suppose there's any point in saying that sometimes it is better for the soul to let things go,' she said quietly. 'But I will say this—please, for the sake of your soul, don't involve anyone else in it. This is between you and the Casillas brothers. Don't let anyone else suffer for it.'

'I don't want you to suffer.' He took another deep breath and looked up at the cobalt sky, the distant wispy trail of an aeroplane the only thing to cut through the skyscape, then got to his feet. 'Come back to the chateau with me. I have something to show you which, I hope, will make you feel more at home here.'

'What is it?'

'The reason I spent an hour searching for you. Your wedding present from me.'

CHAPTER ELEVEN

FREYA FOLLOWED BENJAMIN into the chateau and up the stairs, apprehension colliding with the ache in her heart at all he had confided in her and which she needed to sit down and think about properly to digest.

She had never thought her heart would ache for him but it did. Badly.

How could Javier treat his oldest friend in that way? And she didn't doubt a word of it. What he and Luis had done was so much worse than merely ripping him off of a fortune. It was a betrayal of biblical proportions.

She shivered to think that was the behaviour of the man she had intended to marry.

When they reached the second floor, Benjamin stopped outside a door that was, she judged, positioned above his own quarters. This was a floor of the chateau she had made a cursory search of on her first day when seeking a dance space and quickly forgotten about. All the rooms up there were laid in thick carpet that would act like a grip on her pointe shoes.

His eyes were on her. 'Open it.'

'It's not a cell, is it?' she asked with a nervous laugh.

He shook his head. 'For once trust me and open the door.'

She stifled the instinctive retort of trust having to be earned.

Benjamin had opened himself up to her. Only a small part, she knew, but it was enough for her to see him with eyes not quite so prejudiced.

He'd made an effort to build a bridge between them and for that she would, this once, place her trust in him and do as he asked.

Holding her breath, Freya opened the door a crack and peered through. The smell of fresh paint hit her immediately.

Then she blinked, certain she was seeing things. But no, she wasn't seeing things. This was a dance studio.

She pushed the door fully open and stared in stunned, disbelieving awe at what had been revealed before her.

Benjamin folded his arms over his chest as he waited for Freya's response. Since opening the door and stepping into the newly revealed room, she hadn't moved a muscle. He didn't think she'd even taken a breath.

'What do you think?' he asked roughly. His heart beat heavily through the tightness in his chest, his stomach twisting.

She shook her head, her throat moving, then slowly turned her head to look at him. Her black eyes were wide and shining. 'You did this…for *me*?'

'You're a professional dancer. You need to practise.'

She needed to dance. Freya was a woman with ballet flowing in her veins, ballet the air she breathed. To deny her the opportunity to dance in the chateau was tantamount to torture.

She raised a hand that had a slight tremor in it to her mouth. 'I don't know what to say.'

'You can say whether you like it or not,' he commented wryly.

She blinked and gave a muffled laugh. 'I can't believe this.'

'Is it suitable for your needs?'

'It's perfect. Beautiful. Just beautiful. And it's so light and high.' She drifted forward into the centre of the huge room, her head now turning in all directions, then stopped when she caught his reflection in the walled mirror. Her forehead creased. 'How did you do it? *When* did you do it?'

'This week. When we agreed to marry.'

'But how?'

'By calling the director of a Parisian ballet company for guidance and employing a top building team.'

'But *how*?' she repeated.

'By paying them ten times their usual rate to stop what they were doing to make it happen. I had hoped it would be completed for our wedding so I could surprise you with it then but there was a delay with the flooring.' Specialist flooring for dancers.

'*How?*' she virtually shrieked, bouncing on her toes and waving her arms in the air. 'From conception to finished product in…what? Five days? How is that even possible? How many rooms were knocked down?'

'Only three.'

'*Only?* You knocked three rooms into…*this*, and I didn't have a clue. I didn't hear anything or see anything, not even a single contractor.'

'They used the tradesman's entrance. The walls were knocked down when you were on your walks.'

'But…'

'No more questions about it. It is done and it is for you. I appreciate you will not spend many nights here once your break is over but this is your home now and when you are here I want you to feel at home.'

The animation that had overtaken her limbs disappeared as she stilled. An emotion he didn't recognise flickered over her face. She chewed at her lip as she stared at him, the intensity of her gaze seeming to cut through the distance between them and burn straight in his chest…

Backing away from her with lungs so tight he could hardly pull air into them, he said, 'I have work to get on with so I shall leave you to enjoy your new dance studio. If there is anything you are not happy with, tell me and we shall change it.'

He left the studio in quick strides and had reached the top of the stairs when she called after him. 'Benjamin?'

It was the first time she'd called him by his name.

'Oui?'

'Thank you.'

'De rien. Enjoy your dancing. I will see you at dinner.'

Freya sat in the middle of the wonderful dance studio Benjamin had created, just for her, soaking it all in with a heart thumping so madly she was surprised her ribs didn't crack with the force.

This was a studio every little girl who dreamed of being a ballerina dreamed of dancing in. The left wall was a mirror, the rest painted soft white, a barre traversing the entire room, broken only by a huge round window at the far end, a floor-to-ceiling cupboard by the door and a beautiful high table next to it.

Eventually she pulled herself out of her stupor, got to her feet and opened the cupboard.

Inside it lay rows of pointe shoes, rows of ballet slippers all lying below a row of assorted practice outfits. They were all her exact size.

Further exploration revealed the tools needed to soften the pointe shoes and she pounced on them with glee.

Ignoring the cosy armchair placed in the corner, she sat cross-legged on the floor and began to massage the stiff toe cup, then, when she felt it was softened sufficiently, moved on to the shank, the hard sole that supported the arch of her foot, and gently bent it back and forth at the three-quarter mark. When she was happy with both shoes—by now convinced Benjamin had got Compania de Ballet de Casillas own shoemakers to provide them for her, the shoes' response to her well-practised manipulations rendering the alcohol spray and hammer often used to soften them redundant—she stripped her clothes off, pulled on a pair of tights and a leotard, and put the softened pointe shoes on, binding the ribbons securely.

Atop the table next to the cupboard sat a small sound system. Preloaded into it was the music for every ballet that had ever been created.

She found the music to Prokofiev's *Romeo and Juliet*, still her favourite after all these years, and pressed play.

Music filled the room, startling her into spinning round and gazing up at the ceiling where she spotted small, unobtrusive speakers placed at strategic intervals.

She covered her mouth as fresh emotion filled her.

Benjamin had done this, all of this, for her.

She blinked to focus herself and stood by the barre to begin simple stretching exercises that would warm her body and limber her up. A dancer's life was fraught with injury and not doing enough of a warm-up beforehand was a shortcut to a sprain or strain, as was a hard floor that didn't have any buoyancy for the inevitable falls.

Benjamin had had a semi-sprung sub-floor fitted that would be the perfect cushion for her falls.

The exercises she did were moves she had made thousands of times and the familiarity of them and the comfort of the music settled her stomach into an ease she had begun to fear she would never find again.

Her mind began to drift as it always did when doing her barre exercises alone. She imagined herself dancing the balcony scene where Romeo and Juliet danced the *pas de deux*, imagining it as she always did when visualising this scene, with a faceless partner.

But this time the imaginary faceless partner didn't remain faceless for long.

It was Benjamin's face that flowed through her mind, his strong arms around her waist then lifting her into the air, his green eyes burning with longing into hers…

An ache ripped through her, pulling the air from her

lungs with its force, the strength so powerful that she dragged herself from her trance-like state to rush to the sound system and skip to the Dance of the Knights, breathing heavily, fear gripping her.

A knock on the door should have been a welcome distraction but what if it was him, catching her now, at this moment when she couldn't trust herself not to fly into his arms and beg him to make love to her again?

Benjamin had *stolen* her, she reminded herself, again, desperately.

She had insisted on this marriage because there had been no other choice.

But Benjamin had knocked down three rooms in his chateau to create a dance studio any ballerina would want to die in, and he had done that for her. He'd been under no obligation. He got nothing out of it for himself.

This was the man who had almost bankrupted himself so his mother could live the last of her life in beauty.

Her heart heavy though a little calmer, she braced herself before opening the door.

Christabel stood there with a tray and a smile. 'Monsieur Guillem thought you would be hungry. Chef has made you a whole grain tortilla wrap with avocado, chicken, tomato and lettuce. She can make you something else if…'

'This is perfect,' Freya interrupted with a grateful smile. Benjamin's chef had proven herself to be a shining star, keen to provide the resident ballerina with the nutritious meals she depended on and make them as appetising as they could be. Freya had never eaten so well and had not been in the least surprised to learn the chef had once been awarded her own Michelin star.

Once Christabel had gone, Freya poured herself a glass of iced water from the jug delivered with her wrap and ignored the armchair to sit on the curved ledge of the enormous round window.

Chewing slowly, she gazed out. The window overlooked the back garden giving her the perfect view to appreciate the stunning landscape, including the cherubic fountain in the centre that wouldn't have looked out of place in the palace of Versailles.

Slowly but surely she was starting to appreciate the beauty of Benjamin's chateau without angry eyes, like a filter being removed from the lens to reveal it in all its glory.

This was a chateau childish dreams were made of.

And now, with this wonderful studio, she had a place in it that was all her own.

Maybe one day it really would feel like home to her.

When she was about to pop the last bite of her delicious wrap into her mouth, her heart leapt into it instead as she saw Benjamin stroll by talking animatedly on his phone.

Her leaping heart began to beat so hard it became a heavy thrum and she found herself unable to tear her eyes away. Her suddenly greedy eyes soaked in everything about him, from the way his long, muscular legs filled the black jeans he wore and the way his muscles bunched beneath his black T-shirt...he had changed his clothing since he had left her in the studio. Even with her distance she could see how untamed his thick black hair had become and the shadow on his jaw hinting at black stubble about to break free... She had never seen a more rampantly masculine sight and it filled her with a longing that kept her rooted, right until the moment he turned his head.

She pressed her back into the curve of the window quickly before he could look up and see her staring down at him.

'You are happy with your studio?' Benjamin asked that evening as they dined together. This evening he had decided to eat the same meal as Freya, pork tenderloin with a lentil salad that he found, to his utmost surprise, to be extremely tasty. It wasn't quite hitting the spot the way his rich meals usually did but that would be rectified by the cheeses he liked to finish his meals with.

She lifted her eyes from her plate to his and gave a dreamy sigh. 'It's…perfect. I'm still rather overawed, to be honest.'

'As long as you are happy with it that is all that matters.' He reached for his glass of white wine. Freya, as usual, had stuck to water, the wine glass laid out for her as usual remaining empty.

'I am.' She looked, if not happy, then more content than he had ever seen her. Her time spent in her new studio seemed to have freed something inside her, all her hostility towards him gone.

'*Bien*. I hope you are as happy with the houses my employee has found for you. I've had him searching for an apartment in Madrid…' he found himself almost choking at the word '…and a house in London as per the terms of our contract. He has narrowed them down to a choice of five for each. I will forward the email with all the details to you later.'

'Thank you.'

'I assume you will want to view your preferred ones?'

'Just the London ones. The Madrid apartment is only going to be somewhere for me to sleep so don't bother with anything fancy as it will be a waste.'

The relief at this was dimmed by what it represented. If she only intended to use the Madrid apartment as a base to rest her head, what did that mean for the London house?

'I have appointments in Greece on Friday but we can fly over on Saturday. Tell me which ones you like the look of and I will get Giles to book viewings.'

He waited for her to respond, his sharp eyes noting she was rubbing the napkin between her fingers.

'Is something wrong?' he asked when her silence continued.

She pulled her lips in together, colour heightening across her cheekbones, then took a number of deep breaths.

'Freya?'

'Can I have a glass of wine, please?' she said quietly. 'There is something I need to tell you.'

Apprehension filling him, he took the bottle from the ice bucket and filled her glass.

She took a large sip then set the glass on the table, clutching the stem in her hand.

Then she took another deep breath and squared her shoulders before squaring her jaw. 'My mother is ill. The house in London is not for me. It's for her. For both of them.'

Now Benjamin was the one to take a long drink of his wine.

'What is wrong with her?' he asked, already knowing from her tone and the serious hue reflecting from her eyes that it was not good.

He watched the signs of her faltering composure, the fluttering of the hand not clinging to her glass, the rapid rise and fall of her chest, the movement of her throat.

'She has a rare degenerative neurological disease that affects muscle movement. There is no cure.'

Banging immediately set off in his head. 'No cure...?'

'It's terminal,' she supplied matter-of-factly but with the slightest cracking of her voice on the final syllable.

Benjamin swore under his breath, a clammy feeling crawling over his skin.

'I want her to end her days in a home that has space and with a garden she can sit out in and listen to the birds and feel the breeze on her face.'

'I understand that,' he said heavily.

Her smile when she met his eyes was sad. 'I know you do.'

His heart ached in a way it hadn't done in seven years, the beats dense and weighty. 'Is there *nothing* that can be done for her?'

'There has been a medical development in America recently, a treatment that slows it down in some cases and in even rarer cases reverses some of the symptoms. Not permanently though. No one has found a permanent reversal.'

Everything suddenly became clear.

Pushing his unfinished plate to one side, Benjamin rubbed his temples. 'That's why you married me. To pay for the treatment.'

'Yes.' She shuffled her chair back a little and stretched her neck. 'It's not authorised for use in the UK because it's unproven and incredibly expensive. The money I get from our marriage is to pay for her to have a doctor fly to England every month and administer it to her in a private hospital. It won't keep her alive for ever, but it might give us an extra year or two, and they could be good years for her. The money Javier paid after we signed the contract on our engagement has paid for two cycles of it. Her speech and breathing have improved a little and she's got slightly more movement in her hands. It's stopped it getting any worse. For now,' she added with a sigh. 'None of us are stupid enough to think it will hold it off for ever.'

'Miracles do happen.' But his words were automatic. Miracles were something he had stopped believing in during his mother's battle with cancer.

Freya shook her head ruefully. 'Not for my mother. When the treatment is developed more in the future they might be able to fully reverse it and hold the symptoms off permanently but that will come way too late for Mum. We're just grateful that she's receiving *any* benefit from it. She's already proving to be one of the lucky rare ones.'

Lucky to be trapped in a failing body with no hope of lasting longer than a year or two?

'And now I can give them a home too.' She paused and blinked rapidly. 'I never told them. I was scared to jinx it. They've wanted to move for years. They live in a two-bedroom third-floor flat in a building with communal gardens that are used by the local drug addicts. They're basically prisoners in their own home now.'

'We can fly to London tomorrow to look at the houses.'

She blinked again, this time in astonishment. 'Don't you have to work?'

'Some things are more important. We can fly out after breakfast.'

He saw her throat move. 'That is incredibly generous of you. Thank you.'

'If I had known why you wanted a house I would have made it a priority.'

'I didn't think you'd care.'

He winced at her unflinching honesty. 'I cannot say I blame you for that.'

'It wasn't just that I didn't think you'd care,' she said in a softer, more reflective tone. 'I'm not good at opening up in any capacity, especially about such personal matters.'

'Your dance does your talking for you.'

For a moment she just stared at him, eyes glistening before she jerked a nod. 'It's the only way I know how. I find it hard opening up at the best of times. I didn't want to share something so personal with someone I hated.'

He hesitated before asking, 'Does that mean you no longer hate me?'

'I don't know.' She took a sip of her wine. 'You're not the complete monster I thought you were. You had your reasons to do what you did. I feel a certain…kinship, I think the word is. I understand what you were going through when your mother was ill because I'm living it myself. You signed a contract without reading the terms and conditions; I signed a contract pledging my life in exchange for an extension to hers. If that makes me a gold-digger then I can live with that.'

He closed his eyes briefly and breathed heavily. 'You are not a gold-digger. I should never have called you that.'

She shrugged, her shoulders tight. 'It doesn't matter. You could have called me worse.'

He'd thought worse. When he recalled the things he had thought about her he wanted to retch. She had married him to extend her mother's life. He had married her out of vengeance against his oldest friend.

'It does matter. I know what it's like to watch someone you love slowly lose their life. You will do anything to help them and give them more time.'

Their eyes met. Something, a flash of understanding, passed between them that, like a switch being flicked, darkened and deepened.

He blew out a long puff of air and got to his feet. 'We'll make an early start tomorrow. Get some sleep and I will see you in the morning.'

There was a smattering of confusion in her returning stare before she nodded. 'See you in the morning.'

CHAPTER TWELVE

THE FAMILIAR RATTLE of the cattle grid woke Freya from the sleep she had fallen into. Covering a yawn with her hand, she cast a quick glance at Benjamin beside her. His face was glued to his laptop as it had been since they'd got into the car from the heliport. The seductive looks and words were a thing of the past.

She felt as if she had lived a thousand lives in the past two days.

They had spent the day in London as he had promised. He'd organised everything. A stretched Mercedes had met them at the airport with Giles, Benjamin's assistant who had been tasked with house-hunting for her, in attendance, and then driven them to all the shortlisted houses.

She had fallen in love with the second property, which ticked every box she'd wanted and more.

Best of all, it was unoccupied.

Benjamin had made an immediate cash offer and got the wheels put into motion for the quickest of quick sales. Her parents could move in that coming weekend. Benjamin was going to take care of everything for them.

He had then taken her to the tower block her parents lived in but had refused to come in with her.

'This is a home you are providing for them,' he had explained without looking at her. 'It is better they hear it from you. I will only be a distraction.'

'But they will want to meet you,' she had said, surprising herself with her own argument. 'They will want to thank you.'

His nose had wrinkled before he'd looked at the building she had called home for the first eleven years of her life.

'There will be plenty of time for us to meet in the future. I have things to organise. Giles will see you in. Take all the time you need. There is no rush.'

She had then spent a wonderful couple of hours with her parents, finally having the confidence to tell them they were going to be able to move out of the flat that had become their prison into a house of their own, and that her new husband was in the process of getting a team together to help them make the move and would be providing them with an unlimited credit card to furnish their new home to their liking.

Javier had been prepared to buy them a home as part of the contract. He had known about their situation for two whole months.

Benjamin had known about it for less than a day and had already gone above and beyond his contractual obligations.

And yet there was a distance between them that had never been there before. He had hardly looked her in the eye all day. And it had been a long day, dinner eaten in silence on the return flight back to Provence.

'It is late,' he said as the car came to a stop in the courtyard. 'I am going to call it a night.'

'You're going to bed?' she asked, surprised at the stab of disappointment cutting through her stomach.

'I have a few more calls to make and then I will sleep. I'll see you in the morning. *Bonne nuit.*'

And that was that.

The man who had devoured her with his eyes, who had insisted they would sleep together every night they were under the same roof, would be sleeping in his own bed without her for the second night in a row.

Feeling nauseous although she had no idea why, Freya carried her heavy legs up the stairs.

It *was* late. Maybe she should get some sleep too.

But after taking a shower and brushing her teeth she

knew sleep was a long way off. There was a knotted feeling in her stomach that time was only making worse.

All she could think was that Benjamin was bored of her after only one night together.

Or, worse, had her confession about her family background turned him off? Had seeing the place she had been raised tainted her somehow too? Did he see her differently now he knew her polish and poise had been taught and were not inherent in her?

And why did her heart hurt so much to think all this?

She shouldn't care. She should be thankful his desire for her had been turned off. Wasn't that the safety she craved where all her passion and emotions were expressed in her dance?

The knot in her stomach tightened, pulling at her chest, and she paced her room until she could take no more and, uncaring that it was the middle of the night, bolted out of her quarters.

Thoughts and questions crowding her head, her heart throbbing, she hurried up the stairs to her studio and threw her dressing gown on the floor. Not wanting to waste time putting on tights and a leotard, she pulled a black, calf-length floating exercise dress off the rail in the studio cupboard and shrugged it over her head.

The pointe shoes she had softened into reasonable comfort the day before were on the floor where she had left them and still had plenty of wear left. She put them on, tied the ribbons, then put the sound system on shuffle and settled herself by her barre.

Inhaling deeply through her nose, she then exhaled through her mouth and repeated ten times, determined to clear her mind while stretching her limbs and increasing her blood flow.

But as she made the familiar comforting movements, her eyes drifted around the studio.

Everything that had been done to create this had been with one focus in mind—her needs. The light she needed. The height she needed. The space she needed. Nothing had been missed, nothing stinted on.

The music she had been stretching to came to an end and seconds later the opening bars to the Habanera from *Carmen* came on in its stead.

Freya paused as the wonderful score, with its seductive Spanish vibe, filled the studio.

The Habanera was the part where the immoral, wicked Carmen danced with such allure that Don José, the soldier about to arrest her, instead fell for the temptress and bedded her.

It was a most sensual of dances and, though she had danced it many times, Freya had never wriggled her shoulders at the start and imagined a real, flesh and blood man watching her and desiring her for real.

Had Carmen desired Don José when she had danced for him? Freya had always assumed not, thought of the dance as a trap to hook him in—one that obviously backfired considering he killed her at the end for loving another man—but now, as Benjamin's features shone brightly in front of her, the dance moves coming back to her, she wondered if in the heat of the moment Carmen *had* felt desire for the man she used for her own ends.

Maybe that was all it was for her and Benjamin too, a desire born through circumstance that now, in Benjamin's case, was spent.

She wished with all her heart that it were spent in herself too but it had only grown. Benjamin had made love to her and only now, as she made a series of jetés across the perfect floor, did she acknowledge the truth to herself that every part of her body ached for him to touch her and make love to her again.

She wished he were there with her right now, that she could pirouette to him and see that hunger in his eyes again.

Benjamin could hear music.

At first he'd thought he was imagining it but there was an echoing, haunting sound ringing through the chateau's thick walls, usually so still and silent in the dead of night.

He looked up at the ceiling.

Freya's studio was directly above his own quarters.

He closed his eyes.

He hadn't slept well the night before. Two bad nights' sleep had left him exhausted.

Three large Scotches in quick succession meant he should have passed out the moment his head hit the pillow but he couldn't even shut his eyes without forcing them.

He opened them again and stared at the ceiling. The heavy beat of his heart echoed in his ears and he put a hand to his bare chest in an attempt to temper it.

All he wanted was to go to her. All he wanted was to haul her into his arms and make love to her, again and again.

He'd spent the day with her avoiding her gaze, knowing that to look into those black depths would pull him back into a place he needed to keep away from.

His head was a whirl of diverging thoughts but the one that flashed loudest was that he should never have married her. If he had known about her mother and her parents' situation he would have paid her off when she'd suggested it rather than tie her into this.

Wouldn't he…?

Yes, he *would* have paid her off, he told himself forcefully. Freya hadn't pledged herself to Javier for her own greedy benefit as he had assumed. None of it had been for herself.

Why wasn't she sleeping? Her conscience was clear.

There was nothing to stop her sleeping as sweetly as he had always been able to do.

But she was awake and dancing above him.

Freya needed to dance in the same way he needed air. There was still so much to learn about her but on the very essence of who she was he had no doubts.

Dieu, he ached to see her, hold her, kiss her, touch her...

She was all he had wanted since he had seen her that first time with the sunlight pouring onto her skin.

Benjamin had pulled his trousers back on and reached his bedroom door before even realising he was out of his bed.

With long strides he climbed the stairs and opened the door to her studio.

She was at the far side by the window, moving like a graceful blur to the beats of the music.

There was only the merest glint of surprise when she caught his eye in the reflection of the walled mirror but no pause or hesitation in her movements.

She continued to dance, contorting her body and creating shapes out of her legs and arms that appeared completely natural and effortless. She'd left her hair loose and it flew around her, spinning in a perfect wheel when she spun on pointe, all the while her eyes seeming to never leave his.

And he could not tear his eyes from her.

He had never, in his entire life, been witness to anything so beautiful or seductive.

Freya didn't dance, she *was* dance; she was the emotion of the music brought to life. She was incredible.

Closer and closer she came, every fluid motion bringing her nearer to him until she jumped with her left leg fully extended and her right leg bent at the knee, creating the illusion of flight.

She landed a foot before him and sank into a bow.

Slowly she raised herself back up to stare at him with a stillness that was as elegant and stunning as her movement.

She didn't speak.

He didn't speak.

They just gazed at each other.

It felt as if her eyes were piercing right into his soul.

And then she flew at him.

At least that was how it seemed in the moment, that she had taken flight to throw her arms around his neck and her supple legs around his waist, holding and supporting herself around him without any effort.

Benjamin gazed at the perfection of her face for one more moment before all the pent-up desire and emotions inside him burst free.

Wrapping his arms tightly around her back, he crushed his lips to hers and was met with her matching hunger. Like two starving waifs finally being given a meal, they kissed greedily and possessively, his hands splaying and digging into her back, her fingers digging into the nape of his neck, fusing every part of their bodies together they could.

His arousal, a simmering feature of his life he had learned to endure since he'd stolen her out of the hotel and her hand had first slipped into the crook of his arm, burned. Everything in him burned, from the lava in his veins to the swirling molten heat of his skin.

From the heat of Freya's kisses and the tightness of her legs around him, he knew it was the same for her too.

This was a need too great and too explosive to do anything but quench. The sensual music only added to the mixture, creating the most potent chemical cocktail that, now ignited, had only one possible outcome.

With nowhere to lay her down, Benjamin carried her effortlessly to the nearest wall and slammed her against it.

Slipping a hand up the skirt of her dress, which had bunched up against the top of her toned thighs, he found her bottom deliciously bare, and pressed his palm to the damp heat of her pubis.

She gasped into his mouth and pressed against him, unhooking an arm from his neck to drop it down to his waist and the band of his trousers.

Until she dug her hand into the opening, he hadn't realised he hadn't buttoned himself up. Like her, he was naked beneath the only item of clothing he wore. She caressed him, biting into his bottom lip with her teeth before sweeping her tongue back into his mouth and kissing him harder than ever.

He grabbed her hand with his and, together, they pulled him free. With no further restrictions, all that was left was to adjust their forms against the wall until he was there, fully hard and fully ready, and thrusting up into her welcome tightness.

There was no savouring of the moment, not from either of them. The instant he was fully inside her, Freya's hand grabbed his buttocks and she was urging him on with her body and with mumbled, indecipherable words.

Their lovemaking had a primal, almost feral quality to it, he thought dimly as he thrust into her. Her nails now dug into his skin as she matched him, thrust for thrust, stroke for stroke, until the hand still on his neck suddenly grabbed at his hair and she cried out, every part of her clenching around him in a spasm that seemed to go on for ever and pulled him even tighter inside her and then he, too, could hold on no more and he let go as the most powerful climax of his life ripped through him.

Freya stretched out her leg and immediately her foot connected with something solid and warm and very, very human. Benjamin's leg.

Her languid limbs wakened properly as all that had gone

on between them through the night came back to her like a glorious cinematic masterpiece in her head.

The ghost dream had come to life. She had danced to her lover. She had danced *for* her lover.

Her *lover*.

How else could she describe him after they had come together like two people possessed?

After the explosion that had rocked them in his studio, he had carried her down to his bedroom and made love to her all over again.

And she had made love to him too.

The song birds were already singing the dawn chorus when they finally sated their hunger.

Incredibly, the familiar ache in her loins fired up again. The hunger hadn't been sated, merely put to sleep.

She could handle this, she thought as she snuggled closer to him. A huge arm hooked around her and in an instant she was wrapped back in the wonderful comfort of Benjamin's strong body, his warm skin smelling of them and the heat they had created between these sheets.

This was no big deal. This was merely two compatible people who happened to be married unlocking their desire for each other.

It didn't mean anything. It didn't affect anything. The rest of their contract would stay the same.

Nothing else would change because of it.

It couldn't. She wouldn't let it.

She would not let these wonderful feelings erupt into anything more.

The risks were far too great.

'No, no, no, *jeté* to the *left*! Freya, *concentrate*!'

'I'm sorry.' Freya stopped moving and put her hands on her hips, leaning forward and breathing in deeply. She was exhausted. The rehearsal had started off badly and gone downhill from there. And it was all her fault.

Mikael, the dancer she was supposed to be *jeté*-ing to before pirouetting into his arms, glared at her. The four members of the *corps de ballet* merely looked embarrassed.

The harassed choreographer sighed. 'Let's take a fifteen-minute break. Come back with heads screwed on.'

Freya went straight to her dressing room. She drank some water and ate a banana, then went back to the studio determined to get it right.

The rest of the rehearsal was even worse. She couldn't even get the basic footwork right and these were moves she had been doing since she was a small child. It was as if her feet no longer connected to her brain and her arms were made of modelling clay.

She returned to her apartment knowing one more bad rehearsal could mean her understudy being given the role of Vicky.

This was a role she had coveted for so long and she was in danger of losing it. Every dancer had a bad day but this had been a bad week, following on from a week that had been only marginally better.

Her dancing was deteriorating and she could not for the life of her think why.

She had one more day to get through and then she had a day off. If she could get through the next day's rehearsals she would then have time away to recharge and refocus her mind.

She checked her phone as she ran a bath and found a message from her father, his daily update.

She read it and closed her eyes with the first smile to cross her lips all week.

At least here was some good news. Her mother had wiggled all the fingers of her left hand and hummed along to a song on the radio.

Her mood managed to lighten even more before plunging when her phone rang in her hand and Benjamin's name flashed on the screen.

'Bonsoir, ma douce.' The rich seductiveness of his tone sent tingles of sensation curling across her spine.

'Hi.'

'Is everything okay?' he asked.

'Yes. All good.'

She would not admit her body was forgetting the basic dance moves that had been ingrained in her before she'd learned her times tables. As far as Benjamin was concerned, everything was fine.

He hated her being back in Madrid. It was a simple, mostly unspoken truth between them and she knew it was a proprietorial thing for him. Benjamin hated his wife working for his enemy.

And she hated it too. Mercifully, she hadn't seen anything of Javier or Luis since she had arrived back to work but she found herself constantly on alert for them, which she knew was stupid as Javier especially rarely bothered to grace them with his presence.

Mercifully too, the new building the company had moved into, adjacent to the new theatre that was undergoing its finishing touches, meant her fellow dancers had been too busy exploring and comparing to bother with her. Freya jilting Javier for Benjamin was already old news. There had been the odd snide comment, of course, but the kind she had inured herself against over a decade ago. It grieved her deeply that Sophie had unexpectedly quit the company and returned to England but what she hated the most, and which she also would never admit, was that her mind was almost completely occupied with Benjamin.

Freya had known that keeping a lid on her feelings for him would be hard, especially after they had become proper lovers, but she had never imagined the strength it would take to keep that lid on. He called her every night, and she would listen to the rich honeyed tones with an ache in her heart that had slipped into her every pore.

She did *not* miss him, she told herself constantly. And she did *not* count down the hours until she would be with him again.

But the precipice she had seen her mother edging towards if she didn't accept his proposal was now inching towards her. She could feel it with every minute spent with him and every communication between them, a drop of unimaginable depths waiting to swallow her whole if she couldn't keep her feet rooted to the ground and that lid on, even if she needed to pull it down with both hands gripped tightly to it.

The days they had spent together as lovers before she had left for Madrid had been the best days of her life.

They had spent most of them in bed, yes, but they had enjoyed themselves out of it too. He had joined her in her studio while she practised, making calls and sending emails with her pirouetting around him. They had eaten their separate meals together and even shared more of the same meals. They had shared stories of their childhoods, very different but fascinating to the other.

And then they had flown to England together and met her parents in their new house.

He had been welcomed with open arms and even wider hearts.

And then she had gone back to her life and found everything had changed.

She had changed.

'*Bien.* I just want to check you have no late rehearsals tomorrow.' It was only when she heard him speak after days apart that she heard the thickness of his accent when he spoke her language. She never heard it when she was with him any more.

'Not that I've been told.'

'*Excellente*. I will get my driver to collect you at six-thirty.'

A few minutes later, Freya disconnected the call and climbed into the huge bath.

Then she laid herself down until she was fully submerged and held her breath for as long as she could.

CHAPTER THIRTEEN

FREYA RAN A brush through her hair a final time and laid it on her dresser feeling much better in herself. Rehearsals the day before had gone much better. Today, after a night of making love to Benjamin, she had taken herself to her studio to practise her solo dance and found herself foot-perfect. Not a single step or movement had been wrong, and she had dressed for their night out feeling as if a weight had been lifted.

Now she could enjoy a meal out with her husband without any cares.

Selecting a red button-down shirt-dress that fell to her knees, a thick black rope belt hooked around her waist and a pair of high strappy silver sandals, she then dabbed perfume behind her ears and on her wrists, applied a little gloss to her lips and considered herself done.

She found Benjamin in the half-inside, half-outside living room where he had first told her she would have to marry him, talking on his phone.

He got to his feet when he saw her and ended his call.

Tilting his head, he studied her with sparkling eyes.

'Madame Guillem, you look good enough to eat.'

The feeling is entirely mutual, she thought but didn't say.

Charcoal trousers, a shirt only a shade lighter and unbuttoned at his throat, and a Prussian blue jacket gave him a dangerously debonair appearance.

'Where are we going?' she asked.

'I've booked us a table at Le Cheval D'Or.'

'Where's that?'

'A restaurant near Nice. It's about half an hour's drive away.'

When they stepped out in the courtyard Benjamin smiled to see the furrow on Freya's brow at the car waiting for them, a bright yellow convertible with the roof down.

She ran her fingers along the paintwork and then suddenly that striking face was grinning widely. 'What a beautiful car.'

'It's a 1949 Buick Roadmaster Riviera Convertible. I bought it at auction four months ago.'

She stepped all around it, examining it with the same reverence he'd first studied it. When she was done, he opened the passenger door for her.

Her brow furrowed again. 'Where's your driver?'

He grinned. 'Tonight, *ma douce*, I am your driver.'

She matched his grin and got in.

Minutes later, they were out of his estate and speeding through the sweeping roads to their destination, Freya's hair sweeping around her.

'This is amazing,' she said, bursting into laughter, a sound he had never heard from her before.

As incredible as it was to believe, he had never heard Freya laugh until that moment.

Her joy was as infectious as it was heart-warming and he laughed with her. 'Isn't it?'

Not much more was said but every time he looked at her she would turn her eyes to him and they would give identical grins.

Benjamin was big enough to admit he was greedy about his time with her. Since she had returned to Madrid she guarded their time together zealously. He wanted her to be happy but seven hours in her studio on her one whole day off?

He'd resented ballet enough for stealing all his mother's attention while she was alive and now he found himself with a wife whose passion for it would more commonly be known as an addiction.

He reflected that next week she had two whole days off. He'd already rearranged his diary to free his time so they didn't have to waste any of it.

Tonight he had deliberately booked a table in a restaurant rather than dine at home as they usually did. Selfishly, he wanted all her attention.

So far his ploy was working.

Ten minutes from the restaurant and the first clear view of the Mediterranean appeared; he looked at her and laughed again to see her head flopping on her shoulder.

'You're falling asleep?' he asked with faux incredulity.

She straightened and gave a yawn that turned into muffled giggles. 'Sorry… Wow! That view is incredible.'

All sleepiness deserted her in an instant as Freya took in the glamorous sight in front of them, so different from the peaceful views that surrounded Benjamin's chateau but equally beautiful in its own right.

But none of those views were a patch on the masculine beauty of the man who sat beside her, driving a car that wouldn't look out of place in one of those glamourous films from the Cary Grant era. It suited Benjamin perfectly, far more than any modern-day Bugatti or Ferrari, cars she knew he had in his underground garage.

The wind whipping through her hair and the feel of the sun soaking into her face had rid her of the last of that go-dawful tightness that had been compressing her all week.

This was *fun*.

She honestly could not remember the last time she had done anything that constituted fun. Maybe the theme park she and Sophie had visited on one of their days off on their European tour last year? They hadn't gone this year. Sophie had begged off with stomach cramps and Freya hadn't wanted to go without her.

She wished she knew what was wrong with her oldest

and closest friend and why she had quit the company so abruptly, but Sophie had clammed up.

Soon the roads became even narrower and steeper and they drove into a town with medieval architecture, coming to a stop outside a high monastic stone building with a red-tiled roof and pillars.

Immediately a valet appeared, opening the passenger door for her and helping her out, then zipping to Benjamin's side. Benjamin pressed the keys in the valet's hand then turned to Freya with a grin. 'Ready?'

'Ready.'

Stone walls and floors greeted them, along with high stained-glass windows and a high vaulted ceiling. A low buzz of chatter rang out from the other diners, all dressed in their finery, low bursts and high bursts of laughter and the most delicious smells.

They were led to a table under a window, menus presented to them by the self-important maître d' with the same reverence as if they were being presented with a first edition of a masterpiece. He then took hold of their napkins and, in turn, flicked them to open them up, his face grave as if performing an act of live art as he placed them on their laps.

Freya caught the laughter in Benjamin's eye and ducked her head down to study the menu lest she start giggling at the maître d's pomposity.

The second he left their table, they covered their mouths so the laughter they'd both been supressing came out like muffled sniggers.

'Were we supposed to applaud?' she said when she'd caught her breath, dabbing a tear of mirth with the napkin.

'I think he expected a standing ovation.'

By the time they'd ordered their food—thankfully their order was taken by one of the lowly waiters—Freya felt thoroughly relaxed and sipped her champagne with pleasure.

The food they were served was incredible, her starter of artichoke served with caviar in a lime broth possibly the best dish she had ever eaten…until their main courses were set before them and she had her first bite of her clay-cooked chicken that came with white asparagus, a rocket salad and little delicacies she didn't recognise but knew would be delicious.

'I have never seen you enjoy your food so much,' Benjamin commented as he tackled his smoked lobster. 'I must get my chef to recreate these recipes.'

'Your chef is amazing,' she protested. 'I'm just exceptionally hungry.'

'So am I.'

Her heart leapt at the gleam in his eyes and the suggestiveness of his tone, sending a hot surge of blood pumping through her.

Would this desire ever abate?

His sparkling eyes devouring her a little longer, he said, 'It is strange to see you eat a meal out without worrying over every ingredient.'

She laughed. 'I allow myself the occasional splurge. I've only had one non-healthy meal since you kidnapped me and that was on our wedding day.'

'You hardly ate any of that and I didn't kidnap you. I whisked you away with deception.'

'If it looks like a duck, walks like a duck and talks like a duck then it's safe to say it's a duck. You kidnapped me.'

'Ducks can't talk and I didn't kidnap you.'

'Okay, you stole me, then.'

'Only with your consent, and ask yourself this—who would you rather be sitting at this table with? Me or Javier?'

'You want me to answer that?'

He flashed her a grin that didn't quite meet his eyes. 'Only if the answer is me.'

It's you, every time, she almost said but cut herself off.

She couldn't lie to him but nor could she tell him the truth.

Instinct told her that to tell the truth would be to drag her even closer to the precipice that frightened her so much.

She never thought of Javier unless it was to compare him unfavourably to Benjamin.

Her brain burned to remember she had agreed to have children with him. The ball had been entirely in her court as to when it would happen so she had decided that she would wait until her biological clock started ticking, thinking by then she and Javier would have forged a friendly marriage.

She no longer believed anything of the sort. How could she when she now believed the heart she'd thought he kept hidden from view was actually missing? The way he and Luis had treated Benjamin and taken advantage of his mother's cancer for their own ends enraged her.

Benjamin's heart wasn't missing. His heart was as enormous as his ego. He was a man who did everything wholeheartedly, whether it was loving someone or hating them. When he set on a path he was relentless until he reached his destination.

They had never spoken of children. It was there in the contract though. The ball would always be in her court for that.

What kind of a father would he be? A hands-on, nappy-changing, kicking-a-ball-around-the-park dad? Or the kind of father who appointed an army of nannies and left them to it?

And why did her heart ache to imagine it…?

'You and Javier are very different people,' she said quietly, trying to be diplomatic without giving anything of her thoughts away. 'When I agreed to marry him I knew he was a cold fish but I didn't realise what a complete bastard he was. It wouldn't have changed my mind though. His proposal was just too attractive for my mother's sake.'

'And what about your sake?'

'I have dealt with colder and crueller people than Javier Casillas. You want to know real cruelty, put a hidden camera in a girls' boarding school.'

'Did you suffer a lot?'

'The other girls took an instant dislike to me. They hated everything about me. The clothes I wore, the way I spoke... even the way I held my cutlery. They took pleasure in humiliating me. Petty, nasty things. Constant name calling, stealing my stuff, tripping me in the canteen when I had a tray of food in my hand—that one was a particular favourite.'

'They hated that you were a better dancer than them?'

Her brow furrowed in surprise.

He explained his thinking with a grimace. 'You had a full scholarship. The school you went to only gives them rarely, for exceptional talents.'

She pulled a rueful face. 'If that was their reasoning then it worked. My dancing went to pieces. That first term I was the worst dancer there because they got into my head. I was an insecure bag of nerves.'

'How did you get through it?' But he already had a good idea. That iron control had started somewhere.

'At the end of the first term one of the dance teachers pulled me aside. She told me I was in danger of losing my scholarship. She also said she knew I had problems fitting in but that, unless I wanted to lose my dream, I had to rise above it and find a way to tune the noise out otherwise they would win.'

She would have been only eleven, Benjamin thought, sickened at the cruelty of children and the ineffectiveness of the adults meant to protect her.

'I took her words to heart,' Freya continued. 'I taught myself to block the noise from my head and focus only on the dance itself. I no longer sought their approval and in time I no longer wanted or needed it. By taking control of my feelings and learning to be completely single-minded, I learned how to survive.' Her face brightened a touch. 'And I did make a friend eventually. Sophie. She helped ease the loneliness but they were still the worst days of my life. If I could get through that, I can get through anything. If marrying Attila the Hun could have alleviated my mother's pain I would have married him and known I would survive it too.'

Benjamin saw so many emotions flickering in the black depths of her eyes that his heart fisted in on itself.

Their backgrounds might have them poles apart but when it came to those they loved, there was nothing either of them would not do.

Having met her parents for himself, he understood even more.

He had been struck with the warmth of their welcome, their gratitude for the home he had given them so stark it had embarrassed him.

It isn't me you need to thank, he'd wanted to tell them. *It's your daughter. She's the one who contracted herself out to marriage for you.*

He'd thought he'd been prepared for her mother's condition but it had been worse than he'd thought. She could do nothing for herself, was virtually paralysed in her failing body, totally reliant on her doting husband. And Freya said this was an improvement?

But she had that spirit in her eyes his own mother had had, a will to fight, and, he had seen whenever she had looked at her only child, fierce pride in her daughter.

Strangely, meeting Freya's father, a humble man with a huge heart, had set him thinking about his own when he so rarely thought of his own father. The only good thing his father had ever done—apart from helping create himself and his sister, even if he did say so himself—was provide maintenance to his mother once he'd left the family nest. His mother had saved all those payments, giving Benjamin his share in a lump sum when he'd turned twenty-one, money he'd used to purchase an old, run-down food-production facility.

He'd left his in-laws' home with a heavy heart, which he still hadn't shaken off.

'How can you stand working for him?' he asked.

Javier had known about her mother's condition for two months and done nothing about it other than sign promises for the future when he had his ring on Freya's finger.

Yes, he had paid for two rounds of treatment but he should have taken them out of that decrepit flat and given them somewhere decent to live.

'I don't work for him. I work for his company,' she answered. 'And it won't be for much longer.'

'Have you started looking for a new company yet?'

'I've been approached by a couple of companies.'

'You never said.'

'My career is not your concern,' she reminded him with a tight smile that immediately made his hackles rise.

'I spoke to the director of Orchestre National de Paris a few days ago,' he said. 'Their theatre has just been refurbished and the owner is in the process of creating a new ballet company.'

'I am aware of that.'

'They want you to be their Etoile.'

'What?'

'Orchestre National de Paris want you to be the star of their new ballet company. I was going to wait until the proposal was confirmed in writing before telling you but now seems the right time. Salary is negotiable and they are prepared to put a clause in your contract that allows you time off to guest star for other companies.'

Silence filled the space between them. She stared at him, totally still, her black eyes unreadable.

'Who approached who?' she asked slowly. 'You or the director?'

'Does it matter?'

'Yes.'

'The director is an old friend who I know through the Casillas brothers. The Orchestre National de Paris's intention to create its own ballet company is not a secret.'

An edge crept into her voice. 'But who approached who?'

'I called him.'

'Did you call him with the intention of pimping me out?'

Anger, already simmering in his guts, cut through him. He controlled it. Just. 'Having a conversation to get my wife a better deal with a better company is hardly pimping.'

She leaned forward ever so slightly. 'And who are you to say what is a better deal for me? Or which is the better company?'

'You are a dancer whose star is in the ascendancy. This move will help you reach the pinnacle that much more quickly.'

'And how will it look when people find out I only got the job thanks to my husband being part of the old boys' network with the director?'

'I don't know that term but I can guess what it means, and no one is going to think that because it is not true.'

'Did you not listen to a single word I just said? Everything I have achieved has been on my own merits and I have worked my toes into stumps to get where I am, without *any* help. What makes you think I need help with my career now? And who the *hell* do you think you are, interfering like this?'

'Interfering?' He was taken aback at her venom. 'I am your husband. It is my job to look out for you.'

'It is *not*. My career is entirely separate to our marriage and you have overstepped the mark hugely.'

How he kept his temper he would never know. 'I am sorry you feel I have overstepped your invisible mark but I am sick of living in a separate country to my wife. I *am* your husband. You married me and took my name. I have an apartment in Paris. Take the job and we can live there when you are working and have a proper marriage.'

There. His cards were on the table.

He stared hard at her waiting for her to respond.

'It's not an invisible mark. It's in the contract we both signed. No interference in my career.' Her voice contained the slightest of tremors.

'If you want us to stick to the contract then answer this— if I were to take advantage of the clause that said I could take a mistress, how would it make you feel?'

Her face turned the colour of chalk. Her throat moved numerous times before she whispered, 'I wouldn't try to stop you.'

'I didn't ask if you would try to stop me. I asked how it would make you feel.'

'I would accept it.'

'Accept it?' he sneered.

'I signed up for a marriage that allows us both to live an independent life and I don't want to change any of it. If I move to Paris it will be because that's what's right for my career.' She took a long sip of champagne and blew out a long puff of air before saying, 'I *do* appreciate you thinking of me. I will speak to the director of Orchestre National de Paris but I'm not going to make any promises. My career comes first, you already know that.'

Wishing he hadn't chosen to drive, Benjamin jerked a nod.

Why had he thought the outcome of this conversation would be any different?

His own parents had both put him second to their needs. Why should he think his wife would be any different?

The drive back to his chateau was a far more muted affair than the drive to the restaurant, hardly a word exchanged between them.

Twenty minutes after they'd left, right on cue, Freya had fallen asleep. A minute after that, her head fell onto his shoulder and stayed there for the final eight miles.

Benjamin had put the roof back up before setting off and, without the wind to drive it away, her sultry scent filled the enclosed space cocooning them. It was a scent that slowly worked its way into his senses and pushed out the anger that had gripped him at her uncompromising attitude.

As he brought the Buick to a stop, her face made a movement and then she opened her eyes.

She didn't look surprised to find her head resting on his shoulder.

'I fell asleep again,' she whispered, making no attempt to move away from him.

'You did.'

Her black eyes stayed on his, darkening and swirling. And then she did move, shifting slightly to bring her face closer to his and to brush her lips against his...

Much later, naked and replete in her arms, Benjamin reflected that if fantastic sex was the most he got out of this marriage then he would be a luckier man than most.

If Freya wanted to stick to the exact letter of that damned contract, then so be it. From now on he would stick to the damned thing too.

CHAPTER FOURTEEEN

FREYA WANTED TO scream until all the fear and frustration that held her in its grip was ripped from her.

She settled on crawling into a ball in the corner of the living room and rocking.

She'd thought she'd cracked the role of Vicky.

That afternoon she had walked into the practice room to overhear a seething Mikael shouting at the choreographer that he would not 'partner someone who cares so little for the dance'.

'We can't replace her,' the choreographer had replied with the exasperation of someone who had already had that conversation. 'Her face is *everywhere*. The opening night is a sell-out because of her.'

'She is a terrible dancer.'

'Usually she is the best…'

And then they had noticed her standing at the door, aghast at what she had just heard.

'Freya…' the choreographer had begun, but Mikael had cut him off to barge past her saying loudly for anyone passing to hear, 'You find your dancing feet or you find a new partner. I will not be associated with this crap.'

She couldn't even blame him. She would feel the same if she were lumbered with a partner who had lost all coordination and couldn't remember the simplest moves in their dances.

In her studio at the chateau she was foot-perfect.

She *did* know the dances. She knew the whole choreography for the whole production. She just could not translate what was in her head to her feet.

So frightened had she become about it that she'd paid a

private doctor to test her for the cruel disease slowly killing her mother.

The fast-tracked results had come back negative.

Whatever was wrong with her was psychological not physiological.

The problem was in her head.

Impulse had her leaping to her feet and flying to her phone.

She would call Benjamin,

Since she had virtually ruined their evening out together by reminding him of the terms of their contract, his daily calls when she was in Madrid had reduced to nothing.

She hadn't meant to anger him but he was breaking the terms of their contract, interfering when he had no business to.

That interference had terrified her but not half as much as his reasons for it had.

He *knew* she couldn't give him a marriage of true spouses. He'd never wanted a true marriage either. This was a marriage he had backed her into a corner to wed herself to and now he was trying to change all the rules. She had given him her name. She had given him her body when she had never thought she would give that to *anyone*. Hadn't he taken enough already?

Why did he have to push things when the career she kept such tight control of was already spinning away from her faster than she could pirouette? And to threaten to take a mistress…?

She would not think about that.

But he *had* called her the other morning as she'd been locking her apartment door to go to work, checking if she would be available to accompany him to a business dinner on her next days off.

She'd found the mere sound of his beautiful voice soothing and that morning's practice had been the best of the whole week.

'Is something the matter?' he asked without preamble when he answered.

'No,' she denied automatically. 'What makes you ask?'

'You have never called me before.'

'Oh. I just wanted…' *To hear your voice.* 'To check what I should wear to your business dinner.'

'I would never presume to tell you what to wear, *ma douce*. Come dressed as Carabosse if you want.'

She disconnected the call with ice in her veins.

Carabosse was the wicked fairy godmother in *The Sleeping Beauty*.

The faint sound of music seeped through the ceiling and into Benjamin's office.

It was a sound that wrenched at him, the sound of his wife under his roof but hidden away from him.

On the nights they were together she made love to him with abandon but the days they were apart she treated him with indifference. She never called him or messaged him or made any effort to keep in touch. Her one call to him had been for advice on an outfit. As if he knew anything about women's fashion.

He knew his reaction had been harsh but when he'd seen her name flash up on his phone for the first time in almost seven weeks of marriage, he'd been gripped by fear for her.

Why else would she call unless there was something wrong?

His wife wanted him for two things. Money for her family and sex for herself. As a husband he was surplus to requirements, a fact he was finding harder to deal with as time passed rather than easier.

Come the morning she would be up and showered by

six, ready to return to her life in Madrid, the life she refused to include him in.

It should not smart. This was what he'd signed up for. Two separate lives.

But it did.

There was a tap on his office door.

Immediately he straightened in his chair and pressed a key on his computer to spring the unused screen back to life.

'*Entrez.*'

To his surprise, it was his wife who stepped inside.

'Do you have a minute?' she asked quietly.

She was wearing the black practice dress she'd worn when he had made love to her in her studio for the first time. Hair had sprung free from the loose bun she had pulled it back into, her whole appearance more dishevelled than he had ever seen her be.

The usual stab of lust filled his loins to know that beneath her dress she was completely naked...

He gritted his teeth and turned his attention to his computer screen. 'One moment.'

He used the time to compose himself.

Freya had never graced his office with her presence before.

'What can I do for you?' he asked after making her wait a little longer than was strictly necessary.

She had taken the opportunity to perch herself on his leather sofa, leaning forward with her elbows on her thighs and her hands clasped together.

'I want to ask you a favour.'

'Then ask.'

The black eyes held his before her shoulders dropped and she said, 'I know this is a big ask but will you come to the opening performance on Saturday?'

'I would rather swim with sharks than set foot in a theatre owned by those two bastards.'

'I know you would. I'm not asking this lightly but I could really do with the support.'

He made sure to keep his tone amiable. 'Show me where in the contract it says I have to support you in any way that isn't financial and I will abide by it.'

'I didn't have to go to your business dinner last week.'

'That is hardly the same thing.'

'Please. Benjamin, this is the biggest night of my life.'

'If it is support you require, Javier will be there. I am sure he will be glad to lend his support to you.'

'I would rather swim with sharks than have his support,' she said with a shaky laugh, her words clearly intended as a joke to defuse the tension filling the office.

It had the opposite effect.

'And how would I know that?' he asked silkily.

Her brow furrowed. 'Know what?'

He drummed his fingers on his desk. 'That you wouldn't want his support. I know nothing of your life outside this chateau. I know nothing of what you do in Madrid. You keep me excluded from it.'

'There's nothing to tell. I go to work, I come home. That's it. That's my life in Madrid.'

'I only have your word for that.'

The furrow turned into grooves. 'What are you implying?'

'You're a clever woman. You can work it out.'

Comprehension glinted in her eyes. 'You're being ridiculous. Do I cross-examine you about your life when we're apart?'

'I spent weeks hoping you would and now I find I do not care that you don't. You are happy to take my money and share my bed but God forbid I want to spend time with you outside our contracted hours or deviate from that contract in any form whatsoever. I had few expectations of what our marriage would be like and the reality is beyond the lowest of them. You are uncompromising and selfish.'

Her mouth dropped open, angry colour staining her face and neck. 'You have the nerve to call me selfish when you *stole* me from another man out of revenge?'

'That *man* and his brother stole over two hundred million euros from me.' The reins of his temper he'd been clinging to finally snapped and he got to his feet, put his hands on his desk and glowered at her. 'You know exactly what they did and now you want me to spend a night under the same roof as them?'

Her entire frame shook, her fingers grasping the material of her dress as if she would rip it to pieces. 'No, I want you to support me. I want you to put *your* selfish, vindictive nature to one side for one night and be there for me.'

'Why do you want my support?' he sneered. 'You don't even want my company. When you're here on your days off you hide yourself away in that damned studio for hours on end.'

'I'm spending hours in there because right now it's the only place I can dance in and remember what I'm supposed to be doing!' Her voice had risen in pitch and she dropped her hold on her dress to clutch at the bundle of hair on the back of her head. 'My dance has gone to pot. My partner hates me, the choreographer is about to have a nervous breakdown and for some reason this chateau is the only place I find my body doing what it's supposed to do. I'm not hiding away from you up there. I'm trying to turn off the noise in my head. I'm terrified that on Saturday night I'm going to step onto the stage and find my feet turned to lead. I'm fighting for my career and you're calling me selfish when all I'm asking is for you to put your vendetta to one side for one night and be there for me. You *owe* me, Benjamin.'

'I do not owe you anything. How long has your dance been suffering?'

'Since I went back to Madrid.'

He stared at her, his heart hardening to stone. 'That's over six weeks. You didn't bother to share any of your worries with me before so why should I care now?'

The coil that had been stretching and stretching the longer this awful conversation had gone on finally snapped and with it the last of Freya's dignity.

Jumping to her feet, she yanked the ruffle holding her bun in place and threw it onto the floor.

'You should care because this is all your fault!' she shouted. '*You've* done this to me. You!'

'How am I responsible for your failure to remember your moves?'

'Because you are! You wanted to know why I was a virgin? Well, this is why! It was the last thing of myself that I could keep for myself, the only thing that wasn't public property. I saw how passion and sex worked, the jealousy and the bitterness, how some dancers threw away their careers because they became blinded and I was scared to open myself up to that. I've worked too hard and my family have made too many sacrifices for me to allow emotions into my life that would distract me from my dance but I had no *idea* how bad it could be. You've got in my head and I can't get you out and it's affecting *everything*! I can only remember the moves properly when I'm here in the chateau with you. If I'm going to have any chance of getting through the performance on Saturday I need...'

'Ask someone else,' he cut in coldly.

'There is no one else!' Fat tears sprang out of her eyes. 'I'm scared, Benjamin. I know you think I'm uncompromising but I don't know how to be any other way. It's the only way I've been able to survive this life. I'm not good at asking for help but I'm asking you because...'

Freya took a deep breath and finally spoke the truth of what lived in her heart, a truth that no amount of denial or putting her fingers in her ears to drown out the noise could deny any longer. 'I need you, Benjamin. I need you. Just you. Even if Mum and Dad and Sophie could all be there I would still need you. So please, I am begging you, for one night, please, put your vendetta aside and be there for me.'

The tightness of his jaw softened, the tight white line he'd pulled his lips into loosening.

And then Freya looked into his eyes and found nothing but enmity.

'*Non.*'

'No?'

'*Non.* I will not be used as an emotional crutch. If it is physical support to retain the dance moves you require I suggest you speak to your choreographer about getting help. If it is emotional support you need then you will have the entire audience on your side and willing you to do well, but I will not be there and I will not be a part of it.'

He spoke as if discussing how to repair a broken car.

The tears that had leaked out of her eyes dried up as comprehension struck home.

Just as she had finally accepted her feelings for him had gone way beyond her control came the stark truth. She had only ever been a tool for him to hurt Javier with.

He didn't care about her.

Her heart splintering into a thousand pieces, fury suddenly cut through the agony and she was filled with the need to hurt him back, to see those stony features flinch and make him feel a fraction of her pain; pain that *he'd* caused.

Right then she hated him more than she'd thought it was possible to hate a living being.

'How many times have you asked me if I would have preferred to have married Javier? I can tell you the answer now. I wish I *had* married him. At least I knew he was a cold emotionless bastard from the off.'

But he didn't flinch. There was not a flicker of emotion to be seen in the icy eyes staring back at her.

He lowered himself back into his seat and folded his arms across his chest.

'Get out.'

She stormed to the door. 'With pleasure.'

'No, I mean get out for good. Pack your things and leave.'

'Are you serious?'

'*Oui, ma douce*, more serious than you could ever comprehend. You are not welcome in my home any more. I should have left you alone to marry Javier. That would have been the best revenge on him, to let him spend his life with Carabosse.'

For an age they stared at each other, all the loathing that had been there at the beginning of their relationship brought back to life for its dying gasps.

'You need to let it go,' she said in as hard a tone as she could muster. 'This vendetta is not going to destroy the Casillas brothers, it's going to destroy you. It's already destroyed your soul.'

Then she walked out of the office, slamming the door behind her.

She was opening the door to her quarters when she heard the most enormous crash ring out from his.

She didn't pause to worry what it could be.

By the time she'd shoved as much of her possessions as she could into her cases, a car and driver were waiting for her in the courtyard.

As she was driven out of the estate she didn't look back.

* * *

Only through iron will did Freya make it through the dress rehearsal.

Her performance was not perfect, not by any stretch of the imagination, but Mikael had only screamed in her face once so the improvement was there.

But she wasn't feeling it. She heard the music but it didn't find her soul the way it always used to do.

Had she lost her soul?

That was a question she had asked herself countless times the last few days.

She had accused Benjamin of having lost his. Had the deal she'd made with the devil caused her to lose hers too?

If he really were the devil then why had he transferred ten million euros into her account the day after he'd thrown her out of his chateau?

Her instinct had been to transfer it straight back but she'd resisted, having the frame of mind to remember her mother.

She had been who he'd transferred the money for. Not Freya.

Benjamin would never let her mother suffer out of spite for Freya because, fundamentally, he was a decent man.

A decent man who had been crossed by his closest friends.

She had asked him to sit in the theatre owned by the men who had caused so much damage to him, when she knew how much he hated them.

She lay back on the huge bed he had never seen let alone shared with her and put a hand to her chest to still her racing heart, her thought drifting to Vicky Page, the role she would perform to the public for the first time tomorrow night. *The Red Shoes* was a fabulous, iconic production but Freya had spent so long learning the choreography and

then frantically working to retain it that the storyline itself
had passed her by.

Or had she wilfully blocked it out because of the paral-
lels with her own life…?

The story, in its essence, was about ambition. In it,
Vicky, a ballerina starring in her first lead role, finds herself torn, forced to choose between love and her career.

Freya had chosen career over everything since before
she had developed breasts.

Vicky chose love.

Vicky made the wrong choice.

Freya feared she had made the wrong choice too.

She had fought against letting Benjamin into her heart
from the beginning because the danger had been there right
from the very first look between them in Javier's garden.
She had pushed against it and fought and fought but all that
fight had been for nothing.

Everything she had feared about marrying Benjamin had
come to bear. That pull she had felt towards him from that
very first glance had grown too strong. Without him she
had become untethered, as if her anchor had been sliced
away and she were drifting out to sea without a way of
steering herself back to land.

If it looked like a duck, talked like a duck and walked
like a duck then it was a duck. That was what she had said
to him.

'Ducks can't talk,' he'd retorted.

No, ducks couldn't talk, but fools could fall in love even
when it was the very worst thing they should do, and she
was the biggest fool of all.

Benjamin hadn't just stolen her body, he'd stolen her
heart.

She didn't just need him. She loved him.

She'd fallen in love with every vengeful, cruel, generous, thoughtful part of him and to deny it any longer would be like denying the duck its existence.

And now her greatest fear about falling in love had come to bear too. Her dancing had gone to pieces. That was why the music no longer worked its magic in her soul, she realised. She'd given her heart and soul to Benjamin.

The music no longer worked its magic without the man who thought she was the reincarnation of the wicked Carabosse.

CHAPTER FIFTEEN

BENJAMIN CLICKED HIS pen moodily. He'd read the news article spread out on the table before him so many times he could recite it.

A burst of something suddenly pummelled him and he grabbed the offending newspaper, scrunched it into a tight ball and threw it on the floor at the exact moment one of his maids appeared to clear away his breakfast coffee.

She looked at him for a moment then walked straight back out again.

He didn't blame her. He hadn't been in the best of moods lately and was aware of it affecting his entire household.

That didn't stop him getting up from his seat and kicking the ball of paper.

He would tell Pierre he no longer needed to send someone into town to collect him a newspaper any more. Who even read their news in this old-fashioned format any more anyway? It was all there on the Internet, news from all corners of the globe available at his fingertips.

If he stopped getting it he could avoid all news about the arts. There would be no danger of him turning a page and seeing a news article about the grand opening of Compania de Ballet de Casillas's new theatre that night. There would be no danger of him turning the page to be greeted with his estranged wife's striking face staring at him, *the* face of Compania de Ballet de Casillas.

The face of the ballet company owned by the two men he hated. The face he could not expel from his mind even though he refused to think about her. He'd had every last trace of her removed from the chateau and her studio door locked.

How dared she ask such a thing of him? She wanted him to put his vendetta aside when she didn't spare two thoughts for him outside their contracted hours?

I need you.

Of course she did. Just as his mother and his two closest friends had needed him, all of whom had only ever wanted him for what he represented or could give them and not for himself. He didn't add his father to that list. He had never pretended he needed him.

And then to say she'd wished she'd married Javier?

If that comment had been designed to cut through him it had...

Suddenly he found his legs no longer supported him and he sat back down with a thud.

Freya was used to doing everything on her own and being single-minded. She'd *had* to dedicate her life to get where she was, turning her body black and blue in the process.

She had lost control in his office.

He had only ever seen her lose control before in the bedroom.

The rest of the time she was fully in command of herself and her actions. She never did or said anything without thought.

She *had* wanted to hurt him with that comment.

Because he had hurt her, he realised with a rapidly thumping heart.

She had come to him for help. She had *begged* him.

Freya had never asked for anything from him before but his jealousy over her love and commitment to her job, his automatic disbelief that she should need him, added to his fury at what she had asked of him, had all done the talking for him. And the thinking.

She was going to star in the most important performance of her life that night and she was terrified.

His beautiful, fiercely independent wife was terrified.

But how could she need *him*?

And after everything he had done to her.

He had called her selfish but that was far from the truth. *He* was the selfish one.

He'd been wrong to think she should change habits formed over a lifetime just to suit his ego in a marriage she had never wanted to a man she had never wanted.

And he was wrong to allow his vendetta to destroy her life.

Slumping forward, he rubbed at his temples and willed the drums and cymbals crashing in his head to abate.

He willed the throbbing ache in his heart to abate too. He had been willing that since he had watched her be driven out of his life.

The press would be out in force that night and the spotlight would be on her, the heir to Clara Casillas's throne.

She would see Javier that night too. Everyone would be watching them both to see how the mercurial Javier Casillas dealt with the dancer who had dumped him for his oldest friend.

No one knew their marriage was already over.

Over...

He had thrown her out.

The banging in his head got louder, his chest tightening so hard he could no longer draw breath.

Dear God, what had he done?

Freya would have to deal with all the press attention and Javier on her own while trying to find a way to get her unwilling body to do the performance of its life.

How could he let her go through that alone?

She *did* need him.

She needed him to fix the damage he had caused with his bitter selfishness and untrammelled jealousy.

Freya sat at her dressing table applying colour to her whitened cheeks. She liked to do her own hair and make-up before a performance, liked that she had a private dressing room in which she could concentrate on nothing but her breathing. She was fully warmed up, her costume had been fitted and in two minutes she would join her fellow dancers in the wings. From the apprehension she found whenever she looked in anyone's eyes, they were as terrified about her performance as she was.

Strangely, admitting her feelings for Benjamin had had a positive effect on her psyche. It had been like removing the weights that had turned her limbs to lead. She felt sicker in her stomach but freer in her arms and legs. She could only pray it translated to the stage.

She blinked rapidly and dragged her thoughts away from Benjamin before the tears started up again.

No tears tonight, Freya, she told herself sternly.

A short knock on the door was followed by one of the stagehands poking her face into the room. 'More flowers for you.'

Her dressing room was already filled with enough bouquets to open her own florist's and this was the largest bunch by a clear margin.

Accepting them with a forced smile, she was about to put them on her dressing table when she caught the scent of lavender.

She put her nose into the bunch, closed her eyes and inhaled deeply, memories of Provence and Benjamin flooding her.

Lavender was the scent she would always associate with him. If she made it to old bones she already knew it was a scent that would still hurt her.

Her hands shook as she sniffed again and looked at the bunch properly.

Flowers of all different colours and varieties were in the beautiful bouquet but overwhelming it all were purple lavender flowers.

Placing the bouquet on her lap, she fought her fingers to open the envelope they had come with.

You are a shining star, ma douce. *Every heart will belong to you tonight but mine will beat the strongest.*

Her heart thumping, she stared around the small dressing room as if he would suddenly appear.

Did that mean he was here?

'Who gave you these?' she asked the stagehand, who was still at her door.

'A tall man in a tuxedo.'

'That narrows it down,' she said with a spurt of laughter that wasn't the least bit humorous. Every person there would be dressed in their finest clothes. 'Can you be more specific?'

The stagehand's face scrunched up in thought. 'Black hair. Thick eyebrows. Scary-looking.'

It *was* him!

Benjamin was here!

She could hardly believe it.

Joy and dread converged together to set off a new kaleidoscope of butterflies in her belly.

He was here! Here to support her. Under the same roof as the two men who had caused him such harm for *her.*

The stagehand looked at her watch. 'They're waiting for you.'

With a start, Freya realised she was in danger of missing her cue.

She ran to the wings, whispering her apologies to everyone she passed.

The orchestra played the opening beats and then it was time for the performance to begin.

From the private box Benjamin, who had paid an extortionate amount of money to procure it from a richly dressed couple in the theatre lobby, large glass of Scotch in hand, watched Freya dance on the stage with more pride than he had ever known he possessed.

Seeing her in her studio practising alone and clips on the Internet were no substitute for what he witnessed now, beauty expressed in its purest form, a witty portrayal of ambition and a heart-wrenching portrayal of love.

Freya flew as if she had wings. No one else watching would believe the pain she put her feet and limbs through to create something so magical and here, seeing it with his own eyes, he understood for the first time why she put herself through the torture.

She captivated him and, from the faces in the rows below him, she had captivated everyone else too. When the tragedy at the end occurred he doubted there was a dry eye around.

He sipped the last of his Scotch to burn away the lump that had formed in his throat.

If anything were to happen to Freya for real...

It would kill him.

She wouldn't give him a second chance, he knew that. He didn't deserve it and wouldn't ask for it. But as long as he knew she was living the life she had worked so hard for and creating the magic he had witnessed that night, he could live his own life with some form of peace.

It was only as he left the box to search for her and caught sight of Javier and Luis that he realised he hadn't thought about either of them once that evening. His entire focus had been on Freya.

This could be his moment, he thought, heart thumping, blood pumping. The opportunity to punch them both in their treacherous faces, to show his utter contempt for them with the world's press there to witness it in all its glory...

He turned on his heel and walked in the other direction.

* * *

Freya accepted the warm embraces from her colleagues and told them, one after the other, that no she wouldn't be attending the after-show party but yes, of course she would keep in touch.

The best embrace had come from Mikael, who had thrown her in the air before planting a massive kiss on her lips. 'I knew you could do it!' he had said in his thick Slavic accent. 'You were magnificent!'

And then she had set off to the privacy of her dressing room reflecting that this would be the last time she would walk these corridors. There was none of the sadness she'd expected that this chapter of her life was over.

She still didn't know what her future held dance-wise. She'd put everything on hold to get through that performance.

And she had done it!

She felt giddy. And sick.

Because the other part of her future was also an unknown.

Now the euphoria of the performance was dissipating, the relief at having Benjamin there somewhere within the packed theatre was leaving her too.

If there was any chance he had feelings for her, and her gut told her he did, she knew it wasn't enough for them. How could it be when they both wanted and needed such different things?

Their ending had been fated from their beginning. How could any union forged on hate ever end in anything but disaster?

But still she longed to see him.

Where was he?

Would he seek her out?

She had no idea how she would react or what she would say if he did.

Her heart sank to find her dressing room empty of everything but the dozens and dozens of bunches of flowers. They would be forwarded to her apartment in the morning.

By the time she'd stripped her costume and make-up off and donned a pair of skinny jeans and a black shirt her heart had fallen to her feet.

He hadn't sought her out.

Unnoticed by anyone, she slipped out of the theatre and hailed a taxi.

The short journey to her apartment took for ever.

Had she imagined the note from Benjamin? If she hadn't then where was he? Why had he not come to find her?

So lost in her desolate thoughts was she that when she stepped out of the elevator across from her apartment, she almost didn't register the figure sitting on the floor by her door.

The keys she had in her hand ready to let herself in almost slipped through her fingers.

Benjamin lifted his head and stared at the woman he had been waiting for.

He got to his feet while she walked slowly towards him. Her face didn't give anything away but her eyes…they were filled with a thousand different emotions.

'I apologise for leaving the theatre without seeing you,' he said, breaking the silence. 'Javier and Luis were there. I didn't want to create a scene so thought it best to leave before anything could happen. Please, can I come in?'

She inhaled then nodded and unlocked the door with a shaking hand.

'Can I get you a drink?' she asked politely, no longer looking at him.

Grateful that her first words to him weren't of the *get the hell out* variety, he answered with equal politeness. 'If it isn't too much trouble.'

'Wine?'

'You have alcohol?'

Her gaze darted to his. The glimmer of a smile quirked on her lips. 'I had a glass last night. There's three quarters of the bottle left.'

'You will have a glass with me?'

'Do I need it?'

'Probably. I know I do.'

A sound like a muted laugh came from her lips but the way she tore her eyes from him and blinked frantically negated it.

In the kitchen, she opened the tall fridge and pulled out a bottle of white. She took two glasses out of a cupboard, filled them both virtually to the rim and took a large drink from one. She gestured for him to take the other.

So she didn't want to risk touching him. He could not blame her for that.

'You were wonderful tonight,' he said softly. 'I could not take my eyes off you.'

A hesitant smile played on her lips. 'Thank you. It helped knowing you were there. I know it must have taken a lot.'

'Do not dare thank me,' he said darkly. He did not want her gratitude. He downed the rest of his wine and put the glass down on the counter.

Her eyes had become wary. 'Benjamin…?'

He held out a hand to stop her. 'First, let me apologise unreservedly for the way I spoke to you and for throwing you out of my home.'

'You hardly threw me out. You got your driver to take me to the airport.'

'Do not make excuses for me.' He glared at her. 'I do not deserve excuses and I will not accept them. My behaviour, everything I have done to you has been abhorrent. I will not make excuses to myself any more. I *did* steal you from Javier. I have been a jealous fool. I saw you in Javier's garden and have not been the same since.'

'What do you mean?' she asked in a far softer tone than he deserved.

'Something happened to me when I first set eyes on you. I could not get you from my mind. I was obsessed with you. I wanted you for myself because I am a selfish, greedy man. I chose you as leverage against Javier, not because I thought it was the most effective way to get my money back but to destroy your engagement.'

'You wanted to destroy us?'

He gave a tight nod. Since making the decision to go to Madrid to support her, he had done nothing but think. It had not been a pleasant awakening.

'I could not bear to think of you in his bed or him touching you,' he told her. 'I salved my conscience by telling myself you were better off without him, but you were right that time when you asked me who I thought I was deciding what was right for you. And you were right that everything I did was to serve my own agenda. *You* were my agenda. If you weren't I would have paid you off when you suggested it. I would have done anything to have you and make you mine. And now I would do anything to make amends. I don't deserve or expect your forgiveness. I have ruined your life. Javier would have been the better man for you to marry, and I do not say that lightly. He would never have tried to control you or influence where you worked.'

'Only because he wouldn't have cared,' she interjected with a whisper.

'But that is what you need, is it not? The freedom to live your life for what is best for you and your career without anything else fighting for space in a life already full with your dance and your parents? I took that away from you. I made what should have been the greatest night of your life a nightmare. When you reached out to me about your troubles I pushed you away because I didn't believe an independent woman like you, who has never needed anyone, could need me when no one has ever needed me before. I was jealous too, of you living under the same skies as Javier, and jealous you had a passion that didn't involve me.'

'You were jealous of me dancing?'

'*Oui*. Your dance. It is who you are, *ma douce*. It is one of the reasons I fell in love with you.' Her eyes widened at his casual admission but he carried on, wanting to get everything off his chest while he had the chance. 'When you commit to something you do not do it lightly. I cannot tell you how much I admire the dedication and commitment it must have taken you to become the woman you are today or how envious I am of the childhood you had.'

'You're jealous of my childhood? What on earth for? We were dirt poor.'

'But rich with love. My father left when he couldn't take playing second fiddle to Clara Casillas any longer—and to think I am anything like him just destroys me—and my mother…' He breathed heavily. This was an admittance he had barely acknowledged to himself. 'She loved me in the way an owner loves its pet. I was an accessory, conceived as a playmate for the children Clara would have. When Clara died she transferred her love to Clara's sons. I could never make her smile the way they did. When my father left he didn't give me a second thought and I didn't give him one either. That's what I mean about never being needed before.

'Your parents love you. Whatever career path you chose they would have done anything they could to support and encourage you whatever the cost to themselves. And you are the same. When you love someone you give them your whole heart and I will never forgive myself for making you a pawn in my vengeance.'

He paused to get some air into his lungs.

Freya was staring at him, eyes wide, her mouth half open but no sound coming out.

'You will have seen the deposit I made into your account. It's the sum I should have paid you to begin with rather than force you into a marriage you did not want. Anything you want, for you or for your parents, message me—I don't expect you to call. I know I can't make things better by throwing money at it but, for the sake of my conscience, promise you will always come to me. I need to be able to sleep again, *ma douce*, and abandoning my plans for revenge on Luis isn't enough.'

She smiled weakly. 'You're going to leave Luis alone?'

'I have done enough damage to spend eternity in hell. I will let his own conscience punish him.'

Her chin wobbled. 'I'm glad. And I'm proud of you.'

'I do not deserve that,' he said with a grimace.

'You could have made a scene tonight but you didn't. You walked away. Your soul isn't a lost cause, whatever you believe.'

'I only walked away because of you. You are more important to me than anything. More important than my hate for them. I can only apologise again and again that it was nearly too late for your performance before I realised it.'

'But it wasn't too late, was it? You were there. You came. That means the world.'

He managed the semblance of a smile. 'You have a beautiful heart, *ma douce*. I hope one day you find a man deserving of it.' He took one more deep breath and gave a sharp nod. 'And now I shall leave you to your rest.'

Stepping over to her, he put his hands lightly on her shoulders, breathing in the scent he had missed so badly for the last time. Brushing his lips to her forehead, he whispered. *'Au revoir, mon amour.'*

He took comfort that she didn't flinch away from his touch.

Holding his frame together by the skin of his teeth, he walked to the door.

He would fall apart when he was in the privacy of his

home. There was a whole bar full of Scotch for him to drown his sorrows in.

'So that's it?' she called after him, stopping him in his tracks. 'You come here to pour your heart out and tell me you love me and then *leave*? What about all the things I need to say to you?'

He closed his eyes. 'Whatever you need to say, I will listen.'

'You can start by turning around and facing me.'

Slowly he turned, expecting to see anger, preparing for the full-scale verbal attack he deserved.

Instead…

Instead he was greeted by the softest, gentlest expression he had ever seen.

She treaded over to him and placed a hand on his cheek. 'I took one look at you in Javier's garden and I fell in love with you. I was obsessed with you. I couldn't stop thinking about you even though they were thoughts I knew I shouldn't have. When you stole me away…' She sighed. 'I have tried my hardest to hate you. There have been times when I *have* hated you but running beneath it all has been my heart beating harder than it has ever beaten before because it is beating for two. It is beating for you. I lost my ability to dance because my heart and soul became yours without my knowing. I could only dance in the chateau because that's where you were. I needed to be near you. I still need to be near you. I can dance again now, I found a way through it, but without you in my life the passion is lost. I do need you, Benjamin. Like a fish needs water. I can't breathe properly without you.'

Her lips found his to press the most tender of kisses to them.

She sighed again. 'I love you. When I dance it is your face I see before me and it lifts me higher than I have ever jumped before. You make me want a life that's more than dance. You bring all the different colours and flavours of life out in me.'

He didn't dare allow joy anywhere near him. 'But can you forgive me? Can you ever trust me?'

'I *do* trust you. As for forgiveness, I can promise to forgive you if you can promise to forgive yourself.'

'I don't know how,' he answered honestly. He would never lie to her.

'By drawing a line in the sand on the past. What's done is done and we can't change it. All we can do is look to the future and the only future I want is with you.'

'The only future I want is with *you*. Without you I am nothing. I will follow you anywhere. To the ends of the earth. You can dance in China for all I care, I will be there with you.'

She kissed him again. 'Then prove it to me.'

'How?'

'By loving me for ever.'

Suddenly feeling as if his heart would burst, Benjamin finally allowed himself to believe…

She loved him! This incredible woman who could move his heart with the tilt of her head loved him.

In his wildest fantasies he had never allowed himself to think that.

But she did. And he loved her.

Parting his lips, he kissed her back with all the love and passion she had filled his heart with, thanking all the deities in the skies for giving him this second chance to be a better man with this woman who completed him.

And he would love her for ever.

EPILOGUE

TERROR CLUTCHED AT Benjamin's heart.

That was his wife, waiting in the wings, ready to come on stage and dazzle the packed theatre of families at the Orchestre National de Paris in her role as the Sugar Plum Fairy for this one-off Christmas production of *The Nutcracker*.

And this was their year-old son asleep on his lap, blissfully unaware his mother was about to perform for the first time since his birth. And in such a monumental, iconic role too.

It would also be her first performance since her mother had died peacefully in her sleep that summer. Freya and her father had consoled themselves that they had been given another two years with her, good years with months in which she'd been well enough to travel to Russia and New York and watch her only daughter guest star with some of the most famous ballet companies in the world and meet her first grandchild.

Benjamin had no idea how Freya was going to pull it off. His darling wife had had a roller-coaster year with tears and laughter, sadness and joy. All the ups and downs had only brought them closer together.

Freya was his world. Christopher, the dark-haired bundle of mischief in his arms, had completed them.

Gasps from the children in the audience brought him back to the present, and he blinked to see the vision in a glittering white tutu take to the stage.

Then the familiar tinkling music began and his wife transformed into the Sugar Plum Fairy.

With subtlety, charm and grace, she moved over the

stage, that illusion of flight she did so perfectly enthralling the whole spellbound theatre.

'She's wonderful,' whispered his father-in-law, sitting beside him in Benjamin's private box.

Benjamin nodded his agreement, too choked to speak. He didn't have to look to know Freya's loving father had tears rolling down his face.

When the orchestra played its final note in the dance, the theatre erupted. Cheers and bellows rang out, a sound so different from what had played before that Christopher woke up.

Bouncing in excitement, he pointed to the stage. 'Mama!'

'*Oui*, that's your mama,' Benjamin whispered into his son's ear. 'And your grandfather is right—she is wonderful.'

* * * * *

THE SHEIKH'S SHOCK CHILD

SUSAN STEPHENS

CHAPTER ONE

SAPPHIRES DRIFTED IN a shimmering stream from the Sheikh's fingers. Backlit by candlelight, the precious gems blazed with blue fire, dazzling fifteen-year-old Millie Dillinger. Seeing her mother cuddled up to the Sheikh had the opposite effect. Toad-like and repellent, he was hardly the dashing hero Millie had imagined when her mother had said they were both to be guests at a most important royal engagement.

Millie had just stepped on board the Sheikh's superyacht after being brought straight from school in a limousine with diplomatic plates, and found this a very different and frightening world. Sumptuous yes. Everywhere she looked there were more obvious signs of money than she'd seen in her entire life, but, like the Sheikh, the interior of his vast, creaking superyacht was sinister, rather than enticing. She kept glancing over her shoulder to check for escape routes, knowing it wouldn't be easy to go anywhere with heavily armed guards, dressed in black tunics and baggy trousers, standing on either side of her, with yet more posted around the room.

Much in Millie's life was uncertain, but this was frightening. Her mother was unpredictable, and it was always up to Millie to try and keep things on an even keel. That meant getting them out of here, if she could. This big room was known as the grand salon, but when she'd seen pictures in magazines of similar vessels, they were light and elegant, luxurious spaces, not dark and stale like this. Heavy drapes had been closed to shut out the light, and it smelled bad. Like an old wardrobe, Millie thought, wrinkling her nose.

The Sheikh and his guests were staring at her, making her feel she was part of a show, and it was not a performance she wanted to take part in. Seeing her mother in the arms of an old man was bad enough. He might be royalty, and he might be seated in the place of honour on a bank of silken cushions beneath a golden canopy, but he was repulsive. This had to be their host, His Magnificence Sheikh Saif al Busra bin Khalifa. Millie's mother, Roxy Dillinger, had been hired to sing at his party, and had asked Millie to join her. Why? Millie wondered.

'Hello, little girl.' The Sheikh spoke in a wheedling tone that made Millie shudder. 'You are most welcome here,' he said, beckoning her closer.

She refused to move as her mother prompted in a slurred stage whisper, 'Her name is Millie.'

As if names were unimportant to him, the Sheikh beckoned again, and more impatiently this time. Millie stared at her mother, willing her to make her excuses so that they could leave. Her mother refused to take the hint. She was still so beautiful, but sad for much of the time, as if she knew her days in the sun were over. Millie wanted to protect her, and quivered with indignation when some of the guests began to snigger behind their hands. Sometimes it felt as if she were the grown up and her mother the child.

'See, Millie,' her mother exclaimed as she raised and slopped a glass of champagne down an evening dress that had seen better days. 'This is the type of life you can have if you follow me onto the stage.'

Millie shrank at the thought. Her dream was to be a marine engineer. This was more like Walpurgis Night than a theatrical performance, with every witch and warlock gathered to carouse and feast at the feet of the devil. Candlelight flickered eerily over the faces of the guests, and an air of expectation gripped them. What were they waiting for? Millie wondered. She didn't belong here, and neither did her mother, and if her mother started to sing it would be worse. A careless approach to her health had ruined Roxy Dillinger's renowned singing voice. She had squeezed herself into a shoddy and revealing floor-length gown, but Millie knew that the best she would be able to manage was a few cigarette-scarred songs for people who didn't care that Roxy had once been known as the Nightingale of London.

Millie cared. She cared deeply and passionately for her mother, and her protective instinct rose like a lion for its cub. Ignoring the impatience of the Sheikh, she held out her hands. 'It's time to go home. Please, Mum—'

'Roxy,' her mother hissed, shooting a warning glance at Millie. 'My name is Roxy.'

'Please… Roxy,' Millie amended reluctantly. Whatever it took, she would get them out of here somehow.

'Don't be stupid,' her mother snapped, staring round at her less than admiring public. 'I haven't sung yet. Tell you what,' she said in a change of tone. 'Why don't you sing for us, Millie? She has a lovely voice,' she added to the Sheikh. 'Not as strong and pure as mine, of course,' she added, snuggling up to him.

The way the Sheikh was looking at Millie made her skin crawl, but she refused to back down. 'If you come home with me now, I'll buy cakes on the way,' she coaxed her mother.

Unpleasant laughter greeted this remark. A gesture from

the Sheikh silenced his guests. 'I have world-renowned pastry chefs on board, little girl. You and your mother can eat your fill—once you've sung for your supper.'

Millie suspected the Sheikh had something else in mind other than singing. With her plaits, spectacles and serious demeanour, she would certainly be a novelty for his sophisticated guests, who had started to chant her name. Far from this being encouragement, as her mother seemed to think, Millie knew it was mockery of the cruellest kind. Her neck burned with embarrassment as she begged, 'Please, Mum. You don't need the Sheikh's money. I'll take an extra shift at the laundry—'

Screeches of laughter drowned out her voice. Desperate now, she glanced longingly in the direction of the marina, where life would be carrying on as normal. If this was how the super-rich lived, Millie wanted no part of it. Tonight had cemented her decision to forge a life she could control.

'Sing for us, Millie,' Roxy slurred. 'You can be my support act.'

Millie loved singing, and had joined the school choir, but her real passion was discovering how things worked. Once she'd passed her school exams, she was determined to put in as many hours as it took, working at the laundry to fund more education.

The crowd continued to chant, *'Millie... Millie... Millie...'* Her mother's eye make-up was smudged, and she looked so tired. 'Please, Mum...'

'You'll stay here,' the toad on the dais rapped. At his signal, the guards closed around Millie, cutting off all avenues of escape. 'Come closer, little girl,' he drawled in a sugary voice that frightened her. 'Dip your hands into my bowl of sapphires. They will inspire you, as they have inspired your mother.'

Millie flinched away as someone shrieked an ugly laugh.

'Touch my sapphires,' the Sheikh continued in the same hypnotic tone. 'Feel their cool magnificence—'

'*Step back!*'

The icy command was delivered like a shot and shocked everyone rigid. Millie turned to see a colossus in travel clothes striding into their midst. The guards snapped to attention as he passed, and even the Sheikh's spoiled mouth remained petulantly closed.

What a devastating man, Millie thought. Much younger than the Sheikh, he was infinitely more attractive, and Millie's ideal when it came to a romantic hero. While the Sheikh overflowed his cushions, this man was lean and fit, like a soldier or a bodyguard.

'Why, *brother*, you're such a prude.'

When the Sheikh drawled this, she gasped. His *brother*? *This* was the toad's brother? There was so little resemblance between the two men it didn't seem possible. While the Sheikh sent shivers of disgust shooting down her spine, his brother inspired a very different response.

She cringed to see the Sheikh wrap his arms a little closer around her mother, as if claiming his property in the face of a challenge. 'Have you never played Bridge the Generation Gap before?' he asked, glancing between the newcomer, Millie, and her mother.

'You disgust me,' the newcomer rapped. 'She's just a child,' he observed as he flashed an appraising glance at Millie.

That brief look seared her to the depth of her soul. She would never forget it. There was anger in his eyes, but also concern, and it made her feel safe for the first time since she'd boarded the yacht.

'I can't believe you'd sink so low as to include a young girl in your debauchery,' he said scathingly.

'Can't you?' The Sheikh gave a careless shrug. 'She's

a pretty young thing. Why don't you take a turn when I'm
finished with her?'

'You and I are very different, brother.'

'Evidently,' the Sheikh conceded. 'But it's no business
of yours how I spend my free time.'

'When you bring our country into disrepute, it is my
business.'

The Sheikh's striking-looking brother had everyone's
interest, Millie noticed, and no wonder, with his skin the
colour of polished bronze, and that thick, jet-black wavy
hair. His body was as powerful as a gladiator's, his eyes
as fierce and unforgiving as a hawk's, while harsh cheekbones and sweeping inky brows added to the exotic picture of a man who commanded the room.

'You sicken me,' he rapped with disgust. 'I return from
fighting alongside our forces, to find you indulging yourself in the most depraved manner imaginable. You won't
be satisfied until you've brought our country to its knees.'

'I'll bring something to its knees,' the Sheikh agreed
with a lascivious glance at Millie.

Millie gasped as the younger man swept a protective
arm around her shoulder. 'You won't touch her,' he warned.

The Sheikh's response was a lazy wave of his hand.
'You take things too seriously, Khalid. You always did.'

Khalid.

Learning her guardian's name, Millie felt a rush of emotion. He remained standing between her and the Sheikh,
to protect her from his brother's crude remarks and lewd
glances. If only he could rescue her mother too.

'Don't bring your bleeding heart here,' the Sheikh dismissed with a scornful look. 'It's not appreciated.'

'A bleeding heart because I care for our people?' the
Prince challenged, stepping away from Millie. 'Where
were you when our country needed you, Saif?' he de-

manded. 'You left our borders unprotected and our people in danger. You should be ashamed of yourself,' he finished with icy disdain.

'It is you who should be ashamed for ruining the evening for my guests,' the Sheikh remarked, unconcerned. 'And it is you who should apologise,' he insisted.

Shaking his head, Prince Khalid assured his brother that he would do no such thing. 'Come,' he added sharply to Millie. 'You're leaving right now. And if you had any sense,' he added to Millie's mother, 'you'd leave too.'

Roxy's response was to turn her sulky face into the Sheikh's shoulder.

'Is this what *you* want?' the Sheikh asked Millie.

'Yes,' Millie almost shouted, 'but I'm not leaving without my mother. Please—' It was useless. Her mother didn't move.

'At least take some sapphires with you,' the Sheikh suggested in a mocking tone.

'Don't touch them!' his brother rapped.

'As if I would!' This time she did shout, and it was so unlike her to lose her temper, but if he thought for one moment she could be bribed with sapphires!

Prince Khalid smiled faintly as he looked at her, and there was almost respect in his eyes, Millie thought, as if he knew she found this situation as deplorable as he did.

'You're a disgrace to the Khalifa name,' her rescuer thundered, turning his attention to Sheikh Saif. 'If you weren't the ruler of Khalifa—'

'What would you do?' the Sheikh queried in an oily tone. 'I stand between you and the throne. Is that what's really troubling you, brother?' Opening his arms wide, the Sheikh drew in his avid audience. 'My poor brother can never get over the fact that he can't have things all his own, dull way. How boring life would be with you in charge of the country, Khalid.'

This was greeted by murmurs of agreement from his guests. Millie risked a glance to see how the Prince had taken this latest insult. Apart from a muscle flicking in his jaw, he remained unmoved. 'I'm taking the girl,' he said, 'and I want the mother gone by the time I return. Her daughter should not be left alone at night with so many unpleasant characters roaming King's Dock.'

A gasp of affront greeted this remark. The Sheikh remained unconcerned. 'But she won't be on her own, will you, my dear? She'll have you,' he added with a sneer for Prince Khalid.

By this time, Millie was consumed with fear for her mother. 'I can't leave her,' she told the Prince when he tried to usher her away.

Gripping her arm firmly, he warned, 'Don't get any ideas. You're leaving now.'

'Not without my mother,' Millie said stubbornly.

'Get her out of here!' her mother yelled with an angry gesture in Millie's direction.

Having finally dislodged herself from the Sheikh's embrace, her mother was standing with her fists tightly clenched. 'You're nothing but a little killjoy,' she railed at Millie. 'You always spoil my fun!'

Gasping with hurt, Millie was barely aware that the door of the grand salon had slammed behind her, making her last memory of that night her mother's voice screaming at her to go.

'What's your name?' he asked the pale, tense child as he escorted her off the *Sapphire*. He needed something to distract her from the ordeal, and wanted to keep her talking. She seemed so unnaturally quiet.

There was a silence and then, to his relief, she said in a strained whisper, 'Millicent.'

'Millicent?' he repeated. 'I like your name.' It suited the girl with her serious demeanour, heavy glasses and neatly braided hair.

'People call me Millie,' she added shyly as they left the shadows behind and exited the vessel into clean ocean air.

The child was as refreshing as the ocean, he thought, and he was determined to do what he could to protect her from harm. 'What do you like to be called?' he asked when she turned back to stare up at the shaded windows behind which they both knew her mother would continue to party.

'Me?' She frowned and then refocused on his face. 'I like to be called Millie.'

'Millie,' he repeated.

'Will you do something for me?' she asked, surprising him with her quick recovery.

'If I can,' he agreed.

They had reached the head of the gangplank, where she drew to a halt. 'Will you tell my mother to leave?' she begged earnestly. 'She might listen to you. Will you find her a cab and send her home? I've got some money. I can pay you—'

'You've got your bus fare home?' he guessed. She was young, but she was sensible. She had to be, he thought.

'Yes,' she confirmed. Her forehead pleated with surprise, as if common sense were second nature to the daughter, if not the mother. 'Of course I do. Well? Will you?' she pressed.

'I'll see what I can do,' he agreed.

'Please,' she pressed. 'Promise me you'll try.'

Something about her steady gaze compelled him to answer in the affirmative. 'I promise. Now go home and do your school work.'

He followed her gaze with interest as something else occurred to her. She was staring at his brother's chauffeur, who was standing stiffly to attention at the side of the royal limousine. He saluted as Khalid approached.

'He's been standing here for ages,' Millie whispered discreetly. 'Could you bring him a glass of water before he takes me home?'

'Me?' he exclaimed.

'Why not you?' she demanded. 'There's nothing wrong with your legs, is there?'

Her cheeky comment took him by surprise. She had spirit, and to spare.

'He brought me here,' she explained, 'so I know he must be tired.'

Completely unaware of status or rank, she was a novelty, and a welcome reminder that their respective positions in life had been decided by an accident of birth. Her cheeks blushed red as he pointed out the iced water dispensers, both in the front and the back of the vehicle. 'He's fine,' he explained in the same confiding tone. 'Give him your address and he'll see you home safely.'

'And my mother?' she said, staring back at the ship.

'I'll do what I can.' He ground his jaw with disgust at the prospect of returning on board. 'Never put yourself in such danger again,' he added in his sternest tone.

She didn't flinch as she retorted fiercely, 'I never will.'

He watched the vehicle pull away with its lonely figure seated upright in the back. With her school satchel at her side, and her hands folded neatly on her lap, Millie stared straight ahead. It was impossible to imagine a greater contrast to her mother, and his last thought before turning to the ship was that Millie was a good girl who deserved better than this.

CHAPTER TWO

Eight years later...

'Okay, it's working again.' Satisfied with her handiwork, Millie stepped away from the boiler she'd just repaired.

'You're a gem,' Miss Francine, the octogenarian who had worked at the laundry since she was a girl, and who now owned the business, beamed at Millie as she enveloped her favourite worker in a hug. 'I don't know anyone else who has the patience to coax these old machines back to life. What would I do without you?'

'We'd go down to the stream and beat the yachties' sheets clean with stones,' a girl called Lucy suggested dryly.

With a grin for her friend, Millie plucked a pencil from her bundled-up hair to make notes on how to start up the ancient boiler should it fail when she had returned to her apprenticeship as a marine engineer.

'You'd better not beat the Sheikh of Khalifa's *golden* sheets clean,' Lucy observed, matching Millie's grin. 'He might keel-haul you, or... *What?*' she demanded when both Millie and Miss Francine froze in horror.

'Nothing,' Millie said quietly, forcing her face to relax as she flashed a warning look at Miss Francine to say nothing. 'I didn't know the Sheikh's yacht had berthed, that's all.'

Lucy flung her arms wide like a proud fisherman demonstrating the improbable size of his latest catch. 'It's enormous! You couldn't miss it, if you hadn't had your head stuck in the boiler cupboard.'

Then, thank goodness she had, Millie thought.

'When did those sheets come in?' Miss Francine asked, obviously trying to distract from a topic she knew Millie would not want to discuss.

Lucy held out the yards of gold fabric overflowing her arms. 'The housekeeper from the *Sapphire* brought them, saying they needed special handling.'

'Ripping up?' Millie suggested beneath her breath. The golden sheets reminded her of one particular night and all its heartwrenching associations.

Miss Francine stepped in to her rescue again. 'If a yacht the size of the *Sapphire* has berthed, we must get back to work. We'll have laundry coming out of our ears,' she enthused, with an anxious look at Millie. 'And it might be the pressing machine that goes next.'

'Well, I'm here if it does break down,' Millie soothed, appreciating the change of subject.

'Are you sure you're all right?' Miss Francine asked discreetly as soon as everyone else was distracted by work.

'I'm fine,' Millie confirmed, 'and happy to take responsibility for those sheets. I'll supervise their care every step of the way,' she assured her elderly friend grimly, 'and I'll take them back on board to make sure they're fitted properly.'

'There's no need for that,' Miss Francine said, flashing Millie a concerned look. 'I'll take them.'

'I want to,' Millie insisted. 'It's a matter of pride.' She had to prove to herself that she could do this, and after eight years of hunting for clues into her mother's death, this was the best lead she'd had.

'Well, if you're happy to do it, I won't argue with you,' Miss Francine confirmed. 'We'll have more than enough work to go round.'

Something about the way her elderly friend had capitulated so quickly rang alarm bells in Millie's head. Which she dismissed as overreaction. Discovering the *Sapphire* was back was a shock.

'What do you think of the golden sheets?' Lucy asked later as they worked side by side.

'Magnificent, I suppose,' Millie admitted, 'but too gaudy for my taste.' Though typical of the *Sapphire*, she thought, grinding her jaw as pictures of gemstones falling from a hand that might have pushed her mother to her death swam into her mind.

'Too gaudy for mine too,' Lucy agreed.

'Try not to think about it,' Miss Francine whispered as she drew Millie to one side. 'Take a few deep breaths,' she advised.

If only breathing steadily could be enough to shut out the past. *'I gave birth at sixteen, you know,'* her mother had told the Sheikh.

Why must Millie always remember the bad things?

But that wasn't the worst, was it?

Ignoring her mother's comment with a derisive eye-roll, the Sheikh had remarked, 'Of course you did,' as he selected a ripe fig with his fat, bejewelled fingers.

'I was never meant to have a child,' her mother had added with a scowl for Millie.

Millie still felt the pain of that comment and remembered how her mother had snuggled even deeper into the Sheikh's reptilian embrace as she'd said it, shutting out Millie completely—

'Millie?'

'Yes?' She forced a bright note into her voice as Miss

Francine came around to double-check she was okay. 'So, he's back,' Millie remarked, trying to sound upbeat.

Her old friend wasn't convinced by her act. 'It seems so,' Miss Francine agreed briskly as she helped Millie to tuck the fabulous sheets into a fine cotton sack they used for the most delicate fabrics before washing them.

'He's been gone a long time,' Millie added in a lame attempt to keep the conversation alive. 'I guess Sheikh Saif had to stay out of the country after the accident.'

'Millie,' Miss Francine interrupted in a concerned tone.

Millie had never seen her elderly friend looking so worried. 'What is it? What's wrong?' she asked.

'I should have told you right away,' Miss Francine explained with a regretful shake of her head. 'It isn't Sheikh Saif on board the *Sapphire*. He died some years ago—of overeating, the press said,' she added with a grimace for Millie, who was too shocked to speak. 'You were away on that oil rig as part of your work experience when he died.'

'Who then?' Millie managed to force out. 'Who's on the *Sapphire*?'

'His brother, Sheikh Khalid,' Miss Francine revealed in a businesslike manner Millie had no doubt was gauged to cause her the least distress.

Nothing helped. Millie felt as if all the air had been sucked out of her lungs as Miss Francine continued, 'Sheikh Saif's death only made a few column inches in the press, and you were so upbeat when you came home that I couldn't bear to dampen your enthusiasm by bringing up the past.'

'Thank you,' Millie said numbly.

'You don't have to thank me for anything,' Miss Francine insisted as she rested a reassuring hand on Millie's shoulder.

There was nothing more to say, and they both fell silent.

Millie had been a Saturday girl at the laundry at the time of her mother's tragic death, Miss Francine had stepped in right away, offering her a place to live. Home had been a room above the laundry ever since.

'Of course, no one mentioned Sheikh Saif's death to me,' Millie mused dazedly, 'because…' She shrugged. 'Why would they?'

Was she imagining it, or was Miss Francine finding it hard to meet her eyes?

'I owe you everything,' she said, giving her elderly friend an impulsive hug.

When Miss Francine left her side, Millie put her work on autopilot, so she could think back to what she remembered about Prince Khalid. Which was quite a lot. Never had anyone made such a strong impression on her. Most of it good. All of it awe-inspiring. And confusing. She'd thought him one thing, which was hero material, but he'd turned out to be something very different. And she must think of him as *Sheikh* Khalid now, Millie amended as images of blazing masculinity came flooding back. The sternest of men was now an omnipotent ruler. She could only imagine the changes in him. A few minutes in his company had been enough to brand his image on her soul. She could still see him striding up the *Sapphire*'s gangplank like an avenging angel to rescue her mother. But he hadn't rescued her mother. He'd let her down. And at some point during that terrible night, Millie's mother had either fallen from the *Sapphire*, or she'd been pushed.

Bracing herself, she stared out of the window. It was impossible to miss the *Sapphire* at rest in its berth. The superyacht was as big as a commercial cruise liner, and easily the biggest ship in the harbour. It was like a call to destiny that she couldn't avoid. She tried not to show how tense she was when Miss Francine came back. 'It's had a complete refit,' her elderly friend explained. 'When Sheikh Khalid inherited the throne of Khalifa from his brother, he insisted that the ship must be gutted and refitted. Gossip on the marina says that everything on board is cutting edge.' There was a long pause, and then she added carefully, 'Nothing ever remains the same, Millie.'

'I'm sure you're right,' Millie agreed. She knew Miss Francine was just trying to help. 'And *I'm* all right,' she added briskly, with a reassuring smile for her friend. 'However fabulous the *Sapphire* looks, it has moving parts that need to be fixed.'

Miss Francine laughed as Millie hoped she would. 'Taking your tool kit on board?' she suggested.

Millie narrowed her eyes. 'You can bet I'll be fully prepared by the time I board.'

'I'm sure you will be,' Miss Francine agreed quietly.

'My life is here with you,' Millie said. 'And it's very different from the life I had at fifteen. You've given me a happy home where I'm safe, and a launch pad so I can work towards a successful career. I'll never be able to thank you enough for that.'

'I don't want your thanks,' Miss Francine assured her. 'I couldn't love you more if you were my daughter.'

As they hugged, Millie reflected that she certainly didn't owe the Sheikh of Khalifa anything, other than contempt for letting her down. He was on board the *Sapphire* the night of her mother's death, and when the authorities had come calling, he'd made sure to keep his brother out of the courts.

'I'll take the sheets on board, and be back before you know it,' she said with confidence. She was grimly determined to do just that, if only to prove to herself that the past couldn't hurt her.

Miss Francine exclaimed with relief, 'Bravo!'

* * *

Dressed in formal, flowing black silk robes trimmed with gold, Khalid was looking forward to reclaiming the informality he enjoyed on board the *Sapphire*, but before he could relax he had business to attend to. He had just received a deputation from the local council asking for his support with its youth plan, which accounted for his dress code of regal opulence. This world tour had lasted long enough, he concluded as he appended a final signature to the document that would fund his latest project. Staring out through the rain-lashed windows of his study, he reflected on the significance of King's Dock. His educational trust had been born here, because of an incident that had changed his life. He had never thought to return, but neither would he neglect an opportunity to help young people gain a foothold in life. He had been asked for help, so he was here, and now he was here he couldn't leave without having reassured himself about certain issues.

Closing his eyes, he eased his neck. He longed for the cleansing heat of the desert and the cooling waters of the oasis, but the truth of that terrible night wouldn't go away. Pushing back from his desk, he stood up, and was glad of a muted tap on the door to distract him.

'Come…'

His housekeeper entered and stood politely just inside the entrance. 'The Gilded Stateroom is almost ready for your inspection, Your Majesty.'

'Thank you. Please let me know when the final touches have been made, and I'll inform you if I require anything else.'

'Of course, Your Majesty.' With a curtsey his housekeeper left the room.

He didn't check every guest room, but this was for a particular guest, his old friend Tadj. Otherwise known as

His Radiance, the Emir of Qalala, Tadj and he had been friends since school and university, and had joined Special Forces together. Khalifa and Qalala were trading partners, with valuable sapphire mines adjacent to each other in the mountains of Khublastan. The boundaries of several countries converged in this same region, which had led to their rulers becoming known collectively as the Sapphire Sheikhs. He was looking forward to Tadj's arrival. Things were stable again in Khalifa after Saif's tumultuous reign, and Khalid had not taken a break for some years. Having built a strong team around him, he could afford to do so now. This trip was an opportunity to build relationships between nations, and also to give him the chance to view the royal marriage mart to see if any of the available princesses would do. Tadj might advise on that—then again not, he thought dryly. Tadj was the devil incarnate where women were concerned.

Not wishing to dwell on thoughts of marriage, Khalid returned in his mind to Khalifa, that most beautiful of countries. Prosperity in the last few years had led to modern cities rising like mirages out of the ocean of sand, and though the desert might seem hostile to a casual visitor, it was teeming with life, especially around the oases where the animals he loved, the ibex and desert oryx, thrived beneath his protection. A crystalline ocean yielded more than enough food for his people, while a dramatic snow-capped mountain range held the precious seams of sapphires that gave them security, wealth, education, and medical care. To him there was nowhere to compare with Khalifa, and his spirits soared as he thought about the country he loved.

The stateroom for Tadj!

As he turned to leave his study something drew his glance to the window where, far below him on the rain-swept dock, a mini-drama was playing out. A small figure cloaked head to foot in sensible oilskins was attempting to gain entry onto the private walkway leading to the *Sapphire*. A sentry stood in her way. He could tell it was a woman from her height and tiny hands, with which she was gesturing vigorously as if to impress upon the guard that her mission was urgent and she must be allowed on board. She had a large, wheeled container at her side, and it was this that his security personnel, quite rightly, was intent on searching.

'No,' she told them with a decisive shake of her head, staring to the sky, as if to point out the obvious: that the rain would ruin her goods. A quick-thinking guard stepped forward with a sniffer dog. Once the dog had made a comprehensive inspection, she was allowed to pass.

Satisfied that she would be accompanied every inch of the way, he pulled back from the window. His guests would be arriving soon for a glamorous evening, so it came as no surprise to him to discover that deliveries were being made.

An officer greeted him as he left the study. 'A message from the mine, Your Majesty.'

'Oh?' Concern struck him as it always did where work underground was concerned. This would mean a delay to his inspection of Tadj's quarters, but the depths of the earth, like the deeps of the ocean, were unpredictable territory and inherently dangerous, and the safety of his staff was paramount.

'Good news, Majesty.'

He relaxed. 'Tell me…'

The officer could hardly contain his excitement. 'The new seam of sapphires is almost ten times larger than first thought, Your Majesty.'

'Good news, indeed!'

Returning to his study, he placed a call to congratulate his team. As he waited for the line to connect, his thoughts returned to the young woman on the dock. She'd be on board by now, with his security guard in attendance. No visitor would ever wander the *Sapphire* unattended again. After the tragedy under his brother's rule, Khalid had vowed that he would never take a chance with another person's life.

'Ah, Jusef,' he exclaimed as the line connected. He enjoyed an upbeat exchange with the manager of his mine, ending with the promise, 'I'll be home soon to celebrate with you.'

It was a good enough reason to postpone his search for a bride, and he left his study in the best of moods. A final glance through the window reminded him of the girl, and he smiled to think of her standing up to his guards, *and* getting her own way. That was no mean feat. His guards were ferocious.

There was just time to check the arrangements being made for Tadj, before taking a shower and preparing for the evening ahead. It would be a very different party from those his late brother had held on board the *Sapphire*, in that the people present would be interesting and stimulating company and there would be no wild excesses of any kind. Saif had been furious to have his pleasure curtailed, and had ordered Khalid off the *Sapphire*. Echoing the words of the girl's mother, he'd accused Khalid of being a killjoy.

Better that than a killer, Khalid had always thought.

CHAPTER THREE

RETURNING TO THE *Sapphire* wasn't as easy as Millie had imagined. Her heart had started thundering out of control the moment she'd set foot on deck. However many times she told herself that this was a rite of passage, and she must get through it, her body's reaction was out of her control.

I'm not a teenager, finding my way and feeling awkward, but a successful woman, confident in my own skin.

She had silently chanted this mantra from the moment she'd entered the locked dock. The past couldn't hurt her, if she didn't allow it to. The emotional scars from that night hadn't weakened her, they'd made her strong. Unfortunately, none of these self-administered reassurances helped to soothe her as she stepped onto the recently swabbed teak and all the memories came flooding back. Her throat dried when the guard beckoned her towards the impressive double doors leading into the interior of the vessel.

Taking a deep breath, she braced herself and walked in.

The first thing she noticed was the lack of a sickly-sweet smell. She hadn't known what it was eight years ago, but now her best guess was cannabis. The air inside the vessel today was as clean and as fresh as the air outside. And there wasn't a speck of dust to be seen, let alone a carelessly stubbed out cigarette, or an empty bottle left to roll aimlessly about. There was certainly no jarring music, or cruel laughter, just the low, almost indiscernible hum of a well-maintained engine of the type Millie loved—

She jerked alert as the guard coughed to attract her attention. 'Sorry to keep you,' she said. 'I was just getting my bearings.'

A steward was on hand to take charge of her oilskins and the wheeled trolley. Watching her oilskins disappear around a corner definitely gave her second thoughts. She wanted to call him back and return to the safety of the laundry.

Don't be so ridiculous!

What about her determination that the past couldn't hurt her? And the note she intended to leave for Sheikh Khalid, asking if he could make time to see her.

Where was he? she wondered. Somewhere on board? Somewhere close?

A ripple of awareness tracked down her spine. Her overactive imagination getting busy again, she concluded as the steward returned to her side. He suggested, and tactfully, she thought in view of the state of her trolley, that it might be an idea to unpack the laundry here.

'Yes, of course,' she said. 'I'm sorry. I didn't realise the wheels were quite so muddy.' Or that they would leave such obvious tracks on the pristine floor. Not wanting to cause extra work for the crew, she was glad of the blue plastic overshoes the steward handed her.

She was sorry about everything, Millie thought, which was hardly the mind-set required to make the most of this opportunity. The steward might pass on a note to someone in authority who had contact with the Sheikh. And though Sheikh Khalid almost certainly wouldn't agree to see her, she had to try.

'I'll help you unpack,' the friendly steward offered.

The Sheikh's staff seemed nice. She took some comfort from that. There were no stony faces—apart from his guards—and the atmosphere was different; very different, Millie thought as she introduced herself.

'Joel,' the steward replied with a friendly smile.

After a brief handshake they got to work, and the familiar actions of lifting the laundry from its nest reassured her. She knew what she was doing, and working side by side with Joel boosted her confidence. His uniform was very smart, and not at all intimidating, as she remembered the black-clad servants at that *other* party. Crisp and white, it was quite a contrast to her comfortable work clothes of jeans, a long-sleeved top and sneakers.

If it came to running for it, she was ready, Millie concluded dryly as she straightened up to announce she was ready to make up the bed. The guard would escort them, he said. Things had certainly changed since the free-for-all days of Sheikh Saif, she thought as they set off at a brisk walk with Millie like a sandwich filling between the two men.

Passing through another set of double doors, they entered a world of unimaginable luxury and calm. Or massive wealth and relentless control, depending on how you looked at it. Either she found some humour in this situation, or she'd lose her nerve and run. She couldn't believe the last time she'd been here her mother was alive. It seemed so long ago. And now her senses were heightened to an unparalleled degree. She felt like a sponge, obliged to soak up everything, whether she wanted to or not. Though she had to admit that the vibrant works of art, tastefully displayed on neutral walls, were beautiful, as were the priceless artefacts housed in glass cases. She would have loved the chance to take a longer look at them. Glimpses

into staterooms as they passed revealed one luxurious setting after another, but the walk was so long, she began to
wonder if they would ever arrive at their destination. The
Sapphire was bigger than she remembered, but then she
had only seen the grand salon eight years ago.

I could get lost here and never be heard of again. Like
my mother.

That imagination of hers was working overtime again.
She was here to work, and when that was done, she was
out of here!

Millie Dillinger, Khalid mused as he strode through the
immaculately maintained vessel in the direction of the
guest quarters. The girl's name would be branded on his
mind for ever. How could he ever forget the dramatic
events surrounding their first encounter? He'd been in a
furious mood that night, too angry by what he'd discovered at Saif's party to spend much time reassuring the girl.
His first impression had been of a quiet and contained
young person, which had made the way she'd stood up to
him all the more surprising. She'd showed no deference
for his rank, or for that of his brother, and, in being completely open and frank, had opened his eyes to a world
where women didn't simper and preen in the presence of
immense wealth and power. If only she'd known it, Millie
Dillinger had consigned every prospective bride of his to
the remainder bin of history. None of them had her spirit.

Even though she'd been just fifteen, the connection
between them had been immediate and strong, his overwhelming need to protect her his only concern. As he
turned onto the corridor leading to what would be Tadj's
suite, he thought back to his attempts to persuade Millie
to leave the *Sapphire* for her own good, and her refusal to
go without her mother. The child had become the carer,

he'd thought at the time. She'd be twenty-three now, and had been an orphan for eight years, but, remembering the fire in those cornflower-blue eyes, he knew she was too strong for life to break her as it had broken her mother.

Wow! Quite literally: *wow!* Millie's jaw had dropped a little more with each step she'd taken on board the *Sapphire*, where every corner revealed a new wonder, but this guest suite was beyond belief. Ablaze with gold, it glowed with sapphires. Every surface that could be gilded was gilded, and every practical item, even down to the tiny waste-paper bin placed at one side of the solid-gold dressing table, was intricately worked, and studded with precious stones. Striking works of art hung on the walls, while soft furnishings begged to be stroked and snuggled up to. Carpets and rugs? Oh, yes. She was sinking in those up to her ankles. And it was brilliantly lit. No dark corners here. No den of vice. Miss Francine was right to say the *Sapphire* had been completely transformed.

And now it was fit for a king, Millie thought as she stood back to review her handiwork. Glancing in the ornate mirror, she reassured herself that, in the unlikely event that the laundress met a sheikh, the sheikh wouldn't look twice at that laundress. In weather-sensible shoes covered with blue plastic overshoes, an old pair of jeans and a faded top, she'd come straight from fixing a boiler, so although she'd washed her hands until her skin had turned red she almost certainly still had the tang of oil about her.

Turning full circle, she tried to record every detail, so she could tell her friends when she got back to the laundry. She had no doubt they would be in fits of laughter when she told them about the erotic hangings above the bed. Though, in fairness, even the most particular guest would be comfortable here. The suite was definitely over the top, but it was also very airy and welcoming. She had to admit, she was impressed.

The guard and the steward had remained outside the door while Millie was working, so she could touch this… lift that…peer behind the curtain at the elegant balcony lit by the warm glow of a lantern—gold, of course—and even quietly open the drawers… There was nothing in them. She hadn't expected there to be, but couldn't resist having a nosey. Unlatching the door to the balcony, she stepped outside. Leaning over the railings, she wondered if her mother had stood here, and had maybe fallen from this very spot. It was possible…

Remaining quite still, almost as if she expected an other-worldly voice to fill in the details, she was finally forced to give up and return inside.

There was nothing sinister about this room, Millie told herself firmly. It smelled lovely, felt lovely, *was* lovely, apart from the lurid hangings. Could people really contort their bodies like that? Angling her chin, she tried to work out the mish-mash of limbs and faces, and had to give up. Anyway, the stateroom looked fabulous with those golden sheets in their rightful place. But who would sleep here? she wondered with a frown. Was this a gilded cage, waiting for another broken bird?

Stop it! This was a particularly lavish suite on board a billionaire's yacht, and nothing more. Millie had merely provided some final touches for a guest—

Khalid's mistress?

Why should she care? He might be married, for all she knew—

'Mademoiselle Millie?'

She almost jumped out of her skin as the door opened, but it was only the steward wanting to know if she needed any help. 'I'm doing fine, thank you,' she reassured him with a smile. 'I've nearly finished.'

Aladdin's cave could take another pop of gold, Millie concluded as the door closed quietly behind the steward. And her overactive imagination could take a hike. The Sheikh probably wasn't even on board. And even if he were, would he have changed that much? He was probably the same, devastatingly good-looking charmer who made promises he couldn't keep; a man who'd spirited his brother out of the country after her mother's death.

Power and money made anything possible, Millie concluded, firming her lips into an angry line. Eight years ago, the headlines had read: 'The Nightingale of London found drowned in King's Dock.' But had her mother drowned? Or was she murdered? And did anyone care?

Millie cared, and was determined to uncover the truth of a night she would never forget. She wouldn't rest until she found justice for her mother. Cause of death had never been established, let alone convincingly explained to Millie. It felt to her as if everything had been brushed under the carpet. Claiming diplomatic immunity, Sheikh Saif had left the country, while his brother, now Sheikh Khalid, had remained in the UK to clear up his mess. As far as Millie was concerned, he was responsible for allowing Saif to get away. The coroner's court had managed to establish that drink and drugs had contributed to her mother's drowning, but who had given her those things? Miss Francine had warned Millie to leave the past alone, but how could she ignore a chance like this? Sitting down at the dressing table, she plucked the pencil out of her hair and began to write a note on the order pad she always carried.

She flinched guiltily as the door opened a second time, and stood, as if to demonstrate her readiness to leave. The guard was talking into his mouthpiece.

'Just collecting up my things,' she said.

If he noticed that she was nowhere by the bed, he didn't respond. He was too busy talking to whoever was at the other end of the line. She relaxed as he left the room. Maybe now she could finish that note.

Maybe not. The door opened again almost immediately.

He deplored ostentation. Even the intricately decorated solid-gold handle of this guest stateroom jarred as he closed his fist around it, but this particular suite of rooms had been kept intact, and was in the traditionally ornate style, favoured by his late brother. It served as a reminder to Khalid that extreme wealth could be extremely corrupting. He thought Tadj would appreciate the irony. The last time they'd stayed together had been in a basic tent when they were both serving in Special Forces.

After his brother's death, Khalid had insisted on a deep clean of the entire vessel, following which he'd brought in several cutting-edge designers to modernise the ship, with the proviso that this vintage suite be left intact. The best palace craftsmen had worked on the project, and the suite had fast become a talking point, both for its recording of unique and authentic historical detail, and for the erotic hangings above the bed.

'Your Majesty…'

He thought his guard seemed slightly uncomfortable. 'Yes?' Khalid paused with his hand on the door.

'I didn't expect you here so soon,' the guard admitted.

Khalid was instantly suspicious. 'Well, I'm here,' he said, opening the door wide.

'Millie?'

He would have known her anywhere, even after all this time. Eight years simply faded away. She'd changed beyond recognition, but the bond between them remained the same. She was a very beautiful woman. The braids were gone, likewise the spectacles, and there was no panic in her steady stare, reassuring him that her vibrant spirit was intact too.

The girl on the dock. Of course!

'Your Majesty!'

She seemed equally surprised, and for a few moments they just stared at each other. Her long, honey-gold hair was still damp from the rain where her oilskins had failed to protect her. Bundled up loosely on top of her head, the messy arrangement boasted an unusual ornament in the shape of a pencil, which she'd just stabbed into it as she catapulted away from the dressing table to stand in front of him, in what he guessed was the best expression of innocence she could muster. 'What are you doing?' he asked.

'Writing you a note,' she said with the frankness he remembered from all those years ago. 'I suppose I don't have to now,' she added.

'A note?' he queried.

'A request to meet with you—to talk,' she explained.

The bright blue eyes were completely steady on his. Her gaze was as direct as ever.

'Hello, by the way,' she added, as if finally realising that this meeting was a bombshell for both of them.

'Do you generally wear a pencil in your hair?' he asked as her cheeks blazed red.

'It's useful for writing notes on how to fix boilers,' she said.

He waved away the guard and steward as they entered the room to see what all the fuss was about. 'Welcome on board the *Sapphire*, Miss Dillinger.'

Her look said clearly, I'm not a guest, and if it hadn't been for these wretched sheets, I wouldn't be here at all.

* * *

Electricity didn't just crackle in the air, it was bouncing back and forth between them. She was so shocked at seeing Sheikh Khalid again, and in flowing robes that made him look more intimidating than ever, she couldn't think straight. What annoyed her most of all was the fact that he'd thrown her to the point where she was quivering like a doe on heat, rather than standing her ground in front of him like a hard-working professional.

It was time to get real. This was not the tough guy in jeans who invaded her dreams most nights, but an all-powerful king in whose water-borne kingdom she was currently—well, if not a prisoner, at the very least, vulnerable, which was not a condition she ever flirted with. No one could call his brutal attraction charm. However divinely warm, clean and sexy the Sheikh might appear, he was in reality a granite-faced titan without a single decent bone in his body. He'd turned a blind eye when she'd begged him for help. So whatever *her* body thought of his blistering masculinity, Millie Dillinger remained unimpressed.

But...

Calm down and think. This was almost certainly the only chance she'd ever get to ask him about that night. Being as different from the women he must be used to as it was possible to be, with her no-make-up face and her long hair piled carelessly on top of her head—not to mention the pencil garnish—she doubted she was in any immediate danger.

'When will you have finished your work?' he asked with an edge of impatience, confirming her conclusion that she was not his ravishment of choice.

'I have finished, Your Majesty. Please call the laundry if you need anything more.'

'I'll be sure to tell my housekeeper what you advise,' he commented with withering amusement.

Fortunately, she'd always been able to take a joke, though the thought that he might have a sense of humour only made it worse. If he was actually human, how had he allowed her mother to die? Whatever he'd done or not done on that night, it had changed the course of Millie's life, and had tragically ended her mother's. She had to dip her head so he couldn't see her angry eyes.

They came from different worlds, Millie concluded. In her world, people were answerable for their actions, but in his, not so much.

This was no milksop princess with a desire to please him, Khalid concluded, but a very angry woman, who was different and intriguing. She made him want to fist that thick gold hair and draw back her head so he could taste her neck. The girlish figure was long gone and had been replaced by curves in all the right places. Her features were pale from lack of sun, but her complexion was flawless. 'We will talk,' he promised as his senses sharpened. 'And sooner rather than later.'

'We must,' she returned fiercely, clenching her fists, which were held stiffly at her side.

She'd had years to ponder what had happened that night, so her anger was excusable. The death of her mother was bad enough, but believing he was involved in some sort of cover-up must be a festering wound. It was a reasonable supposition, he conceded.

'It must have been hard for you to return to the *Sapphire*.'

'Ghosts?' she suggested with a level look.

'Memories,' he countered.

'Life goes on,' she said flatly.

'As it must,' he agreed.

'Forgive me, Your Majesty, but if you don't have time to meet with me now, I have work to do on shore.'

She was dismissing him? he wondered with amusement.

'We're very busy at the laundry,' she excused, no doubt realising she had overstepped the mark.

On the contrary, he thought her a breath of fresh air. It would be all too easy for him to slip into the belief that because everyone else bowed the knee, Millie Dillinger would, or that other people's deference made him special in some way. A dose of Millie medicine was exactly what he needed. 'I will see you in my study in ten minutes' time.'

She seemed surprised and didn't answer right away. 'My time is also valuable, Ms Dillinger. My guard will escort you,' he explained, 'and my PA will call the laundry to explain your delay.'

'But—'

'Miss Francine is an intelligent woman,' he interrupted. 'She'll understand.'

Millie's frown deepened.

'Ten minutes,' he repeated before he left the room.

Millie wasn't sure she had breathed properly for the entirety of that interview. Sheikh Khalid was so much more than she remembered. She needed a big, wide space, and absolute silence to get used to it. And the guard didn't give her any time. He quick-marched her out of the sumptuous suite, and didn't pause until they stood in front of an impressive gleaming teak door. The entrance to the hawk's eyrie, Millie presumed. Squeezing her eyes tightly shut, she sucked in a deep, steadying breath, and prepared for round two.

At some silent signal, the guard deemed it appropriate to open the door. Standing back, he allowed her to enter.

Sheikh Khalid was seated at the far end of his study behind a sleek modern desk where he appeared to be signing some documents. He didn't look up as she walked in. The scratch of his pen was a stark reminder that this was his territory, his kingdom, where things ran to his schedule, and she would have to wait until His Majesty was ready to receive her.

Forget pride. Any opportunity to interview a potential witness from that night had to be seized. She glanced around with interest. Order predominated. There was no clutter, no family photographs to soften the ambience—a fact that filled her with unreasonable relief—there was just a bank of tech and the desk piled high with official-looking documents.

Shouldn't he invite her to sit?

This might be the private space of a very private man, but Sheikh Khalid had invited her to come here. What about the so-called politeness of Princes? She'd explained that she was busy too. Ten minutes, he'd said. Did he time-keep to the second? That wasn't a bad thing, Millie counselled herself, because if Sheikh Khalid was so meticulous, he could hardly deny what he remembered of that night.

'My apologies,' he said at last, straightening up to fix her with his hawk-like stare. 'Millie,' he added softly.

His husky tone could have been a caress to her senses if she hadn't ruthlessly banished such nonsense in her thinking. 'That's right,' she said. 'We meet again.'

One ebony brow quirked, challenging her resistance to his blistering appeal. Their stares only had to connect for her body to respond with enthusiasm. Determinedly, she took an objective view. This study, this impersonal workspace, was deceiving. Designed to keep visitors at bay. She wasn't fooled. This was no cold, remote man who chose not to reveal his inner self, but a smouldering volcano, who surrounded himself with a sea of ice.

'You've been patient,' he commented with monumental understatement.

'For eight years,' she agreed.

They both knew that wasn't what he'd meant, and as they stared at each other across the desk she thought they were like two combatants facing each other across a ring.

CHAPTER FOUR

'ARE YOU SURE you wouldn't like to sit down?' the man she knew so well, and yet not at all, invited.

Sitting so he could tower over her was the last thing she wanted to do. 'If you're standing, I'm standing too,' she said as he left the desk. This seemed to amuse him. And he still towered over her. So be it. She had no intention of allowing His Majesty to win every point, even if her pulse was racing out of control.

'Forgive me for keeping you,' he added with a penetrating look. 'I have a lot of work.'

'So I see,' she replied calmly.

He studied her face. She studied him. Anything to take her mind off those mesmerising and all-seeing eyes. His headdress was called a keffiyeh. It moved fluidly as he moved, before falling back into place. She could try to be as objective as she liked, but when he angled his stubble-shaded chin to stare down at her, the lure of those eyes was irresistible, and as much as she wanted to hate him, the woman inside her wanted him more.

'And now I'm all yours,' he declared with the faintest of smiles.

She doubted that, and, for the sake of retaining her sanity, returned to studying his stylish robes. The keffiyeh was held in place by a rope-like *agal* made of tightly plaited gold thread that gave it the appearance of a crown. It could barely contain his wild hair, which was just as thick and black as she remembered, both from that night long ago, and from her forbidden dreams, when she had often run her fingers through those springing waves. Each time she woke when that happened, she was consumed by guilt.

How could she consider touching a member of the despised Khalifa family?

Just the thought made her angry. Yet here she was, standing in front of this same man with her body yearning for his touch.

'I don't have much time, Ms Dillinger,' he informed her sharply.

'And neither do I,' she replied, lifting her chin.

Calm. She must remain calm, Millie thought as his eyes drilled into hers. After Saif's profligate reign, she could understand that Sheikh Khalid was in a race against time to both put things right, and keep things right in his country. But that didn't mean she had to cut him too much slack.

'It's been a long time, Millie,' he said as if they were the best of friends. Of course, he had no reason to resent her. She'd kept out of his life, and got on with her own. 'You've done well,' he remarked. 'Engineering, isn't it?'

That shocked her. How much did he know about her?

The Sheikh of Khalifa would make it his business to know everything about the people he encountered, she reasoned. 'Marine engineering,' she confirmed in a tone that didn't invite further questions.

'You haven't strayed far from King's Dock.'

'Why would I?' snapped out of her before she had worked out whether he was stating a fact or asking a question. Either way, how and where she lived was none of his business. 'I owe Miss Francine a debt of gratitude I can never hope to repay. And I love her,' she added with some challenge in her tone.

Instead of taking offence, something mellowed in the Sheikh's eyes and, turning, he asked, 'Would you like a drink?'

'Yes, please.' She hadn't realised how dry her throat had become, and was half expecting him to suggest she get it herself, or, failing that, he might ring a bell and have a steward bring it for her. It was a pleasant surprise when he pressed a panel on the wall behind his desk to reveal a comprehensive wet bar. He poured two glasses of water and, when he held hers out, their fingers brushed and she inhaled swiftly.

'We need a lot more time than I can spare for you to-night,' he said, appearing not to notice her response. 'And I suggest you learn to relax and trust me.'

Trust him? Was he serious? They were a long way from that. Sheikh Khalid might be much older and more experienced, but she was not a fool, and would work on keeping a clear head. That was far more important than relaxing.

Try thinking clearly in front of all this darkly glittering glamour. How could she avoid noticing the sharp black stubble coating, not just his chin, but the thick column of his neck when he tipped his head back to drink. She could only imagine what he'd look like naked—

She had to stop that right now. Thoughts like that were dangerous and inappropriate.

'A refill?'

'Yes, please.'

Their fingers brushed a second time. He knew, she thought, and could sense her arousal as sweet clenches in secret places begged her to forget the past. It was almost a disappointment when he chose to put distance between them, by moving away to lean back against the wall.

'Why are you frowning?' he asked.

Was she? 'This meeting has obviously come as a big shock for me.'

He shrugged disbelievingly. 'And yet you must have volunteered to come on board with the laundry, and when I invited you to chat in my study, you accepted.'

She should have found a member of staff to question about that night. Why hadn't she?

It was too late to wish she'd played this differently, Millie concluded. So, what now? How would it end? She shivered involuntarily. There was something in Sheikh Khalid's eyes that stripped her bare, right down to the depths of her soul.

He had been forced to put distance between them. Millie's allure was like an atomic charge to his senses. All he could think about was taking her over his desk…parting her legs and bringing her the release the hunger in her eyes said she so badly needed. Pressing her down beneath him, hearing her whimper with pleasure when he cupped her, worked her, before stripping her, so he could press his hard frame against her yielding softness—

He refused to submit to such carnal urges. Millie might be a beautiful woman, and the bond between them might have strengthened beyond belief, but the desire to protect her was intact. As was the desire to soften that stubborn mouth and turn her limbs languid with contentment. He was a stranger to hesitation and yet found himself contemplating a lengthy seduction, when what he should be doing was sending Millie back to the laundry without delay. It would be kinder for her. He must concentrate on choosing a bride, not a mistress.

But there was a yawning gulf between right and desire. 'Please,' he invited, indicating the chair opposite his at the desk. 'Why don't we both sit down and make the most of this short interview?'

Reluctantly, Millie sat down. I can handle this, she told herself firmly, but when the Sheikh sat across from her and steepled his lean, tanned fingers her mind was full of sex. She blamed the erotic images hanging on the wall in the gilded stateroom.

There was no one to blame but herself, and she'd feel worse if she didn't confront him with the real reason she was here. 'I want to know what happened that night,' she said. 'After I left the *Sapphire*, what happened?'

The Sheikh stared at her without speaking until all the tiny hairs on the back of her neck prickled. And then, instead of answering her question, he stood and came around the desk.

'What makes you think I saw what happened?' he demanded softly. 'I could have heard about the accident second-hand.'

'Accident?' Bridling, Millie shot to her feet.

'The coroner's court agreed with that supposition,' the Sheikh pointed out calmly, in no way rattled by her response.

'And closed the case,' she agreed, angrily clenching her fists. 'Does that seem fair to you?'

'I saw no reason to argue with the coroner's verdict.'

'I'm sure you didn't,' she said with a bitter laugh. 'But even if you didn't see what happened, I hope you're not asking me to believe that you never once questioned your brother.'

'We didn't share the close relationship you seem to imagine.'

'Even so, that's no excuse.'

She couldn't keep calm. She'd tried. And failed. This meeting could only play out as she'd planned if emotion could be kept out of it. And how could that happen now she'd plunged back into all the grief and guilt of learning about her mother's death?

In danger of wasting questions, she was also in danger of wasting precious time, but what would it take for Sheikh Khalid to tell her the truth? She had to find a way to make him, though dredging up the past would be the last thing he'd want to do.

She resorted to pleading. 'Can't you tell me anything?'

'Nothing you'd want to hear,' he said.

'Try me,' she said tensely. 'I know my mother had a problem with drink, and wasn't always responsible for her actions—that's why I asked you to go back and bring her out.'

'And if she didn't want to leave?' he asked evenly, keeping her locked in his stare.

'Surely, you could have done something? Or was my mother such an entertaining sight, you laughed along with everyone else?'

The Sheikh's expression turned stony. 'I hope you know that's not true.'

'How do I know anything?' Millie demanded heatedly. 'You won't tell me what happened. And now you're going to send me away without answers.'

'I sent you away that night for your own safety.'

'And then you broke your word,' she said bitterly.

'You don't know me and yet you judge me,' he said in a quiet and unnerving tone. 'You surely can't imagine I condone what happened on board the *Sapphire* that night?'

'I don't know. I don't know you!' Millie exclaimed, all the calm reserve that had kept her safe for all these years, deserting her completely. Its place was soon taken by drowning grief and corrosive guilt at the thought that, fifteen years old or not, *she* should have done something more to help her mother.

'Calm down,' the Sheikh advised as she clenched her jaw and wrung her hands.

This had the opposite effect. When he took hold of her shoulders, she shook him off angrily. 'Don't you dare tell me how to feel!' she raged as the emotion that had been bottled up for eight years erupted in fury. That terrible night could not be changed, and it was all coming back to her in vivid detail, and he was part of it.

'What are you doing?' she protested as he bound her close. 'Let go of me this instant!'

'I'm keeping you safe,' he ground out, his minty breath warming her face.

'So, I'm your captive now?' she derided. 'If you think you can keep me, as your brother would have kept my mother—?'

'Your imagination does you credit,' he said in an annoyingly calm tone, without making the slightest concession when it came to letting her go. 'I would remind you that your mother remained on board the *Sapphire* of her own free will.'

I don't want to hear this!

'And you can leave any time you like,' he added in that same maddening voice.

'All right—I will!'

It was surprisingly easy to break away. The Sheikh simply lifted his hands and let her go. And now she thought she must be going crazy to miss feeling safe in his arms. He'd made her feel safe that night eight years ago, and look what had happened then!

'I hate you!' she exclaimed.

'No, you don't,' he said. 'You're bewildered by the power of your emotions, and by the fact that you can't change anything about that night. You hate yourself, and there's no reason why you should.'

Burying her face in her hands, she accepted that he was right. She would never forget the morning after the party. She hadn't heard the news and had taken the bus to the marina to search for her mother. Determined to board the Sheikh's yacht, she had been all fired up. The bus had stopped short of the dock, and the driver had apologised, saying he couldn't take his passengers any further as there were ambulances and police tape in his way.

She'd known then. She'd felt the disaster like a cold, numbing mist that crept up from her feet until it took over her entire body. Miss Francine had been waiting outside the laundry. Ushering Millie inside, she had plied her with a cup of hot, sweet tea, before confirming the awful truth.

She must have been quiet, thinking about this for quite some time, Millie realised as she slowly became aware of the Sheikh staring down with concern. How dared he care about her now? His concern came too late. But instead of resisting his dark, compelling stare, she met it and felt tremors of awareness run up and down her spine.

'I'm sorry, Millie,' he said softly.

'Are you? Do you care?'

'You won't do anything silly when you leave here, will you?' he said without answering her question.

'Like my mother?' she suggested.

'Every story has more than one viewpoint,' he observed.

Lifting her chin, she gave it to him with both barrels. 'In this instance, a viewpoint that's convenient for you, and another that's not so convenient?'

His stare hardened again. 'That's your interpretation.'

Maybe, but Millie's vision encompassed the Sheikh striding back on board the *Sapphire* just before the royal limousine taking her home had turned a corner and she hadn't been able to see him any more. She'd craned her neck for one last glimpse of the man in whom she'd placed her trust, believing he'd put everything right.

'I'm sorry to rush you,' that same man said now as he glanced at his state-of-the-art wristwatch. 'I have another appointment.'

Millie's cheeks blazed red as she followed his glance to the door. 'Of course.' Time up. And what had she achieved? Precisely nothing.

'I have a party to prepare for,' he explained. 'Why don't you come back?' he said, startling her with this suggestion. 'I'll make time to speak to you.'

A *party* on board the *Sapphire*? Just the word was enough to invoke terrible memories and make her stomach churn with dread. 'I won't take up any more of your time,' she said tensely, turning for the door.

'But we're not finished,' he said. 'If you come tonight we can talk.'

Was he mad? Was she? Attend *a party* on board the *Sapphire*? Why was she even hesitating? Obviously, she had to say no.

'Thank you,' she said. 'What time shall I arrive?'

He shrugged. 'Any time after eight. It's a relaxed evening all across the ship. You might enjoy it.'

She might not.

'Until tonight,' he said before she had chance to change her mind.

'Until tonight,' she echoed. Something made her turn at the door, hoping this was her last big mistake. Staring into the Sheikh's knowing eyes was as dangerous as staring at the sun.

Dismissing his staff, he took the unusual step of personally escorting Millie off the ship. It was a reminder of why she was branded on his mind and always would be. The past had locked them together in a troubling set of memories, and in spite of his words to Millie, he was in no hurry to see her go. They took the stairs. Having the two of them confined in the cab of an elevator would be far too much too soon. However much he wanted to protect this new, older Millie, he wanted to seduce her more. They chatted politely about this and that as they walked through the *Sapphire* like two strangers who'd only just met. There wasn't just one elephant in the room, but two. Sex and death were a potent combination, and all that was needed for him to see her again.

'You're happy living above the laundry?' he asked.

'Of course I am,' she declared with a frowning, sideways look. And that was all she was going to say on that subject, he guessed, until they met later, when he was determined to find out more.

'How do you know where I live?' she asked.

He cursed himself for his carelessness. 'I presumed,' he fudged.

'The same way you know I'm studying engineering?' she queried. 'Should I be flattered by your interest, or accept that a man like you must know everything about people you meet?

'Whichever,' she added with a shrug. 'I'll just mention that you seem to have more insight into my life than I had expected.'

Was the Sheikh having her watched? Millie wondered. If so, why? And how long had it been going on? Did he think *she* knew something about that night—some fact or gossip, or perhaps a careless remark made by one of his crew when they were on shore?

It was a relief to step out on deck. Being too close to a

man like the Sheikh was unnerving. And exciting. It was as if she had been plugged into a power source. And that was dangerous, Millie concluded. No one with any sense played with fire.

'I imagine your engineering skills must be very useful to Miss Francine,' he remarked as they stood in that awkward moment before parting.

Awkward for her, at least, Millie concluded. Once again, he seemed frighteningly composed. While her mind had just clicked into gear. 'You remember the name of the laundry and its owner after all these years?'

'Your trolley?' he said, tamping down on a smile. 'Until later, Millie.'

'Yes,' she murmured distractedly, already having second thoughts. There was something not right about this.

'Don't forget you're coming back.'

'How could I forget?' she called back, subduing the brief spike of panic. She might not have achieved her goal to learn more about that night yet, but the Sheikh had given her a second chance. She had no idea what to expect at his party, but she wasn't a teenager now and could handle it.

What if the Sapphire *slipped its moorings and sailed away?*

She'd reach for her mobile phone and call the coastguard. She wasn't an impressionable teen, but a soon-to-be successful woman who decided her own fate.

The security guard had brought her roll-along bag dockside and she followed him without a backward glance. But once outside the dock gates, she paused and turned, to see the Sheikh still on deck, watching her.

'Until tonight,' he called out, raising a relaxed hand.

Decision time. Bottle out, or opt in. Her choice. 'Until tonight,' she yelled back.

CHAPTER FIVE

THERE WAS UPROAR at the laundry when Millie got back. Everyone wanted to know why she'd been delayed. Miss Francine hovered anxiously while the younger women clustered around Millie with endless questions, outrageous suggestions, and raucous laughter, as well as enough racy jokes to fill the playbill at a comedy show for a week.

Before she said anything, Millie brushed the hair out of her eyes and shed her oilskins. Hanging them up on the peg by the door, she grimaced. 'I'm drenched.'

'With passion?' Lucy suggested, nudging her closest companion.

For the sake of good humour, Millie adopted a mock aloof air. 'I hardly think the Sheikh invited me back to-night so he can seduce me.'

'He invited you back!' Lucy shrieked with a meaningful look at their colleagues.

'Out of politeness,' Millie insisted, catching Miss Francine's attention to reassure her with a look that Millie was okay with this comedy sketch. 'Something about making up the numbers,' she said vaguely.

'At the ruler of Khalifa's party?' Lucy exclaimed with obvious disbelief. 'You don't expect us to believe he left something like that to chance, do you?' she demanded with an eye roll.

'I'm just not seduction material,' Millie insisted, turning serious. At least that much was true. Her mother's looks might have been ravished by pain and abuse, but Roxy Dillinger had always been beautiful, while Millie made the best of what she'd got, which wasn't much. But what she lacked in kerb appeal, she tried to make up for with zest for life.

A barrage of questions about her time on the *Sapphire* hit her from every side. What was the Sheikh like? What was it like on a billionaire sheikh's superyacht? Editing heavily, Millie gave as full an account as she could.

'Why you Millie?' Lucy demanded in a teasing tone. 'What have you got that the rest of us lack?'

'The rest of you have got too much work to do, to be gossiping like this,' Miss Francine insisted above a chorus of groans. 'We'll have our own party when the work's completed,' she promised to a second chorus, this time of cheers.

'I'd rather be Millie,' Lucy called out cheerfully as she got back to her work.

Everyone took the hint and got their heads down, though Millie still had to field a whole host of questions, as well as the teasing remarks of her co-workers, but it had the good effect of making time fly. Good for everyone, Millie concluded, but herself, as, before she knew it, work ended and she had to get ready for the party. Suddenly, she didn't feel so brave.

Don't be such a *wuss*, she told herself impatiently as she ran up the stairs to her cosy bedsit. She had no excuse not to know how fast things could change from hope to tragedy. She had to seize the moment and make the most of it.

Relax. Chill, Millie mused, eyes tightly shut as she stood beneath the shower. If she didn't take this chance to find out the truth about that night, she'd spend the rest of her life wishing she had.

What to wear to a billionaire's party when you wanted to blend into the crowd? That was the burning question. Millie should have asked about the dress code, she realised now. Sheikh Khalid had mentioned something about a casual evening. Good. Casual she could do. An apprentice engineer had more overalls in her closet than frocks, but she did have one nice dress.

It was red, which was unfortunate. Would it make her stand out too much? She didn't want to look as if she'd tried too hard. She'd bought it in the sales, thinking it perfect for the next Christmas party. At least it was an unfussy style, just a simple column of bright red silk. Having made her decision, she hung the dress on the back of the door.

Hair up or down? She'd tie it back, Millie decided. Tossing her long, honey-gold hair for effect wasn't her style. Having trialled a few different looks, she settled on her customary messy up-do. She'd got the knack of arranging that now, but she swopped out the infamous pencil for a simple mock tortoiseshell clip.

Shoes?

Wearing high heels on a ship grated, somehow. She compromised with a strappy flat.

Underwear. She rootled through her drawer. Sensible big knickers, obviously…

So why was she holding a flimsy thong?

Who was going to see what she wore? No one. So she settled for the thong. It wouldn't show any lines beneath the dress.

As she got ready she kept on glancing out of the window to where the *Sapphire* was berthed and blazing with light. When she'd finished she leaned back against the wall, eyes closed, trying to blot out that other party and replace it with the new. If she didn't, she'd never have the courage to step back on board the *Sapphire*.

Music from the superyacht wafted over the marina and into Millie's bedroom. It was tasteful, tuneful music. She'd be all right. She had to be. No one could pick up the pieces. She had to do that for herself, and owed it to her mother to move forward, which was exactly what she intended to do.

Checking her appearance in the mirror one last time, she declared, 'No problem. I'm ready to enter the lion's den.'

Khalid frowned as he paced the deck. The band was playing, and his stewards were putting the final touches to place settings as his guests began to arrive, but there was no sign of Millie. He wanted to see her. They had a lot to discuss.

Discuss?

All right, he snarled at his moral compass director, but she'd be here. She wouldn't be able to resist what might be her last chance to question him, and, if the temptation to interrogate him wasn't enough, he had to trust that the same primal energy drove both of them, and that was an irresistible force.

An eclectic mix of specialists from the arts, sciences, and the charities he supported, as well as tech kings and a few fellow royals, had gathered on the deck below his quarters. It was an interesting crowd. He was keen for her to see the changes his rule had brought about. It had always been important for him to draw a clean line between the way his brother Saif had ruled, and his own very different approach. Had he mentioned the dress code for her evening would be casual? He couldn't believe he was worrying about something so trivial, but he wanted Millie to fit in and relax, and if she arrived in a ball gown—She wouldn't arrive in a ball gown. She had more sense. There was more risk she'd arrive straight from work in a boiler suit smeared with oil.

'Your Majesty seems particularly distracted tonight—'

'Tadj!' He whirled around to greet his friend. 'Forgive me. I didn't see you and your companion arrive. Good evening, Ms…?'

'Lucy Gillingham, Your Majesty. I work at Miss Francine's with Millie.'

'No need to curtsey,' he said, raising Lucy to her feet with a smile. 'Welcome on board the *Sapphire*.'

'It must be a very beautiful woman to distract you to this extent,' Tadj teased him discreetly. 'May I ask who she is?'

'No. You may not,' he told Tadj. 'Your reputation goes before you, my friend.' He had no intention of sharing his interest in Millie with a man known as the Wolf of the Desert for a very good reason.

'The party's already a success,' Tadj observed, glancing down to where the good-natured throng was mingling easily.

'Seems so,' Khalid agreed, scanning the crowd for Millie. 'Excuse me—I can see some more guests arriving—'

'A *very* beautiful woman,' Tadj called after him with amusement, no doubt having spotted where Khalid was heading.

Millie was trying to find her way through the crowd jostling around his stewards as they offered his guests a welcoming flute of champagne. She looked sensational in a slender column of bright red silk. The crowd parted for him, so he quickly reached her side. 'You decided to come?' he remarked.

Running her eyes over him from top to toe, she looked up and smiled. 'It appears so, Your Majesty.'

'Have you been practising?' he asked with amusement as she attempted to bob a curtsey.

'Only as much as you've been working on your boilers today,' she countered, directing this into his eyes as she straightened up. 'Actually, I'd love to see the engine room.'

'Another time,' he said.

'You're inviting me back?' she challenged with amusement. 'I would have thought you'd seen enough of me by now.'

'By the end of the evening, I probably will have done,' he replied in the closest to humour he intended to come. In truth, he couldn't wait to get away from her. She was affecting him like no aphrodisiac known to man.

'I imagined you'd be leaving soon?' she said, clearly unaware of his physical discomfort.

A flowing robe would have been more accommodating than designer jeans, he acknowledged, masking his discomfort. 'And so I shall. My work is done,' he confirmed, sounding harsher than he'd intended, but the need to rearrange himself was becoming more pressing by the moment.

I will not allow myself to be distracted by a pair of knowing black eyes, Millie determined. And if Khalid thought he could just walk away from her, he was wrong. 'I find older vessels fascinating,' she said, determined to keep him in front of her. 'So much experience under their belt.'

He actually groaned as if he were in pain. 'I hope you're not referring to me?'

His voice sounded strangled, but if that was an attempt at humour, it saved him. He might actually be human. 'I hardly think so, Your Majesty.'

People were watching them with interest, she noticed. Gossip would spread quickly on the marina. The ruler of Khalifa and a local laundress, chatting together like old friends. She didn't care, but did he? And if he did care, he might bring this to an end at any moment, before they had chance to arrange that private talk. 'You invited me here to talk,' she said. 'When can we do that?'

'I need time with my guests. At least an hour.'

'Of course,' Millie agreed promptly. 'And my apologies if I'm keeping you.'

'I choose to talk to you.'

And when you no longer choose to do so, you'll move on, she thought. Determined to pin him down, she confirmed, 'An hour. Where?'

'I'll send someone to find you.'

'Do you delegate everything to someone else?'

The words just popped out of her mouth, and there was a moment when she thought he wouldn't answer, but then he said, 'Not all things, Ms Dillinger.'

And now she really, *really* wished she hadn't asked the question, as the expression in the Sheikh's eyes took hold of every nerve-ending in her body and rattled it until it squeaked.

'Don't worry about me,' she said on a dry throat. 'I'm happy people-watching, just so long as we have that promised talk.'

'I won't forget,' he said in a way that left her in no doubt that he meant it.

'Okay.' She shrugged and smiled politely as he left.

That shrug. That smile.

Millie's wildflower scent taunted his senses as he walked away.

It stayed with him—*she* stayed with him as he met and chatted to his guests. To a casual observer, the ruler of Khalifa had been exchanging small talk with a beautiful local woman who had happened to catch his attention.

There was nothing unusual about that. On the surface, maybe, but beneath the apparent calm there was a lot more going on, like a fault line in the ocean with a volcano simmering underneath.

She needed a lot more time to relax on the *Sapphire*. Being back here was upsetting, and disturbing, Millie thought as Sheikh Khalid walked away. Needing something to take her mind off the past, she began to circulate and introduce herself around. She might have worried that she was walking in her mother's footsteps, if the guests at this party hadn't been so very different from those of eight years ago. Millie gave no explanations and none were needed, other than the fact that she lived locally, as the Sheikh was a generous host and had invited people from all walks of life. His guests were so open and pleasant that for a while she lost herself in conversation, but revisiting the place where she'd last seen her mother alive had affected her more than she'd thought.

She kept hearing her mother's last words ringing in her head. *'Get her out of here! You're nothing but a little killjoy. You always spoil my fun!'*

Her mother had been a victim and Millie was anything but, she reasoned, and she had to be strong for both of them. But that wasn't easy when her feelings were in turmoil, and the past kept rolling over her like a storm that threatened to engulf her in grief and guilt. The Sheikh had the knack of putting everyone at ease, she noticed. She also couldn't help noticing that he looked amazing. He had no need of royal robes to point up his blistering masculinity. Dressed casually in jeans and a shirt, he was every fantasy hero made real. Tall, tanned, hard-muscled and obviously super-fit, he radiated undeniably compelling sex appeal.

The biggest shock of all came when she bumped into

her friend Lucy. It was a double shock to identify Lucy's stunningly good-looking companion.

'Isn't he gorgeous?' Lucy exclaimed as they hugged.

'You're on a date with the Emir?' Millie whispered back.

'Don't sound so alarmed. We met dockside. He's a man, I'm a woman. What's wrong with that?' Everything and nothing, Millie thought as Lucy added, 'How are you and the Sheikh getting on?'

'There is no me and the Sheikh. I already told you, I'm here to make up the numbers and nothing more.'

As if sensing their interest in him, Khalid, who was some distance away, turned to look at Millie and frowned. If she didn't know better, she'd think he was surprised to see her at the party. Was she supposed to go home until the hour was up and then come back? He'd invited her, and she'd rather be here, dicing with danger, than fretting about all the questions she wanted to ask him, back at home.

'He shouldn't be allowed to wear robes—'

'Sorry?' She glanced at Lucy, who had been having a one-sided conversation, Millie realised now.

'The robes?' Lucy pressed. 'They hide his body. Sheikh Khalid owes it to the world to only ever wear snug-fitting clothes, like the ones he's wearing now.'

'Oh, yes,' Millie said vaguely.

'You're not listening, are you?' Lucy teased. 'What's a nice girl doing staring at the Sheikh?'

'I'm not staring at the Sheikh,' Millie defended. 'It's what's inside the package,' she murmured distractedly.

'Depends on the package,' Lucy put in. 'Personally, I can't wait to unwrap Tadj.'

They said laughing goodbyes, and as Lucy walked off Millie reassured herself that they could both look after themselves, even in the company of these devastating-looking men.

'Are you ready to talk now?'

She almost jumped out of her skin, hearing Khalid's voice so close behind her.

She could handle this.

'Has an hour passed already?' she asked lamely as his heat invaded every inch of her body.

'I thought you would have been eating by now.'

'But…' She looked at the dining table and frowned. His guests were only just sitting down. 'The canapés did look delicious,' she admitted, thinking he must mean the trays of bite-sized appetisers the stewards had been handing round, 'but I didn't want to spoil my dinner.'

'Quite right,' he said, but now it was the Sheikh's turn to frown.

What was going on? He'd invited her to supper.

Leading the way through his guests, he greeted everyone who wanted to speak to him. He even introduced Millie as an old friend. *An old friend?* she thought as they mounted the companionway to a higher deck.

'It's a beautiful night,' he remarked as he paused at the top.

It was. The rain had cleared, and it was crisp and clear with stars glittering overhead. A magical night, Millie thought.

And on just such a night, her mother had drowned in this same marina.

'I want to show you something,' he said, distracting her before that thought had a chance to take hold. A dart of apprehension still struck her hard. Maybe it was his tone of voice. Following him to the stern, she followed his stare and frowned. 'A lifeboat?' she queried.

'This is the last place I saw your mother alive.'

Millie's fingers tightened on the cold, steel rail. She must compose herself, and must do so fast, or lose any hope she had of getting to the bottom of this.

'Are you okay?' the Sheikh asked.

'Yes,' she managed in a clipped tone. She didn't trust herself to say anything more. 'What was my mother doing here in a lifeboat?'

'Sleeping,' he said.

Sleeping it off, Millie thought, but she was glad he hadn't said that. It hurt to hear her mother criticised, even now. Her mother deserved respect, though she'd had none for herself.

'You let her sleep?' she said, trying to get a picture of what had happened that night.

'But with a guard watching over her,' he said.

'What happened next? What went wrong?' she pressed. 'You said she slipped away. Didn't anyone miss her? What about your brother? Wasn't he expecting my mother to sing for his guests?'

'My brother—'

'Your brother *what*?' she cut in impatiently, unable to hold back as her emotions surged out of control.

'I can't answer for my brother's whereabouts at each precise moment during that night.'

'You must have some idea,' she insisted. 'And if you can't tell me, I don't know why I'm here—'

The shock when he seized hold of her arm, as she was about to walk off, flashed through her like a lightning bolt. 'Let go of me!' Wrenching her arm out of his grip almost threw her off balance, and she had to hold onto the rail with both hands to steady herself. It felt cold and as un-yielding as he was. How he had to be, she thought. He'd had to handle the authorities at the time, and give his lawyers a story they could run with. He was hardly going to tell her another story now.

But still she wondered… *Did my mother touch this rail? Did she cling to it and try to save her life?*

'Did she fall here?' she asked at last. She turned to face him, her grim expression demanding the truth.

'Your mother had had too much to drink. I was surprised she was even capable of moving.'

'Something must have prompted her to climb out of the lifeboat.' Millie shook her head. 'It had to be something so urgent she found the strength.' She glanced over the rail, and her head swam as her imagination supplied the detail: the scream, the splash, the struggle, and finally silence.

'No.'

She was so wrapped up in her thoughts, she barely heard the single word, and only slowly turned to face the Sheikh. 'There's something you're not telling me,' she said.

'This has been a shock for you.'

'That's no answer,' she said tensely.

Happy sounds from the party rose all around them, mocking her state of mind. This was bizarre, tense and horrible. Learning details about that night, while she was battling feelings she shouldn't even have for this man, left her swamped in sadness and tortured by guilt. She couldn't stop thinking that if only she'd been older and more authoritative at the time of her mother's death, maybe she could have saved her.

'My brother could always find women to entertain him,' Sheikh Khalid was saying. 'It's not surprising that he lost interest in your mother's whereabouts.'

'As you did,' she flared.

'I put guards on watch,' he reminded her.

'They couldn't have been much good,' she observed acidly.

'Your mother asked to use the facilities, and of course they let her go.'

'In a drunken state on board a yacht without following her?' Millie exclaimed. 'That sounds like gross dereliction of duty to me.'

'You weren't there,' the Sheikh interrupted. 'Therefore, you're in no position to pass judgement on my staff. I'm satisfied they did all they could.'

'How can you say that?' Millie demanded hotly. 'I've been followed every step of the way since I boarded the *Sapphire*, yet you're asking me to believe my mother could wander at will.'

'As I've tried to explain, times were different, and there were no witnesses.'

'But someone must have seen something,' she insisted.

Ignoring her interruption, the Sheikh continued. 'I was clearing the grand salon at the time of your mother's disappearance. Saif had tried to have me thrown off the *Sapphire*, but his guards had refused to do this. They supported me rather than my brother, though even with their help it still took time for all the guests to leave. As soon as I was free, I went to look for your mother. I wondered at first if she'd returned to my brother, but his attendants hadn't seen her. I can only conclude she slipped away with the rest of the guests leaving the ship.'

'So, you're saying your brother had nothing to do with my mother's death.'

'That's what I told the authorities.'

That's no answer, she thought. 'I can see it would be convenient for you to hear nothing and see nothing.'

'Have you finished?' he asked coldly.

'Why? Are you going to have me drummed off the ship?'

'No part of this tragedy could ever be described as convenient,' the Sheikh assured her.

'For your brother, then,' Millie said.

'My brother's dead.'

'And does that absolve him from blame? If you're saying he deserves respect, simply because he's no longer with us, then so does my mother. And you might as well know, I intend to clear her name—'

'That's as it should be,' he said.

'What's the point in talking further?' Millie asked. 'You're not going to tell me anything.'

'You're leaving?'

She'd thought about it. 'No,' she said, 'not unless you have me thrown off. Eight years ago my mother had no one to protect her, but now she does, and I'm not a biddable teenager who'll go home when she's told.'

'You have always defended her,' he said with the closest to admiration he'd come yet.

'I trusted you,' she said quietly. Lose her temper lose the battle, Miss Francine had always said, and the *Sapphire* provided valuable business for the laundry. Millie must manage her quest for justice and look at the bigger picture.

They stared at each other unblinking for a few moments, which was as troubling as it was a sign of Millie's intent. Her determination to get to the bottom of the mystery surrounding her mother's death had crossed her path with that of a man whose potent persona was wreaking havoc on her control. There was no such thing as a meaningless glance where the Sheikh was concerned. He could convey more in a look than any book of words, and his dark eyes suggested an agreement of a very different kind, one that had no connection with the past, and everything to do with the here and now.

CHAPTER SIX

MILLIE WAS RIDICULOUSLY appealing and passions were high. Drawing her close, Khalid looped an arm around her waist and tipped up her chin until their mouths were only a hair's breadth apart.

'Don't you dare touch me,' she flared.

Her struggles only brought them closer. This first, real physical contact between them was an incendiary device to his senses. His greedy flesh was aroused to the point of agony. She rested, panting, for a moment, blazing her defiance into his eyes. A lithe young flame to his dark, smouldering passion, she was as much a slave as he to primitive forces that made her eyes shoot sparks of fury at him, even as they darkened.

'You're to blame for all of this!' she raged. Reaching up, she seized hold of his shoulders, which only brought them closer together.

He held her at arm's length. 'I think you're over-wrought.'

Savouring her fresh, clean scent while she vibrated with awareness beneath his hands, he thought, *Not yet*. She was all eagerness, and ready to channel her anger into a different sort of passion, but he favoured trial by frustration. Pleasure delayed was pleasure enhanced. She deserved nothing less.

He was actually considering seducing her?

Yes. It seemed inevitable, though his family had destroyed hers, and he had no doubt that coming back to the *Sapphire* and reliving that night had made her hate him. But hate was a strange and adaptable emotion. His desire to protect her was as strong as ever, but the desire to make love to her was even stronger, Millie's passion could change into something very different. Gently, but firmly, he removed her hands from his body and stepped back. He could not have predicted her reaction.

'Don't,' he rapped as she covered her face with her hands. 'You have nothing to feel guilty about.'

'Don't I?' she said bitterly, raising her chin. 'Not even when those feelings involve you?'

She shocked him with words that sounded wrenched from her soul. Her frankness had always been Millie's greatest appeal, he reminded himself as he observed, 'This has been an ordeal. You should go home now and rest. We'll speak on another occasion.'

'And if the *Sapphire* leaves?' she said, her eyes glaring into his.

'Go home, Millie.'

'Why should I make it easy for you?'

'Go home,' he repeated. 'I'll have one of my guards accompany you.'

She laughed at this. 'To make sure I'm safe?' she said. 'I think we can assume I know my own way home, and there's no need for you to have me escorted off the *Sapphire*.'

Her face was pale and defiant as they confronted each other. 'You're not being removed from the ship,' he stated evenly. 'It's dark, and I'm concerned about you. It can be dangerous on the dock.'

'As my mother discovered,' she agreed tensely.

'You will accept my guard,' he instructed quietly. 'He'll be discreet, and I won't argue about this. I insist.'

Her mouth flattened stubbornly, but she could see the sense in what he said, and eventually she grudgingly nodded her head. 'So, when will we talk?' she pressed. 'Or have you changed your mind about that.'

'I haven't changed my mind,' he said as he waved a guard over. 'Before I leave King's Dock we'll meet again and talk calmly. A party isn't a suitable venue for a discussion as weighty as ours.' He wanted her behind closed doors, to navigate both their feelings and the past.

She huffed a short, and, he thought, disbelieving laugh. 'Thank you, Your Majesty. Goodnight,' she added briskly.

When she extended her hand for him to shake, he took hold of it and brushed it with his lips, and felt her tremble. As he watched her walk away, he knew this wasn't over and that it had only just begun. His hunt for a bride would have to wait.

What the hell was I thinking going back on the *Sapphire* with some crazy notion to get in touch with the Sheikh?

Dropping down on her bed, Millie kicked off her shoes and sent them flying across the room. Instead of learning more about the night of her mother's death she had almost *kissed* her greatest enemy? What was that about? This was a man who must have lied to the police, and whose lawyers had glibly lied to the coroner, which had allowed his brother, the late Sheikh Saif, to leave the country without so much as having his wrist slapped.

Someone must pay for her mother's death. Was Millie supposed to believe that Roxy Dillinger had crawled out of a lifeboat dead drunk, used the facilities, as Sheikh Khalid had so tactfully put it, and then fallen into the sea? Had anyone seen this happen? What about security cameras?

From what she'd seen when she was on board the *Sapphire*, the big ship was bristling with cameras. Someone had to know the truth. And that someone wasn't telling.

Springing up, she paced to the window and pushed back the blind. The *Sapphire* was even more awe-inspiring at night when it was lit up prow to stern. The classy party would last until the early hours of the morning, she guessed. It was certainly going full swing now. She could have kicked herself for not finding out when the *Sapphire* was due to leave King's Dock. It could slip away in the night while she was asleep, and she'd be none the wiser, and that would be her chance to discover the truth gone for ever.

And she might never see Sheikh Khalid again.

Good!

Not good. She'd miss him. Seeing him again had really affected her, Millie realised. She hadn't been exaggerating when she'd admitted having feelings for him.

Feelings? The heartache she was experiencing was a real physical pain.

Love hurt? You bet. Love for her mother and confusion where Sheikh Khalid was concerned. And she'd blown her one and only chance. Saying he'd make time to see her again was just a throw-away comment, a pleasantry, *the politeness of princes.*

Maybe, but she wasn't a quitter, so what to do now?

'Okay,' she informed the empty room. 'There's only one thing for it…'

Reaching under the bed for her shoes, she slipped them back on. Smoothing her hair, she glanced in the mirror. Drawing a deep breath, she announced, 'I can do this.' Turning for the door, she headed back to the party.

It was easy to convince the guard to let her pass through the locked gate guarding the *Sapphire*'s berth with nothing more than a smile and the truth. 'I left something at the party,' she explained. Well, she had, if you counted her heart and a whole pile of questions.

'No problem, Miss Dillinger,' the guard told her politely as he unlocked the steel gate and swung it wide.

She was checked a second time at the foot of the gang-plank, and again at the entrance to the ship, by which time her pulse was going crazy. What would Khalid's re-action be when he saw her? Too late to worry about that now, Millie thought. She was here and she was going to go ahead with this.

She wasn't sure what made her glance up as she waited for another tick to be placed against her name on yet an-other clipboard in the hands of a flint-faced guard. Was it animal instinct? An invisible bond? Or a silent whisper, she mused romantically, to take her mind off the compel-ling individual staring down in her direction.

'Come up,' Sheikh Khalid indicated with a jerk of his chin, before stepping back into the shadows behind the rail on the top deck.

Triumph surged through him as Millie boarded the *Sapphire*. He'd known she'd come back. He'd been waiting for her. She wasn't stupid. Millie knew there was some-thing he hadn't told her and she couldn't take the chance he'd sail away. She wasn't here to sell herself for informa-tion. Millie wasn't like her mother with desperation as her only driver. She was a seeker of justice and truth, and she was principled. The urge to protect her was stronger than ever, as were his feelings of guilt. The chemistry between them was insane. Raw, physical hunger surged through his body, a warning to protect her from him, as well as the past. Whatever she was expecting him to tell her to-night, he would not destroy her with the truth. It was so much worse than she could imagine. Millie had forged a new life, and he was glad of it. There was nothing to be gained by making her look back at the past.

Millie was intuitive as well as beautiful, and she was right to come here tonight. As she had suspected, the *Sapphire* would be leaving King's Dock soon. Spending these last few hours in her company would have to be enough. But as she ran up the companionway towards him, he thought there was only one way, a visceral way, to get Millie out of his system. Unfortunately, that was an indulgence he must deny himself. There were other pleasures to distract him. He'd been away from the desert too long. A Bedouin at heart, he would always be restless, and had never craved the challenge of his native land more.

When she appeared framed in the doorway, it was as if the air changed and freshened all around him. Waiting until her eyes had adjusted to the much dimmer lights on this deck, she appeared ethereal and vulnerable. He knew nothing could be further from the truth. Millie was no victim. She was very much together, and tonight determination showed in her expression as if she believed destiny was on her side.

'Over here,' he called out.

Her chin lifted and her gaze landed squarely on his face. His biggest problem was remembering she was innocent in all things, as a fierce carnal hunger did its best to wipe out his previous saintly thoughts.

I know what I'm doing, Millie intoned silently as the security guard who had accompanied her on board the *Sapphire* retreated and the door closed behind him with a soft click, leaving her on a deserted deck with only his most regal majesty, Sheikh Khalid of Khalifa, for company. Security had improved over the years, she'd noticed as she'd passed through the ship. The party that she and her mother had attended had been a free-for-all, but tonight a good mix of people, who could enjoy themselves without getting drunk, were hosted and protected, rather than guarded, by the Sheikh's most excellent staff. But that didn't make her soften towards him. She would settle for nothing less than the truth. He could forget the edited version. Learning what had really happened that night was the only reason she was back here.

The only reason?

'Welcome,' he said.

As his husky and seductive tone took a leisurely stroll across her senses, she told herself firmly that Sheikh Khalid was nothing like his brother, and she was safe. Sheikh Khalid had let her mother down, but had saved Millie. Would he save her again by filling in those gaps that had lashed her with guilt for eight long years?

She was here in search of the truth, but also, Millie silently admitted as she raised her face to his, because she couldn't stay away. There was something between them that wouldn't allow her to. The *Sapphire* was in dock. Sheikh Khalid was close, and, as many times as she told herself that she couldn't miss this opportunity, it was far, *far* more than that. She couldn't breathe easy. She couldn't think straight. She couldn't function properly. Only when she knew everything would they part and go their separate ways.

And was that all it was?

That was all it could be, she told herself as his dark, all-seeing eyes drilled down into hers. What else could it be? Arousal, sadness, guilt and anger collided inside her, making her long and loathe, and feel a type of passion she had never experienced before. They had no future together. That was the bottom line. Even if she could get past her simmering suspicion that he could have done more to save her mother, they were worlds apart, with an unbridgeable gulf between them.

But as the Sheikh's confidence and sexual energy enveloped her in erotic heat, she became more confused than ever. He was so big, so brazenly masculine; in every way, he was different, and on a completely different scale from other men. She trembled with awareness of his brute strength. Sheikh Khalid had no need of royal robes to stamp him with the majesty of power. His authority was unparalleled. And there was a part of her, a reckless part, that wanted nothing more than to battle with him.

Go head to head, at least, she reasoned. That was why she was here, after all.

'We'll talk inside,' he said, leading the way into the shadows of his apartment on board the *Sapphire*.

She had started to follow, but for some reason stepped back instead of forward, and managed to trip over a cleat sticking up from the deck. His reflexes were lightning fast. Whirling around as she yelped and stumbled, he yanked her hard against his chest.

'Steady,' he murmured as their bodies collided.

It was a few moments before he released her, and she was in no hurry to move away. 'What do you really want?' he asked, staring deep into her eyes. 'What do you want of me, Millie Dillinger?'

Her only thought was, *You*. And the truth shocked her. She had been fighting her attraction to him since the moment they met again, Millie realised now, but this was something more, so much more. The worst of it was, he gave a smile as if he knew.

Freeing herself, she pulled away. At best he must think her gauche, and at worst he might think her her mother's daughter. Even in the middle of these two poles apart was a world of 'you're wasting the best chance you ever had to clear your mother's name'.

'I don't know what happened that night,' she said, feeling she must say something. 'But I can tell you this. My mother wasn't weak, she was desperate, and vulnerable, and your brother took advantage of that.'

'We need to talk,' the Sheikh told her in a calm, unthreatening voice.

'Too much has been brushed under the carpet,' she continued as soon as they were inside.

They were in a lovely room, she registered vaguely; it might have been called a snug in a cosy, suburban home, and was the first real sign that the imposing figure towering over her relaxed occasionally. Enough to tell her the truth? That remained to be seen.

'You seem so sure that things have been hidden from you,' he said, indicating that she should sit on one of the two facing sofas.

She remained standing. 'Wouldn't you?'

'Maybe you're overthinking things,' he suggested, staring down. 'And maybe you're not telling me all of the truth.'

Something flickered in his eyes, suggesting she'd hit the mark.

'And maybe I'm trying to protect you,' he countered softly.

'Perhaps that's what you'd like me to think.'

'You're beautiful.'

As he murmured this, she drew her head back and gave him one of her looks. 'I came here for a serious discussion.'

Which was true, but a thrill of excitement still ripped through her as the Sheikh's hard mouth tugged in the faintest of smiles. 'I'm being absolutely serious,' he assured her at the same mesmerising low volume.

There was a scar that cut down the side of his cheek to his mouth, she noticed now. His stubble usually covered it, but he must have shaved quite recently for the party. *Or for her?* The party, Millie told herself firmly as she progressed the thought; everyone had some sort of scar, it was just that some hid them better than others.

'We have all evening to talk,' he said with an easy shrug.

Talk, when she was drowning in testosterone?

Millie could have stepped away when he reached out to find the clip in her hair and release it, but she didn't, and long, silken skeins fell tumbling to her waist.

'Beautiful,' he whispered again as he tossed the clip aside. He combed his fingers through her hair, soothing and exciting her in turn, but she tossed her head, as if pleasure were a sin. 'Guilt?' he asked. 'Why, when you've no reason to feel guilty? Desire is a natural human emotion—'

'That I can resist,' she assured him as she stepped away.

He laughed softly and saw her hesitation. 'You have the same spirit I loved eight years ago.'

'Spirit prompted by my desperate concern for my mother,' she reminded him. 'You promised to go back on board and save her.'

'I did all I could,' he said steadily. Her voice was shaking with emotion. Too much had been bottled up inside Millie for too long. He could imagine the child growing to be a woman, and never once losing control, because if she did the grief would break her. He wanted to comfort her and make love to her all at one and the same time, but his self-control would not allow it.

'So, what do you want of me, Millie Dillinger?'

'I might ask you the same question,' she fired back with surprising passion.

That was it. The dam was breached. 'I want you,' he said.

Millie gasped. Sheikh Khalid wanted her. This was

every dream come true, and every nightmare made real.
Guilt and desire battled inside her. His grip was both gentle
and firm. She wanted this, wanted him. He was holding
her in front of him with a message in his eyes that even a
relative innocent like Millie could not possibly misinter-
pret, and that message surged through her senses, urging
her to act. He wanted her. She wanted him. As amazing as
it seemed to someone whose sexual experience was limited to a few fumbles in the back of a car, Sheikh Khalid
wanted to seduce her, and she wanted to be seduced. To be
introduced to the world of sensuality she'd only dreamed
about, by a man who could teach her everything, was—

Madness.

'I should go—'

'And find out nothing?' he said.

What was he talking about now? That night? Or sex?
She shook her head, as if to shake some sense into it, but
primal hunger was a merciless force. What harm could one
night do? And once they were truly intimate who knew
what she might learn?

I'm going to interrogate him as he seduces me? Did
she seriously expect Sheikh Khalid to betray his brother?

'Well?' he prompted. 'Are you staying?'

'I think you underestimate me,' she said tensely.

'That's not an answer.' And then he laughed, a blaze
of strong white teeth against his swarthy skin. 'I would
never make that mistake, Millie, but I suspect you might.'

The Sheikh's face was dangerously close as he dipped
his head. She didn't know what to expect and remained
frozen as he brushed her lips with his. But frozen wasn't
an option for more than a split second, as he tested and
teased and made every atom in her being long for more.

She had thought she was stronger than this, but she had
never encountered a force of nature like Khalid before.

From teasing, he moved seamlessly to kissing and with so great a skill that she could never have been prepared for it. Even in her most erotic ramblings, she could never have dreamed this. When he pressed her back against the wall, animal instinct consumed her, until there was only one thought in her head, and that was for him to take her. She wanted everything he had to give, the searing kisses, the physical pleasure. The past was obliterated by the searing heat of the present as Khalid teased her lips apart and took possession of her mouth.

With that one kiss he had crossed an invisible line. There was no going back. What had been done could not be undone. But he'd take this slowly. Millie deserved nothing less. She would be properly prepared for pleasure when he took her. Cupping her face in one hand, he mapped the swell of her breasts with the other. They were so full, so firm, he searched for a reaction in her eyes and he wasn't disappointed. She groaned, and covered his hand with hers to urge him on as he lightly abraded the tip of her nipple with his thumbnail before attending to the other breast. Her legs trembled as he moved on to stroke the smooth line of her belly. She sighed rhythmically with approval in time to what he knew would be delicious little twinges of pleasure, and gasped out loud when he captured the swell of her buttocks to press her hard against his straining body. Arching her back, she positioned her bottom high for more touching, but he had decided that that was enough for now.

'Why?' she asked, her voice ringing with disappointment when he stopped.

'Because greedy must learn to wait,' he murmured against her lips.

'I don't want to wait,' she exclaimed.

He could change his mind. An excited breath rushed

out of her as he eased her legs apart with his thigh. Having spread her, he allowed his fingertips to trail tantalisingly lower. As he had expected, she gave a sharp cry of need. 'Not yet,' he whispered, teasing her ear lobe with hot breath and his tongue.

'When?' she demanded on a shaking breath as he swung her into his arms.

He carried her deeper into the privacy of his suite, into his bedroom, but as the door closed behind them, enveloping them in opulent silence, he was aware of his body like never before. It felt like a brutal weapon against the yielding accommodation of Millie's soft frame. He had always prided himself on his steely control, but having her here took things to a knife's edge. If Millie had been a different, more experienced woman, his physical hunger was such he would have had her up against the door by now, bringing them both the release they so badly needed.

'I want you,' she whispered urgently against his neck, adding to the torment.

'Temporary relief?' he suggested.

'More than that,' she assured him. 'A lot more,' she added in a voice shaking with excitement. A wild flame of passion burned in her eyes, wiping out reason. It threatened to do the same to him.

'When I decide,' he told her firmly.

'Okay,' she agreed, gulping convulsively. 'Whatever you say.'

She'd agree to anything in her present heightened state. It was up to him to set the pace.

'Please,' she begged, reaching for his belt buckle. Her hands were trembling as she wrenched and tugged until finally the buckle yielded. She gave a little growl like a tiger cub with a thorn in its pad, and then yanked the belt out of its loops. *Oh!*

His zipper didn't just slide down, but burst open as he

sprang free. Her lips were parted in an expression of such surprise, he wanted to laugh, but that would definitely have broken the mood. Then, she surprised him by exclaiming, 'I can't possibly accommodate *that*.' And now they were both laughing.

'What are you doing to me, Millie Dillinger?' he demanded. This was turning into something far more than a seduction; it was a getting-to-know-you process such as he'd never experienced before, laced with a surprising degree of, *I really like this woman.*

'I mean it,' she said. 'I can't.'

'You might surprise yourself.'

'You'd like to surprise me,' she corrected him. 'Are you a freak, or is this normal?'

'You don't know?' Alarm bells rang loud and clear. Millie was either a virgin, or she was inexperienced beyond any woman he'd ever known. 'This,' he said, 'is normal for me.'

'Hmm.' She considered what he'd said. 'That's what I thought. And I'm glad you think it's funny,' she added when he laughed out loud.

'Funny?' he queried as he moved away to rearrange his clothing. 'I'm not laughing at you. It's your unique take on things that amuses me.'

'Well, I don't know who you've known before me—'

Her outrage amused him even more, but he curbed the smile in favour of cupping her chin and bringing her close. 'Your expression amuses me, *habibti*. But there is one thing I must ask: are you always this reckless?'

She trembled as he whispered this against her mouth, but he could feel her relief that he'd backed off. 'Never,' she admitted frankly.

Relief, Millie thought as Sheikh Khalid backed off. Narrow escape. And huge disappointment. She couldn't pretend that vigorous, fabulous sex with the best-looking man alive didn't hold enormous appeal, but when he also happened to be her historical enemy, the bogey-man she'd fantasised about pummelling into the ground—when she hadn't been making passionate love to him in her dreams—this shouldn't be happening. And now she had to find a way to exit with dignity.

'There's no need to feel embarrassed,' he said, touching her cheek with tenderness as she awkwardly smoothed her ruffled hair.

'I shouldn't have come back here,' she admitted.

'Yes, you should,' he argued. 'In fact, I'd have been more surprised if you could stay away when there are so many more questions you want to ask me.'

I can't stay away, Millie silently admitted. While the *Sapphire* was in dock and Khalid was close by, she was always going to be drawn to the disaster, to the fact that her mother died here, and to him, the only person who could tell her more about the events of that night.

'This is part of your history,' he said, gesturing around. 'You shouldn't expect to forget. It wouldn't be natural. You have to learn to handle how you feel about this place.'

'Not if you sail away,' she said. Guilt overwhelmed her as she tried to block out how they'd kissed, how he'd touched her, and how she'd responded to him like an animal on heat, and failed utterly.

Inexperience had let her down, and now Khalid was giving her an out. Perversely, she didn't want that. She wanted to stay with him. She wanted more of his time, and more of his touches. More of him. A spear of jealousy so real she actually gasped with pain pierced her at the thought of all the women he must have known; women who'd felt his hands on their bodies, and who had seen that same desire in his eyes.

'I suppose your score card's off the scale,' she commented spikily on the back of this thought.

His hard face softened into laughter. 'I'm not so bad.' He paused a moment, and then admitted wryly, 'I'm worse.'

'And shameless.' But there was no venom in her comment, only a growing fondness, which was dangerous; she had no doubt the Sheikh was as shrewd in his dealings with women as he was in every other area of his life. 'So, what is your score?' she pressed, bracing herself for the answer.

'Sheikh undefeated,' he said.

CHAPTER SEVEN

MILLIE SAT ALONE in the suite, waiting for Khalid to return from attending to his remaining party guests, her body still thrumming from his expert touch. She shifted uncomfortably on the sofa, before glancing at the time on her phone. It was getting late—surely Khalid had seen everyone he needed to see by now?

She was on the point of going to find Khalid at the party when there was a discreet tap on the door. When she opened it, a young maid called Sadie introduced herself. 'His Majesty's PA sent me to direct you to the Pig and Whistle,' Sadie explained.

For a moment, Millie was confused. 'His Majesty's PA sent you? The Pig and Whistle?' she queried, feeling like a fool as she shook her head.

'The Pig and Whistle is what we call the staff mess,' Sadie explained chirpily in a way that immediately endeared her to Millie. 'It's where we hold our parties, and I'm having one tonight.'

'*Your* party?' Millie queried.

'Well, it's not my party, exactly,' Sadie excused. 'It's a tradition on the *Sapphire* that when His Majesty holds a party the staff that prepared everything for his guests, but who aren't required during the actual event, are allowed to celebrate too. To be honest, we don't need much encouragement,' Sadie confided with a grin. 'It's fantastic work-ing on the *Sapphire*. It's such a great crowd.'

But now Millie was worried. Would Khalid find the time to talk to her? He seemed to be passing her on to somebody else. So was that kiss a real kiss, or a power play? She didn't have enough experience to work it out. And Sadie was waiting for her answer. 'I'd love to come along,' she said honestly. Sadie seemed fun. Being invited to the crew party was a hell of a lot better than hanging around on her own, waiting to see if His Majesty could spare the time to talk to her.

'You'll love it. I promise,' Sadie said as she opened the door. 'There's always loads of good food and fun, and lots of dancing.'

Curious about the next adventure, Millie followed the young maid out of the room.

Where was she? Khalid had expected Millie to seek him out well before the party for his guests had ended, but now the night was drawing to a close and shortly his guests would be leaving. He had checked with his guards, but there was no report of Millie leaving the ship. A bolt of dread had run through him as he alerted his head of se-curity to a potential problem.

It couldn't happen again.

A second tragedy on board the *Sapphire* was unthink-able.

Involving Millie?

'I want every inch of this vessel searched,' he com-manded his guards as they lined up in front of him.

'Yes, Your Majesty,' they chanted as one, before sepa-rating and spreading out across the ship.

Nothing must happen to her, he determined fiercely as he joined the search.

* * *

She'd lost track of time, Millie realised. Her stomach clenched as she glanced at her watch. She hadn't had so much fun for ages. The *Sapphire*'s crew came from all over the world, and there was a strong Irish contingent with music and fun and laughter in their blood. The party in the Pig and Whistle had turned into such a riot she'd been up on the table dancing with Sadie for the past half-hour—

Two things happened in quick succession. One of the men swung Sadie into his arms and carried her away, leaving Millie dancing solo, then everyone else turned to stare at the door.

Oh, no!

As if a bagpipe had deflated, the music died to a tune-less hum. Khalid was standing in the doorway. Tall. Dominating. Stern. He was the dark angel from her past, come to wreak vengeance on a woman who had taken a giant leap over the traces. That would be the same woman with burning cheeks and tangled honey-blonde hair, with her skirt lifted high, and a very silly smile on her face.

A smile that just as quickly died.

'Please carry on,' the Sheikh invited as he ducked his head to join them in the crew quarters. 'Please,' he said, turning to address the musicians. 'Play on.'

The fiddler, a guitarist, and a banjo player soon started up again, and the drummer plied his beater on the Irish drum, the Bodhrán, and by the time the traditional flute had joined in it was as if there had been no interruption to the party.

'I'm sorry I—'

She got no further before Khalid demanded in an icy tone, 'Why are you still here?'

'We've still to speak— Your PA—'

'My PA was instructed to mention the party in the Pig

and Whistle so you could get some food. You didn't have the chance to dine before you left my ship the first time tonight, and I thought you might be hungry. I didn't expect you to stay here all night. You should have found some way to tell me where you were, or have you so easily forgotten the risks on a big ship? I've had guards scouring the *Sapphire* for you.'

Millie bided her time until the door had closed behind them and they were alone in the corridor. 'I haven't forgotten the risks, and I'm sorry if I've put you and your guards to such trouble, but I understood we were to talk further. I waited and waited in your suite for you to return and then Sadie knocked on the door, inviting me to come here, at your behest, I'd imagined. Maybe I was mistaken, but would you have preferred me to have hung around on the deck for hours, waiting for a signal from you that it was convenient for us to talk?'

He stared down at her with no expression on his face at all, and then he queried softly, 'Dance?' Opening the door to the party, he stood aside to let her pass.

Millie frowned. 'Are you serious?'

'Never more so,' he confirmed. 'Well?'

She was still shell-shocked, both by the sudden appearance of Khalid, and by his offer. She suddenly became acutely aware that her lips were still burning from his earlier kisses, which made the decision to go or stay one hell of a lot more significant than it might have been. 'I'd like that,' she said.

Sheikh Khalid drew her through the throng and, springing up on the table, he lifted her and steadied her in front of him. The noise had reached fever pitch by this time, making it seem that they were in the middle of some primitive rite, with a dark angel and a virgin in the middle of it. And while some men might have looked foolish dancing on a table, as in everything else he did, Khalid was a natural.

Space restriction forced him to keep her pressed hard against his body. 'I won't let you fall,' he promised.

'You'd better not,' she warned.

She felt safe. Even all the history behind them didn't seem to matter. It was hot and steamy in the Pig and Whistle, and the noise was drumming at her head, but it couldn't come between them. They were so closely linked, both physically and mentally, that even here in this crowded space it was as if just the two of them were dancing with no onlookers at all.

'Enough?' he asked when finally she begged for mercy.

'I'm too dizzy to walk,' she protested, staggering as he sprang down from the table.

Reaching up, he brought her safe into his arms.

'Put me down! I feel embarrassed.'

'There's no need,' he said. 'No one's watching. No one cares.'

Everyone cares, Millie thought as the smiling crowd parted to let them through when Sheikh Khalid carried her to the door. It was only natural that they were intrigued. His Majesty and the laundress dancing in the Pig and Whistle? What wasn't cool about that?

When the door closed behind them a second time, Khalid lowered Millie to her feet and stared down at her. 'Are we going to talk?' she asked. 'I guess you need to say goodnight to your guests first, and I'm happy to wait,' she said, thinking it was the least she could do. 'And then I really must get back,' she added to fill the silence when he didn't speak. 'It's getting late.'

'Did you plan to swim back?'

'What? I... I'm sorry...?' Millie stared up in utter amazement. 'What do you mean?'

'Just that the *Sapphire*'s been underway for over an hour.'

She couldn't speak. She didn't know what to say. There was nothing *to* say, Millie concluded. She was a stowaway on the Sheikh's yacht? What protection did that give her? *What had she done?*

She wracked her brains for a solution, but there was none. She was stranded at sea with the Sheikh. 'What about your guests?'

'They disembarked some time ago.'

'So, we're heading to...?' She wracked her brains for the closest port to King's Dock on the south coast of England.

'For Khalifa,' he said, as if that were obvious.

'Khalifa?' Millie gasped. 'Halfway around the world?'

She was stunned when he confirmed this. Now she was standing still, she could feel the vibration of the ship's engines beneath her feet and hear the faint hum. 'Couldn't you drop me off somewhere?' she asked, knowing she was clutching at straws.

'This isn't a bus, Ms Dillinger.'

'Of course not, I mean...' For once in her neatly organised life, Millie didn't have a clue what to do next. 'Miss Francine will be worried,' was all she could come up with.

'You can call her,' the Sheikh advised.

It was too late; Miss Francine would be in bed.

Bed.

The single word ricocheted around Millie's head. Where was she going to sleep? The thought of spending the night—maybe many nights—on board the *Sapphire* was unnerving, to say the least.

'You'll feel better when you've had something to eat,' Khalid predicted.

'I doubt that somehow,' she said, but her stomach grumbled on cue.

'You'll eat with me,' he said, leading the way down the corridor.

With little choice, she followed him to the grand salon, where it was hardly possible to imagine that a party had taken place. Everything had been cleared away and calm order restored in the magnificent room.

She stared blankly at the phone as he handed it to her. 'Miss Francine,' he prompted, shaking her out of the trance. 'Make your call and leave a message if she isn't up. While you do that, I'll arrange for refreshments.'

Miss Francine was not only awake, Millie discovered, but both thrilled and amused to hear from her charge. 'Make the most of it,' she said to Millie's amazement.

'But I'm *alone* with him,' Millie exclaimed discreetly with a glance at the Sheikh.

'Wonderful,' Miss Francine enthused. 'A world of women will envy you.'

'What are you saying?' Millie asked in the same hushed tone.

'Just that life is full of choices, and you haven't gone wrong so far, Millie Dillinger.'

'I wish I had your confidence in me,' Millie admitted. 'When I boarded the *Sapphire*, I seemed to leave my common sense on shore.'

'That's your opinion,' Miss Francine said firmly. 'It won't hurt you to unplug for a while, and it might do you a lot of good.'

By the time Millie ended the call, she felt that, if she hadn't exactly been given a licence to maybe break a few boundaries, she did have the confidence of someone she trusted implicitly.

A knock on the door heralded the arrival of stewards bearing platters of delicious-looking food. 'I can't eat all this,' Millie protested as they laid it out on the table.

'Don't worry. I'm here to help,' Khalid assured her.

He took hold of a plate and handed it to her, but when she gripped it he held onto the other side so they were joined by a fragile china bridge. 'I'm not—'

'Hungry?' he suggested. When her cheeks flamed red, he added softly, 'Or do you feel guilty about being a stow-away on my ship?'

'I thought I was your guest?' Should his stern look be sending her pulse off the scale?

'My guests have all left,' he reminded her. 'All except one. Don't look so worried. There's no charge for this cruise.'

And at least they'd get the chance to talk, Millie thought as he urged, 'Eat. You need to keep up your strength.'

For what reason? she wondered. 'Are you sure the *Sapphire* won't be docking at a closer port than Khalifa?' Her badly rattled nerves were clamouring for a solution.

'Enjoy the trip,' Sheikh Khalid recommended as he helped himself to food. 'I'll arrange for a private jet to fly you home when we're done.'

'When we're done?' Millie queried hoarsely. 'I can't just disappear off the grid. I've got a college course to complete.' And a world of ugly memories to move past.

'You're on holiday from college,' the Sheikh observed.

She was no longer surprised by what he knew, only that he cared enough to find out.

'And as I said, I will place a private jet at your disposal. You can leave Khalifa whenever you choose.'

'I'd rather take a commercial flight, thank you.' She had no intention of putting herself in the Sheikh's debt. 'And if you can let me off at a closer port, that would be even better.'

'Your virtue is quite safe with me,' he said.

Was he mocking her? She couldn't really see his eyes. His face was turned away from her.

'You can have the guest suite, and the golden sheets,' he added.

Huzzah, thought Millie, grimacing.

He turned in time to see her expression. 'My friend Tadj has been detained on shore by your friend Lucy.'

This was getting worse and worse. Now she had to worry about Lucy.

Lucy could look after herself, Millie reminded herself. She was facing a more immediate problem. 'I don't even have a change of clothes.'

'You're wrong,' the Sheikh told her. 'Your closet is full.'

'You *planned* this?' she exclaimed with outrage.

Throwing up his hands in mock alarm, he gave a lazy shrug. 'Designers from across the world have rushed to accommodate you.'

'And you expect me to be grateful?' she said. 'I feel as if I've been manipulated all along.'

'Touché, Ms Dillinger. Not much escapes you.'

'You admit it?' Millie exclaimed with incredulity.

The Sheikh didn't bat an eyelid. 'What use is massive wealth if it can't be enjoyed? London is a rich source of luxury goods, and only a short hop by helicopter from King's Dock.'

'I'm going to my room.'

'Please do,' he invited with a gracious gesture towards the door. 'I'm sure you won't be disappointed with what you find there. Just don't forget to come back and tell me what you think. And then we'll talk,' he promised with velvet charm.

Infuriating man! Just as he'd said, the fitted dressing room leading off the gilded stateroom was packed full of Milan's finest clothes, Spain's softest leather shoes, and the best of New York's cutting-edge accessories...

And if that didn't prove to be enough to persuade Millie Dillinger to relax and unwind, Khalid thought as he waited to hear Millie's verdict, he would just have to think of something else. He was no saint, and had never pretended to be. Protecting Millie, versus seducing her, had long since passed its tipping point. She was no longer a child, but a hot-blooded woman, and there was a long ocean voyage ahead of them.

CHAPTER EIGHT

WHEN THE FOOD was cleared away and Millie had re-turned—acting cool, but still with the glow of pleasing discoveries reflected in her eyes—he persuaded her to walk out on the deck, where a sophisticated heating system ensured she wouldn't be cold this far north, and sub-dued lighting permitted views of the night sky, as well as a wide swathe of restless sea.

'I'd be happy in the staff quarters,' she assured him as she leaned over the rail...still looking, still searching for the truth, he thought. 'Save the guest suite for someone who appreciates golden sheets,' she said, pulling back as a steward drew out a chair.

'Relax. Enjoy yourself. Sit down,' he encouraged. 'There's nowhere else to go.'

She angled her chin to stare up at him. 'It isn't easy to relax,' she admitted.

'I know,' he said quietly.

She couldn't stop staring at his mouth. She had to stop. But how, when she only had to press her lips together to find they were still swollen from his kisses?

'Don't you want to experience something more exciting than a bunk bed dressed with white cotton for the duration of this trip?' he asked, distracting her.

'If that's your opening gambit, I'm disappointed.' Liar, Millie thought as her pulse careered out of control.

'And I took you for an ambitious woman, Millie Dillinger.'

'I am,' she confirmed, 'but I'll get ahead on my own merit, thank you.'

The Sheikh smiled faintly. 'So no golden sheets?'

He shrugged, and pressed his lips down in a way she found hard to resist.

'I realise I must pay you something for passage on your ship.'

Her prim tone made him laugh. 'I'm sure we'll come to some sort of accommodation.'

'I'm talking about a purely commercial transaction,' she assured him.

'And so am I. What else could I possibly mean?'

Millie firmed her jaw and said nothing.

'And you should know I don't offer credit.'

'This is no joking matter, Your Majesty.'

'I think we've reached a stage where you can safely call me Khalid.'

'Thank you, Your Majesty,' Millie said pointedly. There was nothing safe about any of this. 'If it pleases you—'

'It does please me. Call me Khalid,' he repeated with a slight edge to his voice.

Here was someone who wasn't used to being disobeyed, Millie thought. 'Thank you, *Sheikh* Khalid. I realise the great honour you're doing me, so I will use the polite prefix Sheikh in future.'

This made him groan. 'I'm a man like any other.'

'That's just the point,' she insisted. 'You're not. I'm here because I'm waiting for you to tell me the truth about my mother, and—'

'I'm here because?' he prompted.

'It's a long, cold swim home?' she suggested.

He laughed. It was a wonderful sound. However aloof she tried to be, it seemed Khalid could always cut through her reserve. But what was he thinking now? she wondered as she stared into his brooding face. She could never tell—

She yelped as he cleared the table with a comprehensive sweep of his arm. Everything went flying as he dragged her close and pressed her down onto the cool, hard surface.

'Now what are you going to do?' he asked.

She'd have been angry if it hadn't been for the teasing light in his eyes, because that excited her more than he frightened her. 'Let me go,' she said quietly.

'What if I say no? What are you going to do then?'

'Raise a knee and do you an injury.'

He laughed again. 'And you say that so nicely.'

She held her breath as his wicked mouth tugged into a smile. 'You really are a very bad man,' she observed on a dry throat.

'I really am,' he confirmed, unconcerned.

What a time for her gaze to drop to his mouth!

'Do you want me to kiss you?' he asked.

She drew in a long, shuddering breath. 'It would be nice,' she confessed.

'Nice?'

Now he was frowning.

'Very nice?' she suggested.

The tip of Millie's tongue had just crept out to moisten her kiss-bruised lips in a way he found unbearably seductive. Was it deliberate? He concluded, yes. She had the light of mischief in her eyes.

'And when you've kissed me, I still want the truth, and not the edited version you gave me earlier on.'

She said this so coolly he could only admire her nerve. She had a knack of combining business with pleasure in a way he was beginning to doubt he could do when Millie was involved. Cursing viciously in Khalifan, he let her go and straightened up. 'Are you determined to drive me to distraction?'

'That depends on how long it takes,' she said, and, brushing the creases out of her clothes as coolly as you liked, she climbed down from the table.

'You're playing with fire,' he said as she stared into his face.

'I hope so,' she agreed.

Raking a hand through his hair, he began to laugh. 'You win the prize for the coolest and most infuriating woman I've ever met.'

'Good,' she said. 'I'd hate to be an also-ran.'

'As the mistress of the ruling Sheikh of Khalifa, you'd have no competition—'

'Your *mistress*?' Millie repeated as if she had something unpleasant on her tongue. 'Are you telling me, if that were the case, I'd have no competition for your attention?'

'None,' he confirmed.

'Forget it, Your Majesty,' she flared with an incredulous shake of her head. 'Just tell me what I need to know and we're done here.'

'We're done when I say we're done,' he rapped, all out of patience.

'Perhaps you don't think I deserve the truth?' she said, bridling as she confronted him. 'Or maybe you think I can't handle the truth. Either way, you're wrong.'

He'd never had such an outright revolt to handle, and was enjoying the experience. When she started to pick up the mess he'd made when he'd cleared the table, he couldn't just stand and watch.

* * *

Khalid, Millie thought. As if she could call the titan currently helping her to clear up the floor Khalid. It was one
thing having him inhabit her dreams as a sheikh on horseback, or a hero who took the starring role in every one of
her erotic dreams, but calling the real live man Khalid,
rather than Your Majesty, or Sheikh Khalid, was way too
intimate to even contemplate. If she did that, who knew
where it might lead? Not to becoming his mistress, that
was for sure, she thought as their arms brushed. Having
the Sheikh as her lover might hold huge appeal for her
erotic self, because in her dreams she had nothing better
to do than enjoy the pleasures of the seraglio, the hidden
secrets of the desert, and the sensual pleasures concealed
within a Bedouin tent. But in the real world? No chance.

'You wanted to talk,' he reminded her as, job completed,
they both stood up again. 'So, let's talk.'

She'd wanted nothing more, but suddenly her mind
blanked. 'You don't have to protect my feelings,' she said
as the mist cleared. It had occurred to her that maybe he
really was trying to protect her. 'I went through all the
stages of grief eight years ago.'

'When what happened must have seemed black and
white to you,' he said, staring at her keenly.

'Death doesn't come in shades of grey.'

'Indeed not,' Khalid agreed in the same quiet tone.

'My mother was a victim.' She could never say that
enough times. It was what she had always believed, totally and utterly. 'The gutter press may have labelled her
a pathetic drunk, but she was always a star to me, and she
was my mother, and I'll defend her to my last breath. If
you know *anything* about that night that could absolve her
from any blame or ridicule, I want you to tell me. With the
benefit of hindsight, it's easy to see that my mother was

deluded, and believed that singing on your brother's yacht might revive her career. It was all she'd got—'

'She had you.'

Yes, *yes*, and the responsibility for leaving the one person who had needed her most alone on this yacht would never leave her. 'Yes, and I left her,' she exclaimed, lashed by guilt. 'Then your brother took advantage of my mother's vulnerability. How can you possibly sanitise that?'

'You still hate me,' he murmured.

'Tell me something to change my mind,' she begged, wishing deep down that there could be proof that Khalid had never been implicated directly. There was no excuse for his brother. The late Sheikh Saif was guilty of murder in Millie's eyes, and all she could do now was to obtain justice for her mother.

'Your mother brought you into danger that night, and that's a fact,' he said as she shook her head slowly and decisively, over and over again. 'My brother's parties were notorious. She must have known.'

'That she was putting me in danger? No. She would never do that.'

'It depends how desperate she was, don't you think?'

'You didn't know her, I did,' she insisted stubbornly.

'She was your mother, and you loved her no matter what. I get that. And I won't go on, if you can't take it.'

'Don't patronise me,' she warned. 'Tell me what you know. You can't stop now.'

He stared at her for a long time before saying anything, as if he had to be sure she wouldn't break down. She nodded once, briskly, inviting him to explain.

Another long pause, and then he said, 'Did you know your mother was a drug addict?'

She battled to suck air into lungs that had inexplicably

closed. 'Don't be ridiculous!' she blurted at last. 'Don't you think I'd have known, if that were the case?'

But she did know. At least, she had suspected. And had needed to hear it from someone else, someone who was deeply involved. Miss Francine had always protected Millie from the truth, and she loved her for it. Khalid had done her another type of kindness by not dressing up the truth, and perhaps his was the greater gift, because he'd given her closure at last.

'How did you know?' she asked, feeling the tension seep away as the last piece of the jigsaw settled into place. Her fury at Khalid had been instantly replaced by deep sorrow for her mother.

Taking hold of her hands, he brought them down from her face. 'I'm sorry,' he said quietly. 'I think everyone must have known about your mother's habit apart from you.'

'I think I knew,' she whispered. 'I'd read rumours in the press, but I didn't want to believe them. She was always careful around me, so I never saw any proof. Thank you for telling me. I needed to hear it. Then…' She braced herself to voice the unspeakable. 'If my mother was the freak show, was I the support act? Did your brother ever speak to you of that?'

His intention was not to destroy Millie, but to try and lay her ghosts to rest. His late brother would accept no restraint on his perversions. Whatever Millie asked of him now, he had to edit the truth, or cause her endless pain. 'I didn't know there was a party on board the *Sapphire* that night, until I arrived,' he explained. 'And as for your mother taking drugs? She would hardly be the first great artist to fall foul of ruthless and unscrupulous drug dealers.'

'But that doesn't explain her death,' Millie said, frowning. He wasn't about to explain that he'd chased her mother's drug dealer into the arms of the police, and had been dockside when Roxy's body was fished out of the harbour. He'd checked to see if there was a pulse, and had seen the sapphires spilling over the top of her dress. He'd retrieved them before he was asked to stand back, so at least she could never be branded a thief.

'Did she fall or was she pushed?'

Millie's voice was hoarse, and her face was pale and strained. She deserved an honest answer, and at least he could give her this. 'The dealer pushed her into the water.'

Over her gasp, he told her the rest of it—or his interpretation of what must have happened on that terrible night. He guessed Roxy had tried to pay the man for her fix in sapphires, which the dealer would assume were fake. Khalid guessed that was when he lost his temper. He'd seen little more than the end of the fight. The *Sapphire* was a huge vessel, so by the time he reached the shore, calling the authorities as he ran, he was too late to save Millie's mother.

'You saw this happen,' she stated tensely, 'so you were watching her all along.'

'I witnessed something,' he said honestly. 'I was too far away to see clearly, and when I arrived at the scene it was dark and the water was black.'

'But you called the authorities, so you must have known something was badly wrong.'

'I heard a scream. That was what attracted my attention. It could have been kids acting up. It was only a few seconds later when I realised it wasn't a game, and by then it was too late.'

'I asked you to go back to save her,' Millie said quietly. All her frustration and grief collided. 'You bastard!' she exclaimed, launching herself at him. 'You let her down. And I know there's something you're not telling me. I know it—*I know it*!'

Catching hold of her, he held her still. 'It's over, Millie. It's over now.'

As she fought him and railed against him, he wished he could do more, say more, but with a bride looming in his very near future he would not make any false promises to Millie. He could only wait until her anger burned out, and when it did, and she slumped against him, completely spent, he let her sob.

He waited until she was quiet again, and then tipped up her chin. 'Where are you taking me?' she asked as he took hold of her hand.

'To bed—'

'Are you mad?' she exclaimed. 'Let go of me!'

Ignoring her request, Khalid steered her on through the ship. The elevator was closer than the companionway and he stopped in front of it. Within seconds he'd backed her into the small, plush space. It did no good raging. He stood in her way, blocking her only escape route as the doors slid slowly to.

'My intention is not to make you forget the past,' he said quietly as she stood stiff as a board, pressed up hard against the corner, 'but to help you face the facts and deal with them.'

'How very kind,' she said tensely. Her emotions were shot. She should have realised what a trauma it would be coming back. If she'd stayed on board eight years ago and shadowed her mother, this wouldn't be happening, and her mother would still be alive.

'No,' Khalid instructed in a low tone as she covered her face with her hands. 'No,' he repeated. 'This is not your fault.'

This was all her fault. Snapping around so she didn't have to look at him, she slammed her forearm against the padded wall and buried her face in her arm. But reality had a way of intruding. What chance would she have stood against the toad-like Sheikh Saif and his guards?

Maybe none, but she should have tried.

'No,' Khalid said again, this time in a sharper tone when she reached for the controls to try and open the doors of the elevator before it moved off. 'It's too late for that.'

Too late for everything, she thought as he kept her boxed in the corner as the car began to rise. When she tried to push him away, he caught hold of her wrists and pinned them above her head. Frustration grabbed her by the throat. The need to learn secrets he refused to tell her exploded in fury and she snarled like a wild animal caught in a trap. He had an answer for that too. Dipping his head, Khalid enforced silence with a kiss. And not just any kiss, but one that melted her from the inside out. She only had to taste him, feel him, scent him, touch him, and she was lost. He was everything missing from her life. His touch seared her senses. His kisses rocked her world. Being lost in his arms always blotted out the past. He offered oblivion, and that was exactly what she craved right now. If she thought any more about the past, she'd go mad.

The elevator slowed to a halt, but he sent it down again. He pressed another light on the panel and it stopped between floors. 'What are you doing?' she asked tensely.

'Taming you,' he said, shocking her to her core. 'Helping you to forget…'

What did that mean? Her wrists were still captive in his one massive fist, and with his free hand he began to map her breasts. Stunned, excited, angry, eager; she was all of those things. Her knees actually shook when he kissed her this time. Her body felt as if it had been plugged into a power source. She gasped when he grazed her nipples with his thumbnail. And vocalised her need for more when he weighed her breasts appreciatively before stroking them with the most seductive touch. She was incapable of speech, not that it mattered. Khalid was so intuitive he didn't need any instruction, and telling him to stop was the last thing she wanted to do. Pulses of pleasure streamed straight to her core, leaving her with only one possible destination.

'Need is blazing in your eyes,' he observed, sounding pleased. 'But if you'd like me to stop—'

Her excited laugh gave him the only answer he needed. She was a willing prisoner in Khalid's erotic net, and her reward was the brush of his sharp black stubble against her neck, and then the lightest brush of his lips as he kissed her. When he took possession of her mouth with his tongue, she found it too arousing, too tempting, and as he deepened the kiss she rubbed against him. She needed that big, hard body pressing into hers. Desperate for more contact, she writhed shamelessly against him. He tasted of everything good, and she was putty in his hands. Animal sounds of pleasure escaped her throat as his hand slid slowly up her leg.

Done with begging, she commanded, 'I need you.'

'Open your legs. Wider,' he instructed.

He had never felt such an urge to pleasure a woman. Thrusting his thigh between hers, he spread her wide. Her excited cries greeted his first touch. The change in her was instantaneous. From being her avowed enemy, he was her lifeblood and she would do anything he asked. Sinking onto his palm, she ground her body against the heel of his hand.

'Not so fast,' he cautioned.

Releasing her wrists, he held her securely in place while he traced the hot swell of her sex. Removing her thong, he found the tip that craved his attention and circled it. Teasing Millie was torture for him, but it was also its own reward, and with so many days at sea ahead of them, he could afford to take his time.

'Please!' Millie begged in a voice that was trembling with need. Clinging to him, she worked her hips in a desperate hunt for more contact.

'Do you expect me to obey you?' he asked with amusement.

'You can't leave me like this.'

'Can't I?'

'Please don't.'

He smiled against her mouth as she threatened to make him pay for his cruel neglect.

'I'm counting on it,' he said as he began the slow and deliberate circling as she frantically worked her hips.

'Don't tease me,' she begged in a strangled tone as she tried every which way to bring her body into contact with his hand.

Adjusting the position of his fingertip by millimetres was all it took for him to change the outcome. Increasing both pressure and speed by the smallest degree quickly brought Millie the release she so desperately needed. Her screams of relief were deafening and prolonged. She had waited a long time, he guessed, and would need a lot more before she was sated.

Holding her safe in his arms until she quietened, he kissed her and then murmured, 'Bed?'

'Just more of that,' she said, resting against him as she dragged in air. 'Wherever—'

Sending the car up to his deck, he lifted her into his arms and carried her to his suite.

CHAPTER NINE

HAVING LAID HER down on his bed, Khalid kicked off his shoes. Millie's cheeks were burning as incredulity and excitement washed over her in turn, at what she'd done, and what she was about to do. All thoughts of leaving the *Sapphire* as soon as possible and flying home, forgetting any of this had ever happened, had vanished as surely as mist before the sun. Khalid had freed her. He'd seen her lose control completely and, having given him that, there was no reason now to hold back.

She turned to look around as his clothes hit the floor and felt the blood drain from her cheeks. What was she thinking? He was massive and tanned, hard muscles sculpted like a Michelangelo statue; there was so much of beautiful, perfect him, and all of it in formidable proportion.

'Shy now?' he asked with amusement.

'No,' she defended, but he heard the lie in her voice.

Coming to join her on the bed, Khalid stretched out his magnificent, naked length alongside her and, resting his chin on the heel of his hand, he viewed her steadily as if she were a new and fascinating exhibit on board his yacht. He knew how aroused that made her, and how aroused she still was after his skilful attention. 'You want me,' he said.

The faint smile on his mouth was all it took to make her want him even more. 'Not as much as you want me,' she countered, determined, even at this late stage, to fight her corner.

He shrugged and his lips pressed in response.

'If you didn't want me, why are we here?' she asked with perfect logic, she thought. 'Unless you invite all your female guests to share your bed?'

This made him laugh. 'Millie, Millie, Millie. Do you think I make a habit of stopping my elevator between decks?'

'I don't know. I'd rather not think about it,' she admitted. 'I'm sure there are those who think there are advantages to be gained by sleeping with you, but I'm not one of them.'

'No,' he whispered, 'You're not.'

He'd been toying with a lock of her hair as she spoke, and now he drew her into his arms. A great hunger swept over him for more than sex: to be joined, to be close, to give pleasure. This would be a sensuous and lengthy seduction. Millie was young and inexperienced, and deserved nothing less. The reward would be extreme pleasure. The thought of sinking into her hot, eager body was—

'Where are you going?' she asked as he moved away. Reaching for his hand, she caught hold of his wrist. Her boldness made him smile. She was a tigress.

'I'm twice your size.'

'Good,' she said, her grip firming. Her gaze was steady on his face.

Physical pleasure was a gift, to be cherished and worked on. It was not enough to become a great warrior, he had been told by the elders of the desert; a man must prove himself a great lover too. Eroticism was valued by the travelling tribes he'd joined as a youth, when he'd had no expectation of becoming the ruling sheikh of Khalifa.

'Your Majesty seems distracted.'

'By you,' he said, staring down into Millie's laughing eyes. 'You distract me.' He toyed thoughtfully with a strand of her long, silky hair. 'I'll keep you safe.'

'I don't want to be safe,' she whispered fiercely.

'What do you want?'

'To forget,' she said as she closed her eyes.

Coming back to lie close, he soothed her trembling body with long, rhythmical strokes. The bond between them was tightening. Was that fair to Millie?

Being naked in bed with Khalid was a recipe for skewing her thoughts. Drugging and amazing, it was as if every nerve ending she had were standing to attention. Moving her body with increased confidence against his heightened her senses as never before. The lights were out and night enfolded them in a thick black velvet blanket. His soothing strokes and the almost imperceptible movement of the big ship added to her arousal. Cupping her face in his hands, he kissed her in a way that made tears spring to her eyes. She was glad of the dark, shielding her. Her emotions were raw. She forgot her concern as he mapped her body with knowing skill. 'How long does the teasing go on?' she asked, aching with need.

'As long as I deem it necessary—'

She gasped as he swung her on top of him. There was no avoiding the thrust of his arousal, and no way to call this safe. She was equally intimidated by his size, and excited by it. Her body quivered with expectation, though she wasn't even sure she could take him. On the edge, hovering dangerously close to plunging over, she thought, Spread me wide and take me. Make me forget.

'Will you teach me all you know?' she asked. 'Stop it,' she warned when she saw his teasing expression. How could she not want this man? Outwardly stern, privately human—even warm, she thought. He might be twice her size, but the time for caution was over. Winding her legs around his, she proved her trust. He brought them even closer to kiss her lips, her neck, and then her breasts, as he continued to tease her with feather touches. Moving down the bed, he treated her breasts to a feast of pleasure, and with each insistent tug, she experienced a corresponding pulse between her legs.

'Is this what you want?' he asked, raising his head. He smiled faintly, teasing her again with delay.

'As if you don't know,' she whispered.

Running his fingertips over her breasts, he moved on to stroke her belly, which was incredibly arousing. 'And this?' he asked as he parted her legs.

'So much,' she gasped out.

Lifting her buttocks, he rested them on a soft pillow to spread her wide, and then he arranged her legs comfortably over the powerful width of his shoulders. She almost lost control at the first touch of his tongue. She'd never experienced anything like this. Sensing how close she was, he pulled back, his expression stern.

'When I say you can and not before,' he warned. 'The delay is for your benefit,' he added.

She didn't doubt it as eager forerunners of that bigger release gripped her repeatedly. She had everything to learn, and was a most willing pupil. But nothing— *nothing* could have prepared her for this. Khalid knew exactly how to prolong her pleasure, and when to hold back, until she felt as if every delicious pulse of sensation she had ever experienced had gathered and was waiting to be unleashed.

'Now, please,' she begged.

This resulted in a little more attention on his part, but not enough to tip her over the edge.

Resting back, she closed her eyes, temporarily defeated. When she opened them again, the expression in

Khalid's eyes was enough to send her over, but he was the master of pleasure, and knew how to keep her under control.

Short, sharp, noisy gasps shot from her throat as he returned to teasing her with his tongue. She gripped the bed, fists turning white. How much longer was she supposed to hold on? She loved his hands on her buttocks, so firm, so sure as he lifted her to his mouth. A fierce desire to isolate the place where sensation ruled consumed her. Reaching down, she helped him by pressing her legs apart even more, and now she was floating, suspended on a plateau of sensation, where there was no possibility of rational thought and only one way down.

'Now.'

He spoke the single word so softly. It was the only prompt she needed. 'Now!' she agreed fiercely.

Her body worked with wild abandon to capture the waves of pleasure as Khalid buffeted her rhythmically. He was amazing, launching her into a world of pleasure that beat at her senses; he showed no mercy when she wailed, and made sure she experienced every last throb of ecstasy until she fell back, utterly exhausted and yet hungry for more.

'You are so aroused,' he remarked, staring down. 'So warm and plump and pink, and accommodating. Good,' he approved, holding her firmly in place when she surprised herself with a second release that didn't require his involvement. He had unlocked something in her that demanded to be fed. 'Hold yourself wide,' he instructed.

She was eager to do so. It was a sign of how far she'd come. All she wanted was this, and Khalid deep inside her, pressing her down into the bed. She could think of nothing else.

Protecting them both, he teased her with his body. She

wailed with disappointment when he pulled away, and was instantly hungry for more.

'Yes?' he asked, giving her a little more.

Grabbing hold of him, she worked her hips as he circled her core with the same teasing skill, before entering her again, just an inch or so. 'No!' she complained angrily when he withdrew.

'We take this slowly,' he explained in a husky whisper.

She didn't want 'slowly'. She wanted firm and fast and hard. And deep...so deep. 'Please,' she begged, writhing provocatively beneath him.

Pinning her wrists above her head, he teased her repeatedly, each time sinking a little deeper. 'Yes,' she groaned as he took her by thrilling degrees, 'Oh, yes...'

When he was lodged to the hilt, he worked his hips round and round and from side to side, making it impossible not to claim a greedy release.

'That was naughty,' he scolded when she quietened. 'Did I say you could?'

'You didn't say I couldn't,' Millie countered. 'And it's your turn now.'

'Not for a long time yet,' he said, starting up a rhythmical pattern that made further argument the last thing in her head.

She didn't wait, and as she greedily flew into pleasure, he remarked, 'You *are* on a knife's edge,' making it sound like the best sort of praise.

You have no idea, Millie thought as she bucked back and forth to claim the very last pulse of pleasure. She'd had no idea she was even capable of such extremes, or that this would fast become as necessary as breathing to her. 'I'll never get enough of you,' she admitted, her voice muffled against Khalid's chest.

'I look forward to putting that to the test,' he said. Raising her face to his, he kissed her with such lingering intensity that this time she couldn't hide her tears.

What the hell was he thinking? Khalid mused as he paced the deck outside his stateroom. Dawn was breaking. Millie was still sleeping, so at least he had a chance to think. Was he going to trample her feelings a second time? Crumpling the note handed to him by his aide de camp, he cursed viciously. In the shower before he'd received the note, he had pictured taking her to the desert, but now everything had changed. A rumble of thunder drew his attention to the sky where storm clouds were gathering. The change in the weather was a reminder that nothing remained the same. A prospective bride had arrived uninvited in Khalifa, and was waiting with her family in the guest wing of his palace in the capital. It was politically expedient to meet her, for her brother was one of the Sapphire Sheikhs.

However many times he tried to tell himself this voyage was an entertaining interlude and nothing more, Millie's trusting face appeared in front of him. A slave to duty, who was determined to give his people better after Saif had almost ruined Khalifa with his excesses, Khalid owed it to his people to marry and provide them with an heir. He was expected to make a political alliance, a business transaction between neighbouring countries to strengthen borders and improve trade. His personal wishes didn't come into it.

Then change tradition.

He laughed out loud as the thought occurred to him. It was so simple in theory, and yet impossible. Things moved too slowly; they always had.

Then change them.

He placed the call.

'I will be in the desert for the next month,' he informed one of his aides at the palace. 'Please give my apologies to the Princess and her family. I will endeavour to make up for this confusion with a substantial donation to their wildlife protection scheme.'

He felt a surge of triumph when he cut the line, then wondered if a month in the desert with Millie would be too long. She commanded his attention like no one else. Maybe a month wouldn't be long enough! When she came out on deck to join him, swathed in a cashmere throw because the *Sapphire* was still heading for warmer climes, he knew he'd made the right decision. Bathed in the clear, early light of dawn, she looked so young and innocent, and yet her cheeks were flushed with a new understanding of pleasure.

'I missed you,' she whispered, clinging to him, and when she raised her face, her eyes were bright with love.

'Did you sleep well?' he asked.

'What do you think?' Millie murmured, and instead of looking behind them, to where there was no longer any British shore to see, she stared ahead with him, to the future and to Khalifa.

They kissed and he wound his hands through her soft bright hair. It fell in lustrous waves to her waist, though it was a little tangled, and he loved that, because it reminded him of the pleasure they'd shared. Linking fingers, he kissed her again, and when finally they broke apart his decision had been made. 'Be ready in half an hour,' he told her.

'Ready for what?' she asked.

'For the adventure to continue.' When she looked at him for more information, he added, 'We'll travel by helicopter first, and then on by private jet to Khalifa.'

'Khalifa,' she breathed. Worry and anticipation battled for supremacy in her eyes.

'Don't change your mind now,' he warned good-humouredly. 'I know you're as impatient as I am to see my homeland.'

'I'm curious,' she agreed, biting her lip as she admitted this.

'More than that, I think. Pack a small case with essentials.' When she started to question him, he said, 'You'll only need a small bag. You'll find one in your dressing room. Everything else will be waiting for you at our destination.'

'Khalifa,' she repeated, still a little wary, but unable to hide her growing excitement.

'Now, be quick,' he urged as he kissed her.

Millie's first sight of the desert knocked the breath from her lungs. Whatever she'd been expecting, this was more. After swooping low over a bright blue sea, they had landed on a small, private airstrip close to the beach where a large marquee had been erected, and uniformed attendants stood in an orderly row, waiting to greet them. The men were dressed in black, their faces covered apart from their eyes. Dressed in tunics and baggy trousers, with long, curving daggers secured inside their belts, they were an intimidating sight. A sense of unreality struck her as she looked around, trying to take everything in. With a backdrop of burnished blue sky, blazing sun and endless sand, the scene was like something out of a thrilling and exotic movie. And she was playing one of the leading roles with a man at her side who made every film star seem like a pallid sham. This was real, and this was incredible.

A red carpet led from the steps of the jet to the enormous white tent, on top of which fluttered Khalid's personal insignia: the hawk of the desert in black and gold on a red ground. Having piloted the helicopter from the superyacht, Khalid had flown them in one of his private jets from the large international airport. There was no sign of a limousine or sleek SUV waiting to take them on to their next destination. Instead, a number of horses were tethered beneath the shade of a large awning...

'Welcome to Khalifa,' Khalid said, distracting her from the lavishly caparisoned horses as he urged her forward.

Everything was very new and very strange and very wonderful. His hand on her arm was reassuring. And arousing. The look in his eyes was hypnotising. After so many hours of enforced separation in the jet, she longed for his prolonged attention—time alone, to confide and make love. His steadying hand was both a curb on those thoughts, and a reminder of the pleasure they'd shared.

'What do you think?' he said as he turned to look at her at the entrance to the grand pavilion.

'Amazing.' She stared past the guards to the rich colours in the womb-like, shadowy interior. 'It's certainly a contrast to home.' Where a subdued colour palette ruled at King's Dock thanks to the regular rainfall.

'Millie?'

Having no experience of the desert, other than in books, she was overcome by the vastness of the sand stretching away on every side for unseen miles. She was nothing more than a grain of sand in the grand scheme of things. 'I'm disorientated,' she confessed. 'I've never seen anything on this scale.' And she was a long way from home.

This journey was reckless. She was miles away from anything familiar, with only a mobile phone and a failing battery between her and complete isolation. She must place her trust in Khalid. And her own, keenly developed sense of survival, Millie reminded herself as she followed him into the shade.

'You'll be cooler in here.'

He was right. With no obvious sign of air-con, the billowing tent was cool and airy inside.

'Well?' he asked as she stared around.

'It's wonderful. I can't believe I'm here,' she exclaimed as she walked across the rugs to admire some ancient wall hangings. 'It's such a soothing setting.' The stench of aviation fuel had been shut out, and was replaced by the evocative scent of spice. 'I love it,' she said, turning back to face Khalid. This was no Hollywood replica of a warrior king's tent, but a shaded sanctuary, illuminated by the glow of golden lanterns. Fabrics in a rich variety of jewel shades made it welcoming, while bowls of freshly picked fruit, and jugs of juice waited on a pierced golden table to tempt them. 'All this for us,' she said. 'For you, anyway,' she amended with a wry smile.

'This is for your pleasure,' he argued softly.

'Well, it's fabulous. It's a travelling palace.'

'That's exactly what it is.'

'Lucky man,' she murmured.

As Khalid gave a rueful and accepting shrug, she knew in her gut she'd be okay. There was no need to be overawed by any of this. This was as much his reality as her bedsit in King's Dock was hers. Everything she'd seen so far spoke of care, and appreciation for the craftsmanship and the materials of his country. Photographs of Bedouin tents did them no justice at all.

'You must change into robes before we leave,' Khalid said, distracting Millie from examining the many beautiful examples of art from his homeland.

'You don't expect me to ride, do you?' she exclaimed, remembering the horses. 'I'm not a horsewoman.'

'You might surprise yourself,' he said. 'I'm going to change. I suggest you do too.' He indicated another area of the tent. 'You'll find some clothes in there. I'll help you with the headdress. It takes some getting used to,' he explained as she went to investigate.

Millie's eyes widened at the sight of a beautiful silver-grey robe in the finest of fabrics laid out on a leather daybed. Delicate silver embroidery around the neck and hem, ornamented with tiny seed pearls, had obviously been painstakingly hand-stitched.

'Ready?' Khalid called out while she was still running her fingertips reverently over the intricate work.

'Yes,' she lied.

When he thrust the cover aside it was too late to take those words back. When he strode in, her voice deserted her, anyway. Having changed out of the jeans and shirt he had worn for piloting the plane, Khalid was once again dressed in robes. A true master of the desert, he was a stunning sight. Picking up the glorious grey robe she was to wear, he maintained eye contact as he dropped it over her head. 'It suits you,' he remarked. 'Now take all your other clothes off.'

'Everything?' Millie blinked.

'This is the desert, not the high street, and you're not about to catch a bus.'

She frowned. 'Okay—' But before she could do as he instructed, Khalid had reached down to lift the hem of her robe. Deftly removing her top and jeans, he indicated that she should step out of them. Her underwear followed, leaving her naked beneath the flowing robe.

'What are you doing?' she asked as he lifted her. For a moment she thought there was some other garment he was about to help her to put on.

'Being an extremely bad man,' he said.

She laughed with excitement as his beard-roughened jaw raked her neck.

'No one will disturb us here,' he explained, 'and I'm not going to waste time teasing you, or preparing you.'

'No need.'

But he did test her for readiness. Always so caring. And he protected them both. She had to muffle her cries of pleasure against his chest as he took her in one firm thrust. Needing no encouragement to work furiously with him, she ground her buttocks against his big rough hands. They were both noisy and fierce, both craved fast release. She wrapped her legs tightly around his waist, while her hands gripped his shoulders as if she would never let him go.

'Yes!' she cried as he upped the tempo and force of his thrust. 'I need this—need you! *Ah...!*'

'As I need you, *habibti!*' Khalid ground out, working dependably, rhythmically, firmly.

'Oh...!' Her cries went on and on, as sensation exploded between them in the same instant. How could anything be this amazing, and fantastic and essential to life?

'Again,' Khalid suggested against her ear, in a seductive, warm and teasing tone when the first storm had passed and she had begun to quieten.

'Oh, yes, please,' she agreed.

Settling deep, she gasped, 'Need more...need more...'

Incredibly, with his own release only moments behind him, Khalid was still fully aroused, and as hungry as she was. He thrust firmly and deep, moving persuasively as his big hands helped her to thrust her hips in time with his. 'Must be your turn again?' she gasped after he had satisfied her several times more.

'Like this?' he said, starting over.

'Exactly like that,' she confirmed, howling with pleasure as he upped the pace.

It was a long time later, when they had both taken a shower *and* each other *in* the shower, in a bathroom in the pavilion that surprised Millie by being extremely well equipped, that Khalid towelled her dry, and when that was done he stood before her completely naked.

'Not this time,' he scolded when she reached for him. 'But soon,' he promised.

That had to be enough for her. For now. The desert suits him, she thought as Khalid dropped the black robe over his head. Securing a different type of headdress from the usual—she knew this was called a *howli*, and called for yards of fabric to be expertly wound around his head and face—he was instantly transformed from a passionate lover, into passionate lover who was also an imposing desert king.

'You can't be cold,' he remarked as she shivered with unadulterated lust.

Khalid's physicality was staggering. Having thought herself sated, she wanted him again, and with a hunger that threatened to overwhelm her.

Even though she could only see his eyes, they were knowing, and quite capable of delivering a message through the narrow slit he had left for his eyes, and that message said, no chance. 'I'll help you put your headdress on,' he said as he gathered up her scarf. 'It will protect you from the sun, and from the sand.'

Alone with her thoughts as he did this, she questioned her feelings and her behaviour. She was having the most wonderful adventure, but what then? However wonderful this was, he was, there was no future for them. Khalid was the powerful ruler of a fabulously wealthy country. She was a laundress from the docks. He couldn't hold off his marriage for ever, and that would have to be a formal and very public affair, and where would that leave Millie? This wasn't going anywhere except back to Khalid's bed, she accepted as she followed him outside; a thought that excited her far more than it should have done.

'You'll ride with me,' he said. 'If you're as inexperienced on horseback as you used to be in bed, it's the safest way to travel,' he murmured discreetly, though she wasn't sure his guards weren't actually mannequins dressed for the role, as they maintained their distance and their silence, and their stillness, admirably. 'As you have discovered,' Khalid added with a wicked smile, 'neither condition needs to remain permanent. Now come closer so I can put the final touches to your head covering to protect you from the sun.'

She had pulled it back a little, and now asked, 'Is it safe?'

'I've never known scarves to bite.'

'I mean you. Are *you* safe?' she scolded. 'Coming close to you, I mean.'

'It's never stopped you before.'

Her body thrilled with memories as he rearranged her headdress, and then led her towards the horses. And the desert.

CHAPTER TEN

'THERE,' KHALID SAID, standing back to examine his handi-work. 'Apart from your striking blue eyes, you look like a real Khalifan.'

She felt unrecognisable: exotic, unusual, and so unlike her usual self.

'Well?' he prompted. 'What do you think?'

'It feels wonderful,' she admitted. 'Cool and comfort-able.'

'I sense a but?' he queried.

Only that same niggle of doubt that had struck her in-side the tent. What was she doing here, living a dream that didn't belong to her? And never could?

Miss Francine's voice came into her head. *If things ap-pear too good to be true, they generally are.*

She had to shake that thought away, and enjoy each new experience to the full otherwise her time here was wasted. There were never any guarantees in life, so why not make the most of this? She was under the protec-tion of the hawk of the desert. What could possibly go wrong? Millie thought as Khalid's attendants brought up the horses. The air was warm and scented with the tang of the ocean, and adventure in the desert beckoned.

'I'm ready,' she confirmed.

Khalid's snorting, frothing, fearsome-looking animal

was definitely not her mount of choice. 'You don't seri-ously expect me to ride on that?' she said as he beckoned to her to come closer, so he could lift her onto the saddle in front of him. 'That isn't a horse, it's a muscle machine with evil intentions.'

'Play nice, Burkan,' he said as the horse flattened its ears.

'What about me?' Millie pointed out. 'I'm prepared for nice, but preferably when it arrives on four wheels.'

'You'll be fine,' Khalid assured her as he held out his hand.

Black as night, and as hard-muscled as his master, his stallion was grandly caparisoned in red and gold as be-fitted the favourite mount of a mighty ruler. And had the temperament of a snake someone had poked with a stick, Millie concluded. 'He's a monster. No way. Don't you have a mule, or a donkey?'

'*Burkan* means volcano in your language,' the mon-ster's master explained fondly as he caressed his mount's suddenly pricked-up ears.

'I see he responds to flattery like most males,' Millie commented dryly.

Khalid laughed, the sound muffled behind the *howli*, making it sound like a deep rumble of thunder, while his big black stallion raked the ground and gave her the dead eye. 'He's a pussycat,' he soothed.

'Of the big cat variety, with a thorn in its paw,' Millie agreed.

'I'm right out of donkeys,' Khalid told her, 'so are you coming, or not?'

She gazed around at the desert. This might be his home, but it looked like hostile territory to Millie. Re-sistant though she was to the idea of riding half a ton of power-packed, mean-eyed horse, she took hold of Khalid's hand. No stallion with a personality disorder was going to frighten Millie Dillinger.

The next moment they were off. There was no slow build up to a flat-out gallop, so she could get used to the stallion's gait. Burkan only knew one speed, and that was rocket-propelled. She yelped with fear as he galloped on, and for a few moments she was sure she'd fall off, but as Khalid's arms tightened around her, her confidence grew.

'Good?' he demanded as Burkan's hooves ate up the desert at a pace she could hardly believe.

'I'm alive,' she yelled back. And that was enough. But soon she realised it was fabulous. There could be nothing better than this wild ride through the desert in the arms of a desert king.

Dunes rose on either side of them, and Millie had no idea how anyone could navigate their way around when everything looked so similar. Khalid had no difficulty. He spearheaded the troop of men. Seeing the land he loved like this told her more about a complex man than hours of conversation ever could. Khalid might be hugely civilised on the outside, but in his heart, he was a fierce desert warrior.

Seeing his land through Millie's eyes was a wonderful experience, like seeing the desert for the first time. Slowing Burkan, he pointed out the signs he looked for in a landscape, that at first sight appeared confusingly similar, and had the added complication of changing day by day as wind shifted both the shape and position of the dunes. He reined in at the top of one of these sand mountains to give Millie a chance to appreciate the extent of the sea of gold surrounding them. Dismounting, he lifted her down. Kneeling, he showed her the animal tracks in the seemingly sterile environment. He could tell she was fascinated as she knelt down beside him, and they were soon fully engrossed in discussing his plans to turn part of the desert into a fruitful garden, and how he intended to expand his nature reserves in order to protect the most endangered species. When he looked at her to weigh her reaction, and saw how intently she was listening, he felt a swell of emotion akin to love. This was dangerous, he thought as he sprang to his feet.

'Khalifa is *so* beautiful,' she said, standing by his side. 'You're a very lucky man.'

'Yes, I am,' he agreed, striding away to remount Burkan before he said something to make things worse. His growing feelings for Millie were not only inappropriate, but unfair to her. His future was fixed. If not this latest contender who had arrived unannounced at the palace, he must find an appropriate bride soon. It was his duty to settle down and have children, to forge the stable dynasty his people longed for. He could offer Millie nothing in the long-term. He had to content them both with this short desert adventure.

'Come,' he said, reaching down from the saddle. 'We have some miles to cover before we reach the oasis.'

'The oasis?' she exclaimed. 'How romantic.' She stared up with eyes full of wonder, like a child at Christmas, making his decision to follow duty even harder.

'It's where we'll sleep,' he said crisply, trying not to think about the moment of parting, which must come soon, when they would both return to stark reality.

She felt better this time, on the horse, more relaxed, and at one with Khalid. She was excited as they cantered on through the desert towards the promise of a cooling oasis. Having seen this other side of her desert lord, a side that was tender and caring, and deeply committed to the welfare of his country, she loved him more than ever. Yes. Love.

There was no other way to describe her growing feelings for Khalid. She didn't want to leave him, or his country, and she was hungry to know more, about him, about Khalifa. Everything that mattered to him mattered to her.

'Isn't it beautiful?' he asked as they rode on through golden dunes with chocolate shadows.

'It's fabulous,' she said as a hawk soared overhead, calling piercingly to its mate.

Everything she'd seen so far was fabulous in Khalifa. The sun, as it dropped lower in the metallic blue sky, was fabulous. The warm scented air was fabulous. This experience of riding a horse that she'd been so scared of and now loved and appreciated was fabulous. Khalid loved Khalifa and she loved him.

So much, so dangerous, Millie thought. Where did she imagine this was leading? She wasn't stupid. She'd be going home soon. Her dreams of becoming a marine engineer had been put on hold, but she'd pick them up when she went home, while Khalid's destiny kept him here, wrapped up in a life of duty, which he would never renounce.

He would need a wife to sit beside him on the Sapphire throne.

She actually shuddered at the thought, and couldn't bring herself to picture the woman who would support him in everything he did; give him children, live with him and love him. His marriage was sure to be reported in the press, and she would have to be happy for him. It wouldn't be easy, but was the price she had to pay for this...

She stiffened with misery, and that was enough to alert Khalid to a problem. 'Are you all right?' he asked. 'There isn't far to go now.'

She'd gone far too far already, Millie thought. How would this highly charged expedition end? In tears? Or triumph? In understanding? Or in the same fog in which she had instigated their meeting when the *Sapphire* returned to King's Dock? She had never been happier than she was now. Wasn't that enough? Some people didn't have this much. Was she being greedy? Weren't a few days of true happiness better than none?

Khalid had slowed the pace of his stallion, and his arms were gentle as she rested back against his chest. Did he feel the same need she did to stretch every second remaining to them into an hour, a day, until there were no days left?

Perhaps sensing that her thoughts were racing on into the future, he reined in at the top of a dune, and asked, 'Why don't you tell me about your ambitions?'

Millie was speechless as she looked at the view. Miles of rolling sand dunes, with what appeared to be a lush, green park right in the middle of them. And in the centre of that, there was a glittering oasis, like a wide, tranquil, crystalline lake, hidden away in the heart of the desert.

'Your ambitions?' he prompted.

It seemed mundane to talk about her college course after that, or the complexities of a boiler and the satisfaction of tinkering with an engine and hearing it throb into life. But that was her life, Millie thought. And she loved her life. This was Khalid's life.

'Miss Francine's been kind to you?'

'Miss Francine is the best woman in the world,' Millie exclaimed sincerely. 'More than a surrogate mother, she's been the grandmother I never knew, as well as my friend and the special person I confide in, and know I can turn to if ever there's a problem.'

'I hear she turns to you.'

'You hear a lot of things,' she remarked with amusement.

'And your ambition to be a marine engineer? You could work on my ships.'

'How many do you have?'

'Enough to keep you busy.'

Millie smiled. Khalid truly lived in another world. 'I love to see the way things work,' she admitted. 'Making them run more efficiently is my passion. A new engine is like a new friend to me. I can't rest until I know what makes them tick, and how I can help them.'

'A noble career,' he commented. 'Lucky friends, lucky engines.'

She laughed. They both laughed. He nuzzled her face in a way that felt so intimate, and then he turned Burkan and rode on.

Millie was quite open about her hopes and dreams when it came to her career, but what did she do for entertainment? he wondered, having discovered that he cared more than he should.

'I'm a bluestocking,' she said when he asked the question. 'I read, study, read some more.'

'But you must go out?'

'Are you jealous?' she asked, turning in the saddle to stare at him.

Yes, he was, he discovered. 'Would you prefer me not to be?'

'I don't think that's in your nature. You're a warrior through and through.'

She was correct. The thought of another man touching Millie roused him to a passion he wouldn't have believed.

'I love Miss Francine,' she volunteered, perhaps wanting to bring the tension level down. 'So I rarely go out during my holidays.'

'You made an exception for me?'

'Of course I did,' she said easily. 'Don't pretend you're surprised.'

'I'm not surprised. Being as devastatingly irresistible as I am—'

'You are,' she said, turning to give him a frank look. 'At least, to me.'

She was so open it twisted the knife in a heart that must turn cold towards her, to protect Millie from the reality of their respective destinies. They rode in silence for a while after that.

'During term time,' she said eventually, 'I'm far too busy studying to have time to socialise.'

He was relieved in one way, but not in another. 'You need a life, Millie.'

'I have a very good life, thank you,' she returned briskly. 'And my private life is—'

'Yours to know and mine to imagine?' he suggested in a relaxed tone.

'Exactly,' she agreed.

There was only one certainty, and that was that she was in over her head, Millie concluded. It was impossible to be this close to Khalid and not care about him, and her caring ran deep. She was falling a little more in love with him with every passing minute. It was no use pretending. She was his, and she was devoted to him. Maybe she couldn't have him long-term, but her heart didn't care about that.

'Look,' he said, distracting her.

She turned her head quickly, maybe too quickly as she followed his pointing finger, and just for a moment she felt dizzy and disoriented. It was a strange feeling... something she'd never felt before, but her head quickly cleared in time for her to agree with him that no photographic images could ever have prepared her for the reality of an oasis. They had rounded the base of a dune, and now she could see it spread out in front of her, like a sapphire set in gold. She couldn't even see the far side, and hadn't imagined it was so big. The water was so clear she could see the dark rocks underneath. And another Bedouin tent had been erected on the sugar-sand shore. The pavilion might have come straight from her dreams with its billowing blindingly white sides set against the blue of the water and the lush of the green shrubbery.

'Swim?' Khalid suggested as Burkan began to toss his head at the scent of water. 'We all deserve it, don't you think?'

He didn't expect an answer, Millie thought as Burkan took off down the dune. She screamed, but with excitement as the big horse almost lost his footing. How they stayed on board, she had no idea. Somehow Khalid managed to control the powerful stallion as it slithered and then righted, before slithering down again, and not for one moment did she feel in any danger. Between Khalid and his big horse, which was almost like an extension of himself, she knew she was safe.

'Okay?' he asked when they finally arrived panting and snorting—she was panting, horse was snorting—on level ground.

Laughing with shock, fright, happiness and excitement, she exclaimed, 'I'm fine. That was amazing.' This adventure might be reckless, and very dangerous to her heart, but every second was blissful, and she would remember it all her life. 'I'm better than fine,' she exulted as Khalid set her safely on the ground.

'But stiff, I imagine,' he said with a keen look as she took her first staggering step.

That feeling was back, and with it an overwhelming tiredness. It had been a long ride, she reasoned. What she needed was a dip in that oasis. 'So long as I don't stay like

this,' she said, laughing as she added a theatrical groan,
'I'll be okay.'

'You need that swim,' he said.

'I truly do,' she agreed as they linked fingers.

'Now, take off your clothes while I untack the horse,'
he instructed, yanking her close.

'Yes, Your Majesty.' She stared up into Khalid's dark,
mesmerising eyes. 'Do you have any more instructions
for me?'

'I will have. You can depend on it.'

She had no doubt.

When she joined him and he gazed down at Millie's naked
perfection, he thought himself the luckiest man on earth.
Showing no fear of Burkan, she scratched the stallion beneath his chin, while the one-man horse, fierce and unso-
ciable, nickered with approval.

'You've won him over,' he said. 'I'll make a Bedouin
of you yet.'

'Burkan won *me* over,' Millie argued, with an approv-
ing look at his horse. 'Maybe I'll make an engineer out of
you,' she added with a sideways look.

'I mine sapphires,' he reminded her, 'and so I always
have need of top-notch engineers.'

'So I can tinker with your boats *and* with your engines
in the mine.'

'Why not?' They both knew this was a game, and would
never happen, but why not play it out? 'You can tinker with
anything you want to,' he said as he brought his robe over
his head and tossed it aside. Taking hold of her hand, he
drew her close as he led her towards the water.

'Is this a dream?' Millie asked him of the oasis. She
dipped her toes as he sprang onto Burkan's back. Swing-
ing Millie into his arms, he rode full tilt into the chill of

deep water. Millie shrieked with the shock of it, and he laughed and held her close as Burkan lunged forward and began to swim. Steering the big horse towards the shade of the overhanging palm fronds, he urged him up the bank and dismounted. Lifting Millie down, he left the stallion to crop grass and rest.

'This is heaven,' Millie exclaimed softly as she rested briefly against Burkan's side to stroke him appreciatively. 'And if it is a dream, I never want it to end.'

And neither did he, but it must, he thought.

How could she not respond to a man as brutally masculine as Khalid? And so gloriously naked. Primal instinct would always triumph over common sense, Millie concluded as Khalid looped his powerful arms around her waist. He was holding her in a tantalisingly loose grip that she could have walked away from at any time, but he knew she had no intention of going anywhere. His seduction techniques were many and various, as she had learned, and she hadn't encountered one yet that wasn't fiendishly effective.

They stood in silence for a while, but that silence was so deep and intense, she could hear both their hearts beating as one.

'I want to make love to you,' he said at last. 'I mean, really make love to you.'

'What are you saying, Khalid?' Hope filled her.

'Don't you know?'

'Not unless you say it.'

'I love being with you, Millie Dillinger,' he murmured as he nuzzled her cheek and neck.

That wasn't what she'd hoped to hear. *Get over it.* Get real, as her friends at the laundry would say. Urgent pulses of sweet pleasure were teasing her body beyond endurance. Why did she have to think further than that? Of course

he wanted to make love—have sex—it was all just termi-
nology; a choice of words. She did too. Their bodies were
tuned to each other's needs, and the urge to mate wouldn't
leave them alone, until they were sated.

And that dose of reality helped her emotions how?

'I want you,' she whispered as Khalid backed her towards the shade. 'So much,' she added truthfully, feeling
tears sting her eyes as he lowered her to the ground.

The grass was firm and warm beneath her back after
the chill of the water. Their faces were close, so close their
lips were almost touching. Her mouth was kiss-bruised and
tingling as her arousal grew. Knowing this, he smiled and
kissed her. She was his to do with as he wished.

Lowering himself carefully, he brushed his body against
hers. Anticipating his weight, his heat, his strength, was
almost the best part.

'No,' he warned as she positioned herself for pleasure.
'I must protect you first—'

'I can't wait!' she protested.

'You must—'

'No!' It wouldn't be the first time with Khalid that she'd
pushed the boundaries. Passion as fierce as theirs could
accept no boundaries or restrictions. Drawing up her legs,
she arced her hips and drew him deep. Holding him secure
with her inner muscles, she worked him mercilessly. Digging her fingers into his arms, she bit his neck and shoulder, growling to express all the frustration inside her. The
end came quickly in a cataclysmic release. Khalid swore
viciously as he fell back on the grass, but when she turned
to look at him, he was smiling.

'Animal,' he said, making it sound like the greatest
compliment possible. 'What are you? A sorceress? A siren?
A witch?'

'A laundress,' she said.

He laughed as he pulled her across to lie on top of him. 'A very special, and very dangerous laundress,' he observed, 'and one whose talents must never be allowed to go to waste.'

'What do you mean?'

'We need teachers in Khalifa, experts in their field who can inspire our young people. I can think of no one better than you to fill that role.'

'I'm not an expert yet,' Millie pointed out.

'But you will be,' he enthused, 'and we need you in Khalifa. We have an excellent engineering college—'

'What are you saying, Khalid?' she interrupted sharply. Couldn't he see the truth? Her future didn't lie in Khalifa. 'I have a course to finish in the UK.'

'And when you have finished, come and work for me.' The fire of desire and bold intention blazed fiercely in his eyes. Khalid was used to conquering problems, and couldn't envisage a situation that wouldn't bend to his will, Millie thought. 'We're always looking for new ideas, and ambassadors to spread the word.'

'No,' she said quietly. How could she be close to him and not part of his life? 'But thanks for the offer. I really appreciate it.' She tried her best to sound sincere, and untouched emotionally by Khalid's suggestion that she could live in his beautiful country, perhaps within a stone's throw of the palace, and not have her heart break in pieces. She didn't want to hurt him, or seem ungrateful, but neither could she face the heartache that would bring.

'My loss,' he said thoughtfully.

And mine, Millie mused.

Khalid's stroking touch was more gentle than usual as he brought her to rest on his chest, as if his thoughts were plaguing him, and he was still on the hunt for a solution. She couldn't bear it, and had to tell herself not to cry. You can't have everything you want, and nor can he, she told herself firmly. *But she only wanted this*, and it seemed so unfair that she couldn't have it, Millie thought as Khalid stroked her hair, reassuring her, as if he sensed her distress.

It was as if they were already saying goodbye, she realised. A great surge of distress accompanied this thought, and threatened to overwhelm her. She had to be strong. She would be.

They swam again, and it was lovely and cleansing, and the tiredness she'd experienced after the long ride had fallen away. But there was sadness too. After a lifetime of carefully guarding her emotions, she was finding it harder and harder to hide them, and this was beginning to feel like the final act in a play. Being alone in the desert with Khalid had undoubtedly strengthened the bond between them. Whether that was good or bad remained to be seen. Feeling like this after making love was wonderful—so why was she crying again? Millie wondered as she floated on her back in the cooling water, gazing at the sky. She had to pull herself together and fast. She'd always known they would have to go their separate ways to live their very different lives. And she would always feel different, as if part of Khalid would never leave her. A sense of rightness and completeness filled her, taking over from the tears. It was a feeling she would have to try and remember for always and ever, she accepted as she tried her best not to think about returning home.

'Come on,' Khalid prompted when she shivered involuntarily. 'You've had enough swimming for today. You must eat something now.'

'To keep up my strength?' she teased, wondering why just the mention of food should make her stomach churn.

Khalid soon made her forget. Drawing her into his arms

where she felt safe, he made sure that the only hunger she felt was for him.

Don't play with fire.

Why not? Brushing away the shadows that briefly darkened her elation, she put on the fresh robe that, miraculously, or so it seemed to Millie, had been laid out on the bank for her, together with a robe for Khalid, as well as towels for both of them, and simple sandals to slip on. Millie's robe was so pretty. Diaphanous rose-coloured silk, it was a perfect foil for Khalid's stark black. What else would a hawk of the desert wear? she thought as he turned to look at her. Then it occurred to her that there must be invisible helpers, and she glanced around red-faced with embarrassment at the thought that they might have been watched. 'I thought we were alone,' she exclaimed.

'We are.' Khalid shrugged, unconcerned.

'And the gold table covered in a crisp white linen cloth?' She'd just noticed it now. 'Did Burkan set the table for us?'

'He's a horse of many talents,' Khalid told her straight-faced.

And the line of tents and portable buildings that had been erected in the shade behind the dune? How had she missed those? She'd been too preoccupied with Khalid, Millie realised. Of course the ruling sheikh of Khalifa would have staff and security wherever he went, and she was naïve for not knowing this from the start. A little more discretion would be required in future, not to mention muffling her screams of pleasure, she thought as Khalid took her by the hand.

'No one will disturb us,' he promised with a long stare into her eyes. He confirmed this with a lingering kiss, but the shadows were back. What was the point of trying to pretend they were lovers on the bank of an oasis, with nothing to stand between them and their passion, when there was an entire tented city at Khalid's beck and call, just a few yards away?

Duty first, duty always, Millie thought as he excused himself to check with his people if there were any outstanding issues to be dealt with in Khalifa before they settled down to eat.

I love you, she thought as he strode away.

Turning, she entered the royal pavilion on her own. She'd better get used to that feeling of being alone. She loved him madly, deeply, passionately, but must keep that to herself. Khalid had always made it clear where his duty lay, and, wonderful though this trip to the desert had been, their time together was almost over.

CHAPTER ELEVEN

DETERMINED TO MAKE the most of whatever time was left, Millie kept a lookout for Khalid's return. She blenched to see him arriving with a group of grandly dressed men. Quickly retreating into the private section in the depths of the pavilion, she remained by the dividing curtain to listen. It could only be a deputation from his court. Khalid brought them inside, and she could tell by the tone of his voice that he was furious.

'I gave clear instructions that I was not to be disturbed while I was in the desert. Speak in English,' he rapped when the leader of the men, with an obsequious bow, began to say something. Khalid knew she was here, and he wanted her to hear everything. It filled her with warmth and confidence to know he was protecting her even now. Though the sense that they would be parting soon hadn't left her, and her heart was aching with real physical pain.

'Forgive me, Your Majesty,' the same man said. 'Urgent news from the capital.'

'Which is?' Khalid demanded, looking every inch the hawk of the desert as he spoke, Millie saw as she stood in the shadows.

'Another bridal party has arrived, this time from a Mediterranean kingdom—'

She heard Khalid's sound of disgust. 'Have these people

no manners? Are they so desperate to offload their daughter? That's enough. They have been told not to come, and nothing has changed.'

'We know you had forbidden this, but the Mediterranean royal family decided to bring the Princess, anyway.'

'In direct contravention of my wishes.'

'Yes, Your Majesty.'

A Mediterranean princess, Millie thought. She could imagine someone beautiful, who had been groomed to rule at Khalid's side—not a tomboy with oil on her overalls. She had always known this would happen. There was no point in getting upset about it. She shouldn't feel so brutally let down. Khalid had done everything he could to protect her, and she had always known what she was getting herself into. He had never misled her for a moment. Her broken heart was all her own doing.

He was still talking, but in a muted tone, and in his own language. To her ears, he seemed calmer, happier. Perhaps the Princess was very beautiful and he'd relented. Digging her fingers into her palms until her nails cut the skin, she was glad he was talking in Khalifan. She couldn't bear to hear the truth as written by her imagination.

'Take refreshments before you go,' she heard Khalid say in English. 'I will follow you back to the palace in due course.'

She clung to the tent pole, feeling dizzy as she waited for the men to leave. Being hidden in the pavilion should have been wake-up call enough. She could only ever be hidden away. She could choose to be his mistress, even now. The offer had never been rescinded. Think of the engines she could work on, while she waited for him to find time for her.

Even humour couldn't help her now, Millie concluded;

she was long past laughing at this situation. And she couldn't fudge how she felt when he came to find her.

'Millie?'

Her head was swimming. For the first time in her life, she didn't feel strong, or capable, she felt faint, physically, mentally, and it must have shown. As if alarmed by her pallor, Khalid took hold of her arm and drew her to him. The pretence was over. A prospective bride with ironclad credentials was waiting at the palace in his capital city. There was no place for Millie in Khalid's life going forward. 'I've always known this had to end,' she said, smiling as she tried to make it easy for him. 'I just didn't think it would happen so soon. But,' she added in a fiercely upbeat tone, 'better now, and quickly, than death by a thousand cuts.'

'What on earth are you talking about?' he demanded. 'Didn't you hear me send them away? This is not the end, unless you want it to be the end. We can have as long as you want.'

As his mistress, she thought. A muscle flicking in his jaw betrayed his tension as he waited for her answer.

'You've spent too long away,' she said, 'and the country is missing you. It's time for us both to go home.'

He held her at arm's length so he could stare into her face. 'I don't regret a moment of this.'

That sounded like a death knell.

Dreams, she mused as she stared into Khalid's harsh, warrior face. They all had to end somewhere, and she would never hurt him by prolonging this. How could she hurt the man she loved?

'Nothing has changed,' he insisted. 'Those men answer to me.'

'But I don't,' she said.

There was a silence, as if he needed to come to terms with the fact that she wasn't a princess to be paraded in front of him for his approval, but Millie, the laundress, soon to be engineer, who made her own decisions.

Millie could deliver a rebuke with her silent defiance more effectively than with a million words. His men would go back to the palace, and send the Princess and her family away, but the damage was done. The expression in Millie's eyes said this idyll was over, and it wasn't up to him to change the rules. He would try to persuade her she was wrong, but Millie was her own woman, and would plough her own furrow. Wealth and status meant nothing to her. She looked for more meaning that that.

'The Princess is one of many my royal council has asked me to consider. Our constitution allows the royal council to choose a bride for me—'

'What?' Millie exclaimed.

'The law didn't trouble Saif. He would have his women and his bride—'

'And you're different?' she said, feeling faint, feeling unlike herself, feeling furious.

'I will change the law,' he said.

'In time?' And when he didn't answer, she added, 'I've no intention of waiting in line to learn if you're engaged or married. I have a life too, and I need to be getting on with it. I can't postpone everything each time you decide to go back to Khalifa to trial a prospective wife.'

'I have no intention of trialling anyone—'

'Then?' she interrupted, tight-lipped.

She brought him up short, staring at him with such trust, when he knew he could offer her nothing. There would be an engagement. His country expected him to make an advantageous marriage, and he couldn't put it off for ever.

'So, it's definite, then?' she said.

He couldn't lie to her and only briskly nodded his head.

'Why prolong the agony?' she demanded, lifting her chin, strong for both of them now. 'I should go, and so should you. This is over.'

Something tore in his heart as she said the words that needed to be spoken. 'I had planned to show you the desert.'

'As I had planned to learn more about Khalifa,' she agreed, 'but that will never happen now. I think we both have to be realistic.'

She'd come through so much. Why must he be the one to hurt her like this?

'Can you call for the helicopter, please?' she asked briskly. 'I'd like to leave now, or as soon as possible.'

He admired her so much. Nothing knocked Millie down, or, if it did, she soon bounced back again. 'I'll drop you at the airport when I leave,' he agreed stiffly, knowing she was giving them both an easy way out. But she flinched, and he supposed he must have sounded clinical. After the wild passion they'd shared the contrast to this was just too stark. But he couldn't hurt her, and the surest way of doing that was to keep her close.

'One more night,' he insisted, catching her close. 'I'm not asking your permission,' he added. 'This is a direct order. We have one more night in each other's arms.'

'No. I can't,' she said, shaking her head.

'Or, you won't?' he asked softly.

'Khalid, please, don't you think this is hard enough without spinning out the agony?'

He now proved how ruthless he could be, and seduced her.

'You don't play fair,' she complained in a shaking sigh.

'That's right, I don't,' he agreed.

The bed Khalid was backing her towards was composed entirely of down-filled pillows, covered in the softest, fin-

est silk. In this fragrant shaded cool, he laid her down
and then joined her as he continued to soothe and arouse.
She knew it was wrong, but who could resist him when
he lifted her and rested her buttocks on the cushions, and
spread her legs wide?

'No, we mustn't,' she said, thrashing her head.

'I'd say, we must,' he argued.

'It will only make things worse,' she said as she wa-
vered between reason and need.

'For you or for me?' he asked as he paused to protect
her.

'For both of us,' she gasped against his chest as he moved
over her.

It was always a shock when Khalid took her, he was
so big, but he was also careful, knowing that his size
was a consideration, before it became a pleasure. He'd
always taken care of her, she acknowledged as he sank
deep. Relaxing, she tightened her inner muscles around
him to hold him firmly in place, but he had an answer
for that too. Rotating his hips, he buffeted the tiny area
that always needed him. 'Now,' she begged. 'Don't wait.
I need this.'

Pulling back, he stared down. 'Are you ready?'

'Find out?' she said.

Bracing himself on his forearms so his weight didn't
crush her, Khalid thrust his hips forward and took her in
one, deep plunge to the hilt.

'Faster! Harder!' she cried to encourage him, and he
rewarded her by doing just that. Maintaining a steady
rhythm, he made sure that she extracted every single pleasure pulse, before launching her into an atomic release.
Even before she'd quietened, he'd turned her on her stomach. She lifted her buttocks to encourage him. Nudging her
legs wider, he pressed his hand into the small of her back

to raise them even more. Taking a cheek in each hand, he controlled her steady movements back and forth.

They made love through the night as if each second must be savoured, because very soon it would be their last.

'Wake up. It's time to leave.'

Millie blinked groggily as she slowly came to. At first, it seemed she didn't know where she was, only that Khalid was beside her. Groaning with contentment as the new day began, she reached for him.

'Not now,' he said, starting to get out of bed.

'Yes, now,' she argued. He'd made her insatiable. Something had changed in her body that made her need him more than ever.

'We have to leave soon,' he explained, but as their eyes met and she smiled into his, he relented. Drawing her into his arms, he kissed her with the utmost tenderness, and when he took her this time he was equally thorough and caring. 'I'm going to find it hard to be parted from you,' he admitted when they finally rested back with a contented sigh.

'But part we must,' she said, forcing brightness into her tone.

Was she laughing through her tears, or did she not care that much? This was a unique situation for him. He was always so sure of everything, but Millie was an enigma it would take a lifetime he couldn't give her to unravel.

Dropping a kiss on Khalid's shoulder, she tried to show that she could handle this. 'Shall we have one last swim?' she asked. She shrugged. 'We need to shower, so…?'

'There's no need to leave the tent,' Khalid explained. 'There's a bathing platform behind that curtain.'

'All mod cons,' she said lightly, turning to look to hide her tears. 'You've thought of everything,' she confirmed, turning back to face him as soon as she'd got her emotions under control.

'I try to,' he said, making things worse by dragging her close for a fierce, and maybe final kiss.

They linked fingers to walk the short distance across the rugs to the decorative cover he had indicated. Drawing it back revealed the shining lake of water.

'Wow,' Millie breathed. 'I'm never going to get used to this, and I'm going to miss it so much.' How much he'd never know.

'You can swim in the shallows without anyone seeing you,' Khalid said as he led her forward. 'I hope your private bathing area meets with your approval, Ms Dillinger?'

He swept her a mock bow and now those tears were threatening again. But no way was she going to weaken. They should part as friends, not discontented lovers.

All well and good, she thought as they stood in the pearly light of dawn, staring out over the most incredible panorama of waking desert and limpid oasis. If this was the last time they swam together, she was going to make the most of it and the future would have to wait.

Khalid's outstretched hand invited her to join him. They linked fingers again and walked to the water's edge. One last time, she thought as they waded in together. The water was like a warm bath, but they were silent as they swam, as if both of them knew that the time for games and laughter was done. They returned to the tent to be greeted by the delicious scent of cooked food and good coffee. A stack of clean towels and fresh robes were waiting for them. Khalid's people were discreet, and intuitive too, she thought.

'The best staff in the world,' he confirmed when she expressed her gratitude.

Removing the beautiful robe, she hung it up with care, regretting the fact, for the first time in her life, that it was back to oil-smeared overalls, and she would never wear a beautiful Khalifan robe again. She dressed quickly in travel clothes, just jeans and a top, and a sweater because it would be cold when she arrived in England. She took one last look around at the beautiful tent filled with exquisite artefacts. Even the sapphires in the gold bowls didn't trouble her now. The past was the past, and it was time to face the future.

'Do you mind if I take a picture?' she asked.

'Why?' Khalid said, frowning.

'To remember all this,' she explained.

'Will you forget so easily?'

There was hurt in his eyes. Goodness knew what he could see in hers. 'No,' she said. 'I won't forget. But when I'm an old lady, it will be nice to reminisce.'

'To remind yourself that this actually happened?'

They stared at each other, both wanting to say more, but the sound of rotor blades intruded. Perhaps as well, Millie thought. 'Is that our lift?' she said, trying to sound casual.

'Yes,' Khalid confirmed.

That single word, and the way he said it, ripped the heart from her chest and made her wonder how much more she could take without breaking down. Everything, Millie thought. She'd take everything. She was strong and would remain so. It was the only way to be.

'Are you tired of my company?' Khalid teased.

Never. She would never tire of him, never forget him, never fall out of love with him, she thought as his hawk-like stare burned steadily into hers. But she was aching with tension and needed to leave. Why prolong the agony for either of them? Khalid was as tense as she was. She had never seen him so tightly wound.

'This is torture,' she admitted.

There was a moment when they stared at each other, and

the next moment she was in his arms. 'I'm not ready to part with you!' he ground out in a voice hoarse with passion.

'Then, you're not being fair,' she said. Removing herself from his arms, she stared up. 'You can't always have what you want, Your Majesty. A country depends on you.'

Khalid had to be strong for everyone, she thought as his hawk-like stare stabbed into hers. 'I don't want to hurt you, Millie. You've had too much trouble in your life, and I hold myself responsible for much of that.'

'Then, don't,' she said. 'I'm responsible for my actions. I chose to be here. I chose to listen to what you had to tell me about my mother, and it was my decision to stay. But I've always known we can't have a life together. Don't worry,' she added brightly, dredging up resolve from the depth of her soul. 'I won't let history hold me back, or you, for that matter. What we had was good, but it's done now. You have to let me go. I mean it, Khalid,' she said when he looked shocked. 'Let me go.'

'Are you serious? That's it? Done? Just like that?'

'I am.' She guessed he'd never been on the receiving end of a refusal before. She continued quickly before her heart overruled her head. 'Did you think I wouldn't be able to live without you? I won't become your mistress. I have a good life back in England, and people who love me. I'm working towards a job I enjoy—'

'So you don't need me,' he supplied.

'Exactly,' she confirmed with a thin smile.

'Good,' he said tonelessly. 'I could ask for nothing more for you.'

Parting from him was the hardest thing she'd ever had to do. Killing off all hope of a future, or reconciliation was worse.

'If that's what you really want,' he said.

He had to be sure, she thought. There could be no going

back now. Her next words would end this. 'It is what I want,' she said. 'We both know it's the only way forward, and best for both of us.'

That might be right, but no one could steal her memories away. They would stay with her for ever.

CHAPTER TWELVE

It was back to earth with a bump when Millie walked into Miss Francine's laundry. She'd gone straight back to college from Khalifa, needing time alone to get her head straight, and had bunked in with a new student who asked no questions, not even when Millie had carelessly left packaging from several pregnancy tests in the bin. Bloating, feeling sick in the morning, suffering from a severe dose of emotional incontinence, as well as sore breasts, could not be ignored for ever and she'd taken her first test the week she got back. And the result was positive. All five had been positive.

Having scoured the news each day, she'd found no announcement of an engagement in Khalifa. But that meant nothing, Millie thought, as Lucy's head shot up with surprise as she walked in. Everyone was staring at her, and trying not to. They must be wondering how she felt about her time in the desert with the ruler of Khalifa. Nothing travelled faster than bad news, but confirmation of her pregnancy was the very best of news, so no one at the laundry knew about that yet, not even Miss Francine. Millie couldn't wait to tell the elderly woman who'd done so much for her that Miss Francine was about to become a grandmother. Now it was just a case of finding the right moment to inform the mighty ruler of Khalifa that he was about to become a father.

Millie and Lucy hugged warmly, and then Millie asked about Miss Francine.

'In her office,' Lucy said, adding worriedly, 'with her lawyers.'

'Lawyers?' Millie echoed with concern.

'Go and join them, and then you can tell me what's happening,' Lucy whispered so their colleagues couldn't hear. 'You're like a daughter and she's missed you. Here, let me take your things. It doesn't look good,' Lucy added with a glance at the firmly closed door to Miss Francine's office.

'Millie!'

Lucy was right. Miss Francine couldn't have been more relieved, or happier to see her, but Millie was disturbed to see how frail she looked. She could feel her ribs through the thin cardigan and blouse as they embraced. When they parted, Miss Francine introduced Millie to the two lawyers sitting in front of the desk. 'Mr Frostwick's firm has worked in my best interest for years,' she explained to Millie, 'but I've given him a real problem this time.'

'Can you tell me about it?' Millie asked her old friend gently, with an enquiring look at the two men. What could have gone so badly wrong while she was away?

Miss Francine lost no time explaining. 'I've been advised by my doctors to retire from the business with immediate effect. And with no one to take over from me…' She spread her arms wide. 'Millie is studying to be a marine engineer, you know,' she told the Frostwick team with all the warmth of a proud mother.

'I'm on holiday from college, so I can stay and help out,' Millie offered.

'It might not be enough,' the older of the two lawyers commented gruffly.

'And I won't hear of it,' Miss Francine said, closing that avenue down. 'You've worked too hard to give up now.'

'I'm not talking about giving up, just taking a longer break,' Millie soothed.

'The business will have to be sold,' the lawyer cut in. 'There's no money to save it,' he added bluntly, 'unless you have a suggestion,' he said as he stared at Millie.

If the business was sold, Miss Francine's name would be lost, Millie thought, and a lifetime's work would count for nothing. 'Could the name be retained, perhaps?'

The flash of hope in her old friend's eyes stabbed Millie in the heart. She could come up with as many suggestions as she liked, but if only money would save the laundry—

'I'm afraid the name can't be kept if an offer is accepted from one of the big chains,' the lawyer was saying, crashing into her thoughts, 'and the creditors will insist on a sale. There's been a lot of interest,' he continued on a brighter note. 'Miss Francine's reputation is second to none—'

'Of course it is,' Millie interrupted, seeing how distressed her elderly friend was becoming. Millie had been too young to help her mother, but nothing would get in the way of helping Miss Francine. 'I'll sort it out,' she said in a tone that brooked no argument. 'And now I think Miss Francine needs to rest.'

'Of course,' the lawyers agreed, standing up. 'We'll be in touch.'

'Don't worry,' she told Miss Francine as soon as the door had closed behind the visitors. 'I meant what I said.'

Miss Francine gave a grateful smile, which at the same time seemed to accept there was nothing *to* be done. Millie had other ideas. There was one person with enough money to put this right, and, after everything Miss Francine had done for Millie, she was going to enlist his help.

Ask Khalid for money when she'd broken off with him? See him again? Speak to him? He wouldn't even take her calls. He'd wanted a clean break too.

She wouldn't let Miss Francine down. Her elderly friend deserved a far better end to her working life than this. She didn't waste any time placing the call to Khalid. The sooner she got it over with, the sooner she could…well, if not exactly relax, at least satisfy herself that she'd tried every avenue.

Khalid answered on the second ring. She might have thought he'd been waiting for her call, if his comment hadn't been quite so crisp and short. 'I'll send transport for you,' he said.

'That's not what I want,' Millie said tensely. 'I'm not coming back to Khalifa.' She drew a deep, steadying breath. 'I'm asking for your help.'

'Money?' he said flatly.

'But not for me,' Millie said quickly, going on to explain the situation.

'Is money all you want?'

'Should there be anything more?' Of course there should! She had to tell him about the baby— Over the phone? No. She couldn't do that to him.

'Anything more?' he queried. In the pause that followed, she could picture him frowning.

'No. There's nothing more,' she confirmed, knowing she could never agree to his terms. Becoming Khalid's mistress while he lived with an arranged bride would break her, and that was even supposing he hoped for something more.

Millie's heart was in pieces to hear Khalid sounding so unemotional. It was as if he hadn't missed her at all— and why should he? They were still worlds apart, Millie concluded sadly, not only in the physical sense, separated by thousands of miles, but by a yawning gulf in their destiny. But she couldn't allow any of that to matter now. She had to try and do a deal with him, to save Miss Francine's laundry. Taking a deep, steadying breath, she hit him with her first idea.

'Would you have any objection to my putting Miss Francine's lawyer in touch with your Development Grant department? I thought that perhaps they could look at the possibility of franchising the business,' she went on. 'It would mean everything to Miss Francine to keep the name.'

'And she could be a figurehead?' the deep, husky voice at the other end of the line said thoughtfully.

'Exactly,' Millie agreed, relieved that he'd caught on so fast. She smiled to herself, thinking, when did the hawk of the desert ever have any difficulty in making a decision?

'I'll think about it, and let you know,' he said.

The line cut abruptly. She stared at the receiver in her hand, and only then realised that tears were streaming down her face.

Millie, Millie, Millie. Just the sound of her voice was enough for him to start cancelling appointments. Since the moment they'd parted, he'd realised that there was only one woman he could ever care for. To be a better man than his brother meant leading by example. It took time to effect change in an ancient constitution like that of Khalifa, but alterations would be made. On that he was determined.

He had omitted to mention to Millie the fact that he was in England. An invitation to dine with royalty in London at the palace tomorrow night to discuss various matters had prompted this visit. After talks and a dinner, a ball was to be held in his honour. Anticipating hopeful parents with a daughter to offload, he had planned to make his excuses and leave the palace before the ball. Hearing Millie's voice again had changed that decision.

* * *

Impatiently knuckling away tears, Millie replaced the receiver in its nest. There was no point cradling it, as if that could keep Khalid close. She had to be patient and wait to see if he would be as good as his word. She believed franchising Miss Francine's laundry would be a good investment, and could only hope that he agreed. But now she had work to do. Sprucing up the laundry to entice any investor was essential. She owed it to Miss Francine to make sure the business looked its best.

Everyone at the laundry was only too eager to repay Miss Francine's kindness by pitching in to touch up paintwork in rooms that hadn't been decorated for years. Millie's job was to check the machinery was working smoothly, and when they finished Miss Francine had promised a special supper to celebrate what she was already calling 'a new era' in the laundry's history, as if the deal to save it were already done.

Much to Millie's relief, her elderly friend seemed to have regained her former vigour, and brightened even more when Millie mentioned another idea she'd come up with, which was for Miss Francine to invite some of the workers to move into her spare bedrooms, much as Millie herself had done after her mother's death. Miss Francine was known for her soft heart, and many of the girls had experienced unpleasantness in their past like Millie. This would not only provide those who needed it with stability, but would give Miss Francine company and a little extra cash.

When their long day had finally ended, Miss Francine hurried out of the office with a printout in her hand. 'This has just arrived from the Sheikh's office,' she explained in a voice trembling with hope. 'His business development team is coming here to look us over!'

'That's wonderful,' Millie exclaimed as excitement rose around her.

Khalid hadn't let her down.

Maybe jobs would be saved, and the name of the laundry kept intact. The expression in Miss Francine's eyes was so full of happiness that it took hold of Millie's heart and twisted it hard.

'Do you really think we'll be okay?' she asked Millie.

'I know we will,' Millie said confidently as she plucked the pencil out of her up-do to tick another job off her list.

Everyone was laughing at each other's paint-streaked faces, especially at Millie's face, as she had added a good dose of black, greasy oil, and not just to her face, but all over the dungarees she'd been wearing to work on the boiler.

'I need to check one more thing,' Millie said as she climbed back into the tiny, spider-infested cubbyhole where the ancient boiler was housed. She would clean it out, once she had a minute—if that ever happened, Millie thought, grimacing as she stared around in the gloom. Brushing a web out of her hair, she checked the valve she'd replaced was working smoothly, and then carefully backed out of the confined space on all fours.

'Phew, it's hot in there,' she exclaimed as she emerged into the light. 'I'll have to set up a fan or something before the Sheikh's team arrives—'

It was the silence that alerted her to something out of the ordinary. Standing, she turned around. *'Khalid?'*

Millie's stomach clenched alarmingly and, turning away, she was forced to put her hand over her mouth.

One. Two. Three. Time up! Turn around.

'We were only speaking on the phone an hour or so ago,' she exclaimed heatedly, as if he were in the wrong. 'How on earth did you get here so quickly?'

'I'm overwhelmed by my welcome,' he said dryly.

His smoky, mocking tone, and those eyes...those all-seeing, darkly amused eyes, made her heart beat off the scale.

Was he really here? Their baby! How would he take it? I love you—so, so much. Oh, good grief, what do I look like with webs in my hair and oil on my face? I never thought to see you again, and now you're here—

And breathe.

'*No!* Don't touch me!' she yelped, backing away as Khalid, looking like the master of the sexual universe in a rugged jacket and jeans, advanced. 'I'm covered in oil and spiders' webs.'

As she spoke the room cleared as Miss Francine quickly ushered everyone out.

There was no stopping Khalid now. Closing the distance between them in a single step, he took hold of her arms in a non-negotiable grip, and, blazing a fierce look into her eyes, he demanded, 'Do you really think I care about a few spiders' webs?'

'You should—I mean, your expensive jacket—'

He snarled something in Khalifan that needed no translation, and dipped his head; he savaged her mouth with a kiss so deep, so firm and passionate, she almost swooned in his arms. When he let her go there was a moment she would never forget, when they stared at each other. So many frustrated hopes and dreams must be reflected in her eyes, while his were stonily determined. 'I can't do this again,' she whispered.

'Yes, you can,' he said. 'And you will.'

He was to marry some suitable princess. Why pretend? Millie's heart had already been dashed to pieces on the harsh rock of reality. But that didn't stop her heart aching with love, even as the more sensible part of her wished they could have remained continents apart, so she would never have to go through the grief of losing him again.

'You're coming with me,' he rapped.

'No, I'm not,' she argued, incredulity ringing in her voice.

'That wasn't a suggestion,' Khalid assured her. 'We've wasted enough time. Do you want my help or not?'

'At the laundry?' she said in confusion. 'Of course, I want your help. But not if you're blackmailing me—I'll find some other way.' She stared at him tensely. They had to get this straight.

Neither was prepared to back down, or give in. They were perfectly matched, she thought a little wistfully.

'You have a decision to make,' Khalid told her.

Think—think straight—make the right call.

She only had one shot at this. A lifetime of work had gone into the laundry, as well as all the precious lives Miss Francine strived so hard to put back on track. It wasn't just jobs at stake here, but people's futures and their happiness, and maybe even survival for some of her friends. She had to get this right. It wasn't about her feelings for Khalid, or even for her own self-respect; it was a bigger decision than all of that.

'Where are you going from here?' she asked tensely.

'To my London home,' Khalid told her succinctly, his eyes stern, his mouth firm.

Well, that wasn't too bad. It wasn't as far away as Khalifa. 'Can't we talk here?'

With a sound of impatience, *Sheikh* Khalid—for she could think of him as nothing else now, and in this setting—raked his hair. 'I can't just book into the local motel.'

He had a point.

'You wanted to discuss Miss Francine's case,' he reminded her. 'And *you* convinced me this meeting can't wait. *I* can't wait,' he added in a clipped tone. 'I have a country to run, and business at the palace in London. Either you come with me now, or I return to the capital without you, in which case you can go through the usual channels to apply for the grant.'

Millie's jaw dropped. 'You *are* blackmailing me.'

'I'm telling you how it is,' Khalid stated without emotion, though there was fire burning behind his eyes.

So much for romantic reunions, Millie thought, feeling her spirits dip even as her determination to do something right strengthened. 'I'll have to change my clothes—'

'No time,' he rapped. 'Everything will be waiting for you when we arrive. Go and say goodbye to your friends.'

Millie's mind was in turmoil. This was crazy. She was still getting over the shock of seeing him. And coming to terms with how much she'd missed him, she silently admitted. Khalid's stern expression held nothing but impatience, though his kiss had suggested he was pleased to see her, she accepted wryly. If she had a chance of saving Miss Francine's business, she didn't have a choice, and better she told him about the baby when they had some prospect of privacy in his London home. 'Ten minutes,' she said.

'Five,' he countered.

She fired a look into Khalid's fierce dark eyes, to let him know she'd do this, but was no pushover. He held her stare locked in his, and in that split second she knew there would be trouble ahead. Putting down her tool bag, she headed into the next room to break the news that she was leaving to her employer and friends.

CHAPTER THIRTEEN

NOTHING IN KHALID'S life was slow or ordinary, Millie accepted as she ducked down beneath the rotor blades before climbing into his helicopter. Having seen her harness was correctly fixed and her headphones in place, he took the pilot's seat, and before she knew it they were soaring over London.

Green areas were at a premium in the centre of the city, but the Sheikh of Khalifa owned a very large swathe of green, with an impressive dwelling, a palace, really, set like a jewel in the middle of the most fabulous grounds. There was even a lake, she noticed, and as the aircraft swooped lower she could see the bustle of a big city beyond his perimeter walls. The haven inside those walls reminded her of an oasis in the middle of a glass and concrete city.

What else did she expect of the hawk of the desert? Millie wondered as Khalid hovered the aircraft over the helipad set in a courtyard the size of two football pitches, before landing it precisely in the centre of the cross.

His voice came through the speakers. 'The building dates from Tudor times,' he said as he closed down the engines.

At least he seemed to have relaxed. 'I'm impressed,' she said truthfully.

'Wait until you see inside,' he added as the engines fell silent.

Khalid was right about the inside of the building. It was the most spectacular interior she'd ever seen. It was a disappointment when he didn't offer her a tour, and simply handed her over to the care of a smiling housekeeper.

She had thought they'd have some time together, Millie reflected as he jogged up the stairs. When was she going to tell him about the baby? Would she have to make an appointment to see him? This entrance hall was so grand, with its vaulted ceiling and acres of marble floor, that she felt like a very tiny cog in the huge engine of his life.

But the housekeeper was friendly as she escorted Millie to her suite of rooms. To her *fabulous* suite of rooms, Millie amended, trying not to overreact at each new revelation. While meticulous attention had been paid to ancient architectural detail, every gizmo and tech advancement was available to make life easy, though, of course, discreetly hidden away, she saw as the housekeeper opened a drawer in an antique chest to show her the controls for lighting and blinds, and heating and air con.

'You should be comfortable,' the housekeeper said with monumental understatement. 'And if there's anything more you need, please don't hesitate to call on the house phone.' Which was also cunningly concealed in a drawer in the nightstand.

Old English panelling gleamed with loving care, while Millie's feet sank into soft rugs as she stared around. She had loved the rich, vibrant colours of the desert, but she loved these muted pastels just as much.

'I hope you like your accommodation,' the housekeeper said warmly as Millie stared up at the colourful frescoes and took in the intricate plasterwork, and walls covered with silk, rather than paper or paint.

'I love it,' Millie enthused. 'These are the most beautiful rooms I've ever seen.'

'There's a view to the lake,' the housekeeper revealed as she drew the floating voile drapes aside.

'This is just exquisite,' Millie breathed as she trailed her fingertips across the top of a mahogany dressing table. And a world away from what she was used to. It only made the gap between her and Khalid seem wider.

'I ordered the scents—' she'd been trailing her fingertips across, Millie realised now, drawing her hand back fast as the housekeeper mentioned them '—from our most famous store in London. I wasn't sure of your taste, so I hope you like at least one of them?'

'I like all of them, and thank you for your trouble.' As gilded cages went, this surely had to be one of the most opulent and refined, though it was hard to see this as a cage or a trap. Khalid's housekeeper couldn't have been nicer. Any guest would feel welcome here.

'Nothing is too much trouble for His Majesty's guests, Ms Dillinger.'

And this was said so warmly it wasn't easy to think Millie was just the most recent in a long line of His Majesty's female guests. 'I'm sure not,' she agreed, returning the housekeeper's smile.

The tour continued into the bathroom, and then into a fully fitted dressing room.

'I have also taken the liberty of ordering a number of gowns for you to choose from for the ball tomorrow night.'

'The ball?' Millie queried. She gazed in incredulity at the glittering collection of fabulous gowns.

'His Majesty has been invited as guest of honour to a ball at the palace tomorrow evening,' the housekeeper explained. 'He thought you might like to accompany him.'

Millie was speechless. At first, she thought, I'd be like

a fish out of water. But then she remembered her friends at the laundry. They'd give their eye teeth to take a look around the palace, and she could tell them about it when she returned to King's Dock.

'I can't thank you enough for all the trouble you've gone to,' she told the housekeeper.

'Don't thank me, thank His Majesty—who sends his regrets, but he has business to attend to for the rest of the day and evening, and so he will meet you tomorrow evening at the ball.'

No chance to talk to him about the baby before then?

Arriving at the palace without an escort tomorrow night seemed an insignificant challenge compared to that.

'Would you like me to send up some food?' the housekeeper asked as she prepared to leave.

The mere thought of food was enough to make Millie's stomach churn. 'Some water would be nice.'

'And a light meal, surely?' the kindly housekeeper pressed.

She had to force herself to say, 'Thank you, that would be lovely.'

'Call down on the house phone if you need anything else. It's manned twenty-four hours a day, but there's iced water in the fridge in your dressing room, as well as a selection of soft drinks and snacks.'

Soft drinks and snacks? Millie's stomach turned over. In her current condition, fatty, sweet things were as attractive a prospect as a stomach bug at the ball, but she thanked the housekeeper with a warm smile, and when she'd left, walked into the bathroom to splash her face with cold water. Staring into the mirror, she knew she had to tell Khalid now. It couldn't wait. Not if she wouldn't see him until the ball.

'I need to contact His Majesty,' she told the impersonal voice on the other end of the house phone.

'I will inform his PA, madam. Is there anything else?'

'No. Thank you.'

She sat by the phone, and didn't have long to wait. 'Millie?'

'Khalid! Thank goodness.'

'Is something wrong?'

'No, but I need to talk to you, and not over the phone.'

'I thought the housekeeper would explain that I'm tied up.'

'She did, and I'm sorry to call, but—'

'Is it something urgent or can it wait?'

For nine months, Millie thought. Her blood was beginning to boil. Khalid had never had any difficulty making time for her when he'd wanted her in his bed. For the sake of the child inside her, she bit back her angry words. 'It's nothing urgent,' she confirmed.

'Then, I'll see you at the ball,' he said, sounding vaguely irritated.

'Until tomorrow night,' she agreed, directing this to an already dead line.

He had been granted the singular honour of standing next to the ruling monarch of the United Kingdom to receive the guests, but all he could think about was Millie. Their reunion had been disjointed and unsatisfactory, and now their second meeting would be carried out in front of a crowd. He hadn't realised how much he'd missed her until they were standing in front of each other and he'd stared down into that intelligent, combative, beautiful oil-stained face. He loved everything about her, even the pencil sticking out of her hair.

As good manners demanded, he returned his attention

to the line of guests as they moved at a snail's pace in front of him, but his attention kept straying to the grand entrance doors to the ballroom, with impeccably dressed attendants flanking them at either side. Millie would appear at the top of that gracious sweep of marble steps.

He hoped.

Each new arrival was announced before being escorted down the stairs by their companion. Millie had no one to do that. He had hoped to return to his London home to surprise Millie and escort her to the ball, but his meetings had run over. They were too important to miss when the future of Khalifa depended on their outcome.

He turned as his aide whispered in his ear, 'Ms Dillinger has arrived, Your Majesty.'

'Excellent,' he murmured, instantly on high alert.

From that moment on it was an ordeal to greet the guests politely and give them his full attention, when all he wanted to do was hunt for Millie. How frustrating, he thought with some irony, that of all the many things available to him, the one thing he wanted most was out of reach.

Light blazing from countless chandeliers had momentarily blinded Millie. When her vision adjusted, she took in the glittering throng in the ballroom, resplendent with light and gilding, and the glittering jewels of the guests. A vaulted ceiling stretched a dizzying height above her head, and was decorated with the most exquisite colourful frescoes. An orchestra was already seated, and waiting for the instruction to play. Even with these distractions, she needed no prompting to find Khalid. Her gaze flew to him like a heat-seeking missile, and as he turned to look at her she wasn't disappointed.

But had she chosen the right dress?

Maybe not…everyone was staring at her, and a hush had

fallen over the ballroom. Feeling exposed, she reviewed her choice of gown. She'd been careful not to choose anything too brightly coloured, or low-cut, or tight-fitting, and definitely not white. She didn't want Khalid getting the wrong idea. She needed his help at the laundry, and had to focus on that. She had to tell him about their child, and still dreamed that when she did he would be as excited as she was at the prospect of creating a new life.

The dress, Millie reminded herself as her name was announced and she started down the stairs. *It was fine.* Careful as she was, she'd still had a wide choice of gowns, and had chosen a dream of a dress in a subtle shade of forest green, for no better reason than it reminded her of the lush banks of the oasis. Composed of floating lightweight silk chiffon, over a foundation of the same shade, it was covered in tiny crystals that shimmered beneath the light of countless chandeliers, like sunlight on the ripples of a lake. It fitted her like a glove, but as she wouldn't be able to wear a close-fitting gown for much longer she'd looked at herself in the mirror before setting out, and thought, Why not?

Millie's presence had caused an electric response in the ballroom. Everyone felt it as they stared towards the entrance where she stood. She had no need of diamond tiaras or a royal title to cause a buzz. Her warm smile to the footman who'd shown her in said everything about Millie. She made people want to get to know her, and for her to share some of that magic dust. She was more than a beauty, she was a kind and lovely woman, and even as Khalid was thinking this an ambassador leaned across to ask him if he knew her. He was about to answer when an upstart prince seized his opportunity and, leaving the receiving line, strode at speed towards Millie, no doubt intending to escort her the rest of the way down the stairs.

She's mine!

The thought hit him like a freight train.

'Excuse me, Your Majesty... Ambassador—' A brisk dip of his head, and he'd left the line to chase after the Prince. Guests fell back at his approach, but his stare remained fixed on his goal.

Millie watched as the crowd below her on the dance floor parted like the Red Sea, first to admit the royal Prince, and then a tall, brutally masculine man in flowing black robes.

Khalid *and* the young man she didn't recognise were both heading her way!

Something made the younger man turn around. Seeing Khalid, he glanced at Millie. Quickly assessing the situation, he stepped back. 'You're a lucky man,' he said as the hawk of the desert swept past him.

Riveted by the drama, the crowd now turned to stare at Millie. She was halfway down the stairs, and had no alternative but to stand and watch. Or did she? Taking one of her famous executive decisions, she continued on down the stairs.

Khalid waylaid her. 'Take care,' he instructed, 'or you might tumble in those high heels. You look fabulous, by the way.'

For an instant, it was such a thrill to see him, hear him, smell him, touch him—and he was right about the risk of her tumbling down the stairs, while she was distracted by him—she didn't say a word. But then, making another executive decision, she placed her hand on his steadying arm. Fire streaked through her. She smiled. She should have known the effect he would have on her. 'Shouldn't you be with the royal party?' she asked, struggling to maintain her dignity while her body insisted on behaving with no dignity at all.

Touching Khalid sent pulses of excitement racing through her. This was the father of her child? It hardly seemed possible. The same man who didn't know yet, Millie reminded herself. The thought was like taking an ice-bath. She would tell him as soon as she could. It was important to let him know she wanted nothing from him.

But she smiled and the ball went on. No one, not even Khalid knew the thoughts in her head tonight. Taking his cue from their arrival on the dance floor, the conductor turned to the orchestra and raised his baton.

The rest of the night passed in a series of images she would never forget. A ball at the palace was everything she had dreamed it might be and more. The food was delicious, the music was sublime, and Khalid was...too perfect, at least for her, and that made her heart ache more than ever.

Being the Sheikh of Khalifa's guest was like holding the golden ticket, Millie discovered. Everyone greeted her with warmth, and a rustle of interest followed them around the ballroom. It was a very different world, and she appreciated the chance to be here, but tucked away inside her enjoyment of the evening was the niggling suspicion that people assumed she was just another conquest of an immensely powerful man.

'You're not fooled by any of this, are you?' Khalid remarked with his customary intuition as he escorted her to his table.

'Can you read my thoughts?'

'Always,' he said.

Now she knew that wasn't true, and smiled, relaxing. 'I keep some thoughts hidden,' she admitted.

'And I wouldn't change you,' he said in a serious tone as he waved the palace attendant away so he could hold her chair himself. 'I like you just the way you are.'

Their eyes met briefly, and Khalid's stare was so direct, she thought this was the moment to tell him—in a crowded ballroom, full of people who would love to overhear what they said? It would have to wait. 'Will you stay much longer?' she asked instead.

'I'm in your hands.'

That comment was no help at all. And then the rest of the dinner guests joined them, and it was impossible to get away, so she sat and talked and ate and danced, as if everything were as it should be.

When the royal party left, it was a sign that everyone else could leave, but she had to be sure that Khalid wouldn't disappear again when they reached his London home. 'Can we talk when we get back?' she pressed as he escorted her out of the ballroom.

'Of course,' he reassured her with a slight frown. 'I hadn't forgotten you wanted to speak to me.'

Though he could have no idea about the subject of that talk, she thought as he helped her into the rear seat of the royal limousine, with its flag of Khalifa flying proudly from the roof. And a uniformed chauffeur seated only feet away from them, which made confidential conversation impossible.

'You're very quiet,' Khalid commented as they drove smoothly through the London streets. Raising the privacy panel between them and the driver, he turned to face her. 'What's wrong, Millie?'

'I'm just tired,' she said, unable to meet his eyes. Telling him such momentous news in the back of a car, however grand, didn't sit with her any better than in a crowded ballroom.

'And you look quite pale,' he observed as the street lights flickered across her face. 'But I don't buy you being tired. You were the star of the ball. Adrenalin must be pumping through your veins.'

And it was, Millie thought, but for all the wrong reasons. After the intimacies they'd shared, telling Khalid that she was pregnant should have been the easiest thing on earth, but instead it was turning out to be the hardest.

'What is this mystery?' he asked. There was a pause, and then he said, 'Are you pregnant?'

Millie gave an audible gasp. Never one to shirk the truth, she could do no more than admit, 'Yes, I am.' She could only wait for his reaction and play off that, but Khalid remained silent until they reached his London home, where he helped her out of the limousine as if he'd learned nothing unusual that night, and ushered her up the steps with his usual care.

'Ten minutes,' he said, turning to face her when his butler opened the door.

She watched him jog up the magnificent mahogany staircase. He didn't look round, and there was no offer of a steadying hand. It should have been a relief to have her wonderful news out in the open, but instead she felt more diminished than ever as she stood in the magnificent vaulted hall.

Rubbish! She was about to become a mother. And that took guts. This was no time for feeling anything other than confident about the future. Once she had reassured Khalid she wouldn't make any call on him, he was sure to see she meant it and be relieved.

A child. They were having a child. Shocked at the enormity of this turn of events, he was fiercely excited. A baby was the natural consequence of so much sex, he reflected, and however careful he'd been, there had been times…

Releasing his grip on the back of the chair, he began

to pace his study. He needed time to think. Ten minutes wasn't long enough. This was as much emotion as he'd ever felt. Having grown up in a home where displays of emotion were frowned upon, his older brother, Saif, had been indulged, while Khalid, as the younger son, and by far the more spirited child, had largely been ignored, and consigned to the care of servants. By the age of seven he had learned not to yearn for the love of his parents, and had known that he would have to make his own way in the world. He'd studied hard to be the best he could be, and had gone on to serve his country in the forces, before going into business. Saif had never shown any interest in the sapphire mines, only in spending the money they produced, so it had been up to Khalid to bail out the royal treasury.

Duty remained as vital to him now as it had been then. The chance to have anything more than a formal royal life had never occurred to him, but before he could reassure Millie, he must open Pandora's box. He had no option now, but telling her everything about that night was a risk. It could destroy her; destroy all the trust she'd built and the confidence she'd gained. Withholding the truth would almost certainly drive her away from him, but he would never contemplate building a child's future on lies and evasion.

Having received the call to join Khalid in his study, she knew after he'd only been talking for a few minutes why he had wanted to keep things formal between them. 'Let me get this straight,' she said, holding up a hand to silence him. 'You've been receiving reports on me since that night?' She hated the way her voice quavered with shock.

'Every school report,' he confirmed evenly, as if this were completely normal, 'and every course you ever took. Every friend you made—'

'How *dare* you snoop on me like that?' she demanded, incensed.

'You were made an orphan that night,' he continued, ignoring her outburst, 'and I hold myself responsible for that. I felt protective towards you from the start, and I couldn't just turn my back on you and walk away.'

'So you paid for everything throughout my entire life.'

He remained silent.

'You thought it your duty,' she guessed bitterly.

'Miss Francine was more than eager to give you a home,' he argued in the same calm tone. 'She was already very fond of you, but that isn't an excuse for either of us to expect an elderly woman to bear the additional cost of housing you.'

'I never did,' Millie exploded. How dared he suggest such a thing? 'I always paid my way.'

'Yes, you did,' he agreed, 'but Miss Francine's finances were perilously balanced, and she still refused to take any money from me. The least I could do was cover your education.'

'So my scholarships—'

'You earned every one of them,' he stated firmly. 'Khalifa does not bestow grants where they are not deserved.'

'Khalifa?' One shock on top of another. 'I thought my awards came from the college. There was never any mention of Khalifa.'

'Nothing is ever done in Khalifa to garner public acclaim. Everything is low-key.'

The way he liked it, she thought, still trying to come to terms with the fact that Khalid of Khalifa had been a major player in her life since the day of her mother's tragic death.

There was a question she had to ask him. 'Was it guilt that made you do this?'

'Partly, yes,' he admitted.

'I would rather you'd told the truth to the court, than be here now.'

'I did tell the truth to the court.'

He had just left a lot out, knowing it would make the headlines and those headlines would live for ever, taunting Millie with the truth of her mother's death.

'You told your version of the truth,' she accused him.

'Doesn't everyone?' He opened his arms wide. 'The truth is always open to interpretation.'

'Not in my world,' she shot back bitterly.

'Some facts aren't helpful, Millie.'

'Like those that prove your brother guilty of murder?' she suggested with a short, humourless laugh.

'Someone else pushed your mother. I told you that it was her dealer.'

'But your brother drove my mother to the edge—he held that party—his guests mocked my mother. Whatever your lawyers said in court about my mother's fate being in her own hands—her own *shaking* hands,' she added hotly, 'surely someone could have saved her! *You* should have saved her! I should have—'

'You're torturing yourself unnecessarily,' he said as she broke off.

'Says the man who fathered my child!' she raged. 'You lied to me, Khalid. You've been lying to me since the day the *Sapphire* sailed back into King's Dock. I should have gone with my gut then, and stayed away from you.'

'Your gut told you to see me,' he argued quietly. 'And you did the right thing. You've never turned your back on a problem yet, so why start now?'

'Some things are better avoided? And you're one of them! Why couldn't you just tell me that you were going to be part of my life?'

'Would you have preferred me to feed the scandal sheets?'

'I would have preferred the truth,' she flared. 'It makes me wonder what else you're hiding,' she added with an acid glare. 'You saved your brother—'

'To prevent my country from being dragged through the mire,' he defended. 'After that was done, it was all about you.'

'And I'm expected to believe that.' Turning her back, she folded her arms, as if to contain her emotions. 'Well, now it's about me and my child,' she said, whirling around to confront him, 'which must be a considerable inconvenience for you.'

'It's nothing of the sort,' he assured her.

She threw him a sceptical look. 'I can just imagine the headlines: The Sheikh and the laundress expecting a baby, after the ruler of Khalifa returns to the UK to seduce the daughter of his brother's victim.'

'A rather long headline,' he observed, curbing his natural response. He knew it was hormones driving this rant, but that didn't make it acceptable.

'Don't make a joke of this,' she warned.

'And don't you live in the past. We have a child to consider now, and the future of that child is far more important than anything that's happened to us previously.'

Her lip trembled, and now he regretted pulling her up short. But not too much. What he had said was true.

'I'm sorry,' she said. 'I don't know why I thought I could discuss this with you calmly.'

'Because you can.'

'So long as I toe your line?'

'So long as you state your case clearly and I state mine. Now. It's been a long day for both of us. May I suggest we reconvene this meeting in the morning?' Before she could answer, he stood up and walked to the door. Opening it, he waited for her to leave. After a moment's hesitation, she did so.

'Nine o'clock tomorrow morning on the terrace for breakfast,' he said.

Lifting her chin, she walked past him without another word.

CHAPTER FOURTEEN

KHALID HAD BEEN watching over her all these years? Millie didn't know whether to be comforted or furious. Back in the beautiful suite of rooms that had been allocated to her in his London home, she was consumed by blind fury and hormones—and blind fury was definitely winning out.

She'd told him they were expecting a child, and his response had been that they'd talk about it in the morning? What was that about? This was the biggest thing that had ever happened to her: a baby, a family, a ready-made grannie in the shape of Miss Francine, and honorary aunts galore. She didn't need any more time to think about it, and she got his message loud and clear. He wasn't interested.

He thought she was overwrought? Just let him try and pay her off. Then he'd see her angry. No one was going to put a price on her baby. Wrenching her ball gown this way and that, she now discovered that the zip was out of reach. Forced to concede defeat, she realised she'd have to ask a maid to help her.

At one o' clock in the morning?

She couldn't ask anyone to get out of bed to help her undress. Glancing at the house phone—*palace* phone, Millie amended, rejigging her thoughts—she remembered the housekeeper said it was manned twenty-four hours a day.

If they'd tell her where the office was, she could go there and ask whoever was on duty to give her a hand.

Lifting the receiver, she waited for the call to connect. 'Hello, I'm—'

'Millie?'

She would have known that dark, husky voice anywhere. Why was Khalid manning the phones? 'Are you monitoring my calls now?' She sounded like a shrew with a nail in its pad.

A shrew with a hawk watching her?

Everyone knew what happened when a hawk watched a shrew.

'Can't you sleep?' Khalid sounded amused.

'Can't you?' she countered.

'I happened to be passing the office, and was alerted to a call from your room. Is there something wrong?'

'Nothing you can put right,' she assured him.

She had to calm down, Millie realised as the silence stretched on. Her hormones might be racing out of control, but she was a guest here and Khalid was her host, as well as the father of her child, *and* the best hope she had to save the laundry. And she could hardly blame him for her getting stuck in her ball gown. 'It's a practical matter,' she admitted crisply.

'Like you want a cheese sandwich?' he suggested with genuine interest. 'Being pregnant these urges are natural. The kitchens are open. Just call down—or I can put you through, if you like…?'

'If you must know—' and now she felt incredibly foolish '—I can't get out of my dress.'

'I'm sure I can help with that,' he said.

Before she had chance to argue the line cut, and seconds later, or so it seemed to Millie, who was pacing up and down, there was a knock on the door, and Khalid strode in.

'Do come in,' she flared.

He laughed. Why did he have to do that? She could never resist his laugh. He'd obviously taken a shower as soon as he got back, as his hair was damp. He had changed into casual clothes, jeans and a top. That was her clue. He couldn't sleep, either.

'It didn't take you long to get here,' the shrew inside her observed. 'Were you monitoring my door, as well as the phone?'

'Turn around,' he instructed calmly.

Khalid's fingers on the back of her neck were incendiary devices to her senses, creating delicious little shocks that went streaking through her veins.

Okay, so she'd let him help her with the zip, but then he must leave.

'You're very tense tonight, Millie.'

Well, that shouldn't come as a surprise to either of them, she thought as Khalid's hands rested on her shoulders.

'You were a sensation at the ball,' he commented.

'I think the company I kept made sure of that.'

'I disagree,' Khalid argued as he pushed the dress from her shoulders. 'You needed no help. You have your own very unique appeal.'

She stepped out of the dress, and was in his arms before she knew it. And now she was lost. One of the more enjoyable side effects of pregnancy was that it made her mad for sex.

'I can manage now, thank you,' she said primly, attempting to push him away, but her voice sounded hoarse and unconvincing. And when Khalid's arms were wrapped around her, escape was…incidental.

'I'm sure you can manage,' he agreed. 'The question is, do you want to?'

'You not going to dictate terms just because I'm pregnant,' she warned.

'And neither will you,' he assured her in a soft seductive whisper, with his mouth so close to the back of her neck she could feel his warm breath on her skin.

'What are you saying?' she demanded, reclaiming her hold on common sense as she turned to face him.

'Just that tonight you need to sleep, and you will do so in my arms.'

'You're very sure of yourself.'

Much surer than she was that she could resist him. 'And I'm to remain in your arms until you grow tired of me and send me away?' Angling her chin, she stared up at him. 'I don't think so.'

'I've got no plans to send you away,' he said, drawing his hands down her body until the dress fell away. He steadied her as she stepped out of it, and then stepped back.

'What are you doing?' she demanded.

'I would have thought that was obvious,' he said, maintaining caution-shattering eye contact as he cupped her between her legs.

'Sleep, you said,' she accused shakily. 'And then we'll talk in the morning.'

'You will sleep. I promise,' he said.

After sex, she thought as her body overruled her caution.

'You're so deliciously plump here,' he said as he cupped and soothed and teased, applying just the right amount of pressure until she was out of her mind with lust. 'You definitely need my attention before you can sleep,' he observed in a tone she found thrillingly matter-of-fact.

So much, Millie thought as Khalid suggested in an amused whisper, 'Let's go to bed, so I can show you how much you need this.'

'And then?'

'And then you sleep,' he said dryly.

'I mean, when you go back to your life and I go back to mine.'

'That's what I'm going to talk about in the morning.'

'Put me down,' she insisted when he carried her to the bed, but it was only a token struggle. She enjoyed the banter between them, as well as everything else. It was just a pity it couldn't last, but, as he'd once said to her, he was a man and she was a woman; *carpe diem*, seize the moment, or waste more of her life regretting.

Stripping back the covers with one arm, Khalid lowered her against the nest of pillows. Maintaining eye contact, he stripped off. Damn that mix of stern and wicked. She was lost. She wanted him. Even if it was just one last time.

'I won't hurt you,' he promised.

Any more than he had already, Khalid thought.

'Sex won't hurt the baby,' she told him. 'I read up on it.'

Emotions he'd never expected to feel welled up inside him at the thought that this was the mother of his child.

'Words hurt,' she said quietly, staring deep into his eyes. 'Actions hurt. Not telling each other the truth hurts.'

He said nothing, knowing the truth could be destructive, and he would never hurt Millie.

Stretching out his length beside her, he brought her into his arms. 'I'm not joking about sleeping. I don't want to hear another word from you until the morning.'

'Like that's going to happen?' she said.

'Close your eyes,' he instructed.

'Only if you touch me.'

'Hussy,' he growled, moving over her.

'Only for you,' she whispered as she wound her arms around him.

* * *

Millie blinked and realised daylight was streaming through the curtains. 'What happened?' she asked, looking around.

'You're still wrapped in my arms and I'm in no hurry to move away,' Khalid told her in a growly, morning voice. 'I've been watching you sleep.'

'Snoring?'

He pulled a wry face. 'Not that I could hear.'

'What are you doing?' she asked. 'I'm still asleep.'

'Not for long,' he promised.

Kissing and touching, he stroked and soothed her as she whimpered and sighed. It was all too easy to fall under his spell, but when she woke up and came to her senses, what then?

'Better?' he asked as she trembled in anticipation of more pleasure to come.

'No,' she said, trying to regain a grip on reality that didn't include the mighty Sheikh of Khalifa taking up a permanent berth in King's Dock.

'How about now?'

As Khalid sank deep, she lost control immediately, which made reasoned thought impossible. Wrapping her legs tightly around him, she worked as vigorously as he did to bring them both the satisfaction they craved. After making love, they slept again, and she woke in his arms. Khalid was still sleeping—or so she thought—when she slipped out of bed to shower and dress.

'Where are you going?' he asked.

She turned to see him resting his chin on his hand as he stared at her.

'Home,' she said quietly.

There was a pause, and then he frowned and said, 'Why?'

Because this was the perfect ending, Millie thought.

She'd spent so many teenage years dreaming and imagining that she knew exactly when the curtain should come down.

'There's nothing to be gained by staying any longer,' she said. 'We both know this can't go anywhere.'

'So you're leaving before we talk about the baby?'

'I'm sure you'll have your lawyers handle your side of the discussion.'

He looked astounded.

'I'll be ready for them when they arrive,' she promised calmly as her heart began to crumble like an iceberg in the sun.

'Is this because of some silly idea you have about me being a king and you being an apprentice?'

'Well, of course it has something to do with it,' she admitted. 'I'm hardly a suitable match. Don't you have an arranged bride on the horizon?'

Millie's heart shrank to the size of a pea as she waited for Khalid to reply. She could bear this, she told herself firmly. Whatever he had to say, she could take it.

'There's something I should have told you,' he said as he swung off the bed.

She prepared for the worst.

'That time…before the ball,' he began.

'When your meetings overran,' she supplied tensely. 'Were you…?' She had to brace herself to say the words. 'Were you discussing a marriage?'

'Yes, I was,' he admitted.

She swayed. He caught hold of her. 'I was discussing our marriage.'

'What?' she said faintly.

'It takes time to change the constitution of a country,' he explained as she stared up in bewilderment. 'That constitution has been changed to allow the ruler of Khalifa to choose his own bride. It's the way forward, Millie, not just for us, but for our children, and for all the future generations.'

'You did this for me,' she whispered.

'Yes, I did.'

'I don't know what to say,' Millie admitted.

'You're a self-made woman and an inspiration to everyone who meets you. And you're the mother of my child,' he added. 'The simple fact is, you're a woman and I'm a man. Do I need any more reasons?'

Perhaps one, she thought.

'And I love you,' he said.

Yes.

'I can't think of anything more important than that, can you?'

And neither could Millie. 'So…'

'So, you're not going anywhere,' Khalid said as he lifted her into his arms. 'You're staying here with me.'

'Well,' she teased, hardly able to contain her happiness, 'I suppose if I have to be anyone's captive—'

With a laugh, Khalid swung her around. 'That imagination of yours should be bottled and sold, and then I wouldn't need sapphire mines to make a fortune.'

'Another fortune?' Millie commented as her heart threatened to explode with love.

'Think of all the good you can do with my money.'

'Now, there's a suggestion I doubt anyone's heard before,' she admitted.

'Then, it's time you started thinking about it,' Khalid insisted, turning serious. 'You're the love of my life, and I want to share everything with you.'

'Are you asking me to believe that His Majesty the mighty Sheikh of Khalifa loves Millie Dillinger, oil-smeared apprentice, and sometime laundress?'

Khalid's mouth pressed down in the way she loved. 'A man called Khalid loves Millie,' he said, 'and that's the beginning and the end of it.'

'So, what are you proposing?'

Pulling back his head, he stared down at her. 'Marriage, of course.'

'Are you serious?' she gasped.

Lowering her to the ground, Khalid got down on one knee? 'Either that, or you've lost an earring. Marry me, Millie,' he said in a very different tone, 'and stand at my side for ever.'

'As your Queen?' Millie blurted, still shocked.

'As my wife,' Khalid corrected her. 'You're the only woman who is uniquely qualified for the job.'

'What qualification would that be?'

'You love me.'

'Well, yes, I do,' she admitted. 'So much it hurts.'

'Is that a yes?' Khalid demanded, his eyes burning with love and laughter. 'Can I get up now?'

'You *are* serious,' she said.

'Never more so,' he confirmed. 'I knew the moment that the young Prince hurried to escort you that I had to move heaven and earth to push that new law through. No one else could be my wife. No man could ever love you as I do. I intend to spend the rest of my life with you, and I want the whole world to know that I adore you. Starting with you,' he added softly as he cupped Millie's face in his hands.

It was a long time before they broke apart, and when they did, she remembered their talk.

'About this child or the next?' Khalid teased as he stroked her belly. 'Or all of our children to come?'

'Stop it,' she said, laughing. 'But what about my education?'

'I intend to continue that in depth.'

'I mean my college education,' she whispered against his wicked mouth.

'You can continue that at one of the best engineering colleges in the world.'

'In Khalifa,' she said.

'Exactly. If that's what you want.'

'It is what I want.'

'Good.'

'But where will we live?'

Khalid shrugged as he smiled and admitted, 'I have homes across the world. Where would you like to live?'

'In one of the transportable palaces,' Millie exclaimed softly as her imagination took her flying back to the desert.

'Maybe when the baby's a little older,' Khalid suggested. 'But we can take holidays in the meantime,' he added quickly when he saw her disappointment.

As Millie stared up into dark, beloved eyes, she knew there would never be anyone to compare with her Sapphire Sheikh, and that whatever else Khalid had to tell her about the past, they had a lifetime to understand and discuss it.

'I love you so much,' she said. 'I always have—right from that first moment when you came to my rescue like an avenging angel striding into the bowels of hell on board the *Sapphire*.'

'I never doubted it,' he said as he backed her towards the bed. 'And I love you so much, it's going to take a lifetime to prove it.'

'Starting now?' she said hopefully.

'Oh, yes,' Millie's darkly dangerous Sapphire Sheikh confirmed.

CHAPTER FIFTEEN

MILLIE AND KHALID'S arrival in Khalifa was a double celebration. Before their private jet had landed, Millie changed out of casual jeans and a lightweight top into a knee-length summer dress, garnished with a simple straw sun hat with ribbons streaming behind in the same blue as her eyes. Khalid had donned his regal royal robes of black and gold, with the crown-like *agal* holding his flowing headdress in place. They drove through streets lined with flags to herald a much-loved leader's return, in an open-topped limousine to the cheers of his people who were also celebrating the discovery of yet another rich seam of sapphires in the Khalifan mines. It was a sign, the elders had said, Khalid confided in Millie, that their leader's prospective bride would bring good fortune to their country.

'I've never been so happy,' Millie admitted. 'You love me, and that's enough,' she said as Khalid raised her hands to his lips. Which was exactly what she'd said when Khalid had placed the fabulous sapphire engagement ring on her ring finger. But he'd insisted, saying the sapphire was the same colour as her eyes. It was a huge and flawless blue, surrounded by flashing diamonds that sparkled and glowed in the blaze of the sun.

'Sapphires mean many things to many people,' Khalid had told her, when she'd said it was too much, and all she needed was him. 'To some they bring nothing but greed and grief, while to others, they foretell a lifetime of happiness ahead, and that is how it will be for you.'

She believed him, and knew that the wonderful ring was the start of their future together. The past could hold no more terrors for her. Their love had driven those shadows away.

'And now for the intimacy of the desert,' he said as the limousine turned into his private airstrip, 'where I will be joining you tomorrow.'

'The intimacy?' Millie queried, thinking of the vastness of the place she had chosen to pledge her love.

'Wherever we are, it's just the two of us,' he said.

The look in Khalid's eyes as he escorted her up the steps of the aircraft before parting from her thrilled Millie more than she could say. The prospect of being married to him still seemed incredible. 'How can I wait?' she whispered as he turned to go.

'I'll make sure you're well rewarded for your patience,' he said.

This was going to be the perfect wedding with the perfect guests and the perfect bridegroom, Millie thought, tense with excitement as her friend Lucy helped to put the finishing touches to Millie's flowing white lace gown, while Miss Francine made sure the diamond and sapphire tiara was safely secured in Millie's hair. Khalid had only insisted on one thing in his bride, and that was that she leave her pencil ornament behind, and replace it with the priceless coronet for their marriage ceremony.

They were still laughing over his innovative wedding gift, which was a comprehensive tool kit, just to let Millie know that she might be a royal bride, but she could still be called upon to mend a boiler from time to time. And his gifts didn't end there. There was a snowy-white pony waiting to greet her arrival in the desert, and when she joined her group of friends in the bridal tent, she found them cooing over a golden chest, studded with sapphires, which, when she opened it, was full of the most incredible jewels, as well as a stack of pencils. But the best thing of all was the news that Miss Francine's laundry had been saved, and was well on its way to becoming a highly successful franchise.

Not totally the best thing, Millie thought as she stepped out of the tent to find Khalid waiting for her, mounted on Bakran. 'You're not supposed to see me,' she exclaimed.

'Too late,' he informed her. 'And as it's your wedding day, I don't know why you're hesitating.'

'I'm not,' she said, seizing hold of his hand.

In seconds she was on the back of his fiery stallion, and, to cheers from her friends, they galloped across the desert to the shore of the oasis where the crowd of guests were waiting to welcome the Sheikh of Khalifa and his Queen.

EPILOGUE

Eight years, one engineering qualification,
four children, and a newborn baby later...

'A PENCIL IN your hair?' Khalid demanded as their oldest child, Luna, a gorgeous, bubbly tomboy, consulted her clipboard and frowned.

'The entire palace air-con needs a complete refurb,' Luna informed her father in a tone that exactly mimicked her mother's.

'And I know the very person to supervise these works,' Khalid said as he drew Millie close.

'I'm quite capable of supervising my own works,' Luna assured him.

'By pressing your brothers and sisters into work?' Khalid suggested fondly. 'Come on, time for bed.'

Millie helped him chivvy the children out of the family snug they had created in their magnificent palace in Khalifa. 'It's adult time now,' he added with a glance in Millie's direction.

Would she never get enough of this man? Millie wondered as she took in Khalid's magnificent physique, shown off to best advantage in snug-fitting jeans and a close-fitting top. He'd had taught her everything about love and trust, and feeling safe—as well as the most incredible sex.

'It's a very important part of marriage,' he told her when they had finished the bedtime stories and closed the door on their sleeping children.

'I would never disagree,' she said.

'Yes, you would,' Khalid argued dryly. Drawing her into his nearby study, he closed the door.

'I would never argue about this,' she whispered as he kissed her neck and backed her up against the wall. Dispensing with the clothes that stood in his way, he lifted her. 'But can I remind you that we're hosting a royal banquet in less than an hour.'

'Then, you'll have to be quick,' he said.

'With you?'

He shrugged. 'I'll make up for it,' he promised. 'Just concentrate and let me do the work.'

Okay, he was right. He hadn't even touched her yet, and she was already hovering on the brink. 'You've made me mad for you,' she said.

'Are you pregnant again?' he queried. 'That always makes you mad for sex.'

'*You* make me mad for sex,' she corrected him.

'That too,' he agreed.

'Modesty would become you.'

'But it wouldn't satisfy you.' And with that, he proceeded to tease her into an advance state of readiness. 'So. Are you pregnant?' he asked when she was quiet again.

'We can only hope,' Millie whispered.

'And trust,' Khalid added, 'but as we don't have much time, and I feel the need again, we'll talk about this later.'

'Yes, Your Majesty,' Millie said, sharing his smile.

'This is the only time I can ever get you to obey,' Khalid complained as he positioned her for pleasure.

'Be grateful for small mercies.'

'Small?'

'Okay, not small,' she gasped as he took her in one firm thrust. And now it was impossible to speak at all.

She would never tire of this man and the family they were building. This was her life, her love, her everything. 'You're a very bad man,' she scolded as Khalid began to move with real intent.

'Yes, I am,' he agreed. 'Thank goodness I found such a bad woman to match me.'

* * * * *

COMING SOON!

We really hope you enjoyed reading this book. If you're looking for more romance, be sure to head to the shops when new books are available on

Thursday
28th June

MILLS & BOON

Coming next month

THE BRIDE'S BABY OF SHAME
Caitlin Crews

"I can see you are not asleep," came a familiar voice from much too close. "It is best to stop pretending, Sophie."

It was a voice that should not have been anywhere near her, not here.

Not in Langston House where, in a few short hours, she would become the latest in a long line of unenthused countesses.

Sophie took her time turning over in her bed. And still, no matter how long she stared or blinked, she couldn't make Renzo disappear.

"What are you doing here?" she asked, her voice barely more than a whisper.

"It turns out we have more to discuss."

She didn't like the way he said that, dark and something like lethal.

And Renzo was *here*.

Right *here*, in this bedroom Sophie had been installed in as the future Countess of Langston. It was all tapestries, priceless art, and frothy antique chairs that looked too fragile to sit in.

"I don't know what you mean," she said, her lips too dry and her throat not much better.

"I think you do." Renzo stood at the foot of her bed, one hand looped around one of the posts in a lazy, easy sort of grip that did absolutely nothing to calm Sophie's nerves. "I think you came to tell me something last night but let my temper scare you off. Or perhaps it would be more accurate to say you used my temper as an excuse to keep from telling me, would it not?"

Sophie found her hands covering her belly again, there beneath her comforter. Worse, Renzo's dark gaze followed the movement, as if he could see straight through the pile of soft linen to the truth.

"I would like you to leave," she told him, fighting to keep her voice calm. "I don't know what showing up here, hours before I'm meant to marry, could possibly accomplish. Or is this a punishment?"

Renzo's lips quirked into something no sane person would call a smile. He didn't move and yet he seemed to loom there, growing larger by the second and consuming all the air in the bedchamber.

He made it hard to breathe. Or see straight.

"We will get to punishments in a moment," Renzo said. His dark amber gaze raked over her, bold and harsh. His sensual mouth, the one she'd felt on every inch of her skin and woke in the night yearning for again, flattened. His gaze bored into her, so hard and deep she was sure he left marks. "Are you with child, Sophie?"

Continue reading
THE BRIDE'S BABY OF SHAME
Caitlin Crews

Available next month
www.millsandboon.co.uk

LET'S TALK
Romance

For exclusive extracts, competitions
and special offers, find us online:

f facebook.com/millsandboon

⬚ @millsandboonuk

🐦 @millsandboon

Or get in touch on 0844 844 1351*

For all the latest titles coming soon, visit
millsandboon.co.uk/nextmonth